Eleanor gasped against his mouth, her hips surging against his.

Her reaction fired Brahm's blood. He would devour every inch of her if she would allow it.

And she would allow it, of that he was certain.

Of course, that would make them late for dinner.

Dinner. People would wonder where they were. There would be speculation as everyone saw them leave together.

God almighty. What was he doing? If he didn't stop now, he might very well ruin Eleanor. He wanted to woo her, not destroy her.

Reluctantly, Brahm eased himself away from her, lifting his mouth from hers. Her eyelids fluttered. Confused, glazed blue eyes gazed up at him. Her lips were red and softly parted, inviting him to claim them once more.

He swore instead, and released her. "Forgive me."

Other **AVON ROMANCES**

KATHRYN SMITH

Still In My Heart

AVON BOOKS
An Imprint of HarperCollinsPublishers

This is a work of fiction. Names, characters, places, and incidents are products of the author's imagination or are used fictitiously and are not to be construed as real. Any resemblance to actual events, locales, organizations, or persons, living or dead, is entirely coincidental.

AVON BOOKS
An Imprint of HarperCollins*Publishers*
10 East 53rd Street
New York, New York 10022-5299

Copyright © 2005 by Kathryn Smith
ISBN-13: 978-0-06-074074-0
ISBN-10: 0-06-074074-4
www.avonromance.com

First Avon Books paperback printing: September 2005

Avon Trademark Reg. U.S. Pat. Off. and in Other Countries, Marca Registrada, Hecho en U.S.A.
HarperCollins® is a registered trademark of HarperCollins Publishers Inc.

Printed in the U.S.A.

10 9 8 7 6 5 4 3 2 1

*This book is dedicated to
the memory of my grandmother,
Mildred Berry.
Unswerving in her devotion and
in love with my grandfather till the last,
Nanny B. treated life like a dance
and dance she did.
It did not matter if she knew all the steps,
she would make up her own.
It did not matter if she had rhythm,
she got her groove on regardless.
It did not matter that she lost the only partner
she wanted 20+ years earlier.
She learned to waltz alone.
And most importantly, Nan danced
like no one was watching—
living life on her own terms.
I was blessed to have shared
her dance floor for 32 years
and, thanks to her instruction,
am unafraid to cut a few rugs myself.
Thank you, Nan.
Save one for me.*

Chapter 1

Once upon a time . . .

He was drunk.

Not drunk in a silly manner, or even drunk in a vaguely belligerent fashion, but head-spinning, world-whirling, out-of-his-mind drunk. He hadn't meant to get so foxed; it had simply happened. One brandy had led to another and then another, until his feet became as heavy as lead and his entire body was engulfed in woozy numbness.

He liked being numb.

Still, his inebriation wasn't so consuming that it kept him from remembering the promise he had made earlier that day. He had asked the fair Eleanor to marry him, and she had agreed. All that was left was to tell her father, and as the earl was a friend of his own papa, there would be no obstacles to the union. The license would be procured, and Eleanor would be his. Soon he would kiss her sweet lips, feel her luxuriant body against his, and make her his in a way that would seal his claim to her. The very thought of it caused him to stiffen with desire. Perhaps he wasn't as drunk as he'd thought.

Tossing back one more glass, he decided it was time to leave the company of these amiable gentlemen, who seemed more than happy to pour brandy down his throat by the barrelful. He could stay there all night, drinking. It made him feel so very free. Eleanor made him feel free as well. And Eleanor didn't make his head ache the next morning.

The image of her face swimming in his mind put a spring in his step as he made his way through the darkened corridors of the manor house, up the stairs to his chamber. Country house parties were always such fun.

In his room he kicked off his boots and tossed his coat on the floor. Waistcoat and shirt followed. He tripped taking off his trews and fell onto the bed with a gleeful "Oops!" He kicked at the offending garment until his limbs were finally free and lay on the bed gloriously naked and gloriously warm, as a soft summer night breeze drifted through the windows.

The world wasn't spinning, but it swayed a bit as he closed his eyes, and he gave himself up to the sensation. It was like being in a boat on gently rippled lake. He liked boats. He liked this rocking feeling. It lulled him toward the uncompromising darkness of a spirits-induced slumber. No thoughts, no insecurities, no dreams. Nothing but sweet blackness.

He was on the verge of slipping under when something touched his thigh. His brow wrinkled with the effort of trying to will his eyes open. Reluctantly the lids parted slightly, revealing the blurred vision of a woman with long blond hair hovering above him.

He smiled. "Eleanor." Even her name was calming, an audible representation of serenity. What was she doing there? They hadn't made their understanding known yet. She could still be ruined if anyone found her there in his room. He didn't want their marriage to start off with rumors surrounding it. "You should not be here."

"Shh," she replied, her soft hand sliding up between his thighs. She stroked his growing erection until he arched his hips in languid arousal. And when she closed her mouth around him, a groan escaped his lips.

Where had an inexperienced virgin learned such technique? Had he been sober, he might have given the question more thought. Had he been sober, he might have given the woman kneeling between his legs with her lips wrapped around his pole a second glance, but he wasn't sober. And he didn't do either of those things.

Later, as he slipped between her eagerly spread thighs, he thought he heard someone gasp behind him, but the sound was drowned out by Eleanor's welcoming coos and sighs as he nudged her body open and slid into her warm, welcoming wetness. There was no barrier to his possession—a detail that should have given him pause, but didn't. Right now he didn't care if she was a virgin or not. All that mattered to him was that she belonged to him.

The amazing, wonderful Eleanor was finally his.

London, September 1819

"You are not actually entertaining the idea of accepting Burrough's invitation, are you?" The question was asked in a tone both incredulous and vaguely insulting.

Over the edge of the invitation, Brahm Ryland flashed an annoyed glance at his brother. He and Wynthrope had been on speaking terms but six months now, and the slightly younger man still knew how to get under his skin like a festering splinter.

"Actually," he mimicked dryly, "I am doing just that, yes."

Wynthrope's tanned brow creased in a scowl that told Brahm in no uncertain terms what the younger Ryland thought of that answer. "Are you foxed?"

From anyone else, that question would have been the most insulting they could ask. However, Brahm knew his brother was capable of being much, *much* more obnoxious than that. He leaned back in his chair, crossing his freshly polished boots on the top of his desk. "I am as sober as Aunt Jane."

His brother blinked. "Aunt Jane is dead these past twenty years."

Brahm smiled condescendingly. "I imagine it has been a while since she had a drink, then."

"Prior to her death, she was sauced every day of her life—except for Sunday, of course."

"Of course." Closing his eyes, Brahm stifled a sigh. Was his brother deliberately provoking him, or was Wynthrope truly stupid? It had been so long since they'd had a brotherly relationship—not that they had one now—that there were times when he really didn't know what to think of his sibling. He loved him—sometimes he even liked him—but most of the time he thought of Wynthrope as the wind; the only thing constant about him was that he was never, *ever* constant. Not with Brahm, at least. Not with their brothers either. Brahm couldn't speak for Wynthrope's wife, Moira, but if the smile on the woman's face counted for anything, his brother was pleasing in marriage at least.

He didn't have the patience to verbally dance with

Wynthrope this morning. The invitation from the Earl Burrough had come like an unexpected guest—not necessarily wanted, but not entirely unwelcome. And above all else, it had come as a surprise. Why would Burrough invite him, of all people, to his home? Surely the old man couldn't have forgotten what Brahm had done the last time he'd been in his house?

Of course, it wasn't as though Brahm's memory of that night was that clear either—it had happened more than a decade ago. All he knew was that he thought he had been bedding Eleanor, but he had awakened the next morning beside her sister. Of course, Eleanor had refused to marry him. Refused to even speak to him, and Lord Burrough, her father, had him unceremoniously ejected from his country estate. All Burrough seemed to know, however, was that Brahm had broken his daughter's heart, not that he had shagged his other daughter to do it.

The next few months that followed were a blur as well, as he had spent them in a stupor, trying to forget Eleanor's face. He thought it had worked, but there was that night a few years later when he'd seen her at a ball given by Lord and Lady Pennington. He'd watched her dance every dance with some young fop as he himself downed glass after glass of disgusting champagne. One minute he was horribly jealous of the fop, wanting Eleanor to show at least some indication that she was aware of his presence, and the next he was standing on the refreshment table, relieving himself in the cut crystal punch bowl for all to see.

Even through the fog of drink he could plainly remember Eleanor's horrified reaction. There could be no denying that she had been painfully aware of him at that moment.

"You are going to see her, aren't you?" His brother's

tone was faintly accusatory. "You want to see Lady Eleanor."

The sound of her name was enough to send Brahm's heart into a shameful gallop.

Eleanor. Over thirty years of age, she was considered an ape leader by many. An old maid to be pitied and whispered about behind fluttering fans. To Brahm she was a painful memory, so deeply imbedded in his mind that her image was burned into the backs of his eyes. Ever since he had given up the drink, she had started taking up more and more of his thoughts. He dreamed about her, thought of her at the strangest times. She was the one person to whom he hadn't apologized for the hurt he had sown. He owed her that. And maybe once he had apologized, once he had proven to her that he was a changed man, she would cease haunting him.

And yes, if he admitted the truth, perhaps she'd give him a second chance. God, how weak and pathetic that made him feel, but it was true. There had never been another woman who made him want to propose marriage—never another woman who made him smile the same way that Eleanor had. Their time together had been brief, their courtship practically nonexistent, but those weeks spent in her company had been among the best moments of his life.

And moments such as those had been few and very, very far between.

"Your silence is very telling," Wynthrope remarked, bringing him back to the here and now. "You do realize you are setting yourself up for a mighty fall?"

Brahm nodded as he tossed the invitation onto his desk. "I do."

"And yet you plan to follow it through?"

"I would rather fall than continue walking this precipice."

His brother arched a dark brow. "How positively poetic."

If his tone were any drier it would have been a desert. Brahm chuckled. "Do not be jealous simply because I have a more lyrical manner than you do."

Wynthrope's answering expression was dubious. "I am simply nauseous over it."

Again Brahm laughed. He should know better than to verbally spar with his younger brother. Wynthrope had a wit—and a tongue—like a rapier. He could slice someone wide open and the person would never even know he was bleeding. Brahm could have no doubt that his words made his brother ill, and yet he sounded so . . . sincere.

"You have, of course, thought of how badly this meeting could go?"

Ah, here was Wynthrope's genuine sincerity. He didn't know his younger brother that well, and God knew they needed patience and time if they were ever to become friends, but they cared about each other, loved each other. After many years of misunderstandings and resentment, that connection was pleasantly warming.

"Of course." In actuality, he hadn't. He did now, however. He had thought only of what seeing Eleanor again meant to him, not what it might mean to her. Were the situation reversed, he would not be so keen to reunite with a woman who claimed to want to marry him and then frigged his brother.

But if she wasn't open to the meeting, why had he received an invitation? She was mistress in her father's house; the servants listened to her. She planned everything that went on in that house, from menial daily tasks to the grandest parties. She had to know he was invited. Hell, she had to have issued the invitation. Hadn't she?

Wynthrope eyed him curiously, his blue eyes unreadable. "Be careful, brother."

It was a warning in every sense of the word, but Brahm's throat tightened with emotion at the sentiment behind it. "Of course," he repeated. He could be nothing else. He was always careful when sober. It was only when drunk that he was reckless.

Reckless enough to piss in a punch bowl. Reckless enough to allow his father, the former viscount, to enter a carriage race that led to his death—and Brahm's limp. And apparently reckless enough to sleep with his betrothed's sister. He mentally shook his head at that one. Of all the things he had done—remembered and not—injuring Eleanor was the one he regretted most, outside of his father's death.

Wynthrope rose to his feet. "Then I shall leave you to your preparations."

Brahm watched his brother. Wynthrope was so elegant, so thoroughly cool and composed. There had been a time when he thought his brother made of ice, but then Wynthrope had met Moira, and the ice melted. Brahm knew, even if his brother would never want it acknowledged, that Wynthrope ran much deeper than he appeared.

"I will be fine, Wyn," he heard himself assure the younger man.

He was pinned to his chair by a simple, plaintive gaze. "If you find yourself in trouble—any kind of trouble—send for me. I will come for you."

Again Brahm's throat tightened. Wynthrope meant liquor, he was certain of it. "I will. Thank you."

Wynthrope only nodded and took his leave. Brahm sat

there at the desk for a long time after his brother was gone, staring at the portrait of his father that hung above the fireplace.

Of all his father's sons, he was the most like the former viscount. He alone had developed the same vices, perhaps even the same virtues. He had his father's dark hair, the same nose and chin. In one respect, however, he was very much different from the man who sired him. He would never, never marry a woman he did not love simply to increase his fortune and beget heirs. He would not relegate the woman he adored to mistress and allow one of his sons to be born a bastard, as Brahm's brother North had been.

No. Brahm would marry the woman he loved, or he would not marry at all. As the years went on, he began to think the latter would be his fate. But now . . . Now he might have been given a second chance, and he'd be damned if he'd let it pass him by. He was going to accept this invitation. He would go to Burrough's estate and he would confront Eleanor. He would do whatever was necessary to force her to listen to his apology, to prove to her that he was a changed man. And then he would discover whether her opinion of him had changed. Beyond that, he dared not speculate. There could be no predicting what his reaction would be to her, or if either of them would find anything appealing in the other.

All he dared hoped was that if she didn't accept that he had changed, he might be able to finally put her in the past where she belonged. That he would stop thinking of what could have been and start concentrating on what was. She was the last person to whom he wished to make amends. After that, he would truly have a fresh lease on life.

Yes, his future and the path it would take relied almost

entirely on Eleanor Durbane and her forgiveness. If he still drank it would be a sobering thought.

What was she like now? He knew from the few times he had seen her over the years that she had maintained her looks, maturing into a beauty even more heartbreaking than in her youth. She had never married. Was she bitter? Had he ruined her for other men? Somehow he couldn't bring himself to feel much remorse at the thought. What would his reaction be to her after all these years? Would she still fill his heart with joy? Would she still make him want to be everything she desired?

More importantly, he wondered what her reaction would be when she saw him. Would she be pleased? Or would she want his head on a platter?

Chances were he wouldn't be lucky enough to achieve either.

"I must be stark raving mad."

Across the parlor, her sister Arabella looked up from her needlepoint. "What was that, dearest?"

Good Lord, she hadn't said that aloud, had she? Eleanor's cheeks warmed as she met her sister's pale gaze.

"Sorry, Belle. I pricked my finger." That was such a lie. Her own needlework hadn't been touched in almost half an hour. It wasn't that she didn't enjoy stitchery, normally she did very much. She had finished numerous projects, and each had given her a great amount of pleasure and peace in her life. Sometimes the days were so long, she needed something to pass the hours, such as the needle-work in her hands.

But her task did nothing to take her mind off the fact that she was two-and-thirty and well and good on her way to becoming a spinster. And if by chance her mind did stray to thoughts of spinsterhood, she needed something to keep it from straying to the fact that she could be Lady Creed right now, if only she hadn't gone to Brahm's room that night . . .

But she wouldn't think of that awful night, not now. Not with Arabella watching her. Because Arabella did not know that the one man Eleanor had ever entertained thoughts of marrying had bedded their sister Lydia. In fact, to Eleanor's knowledge, even Lydia didn't know that Eleanor had seen her in bed with Brahm. Lydia never would have done what she did—oh, what she did!—if she had known of Brahm's proposal to Eleanor. What sister would?

At times Eleanor rather wished her sister had confessed to her. It would have made forgiving her a little bit easier, would have made her resentment a little easier to live with. But Lydia never said a word.

And truth be told, Eleanor sometimes wondered if her sister even cared. Did Lydia ever wonder if maybe Eleanor knew about her and Brahm? Did Lydia make a habit of betraying her husband, or had Brahm truly seduced an innocent woman?

She knew for a fact that Brahm Ryland rarely had to stoop to seduction. Women used to flock to him like flies to manure. Even now, with his tarnished reputation, he was reported to have his share of feminine attention.

Well, there were obviously a lot of women in England with a total lack of morals and taste.

"Ellie?"

Eleanor's head jerked up. Arabella was watching her with a sympathetic smile on her face. "What has you so distracted?"

Feigning surprise, Eleanor laughed—it sounded sharp

and disjointed in her ears. "Distracted? Why would you believe me distracted?"

Arabella nodded at the needlework sliding off Ele.... .'s lap. "Because you have been staring into space for   minutes."

Elea... knew when she was caught. Only Arabella would notice that she was out of sorts. Lydia and their other sisters, Muriel and Phoebe, were usually too busy with their own lives to have an interest in anyone else's. Arabella was different. Arabella was happy with her life, her husband, and her situation. The others—including Eleanor herself—often were too distracted by their own problems to have an interest in another.

Surely Eleanor had to take some responsibility for that. After the death of their mother, she had practically raised her four younger sisters. If their lives had turned out less than what they had hoped for, couldn't they blame her for some of it?

"So," Arabella prodded when Eleanor remained silent. "What has you so addled? Is it this party of Papa's?"

Unfortunately, Arabella's attention to others often led to her noticing things better left alone.

Eleanor sighed. "Yes." She dropped her needlework into the basket at her feet. "He is determined to marry me off."

Her sister's smile was patient. She spared a glance at her canvas as she slipped her needle through it. "You sound so very displeased at the prospect."

She was. She had only agreed to it because their father was ill and she didn't want to upset him. "I do not need help finding a husband."

Arabella shrugged. "You never leave the house. Obviously, if you are to find a husband, you need him to be brought to you."

"I leave the house!" Even as she protested, Eleanor knew there was little point. She didn't leave the estate that often. She went to church on Sunday mornings, to the village once in a while for thread or ribbon. It was only during the Season that she traveled, and even then it was only to London. She didn't even socialize much while she was there, not now that all her younger sisters were married and there was no need for her to play chaperone.

The truth was, she didn't go out much in London anymore because Brahm was becoming more and more of a fixture among the *ton*. His reputation wasn't as black as it once was, rather a dark shade of gray. Some hostesses even thought him fashionable—and the sight of him proved to be more than Eleanor's bitter heart could bear.

"He invited so many bachelors, Belle." She couldn't keep the whine from her voice. "Everyone is sure to guess why. Our guests will all know that he's trying to sell me off like a broodmare at market."

Arabella's flaxen brows knitted in a fierce frown. "What an awful thing to accuse Papa of! He is not trying to *sell* you to anyone! He simply wants to know that you are looked after in the event of his death."

How could her sister speak so matter-of-factly about the fact that their father would one day die? Maybe it was because Eleanor had spent more time with him, had seen him be so dependent on her after her mother's death, that the idea of losing her papa brought a hard lump to her throat.

She refused to feel guilty. "I will be looked after. My inheritance will ensure that I never want for anything." *Inheritance*, it had such a nice ring to it. Much nicer than, *unused dowry*.

"It is not the same," her sister admonished. "A lady needs a gentleman to look after her, to share her life with.

It is a woman's duty to provide her husband with companionship and children."

Eleanor stared at her. Arabella truly believed that. More importantly, Arabella *lived* it. It was what she wanted, and she had it with her husband. They were expecting their first child, and were one of the happiest couples Eleanor had ever seen. They rarely quarreled, and when they did, it made both of them miserable. They were partners, which was an oddity in itself among their set.

God, how Eleanor envied her sister. She envied her even though she often didn't understand her. Maybe Arabella had turned out so different because she was only two years younger than Eleanor. Arabella remembered their mother better than the other three. Eleanor had been twelve when her mother died. Arabella had been ten, Lydia seven, Phoebe four and Muriel a mere year. Arabella had enjoyed their mother's influence. She even looked the most like her.

Caroline Durbane had been a lovely, graceful woman with pale blond hair and pale blue eyes. Only Arabella was just as fair, just as lovely. The rest of them had darker hair. Eleanor and Lydia shared the same shade of dark and light blond mixed. Phoebe was a brunette, and Muriel's hair was honey gold.

But why was she thinking about her sisters when she should be contemplating a way out of this mess her father had gotten her into?

She agreed to the house party because he wanted it— and the truth was, she was terrified he was dying. She'd walk to London barefoot if she thought it would keep him with her longer. Odd how she couldn't bear to lose him, even though she sometimes felt suffocated by him.

But then she learned that he was inviting unmarried men to the party. There would be several bachelors living under their roof for the next month, bachelors invited with the hope that one of them would propose to Eleanor—and that she would accept.

A broodmare at market, indeed.

She had taken over the responsibilities of running an estate at an age when most girls developed crushes on their dance instructors. She had raised her sisters—granted, she might not have done such a fine job of it. And she had cared for their father. Where had anyone, particularly Papa, gotten the idea that she needed a husband to look after her?

She didn't *need* anyone. Yes, it was true that she sometimes thought it would be nice to have someone to lean on, but that didn't mean she needed a husband. It simply meant she needed . . . someone to lean on.

And she certainly didn't need a husband from her father's list of potentials. Lord only knew the kind of men he had chosen to show her off to. It had been he who had brought Brahm Ryland into their house all those years ago, and look where *that* had gotten her.

". . . your attention."

Eleanor's gaze jerked to her sister. "I beg your pardon?"

"And well you should," her sister chastised. "You have not listened to a word I said!"

"I heard you. A woman needs a man to look after her. A man needs a woman for companionship."

Arabella arched a shapely brow. "And?"

"It is her duty to provide him with children."

"And?"

There was more? Oh dear. "Um . . ."

Arabella waited patiently, despite the pained look Eleanor shot her.

"Fine." Eleanor scowled. Sometimes her sister was so cruel. "I was not listening."

A smug smile curved Arabella's cupid's-bow lips—another trait that had escaped Eleanor—as she deftly pierced the hooped canvas in her lap with her needle. "I said that Papa only wants to see you happy, no matter how you choose to see it. You know he will not force you to marry anyone you do not want."

That was true. None of her sisters had been forced into marriage, and Eleanor knew she would be no different. After all, her father had allowed her to refuse Brahm, and he had been Papa's favorite of any of her suitors.

Of course, there might be something to be said for allowing her father to choose for her—two of her sisters were vocally unhappy with the choices they made, and Muriel, married but a year, showed signs of soon joining them. But not Arabella, who had come to Eleanor the night Henry proposed to ask for her opinion—and for her blessing. Eleanor had been all too happy to give both.

She sighed. This was all so confusing. "I know no one will force me, Belle. It is just so embarrassing. People will gossip about it, you know."

Her sister nodded and added another stitch to her sampler. "I know. That is why I talked Papa into inviting some young ladies from the marriage mart."

"You did what?" Eleanor could not believe her ears. "How did you manage that?"

Arabella smiled conspiratorially. "I told him you might try harder if you thought you had competition."

Eleanor laughed at that. How could she not? "Oh, Belle! Thank you."

Her sister nodded. "I thought that might make you feel a little less pressured. I saw some guests arrive this morning. Were any bachelors among them?"

Eleanor shook her head. "Lord and Lady Boothe. You know how they like to arrive early. And a few families came in early to get settled." Her gaze drifted to the clock on the mantel. "I suspect others will start arriving soon, however. This afternoon and this evening will be the busiest time."

Another dip of the needle. "Does Papa expect you to greet the guests?"

Eleanor shook her head. Normally she would, but even she didn't have enough composure to face all those gentlemen, not to mention the ladies and their knowing glances. "Muriel and Phoebe offered to take turns doing it." More than likely her sisters had volunteered so they could be the first to get any gossip.

"Good. It will heighten their anticipation if they do not see you until dinner."

Anticipation? For her? Eleanor would have laughed if she weren't so close to choking on it. She wasn't ugly by any means, but everyone knew she was the least comely of her sisters. She was too tall to be fashionable, and she often thought her mouth made her face resemble a duck's. There was just something about the way her upper lip was wider and fuller than her bottom, and it curved slightly upward, making her look as though she was always on the verge of smiling—or quacking.

Why would anyone be anxious to see an old maid? She was past her prime. She wouldn't produce as many children as a girl one-and-twenty. The only thing she had to offer for anyone to get excited for was her fortune—and possibly her maidenhead, if that was all that much of a prize. The poor thing probably had dust on it.

As soon as that ludicrous and entirely improper thought

crossed her mind, she knew she was in danger of going as mad as she feared.

"I cannot do this!" she exclaimed, leaping to her feet and pacing back and forth. "I cannot pretend to go along with this. Never mind that it is humiliating, but what if one of them actually wants to marry me?" The thought hadn't occurred to her before this. Good God, what if she played along to please her father and one of these men proposed? Worse yet, what if the impossible happened and a gentleman actually became attached to her? It would be too cruel of her.

Arabella looked up from her work. "What if you find yourself wanting to marry one of them?"

That wouldn't happen. It just couldn't. Could it?

How she wished this party was already over. She had agreed to this scheme of her father's to appease an ill man, but how much was she expected to endure? How much worse could this debacle possibly get?

"Oh my Lord!" Eleanor's sister Muriel barged into the room, slamming the door behind her and bracing her back against it as though something awful lurked on the other side. Her dark blue eyes were wide, her cheeks blooming with high color. Muriel was young enough still that everything seemed to be worthy of theatrical reactions.

"What is it?" Arabella cried, her hand over her bosom. Melodrama apparently ran in the family.

Eleanor would have rolled her eyes at Arabella's dramatics if Muriel didn't seem truly out of sorts.

"Yes, Muriel," she added, hoping that her voice would push their sister to replying. "What is it?"

Muriel's shocked gaze locked with hers. "Viscount Creed is just arrived."

Eleanor's heart came to a lurching halt in her chest. Viscount Creed?

Brahm.

Now she knew the situation could not possibly get any worse.

Chapter 2

The minute Brahm saw Muriel scamper away, he knew he was in trouble. No one was that anxious to run off and report the arrival of an expected guest—not even an anticipated one. He might have received an invitation, but Muriel hadn't known it, and he was willing to bet that Eleanor hadn't issued it.

Muriel's evacuation left him standing in the hall with the other one—what was her name? Phoebe, one of the younger sisters—the brunette. She watched him with an expression of wary curiosity in her blue eyes. She was a pretty girl, but then Lord and Lady Burrough hadn't produced anything but comely children, which was fortunate considering they had all girls. Pretty heiresses were just that much easier to marry off than homely ones.

So why had Eleanor not married? Surely he hadn't left her with such an awful view of his sex, had he?

He was opening his mouth, about to make inane chitchat, when the pitter-patter of hurrying little feet echoed through the hall. Muriel was returning. Would she be armed with a pistol to drive him out of the house? A rapier perhaps?

Neither, actually. She came into view with no defense other than a mischievous—no, malicious—smile. She was far too young to be able to smile like that.

"Lord Creed, would you be so kind as to come with me?"

Ah, so she was going to lure him to his death, was she? Take him somewhere quiet and do him in with no one the wiser? He should be so fortunate. No doubt she was taking him to face either her father or her eldest sister. If his luck ran par for the course, then the entire Durbane family would be waiting to tear him limb from limb.

Still, he followed after the blond woman anyway, his gaze casually drifting over his surroundings. The house looked the same as it had the last time he had visited. Oh, perhaps there were a few new draperies, one or two newer pieces of furniture, but the floor was still Italian marble and the portraits were still of pompous ancestors, and the air still smelled of beeswax and fresh flowers.

Perhaps the most marked difference was with himself. The last time he entered this house it was with nothing to prove and no thought as to whom to prove it to. Now he sought to prove to one woman that he was a changed man. He would have better luck trying to prove to Parliament that England did *not* rule the world.

Muriel stopped beside a door and turned to face him. Her pink lips curved into a peculiar smile, anticipatory and a little bloodthirsty. She was going to take pleasure in watching her sister slowly dismember him, the little wench.

"Wait here," she commanded.

While I get my ax, Brahm silently added for her. If he was going to turn tail and run, now was the time to do it.

Instead he returned Muriel's smile with a wolfish one of his own. If she thought he was going to run scared from her and her sisters, she was going to be sadly mistaken. He had fought hallucinations, trials, and demons far more frightening than the Durbane sisters—and all of them had been of his own making.

Besides, he couldn't run anymore—not just figuratively, but literally as well. The best he could manage was a fast limp.

Muriel did seem somewhat taken aback by his smile, which afforded him some degree of pleasure as she slipped into the room and quickly closed the door behind her. She hadn't allowed him even the slightest glimpse inside. Prepared for a long wait, Brahm leaned most of his weight on his good leg and studied the portraits on the walls.

A few excruciating minutes later, as he was contemplating one particularly amusing likeness of an old lord with a crooked wig, the door opened once more. Smiling at the askew hairpiece, Brahm glanced over his shoulder and was rewarded by Muriel's scowl.

It was then that he noticed that the other sister—Phoebe—had followed them from the hall. He hadn't heard her, hadn't even been aware of her presence. Odd, he would have thought a sharp stinging between his shoulder blades would have accompanied her. Fortunately for him, she seemed to have forgotten to bring a dagger with her.

"You may come in," Muriel informed him, displeasure twisting her otherwise pretty mouth. There was a hardness about her—a trait that elicited sympathy for one so young.

Eleanor had been about this girl's age when he met her, but Eleanor had the look of someone much sweeter and more innocent. When he saw her now, would he find this same hardness in her features? And if so, how much responsibility would he have to take for it?

Brahm bowed his head in acquiescence. Squaring his shoulders, he entered the room with both sisters behind him, feeling very much like a hapless fly stepping onto a spider's web. Eleanor was in this room. Was the other one? How much did the other sisters know of his stupid indiscretion? He had always assumed that Lydia had confessed all to Eleanor, but what about the others? Did they know as well, or had Eleanor kept the truth from them? He would choose the latter. There had never been any gossip about why Eleanor had cried off—none that had been *that* accurate, at any rate. Quite a few loose-tongued matrons had hinted that his penchant for drunkenness played a part, but that wasn't so much a speculation as it was a simple truth.

He had been in this room before. It was still decorated in shades of blue, rose, and gold. The carpet beneath his feet was the same Aubusson that had welcomed him years earlier when he set his gaze upon Eleanor Durbane and his heart gave that mighty thump that told him she was the woman he wanted as his wife.

He found her instantly, his gaze locking with the cool blue of hers. She stood in the center of the room, with one of her sisters behind her. The two that had followed him into the room moved from behind him to come around and flank their sister. Cold they might be, ignorant of his betrayal perhaps, but these women knew he had done something in the past to injure their sister, and they weren't about to give him a chance to do so again. He could respect that—he had three brothers, after all.

But her sisters meant nothing to him. Only Eleanor's reception mattered. She stood there, surrounded by her sisters, but untouched by them. Her spine was iron stiff and straight beneath a gown of cream muslin with blue ribbon around the scalloped hem and beneath her lovely breasts. As always, Eleanor was fashionable but not fussy, another trait that set her apart from her sisters. Her rich blond hair was pulled back from her face and knotted high on the back of her head.

Simple and unadorned, she stood as still and fair as a statue, just as delicately chiseled and smooth. Eyes of silvered blue watched him warily beneath hooded lids. That sharp little nose lifted ever so haughtily, and her mouth—that unusual mouth with its fuller upper lip—was unforgivingly grim.

This was the woman who had haunted his dreams of late? She was the one person whose forgiveness he craved? This woman, who watched him with such disdain, who looked so cold and remote, he thought he might have fabricated the memory of her smile? Was this bitter-looking woman the same one who had once made him entertain the notion of becoming a better man just so he could see adoration in the mirrored depths of her eyes?

Yes, it was, because his heart gave that same damn rolling, twisting, painful thump when his gaze locked with hers.

She was no longer that girl who had made him believe waking up with the same person for the rest of his life might be tolerable. He was no longer that arrogant boy who believed himself happily immune to a woman's charms. Until Eleanor he'd believed himself a good catch, a lofty trophy for any husband-hunting young woman, who would be more than happy to stand by, silent and docile, while he lived his life exactly as he wanted. Then he had met Lord Burrough's oldest daughter, Eleanor, and he began to entertain the notion that there might be such a thing as a "happy" marriage and that he just might find that kind of friendship, support, and passion with her.

But then he had gone and ruined that, well and good. And now she looked at him as though he were something she had just scraped off the bottom of her slipper. But there was something else in her gaze—a touch of wariness that told him his cause was not lost yet.

This uncomfortable silence had dragged on long enough. One of them had to speak.

"Hello, Eleanor." He winced. That hopeful whining wasn't really his voice, was it?

For a split second, her cool mask of composure and contempt cracked, and she looked almost as vulnerable as he felt. Perhaps her forgiveness was too much to ask. Until now he had only thought of what this opportunity might afford him, not what discomfort it might offer her. If she still harbored ill feelings toward him for what he had done years ago, then perhaps her feelings for him had been deeper than he first thought. Perhaps he had wounded her so greatly, she would never find the ability to forgive him. He had bedded her sister after pledging her his troth. Were the situation reversed, he didn't know if he could be man enough to forgive such a betrayal, no matter what the circumstances.

"Lord Creed." Her voice was huskier than he remembered, and her formality brought the sting of shame to his cheeks. And yet . . .

If she was still so bitter after all these years, perhaps there was a chance she too retained some secret regard for him. Perhaps he still had a hold on her heart as she did on his. They were connected in some twisted way— she as the one who rejected him and he as the one who broke her heart. Too many unanswered questions, too many regrets and doubts. Youthful hope combined with youthful heartbreak.

And then there was the fact that she was a woman and he a man, and all he had to do was look at her to know he wanted her, and his past hope of making her his viscount-ess had nothing to do with it.

"Lord Creed," the sister behind Eleanor began in a musical, yet firm voice, "We were not expecting you."

He smiled at that blatantly polite understatement. "I apologize for any . . . *inconvenience* my arrival proposes." That was an understatement in itself. So what transpired now? Was he to be tossed out without so much as a chance to explain himself to this woman, this phantom of his heart who had become an obsession? He could not go back to wondering what might have been, not after coming this far.

He would not go back. He would ask for her forgiveness as they dragged him out the door. Whatever happened after that didn't matter.

Eleanor's gaze remained locked with his. Neither of them had looked away since he entered the room. How much longer could they go on simply staring at each other before one of them cracked?

"Would you mind leaving us?" Eleanor asked. For a moment Brahm thought she had directed the question at him, as her gaze never wavered. Only the warmth in her tone told him otherwise.

Her sisters—three blue-eyed women wearing the same expression of surprise—turned to her. Eleanor's attention remained where it was. It was all Brahm could do not to lose himself in her eyes. They were pools of cornflower blue that reflected so much—more than he wanted to see. Eleanor's eyes weren't just windows, they were mirrors.

Once he had seen himself as she had, and it had pleased him. Now he was glad she was so far away so he couldn't see himself as she did.

"No," Muriel replied resolutely. "We are not leaving."

The soft-voiced sister—Arabella, if memory served—placed a hand on Muriel's arm, but her gaze went to Brahm. He was dimly aware of her scrutiny out of the corner of his eye, as he was determined not to be the one to break the contact between himself and Eleanor. "If Eleanor wants us to leave, we must respect that."

Yes! Alone with Eleanor. It was a small victory, but a victory all the same.

Arabella's hand went to Eleanor's shoulder. "We will be in the corridor if you need us."

Apparently Eleanor wasn't going to be the one to look away first either. She held his gaze as she covered the hand on her shoulder with her own. "Thank you, Bella."

The three Durbane sisters each shot him a look of warning as they reluctantly left Eleanor's side. Thank God Lydia hadn't been present. Her presence would have been a barb for both him and Eleanor—and might have made it all the easier for Eleanor to toss him out on his arse.

Brahm didn't look at the sisters as they filed out, but he knew the minute they were gone—not because he heard the door close, but because the air thickened when he and Eleanor were left alone. Suddenly his mouth became a little dry and the skin beneath his collar a little damp.

He opened his mouth to speak, uncertain of what to say.

Eleanor beat him to it. "You were not invited to this party."

Brahm closed his mouth and tried again. "I was." It wasn't as eloquent a statement as it could have been, but it served its purpose.

Her slender arms folded across her chest. Did she realize that belligerent pose pushed her breasts upward in a most enticing manner? Probably not. "Prove it."

He slipped his hand inside his jacket and withdrew the invitation. He paused before giving it to her, enjoying the heightened emotions playing across her face as she waited. When he offered it, she snatched it from him as though she was afraid his touch might burn. He should have been offended, but he wasn't.

She had to lower her gaze from his to read the invitation, something she was loath to do, he could tell. What did she think he was going to do, pounce on her while her attention was diverted? It wasn't an entirely unpleasant thought, but he preferred willing flesh to unwilling. And he wanted Eleanor willing. So willing he was ashamed of it.

The vellum crumpled in her fingers as the hands holding it clenched into fists. She knew his claim was true. He had been invited. Someone other than he had betrayed her this time.

Those silvered blue eyes flashed, almost blinding him with the force of their emotion as her gaze snapped to his. "How dare you accept."

Brahm chuckled. He couldn't help it. Did she honestly think that he could have refused such an opportunity? "It would have been rude of me not to."

"It was cruel of you otherwise." A catch in her voice sliced at his heart and robbed him of his smile. "I never told anyone what a blackguard you are, and this is how you repay me?"

Repay her? Did she expect him to believe that *he* had been the one she sought to protect?

"If you want retribution for your silence, then speak to your sister. I neither expected nor asked for your secrecy.

The only thing I owe you is an apology, which I am here to give."

She looked as though she might choke. "An apology? After all these years? I do not want it. I would not believe it."

"What about what you owe to me?"

Eyes widened, then narrowed to angry slits. "I owe you nothing." The words fairly seethed out of her.

Did she not? A few moments ago he might have believed that, but heightened emotion now had him thinking otherwise. "You owe me the chance to explain. You never gave me that when you broke our engagement."

"Explain?" A quick glance at the door lowered her tone. "There was nothing to explain. I know what you did."

"You know what your sister told you."

She took a lurching step forward, as though she wanted to strike him but managed to stop herself just in time. "I know what I *saw*."

Saw? Oh dear God. "What did you see?" He had no memory of that night, nothing except waking up beside Lydia and knowing with awful certainty that they had shared more than just pillows.

Her clear skin flushed a deep rose, but she held his gaze. She looked so angry—angry with a touch of humiliation as she obviously remembered with perfect clarity what she had seen that made her reject him. He had thought Lydia had told her what happened. Why had Eleanor not told him this before?

"I saw the two of you together," she replied.

Brahm raised a brow. That statement could mean so much, especially in polite company—which he was not. "Together?" Before, after, or during?

The crimson of her cheeks deepened. Her entire neck

and upper chest matched in hue. She was a proper lady, not used to such talk, and it was cruel of him to taunt her so, but since he had no memory of that night, hers would have to suffice for the both of them.

"You were naked," she informed him in a low, hoarse voice. "My sister was naked. And you were on top of her. Is that description enough for you, or do you wish me to continue? I assure you I remember every detail most acutely."

Brahm swallowed. The hurt in her voice bruised him. The accusation in her eyes stung. There was a hollow feeling in his chest, as though someone had reached in and pulled something out. He could not deny it because he didn't know anything different. If she had nothing but her sister's word, then there was a chance that he could deny it, both to himself and Eleanor, but if Eleanor had seen, then he had no other choice but to believe.

How could he have done something so awful to her? And how was he ever going to even begin to make amends for it?

"Eleanor, I am so sorry."

She made a scoffing noise. "Of course you are." But she didn't sound as if she believed it at all. "I have no idea why you are here, and I'm sure I do not care, but I am going to discuss this with my father, and he will rectify the situation." She thrust the crumpled invitation back at him, and after a moment's hesitation he took it.

Their gazes locked once more, and this time she was close enough that he could see himself in her eyes. He looked lost, stupefied, and very much like the blackguard she knew him to be.

"Until then, Lord Creed," she continued flatly, "please

know that I have given you the explanation you sought and therefore owe you nothing."

Brahm could only watch as she swept from the room, her spine still so straight and regal, while his was surely slumped with shame.

No, Eleanor Durbane owed him nothing. But he certainly owed a great debt to her—one he had no idea in heaven how to even begin to repay.

Eleanor stormed up the stairs to the next floor where her father's bedchamber was located, her sisters scurrying after her.

"What did he say?"

"What are you going to do?"

"Eleanor, say something!"

They were at the landing. To the left were the stairs to the family rooms. To the right were the stairs to the guest quarters. Eleanor spared Arabella the briefest glance as she willed her clenched jaw to relax enough to reply. "Papa invited him."

A collective gasp rose behind her as she neared the top of the stairs. Her sisters were, of course, suitably horrified. Eleanor, however, wasn't horrified. She felt hurt, confused, and more than a little betrayed. There was also a traitorous part that had leaped with excitement at the sight of him, but she wasn't going to address that now.

What the devil had her father been thinking?

Her father, like her sisters, didn't know the truth behind Eleanor's rejection of Brahm years before. Until today not even Brahm himself had known. She hadn't meant to reveal that she had seen him and Lydia engaged in their sordid liaison, but he had made her so *angry.* Normally she wasn't the kind to lose her temper, but Brahm Ryland brought out the worst in her.

He'd always held the ability to make her act out of character. It was an odd ability for someone she hardly knew. True, she had known enough of him to accept his offer of marriage many years ago, but the offer came after but a few weeks' acquaintance. Neither of them had been exactly green, but their courtship had swept both of them away on a giddy tide. It happened so quickly, but it had felt so right.

Which made finding him with Lydia in such a shocking manner all the more painful.

And now he wanted to apologize? *Now?* What was he, mad? Whatever had possessed him? And why would he possibly think she'd want to hear his explanation after all these years? There was no explanation he could offer.

The change of his countenance when she informed him that she had seen him and Lydia was so horrific, it could mean only one of two things: that he had been foxed and had no recollection of the night, or that he had meant to lie to her about what had happened, and she had ruined it by revealing the truth.

It was no doubt the latter, even though a tiny voice in her head suggested the former. No matter that he had betrayed her in the worst possible way, some small part of her never missed a chance to defend his actions. She didn't like to think ill of people, even those who deserved it.

Well, if Brahm Ryland had something to prove, he could prove it elsewhere. If she had her way—and as mistress of the house she always did—he would be gone before the hour.

Her slipper caught at the carpet as she misstepped, almost causing her to tumble to the floor. Her sisters, chattering like magpies behind her, luckily didn't notice, otherwise Eleanor would have to think of an explanation for her stumble. The truth would not do, for the thought that had occurred to her was something she could never voice without revealing everything.

What if the invitation hadn't come from her father, but from Lydia? What then? What if her sister had orchestrated his appearance? What if Brahm and Lydia planned to continue their affair? Eleanor would not stand for it— never mind that what they did was none of her concern.

But if she confronted her father and he hadn't sent the invitation, he would want to know who had and why . . .

And that would be Lydia's problem, not hers. Eleanor's jaw tightened with conviction even as her insides warred against it. She'd been like a mother to her sisters and just as sheltering, resolutely doing all she could to keep them from harm.

But Lydia was a grown woman now, not a young girl. Eleanor had protected her younger sister once where Brahm Ryland was concerned. She would not do it again. For once, she was going to ignore her maternal instincts.

Just as she had ignored them when she noticed that Brahm was still using a cane to walk. Many men used canes as fashionable accessories, and when she first saw him in public she thought perhaps he was just another affected fop, but then she remembered that his leg had been shattered in the accident that had claimed his father's life. Brahm was very fortunate that he had managed to survive. She tried not to remember her own relief when she heard that he had recovered from the ordeal. For a while it had been unclear whether his wounds would kill him, and as much as she resented him, she had secretly prayed for God to spare him.

Her prayers had been answered. Why couldn't God have been so obliging when she begged him to make Brahm's betrayal nothing more than a bad dream?

And why had her heart given such a traitorous leap when their gazes met? She'd wished she'd worn a better dress—to make him see what he'd lost, of course. She'd wished that the years had been as kind to her as they had to him. He was such an unfairly handsome man. He had the kindest face, marked by the humor and bitterness of life. There were lines of laughter around his whiskey brown eyes and lines of sorrow around his always-poised-on-the-brink-of-a-smirk mouth.

His eyes. His mouth. His hair. His hands. She had forgotten none of it. Sheltered and closeted away from society as unmarried women were, she had suffered twice as long as she should have under the weight of his memory. Cloistered as she had been, he had been the first man to truly turn her head, the first man to make her see her appeal and worth as a woman. Whether he had meant the words he'd said, she didn't know. She thought he had. He seemed to genuinely like her, and she had been genuinely infatuated with him. In fact, she'd been on the verge of falling in love with him, so much so that when she caught him with Lydia, she tried to make up a thousand excuses for him. She had wanted to *forgive* him for betraying her with her own sister. What did that say about her own character? She had to be defective to be sure.

His hair was longer now. It made him look a bit like a pirate—or the hero of one of Byron's poems. Oh, it would be so much easier to hate him if he were ugly! But she was so tired of despising him. She was so tired of carrying this secret, and it had felt so good to reveal the truth to him—

as if that huge weight had finally been lifted from her shoulders.

It wasn't hate that drove her to her father's room now. It was fear. She was so very, very afraid that if Brahm remained in their house, she would start wanting to forgive him again, that she would want to believe that he was sorry and that he might have become a different man. She was afraid that she might like him. Worse yet, she was still a cloistered, sheltered woman. Older, yes she was, but she was terrified that she might yet be that naive girl at heart.

She was afraid that if she gave up her hate, if she let it all go, it might turn toward her sister, and she could not hate the child she'd practically raised, not for *that* man— not for any man.

If she gave up her hate, if she believed in him, then he would have the power to hurt her again, to make a fool of her trust once again. That would not happen. Could not happen.

She wanted Brahm Ryland gone. *Now*.

Her sisters gathered around her as she knocked on her father's door. God bless them, they looked so outraged on her behalf. There had been many times in the past when they acted as though they resented Eleanor and her dual role as oldest sister and surrogate mother, but on the odd occasion when she needed them—or they thought she needed them—they flocked to her, doing whatever was necessary to protect and support her.

From behind the heavy oak door, Eleanor heard her father call for her to enter. She turned the doorknob before her courage could desert her.

Jeramiah Durbane reclined on his bed, a great mountain of pillows supporting his impressive frame. At almost seventy years of age, he had pale hair that was more white than blond, but his blue eyes were still bright with life and his physique impressive with youthful vitality.

That was, he had been vital until this illness struck. It was only because of this illness that Eleanor had agreed to this foolish house party. If her father wanted to dress in a frock and walk into town, she'd agree to it if it might keep him with her just a little longer.

He hardly looked like a man with one foot in the grave today, however. He eyed his daughters with a suspicious wariness that only the father of five girls could conjure.

"Good God," he muttered gruffly. "There is only one thing that could bring the lot of you bursting in here like that. I must be dead—or I shall soon wish I was."

Eleanor might have chuckled at her father's wit were she not so prepared to be angry with him.

"A guest has just arrived that I thought you might be interested in, Papa," she informed him, choosing her words carefully.

That her father didn't look surprised sent a tremor of welcome unease down her spine. It had been he, not Lydia.

Which meant that Brahm's arrival would be a surprise to her younger sister as well.

Good.

"And who might that be?" her father finally asked after a few seconds' silence.

Eleanor frowned at his feigned innocence. He wasn't fooling anyone, especially not her. "Viscount Creed."

Her father's attempt at astonishment failed miserably. "Really?"

"Stop it, Papa. I know you invited him. You fairly reek of guilt."

Her father sniffed the air. "That's liniment, Ellie, not guilt. Trust me, I know what guilt smells like."

Someone snickered behind her—Arabella, no doubt, Eleanor didn't bother to look. "Why?"

Her father knew what she was asking. "I was good friends with the boy's father, and one must hold loyal to such connections."

What hogwash. What about family loyalty?

Her father smiled. "Do not fret so, Ellie. I still hold you above all others."

Eleanor's cheeks warmed. How did he know what she was thinking like that? "I want you to ask him to leave."

"I cannot."

Whyever not? Surely her father wasn't going to hold to propriety in such a situation? "You invited him. You can uninvite him," she insisted. "It is very simple."

He admonished her with a gentle look. "Not that simple. Besides, I see no reason to toss the boy out on his ear."

His ear wasn't the body part Eleanor imagined Brahm Ryland landing on.

"Papa," Arabella began in a reasonable tone before Eleanor could begin a litany of reasons. "Viscount Creed and Eleanor's . . . understanding ended badly. That should be cause enough to not welcome him into the house."

Eleanor gave a satisfied nod. She couldn't have put it better herself.

Their father dismissed the statement with a wave of his hand. "That was a long time ago."

"Papa!" Eleanor couldn't believe her ears. Could he shrug off her disappointment just like that? Of course he could. He didn't know the extent of Brahm's villainous behavior. Her father believed her to be bound by her embarrassment and silly feminine pride, no doubt. He had no idea what a slap to the face it was to have Brahm Ryland under the same roof.

Although maybe she should be thankful to her father. This conversation was a reminder that she had every right to despise Brahm, that her earlier fears were totally misgiven. She had nothing to fear from him. Nothing at all.

Her father's gaze was shrewd as it shot to hers. "What is it, girl? Are you worried he might try to renew his addresses? Mayhap you are afraid he won't?"

Heat coursed through Eleanor's cheeks, burning her face with shame she didn't want to dissect. Had her father hit on something with his glib remark? Was she worried that Brahm might try to woo her once again? Or was she frightened that he wouldn't try to woo her? If he paid her no attention, would she finally give in to the realization that she would probably end her life alone, unwed, a dried-up old maid?

No, that wasn't it at all. She was in charge of her own destiny. There was no reason she couldn't marry someday if she wished it. She was simply angry that her father, like so many others of his sex—and her own as well, to be truthful—weighed so much of a woman's self against what men thought of her.

"Neither," she replied coolly. "Papa, I am merely concerned about Lord Creed's past behavior." That was so very, very true—if her father only knew.

Her father shifted against the pillows. "I take it you are referring to behavior that had nothing to do with you?"

If it was at all possible, Eleanor's flush deepened. There had been a few scandalous times when Brahm stole a kiss from her, but no, that wasn't what she meant.

"I refer to his penchant for copious consumption of

spirits. You have witnessed his atrocious antics just as I have. What if he wreaks such havoc here?" It was all she could do not to flash a smug smile. Let her father argue with that logic. After all, Brahm's past actions more than spoke for themselves.

Her father pulled a face. "Rubbish. Haven't heard a story about him since his father died—God rest his soul. Rumor has it Creed's turning over a new leaf."

Eleanor could not believe her ears. "But—"

He cut her off. "Did you not tell me just the other day, when I was determined to never call on Dr. Kerry again, that everyone deserved a second chance?"

Oh-oh. "Yes." It was a squeak of a whisper.

Her father smoothed the expanse of sheet next to him with the flat of one broad hand. "Then surely Viscount Creed deserves the same consideration? Unless, of course, you can offer a reason why he does not?"

Oh, she could, make no mistake! Eleanor opened her mouth, but no sound came out. Her father was watching her—far more closely than she was comfortable with. Her sisters too had closed around her like a cape, their gazes burning into her so she didn't dare spare a glance at any of them.

"Eleanor?" Muriel prodded softly. "Is there a reason Viscount Creed does not deserve a second chance?"

The tone of her sister's voice was hopeful, indicating that if there was such a reason, she wished Eleanor would present it, but Eleanor could not. Brahm might have betrayed her trust long ago, and he might have included Lydia in his betrayal, but Eleanor could not reply in kind. Without admitting the awful truth, she had nothing.

"No," she whispered, an invisible weight pressing down on her shoulders. "I suppose not."

"Good." Her father's pleased grin was painful to look at. "Then the matter is settled." His humor faded as he met Eleanor's gaze. She could only imagine what her expression must be to warrant such a change in him.

"All will be well, Ellie. You will see. Viscount Creed will be no trouble at all. Try to give him the benefit of the doubt. You may even find it within yourself to forgive him."

Eleanor didn't speak; she couldn't. Her own father had sided against her, and she could not reveal to them the one thing that would bring him back.

Perhaps Brahm had changed; it was possible, but she doubted it. Even if by some miracle he had given up drinking to excess, he was still the same person. It wouldn't change what he had done. It wouldn't change the fact that he had made a fool out of her.

A second chance. To do what? Make a fool of her again? No. There was no way she would allow that. As for forgiving him, what a joke that was. She would never forgive Brahm for what he did—for toying with both her and Lydia as he did. Never.

Never.

Chapter 3

~~~ ⌒◯◯⌒ ~~~

She hadn't kicked him out, yet.

By that evening, when his dinner clothes had been laid out by his valet and all other belongings unpacked, Brahm began to suspect that perhaps Eleanor had been unsuccessful in her attempt to have him ousted from the house. It was either that or she hadn't had the chance to talk to her father. It was unlikely that she would fail, as the old man doted on her, but if it was true that Burrough was as ill as the gossips indicated, then he might not have been well enough to have such a discussion with his eldest daughter.

And when Arabella asked the guests to excuse Eleanor from dinner that night because of a headache, Brahm knew it was his presence that caused her pain. The others knew as well. Society might not know why Eleanor had jilted him, but the fact that she had was common knowledge. More than one guest cast an accusatory gaze in his direction after glancing at Eleanor's empty chair. Her fa-

41

ther didn't join them either. The old earl must be ill indeed.

But the highlight of the evening had to be Lydia's reaction to him—and he meant highlight as in the worst possible thing that could have happened. She didn't seem outraged to see him as her sisters had. In fact, she seemed rather pleased, which raised more than a few eyebrows. Her husband remained blissfully ignorant as he chatted up several other guests.

If Lydia had any hopes of renewing their "acquaintance," she was bound to be disappointed. She was a pretty enough woman, but Brahm didn't find her the least bit attractive. Perhaps it was the fact that he knew he could have her if he wished, or perhaps it was because she reminded him very much of a predator in search of her next meal.

It hadn't occurred to him at the time, but now that his mind was clear as he looked at her, Brahm was certain that she had wanted him only because he had wanted Eleanor. And if this party really was a flimsily veiled husband hunt for Eleanor—despite the presence of other unmarried ladies—then Lydia was bound to suspect that he had tossed his hat into the ring. That would no doubt make him—and any other man at the party—very attractive indeed.

The footman came along with the wine, and Brahm allowed him to fill his glass. The claret was no doubt fine, but it would go to waste regardless. But people were more apt to notice an empty glass than a full one, and he had no desire to explain to this bunch that he could not trust himself to ingest even a sip. Fortunately, wine didn't pose the same temptation that other libations did, and therefore presented less danger within his reach.

"Bring me a glass of water, would you?" he asked the

footman. The servant nodded and turned to the sideboard to fulfill his request.

"Lord Creed," a soft voice from down the table spoke. "It seems an age since we last met."

He met Lydia's gaze directly. What game was she playing? "It has been several years, Lady Brend."

"You look well." Her tone was like a warning bell that echoed in his head. Brahm never claimed to be a rake, or any kind of expert when it came to women, but he knew blatant flattery—sexual sycophancy—when he heard it.

"He's unmarried," Lord Brend replied jovially. "Of course he looks well!"

The remark drew laughter from several guests. Lydia smiled coyly, but her attention never left Brahm. "Unmarried. We all know what a close call that was, do we not, Lord Creed?"

Was that Arabella or Muriel who gasped ever so softly at her sister's obvious reference to Eleanor jilting him? But perhaps he simply imagined it because the other Durbane sisters soon met the remark with musical laughter.

"Oh, Lydia," Phoebe tittered. "You really are too droll." There was a tightness to her smile that didn't quite manage to hide her true feelings. She did not approve of Lydia's remark. Brahm didn't either, even though Lydia had done him a great service by making the joke—as had Phoebe by joining in. They were presenting the illusion to the rest of the guests that whatever discord there had once been between him and Eleanor was gone now. In other words, there was no gossip to be found in his being there.

"Indeed," he added, joining the ruse even though it left a bad taste in his mouth. "Especially since I am certain that everyone here knows that Lady Eleanor was truly the lucky one."

He was only saying what no doubt everyone else was thinking, but Arabella flashed him a grateful glance anyway. Regardless of Eleanor's motives for crying off, for refusing to marry him only hours after giving her consent, society never looked pleasingly upon a jilt. If Brahm wanted, he could have made some very disparaging remarks against Eleanor—years ago as well as now—but to what end? He hadn't deserved her when she was his for the having, proving, if to no one other than himself, that Eleanor had been the one in the right after all.

Lydia continued to watch him with that rapacious gaze. Could no one else see it? Or did no one else care? She looked so much like Eleanor, but not even half as lovely. Eleanor might have had the look of an angry woman when she gazed at him, but Lydia looked bitter. While Eleanor had a cool elegance, Lydia was simply unfeeling and overdone. She was like a distorted version of Eleanor. How could he have ever mistaken her for the girl he had wanted to marry? And he must have been mistaken that night, because he never in a million years would have bedded this woman if his wits had been about him.

He remained quiet during the remainder of the meal, speaking only when a question was directed his way. Was it just his imagination, or were people going out of their way to include him in conversation? To be sure, there were those who ignored him altogether—he was bad *ton*, after all—but a few others seemed to pay him undue attention, as though they sought his approval. Odd. It had been many years since anyone treated him in such a manner.

Oh, there were those mamas who didn't care whom their daughters married, provided he had ample fortune; they had never stopped curtsying to him, but these guests weren't greedy mamas, though there were a few mothers and daughters present. They were socially acceptable lords and ladies who would lead others by their example.

Could it be that he had actually changed enough for society to take notice? Or perhaps he was becoming fashionable in his unfashionableness? Did it matter? His brothers and their wives and their families and friends had done so much to bring him back into the world, perhaps their efforts had not gone to waste after all.

After dinner he enjoyed a cigar with the other gentlemen, listening to their ribald stories with a relaxed smile. No one seemed to notice that he didn't drink his port.

He was just about to escape to his room for the remainder of the evening when the butler stopped him in the corridor.

"I beg your pardon, my lord, but Lord Burrough requests that you attend him in his chamber."

This was it. They'd fed him, lulled him into a false sense of security, and now they were going to toss him out on his arse like the offal they believed him to be.

Or perhaps Lord Burrough was going to tell him why he had invited him in the first place. He might even offer him Eleanor's hand.

What a joke that would be.

"Thank you. I shall go right up."

"Do you require my assistance in locating His Lordship's chambers, my lord?"

Brahm shook his head. "I know where it is." He had visited that same chamber on his last visit, sharing a brandy with the old man before retiring to bed.

The butler bowed and left him. Brahm continued down the corridor to the hall, where a wide flight of stairs awaited. He paused at the bottom, staring up the large staircase that split into two separate curving paths halfway up. What rubbish this was. He was afraid to go up, afraid to face the man who had been a friend to his father, and a friend to him. He was afraid to face him because he had acted so very badly the last time he was in this house, and he was ashamed of it. He was ashamed of so very much. Every time he was confronted by another person he had wronged or slighted, it was like a knife twisting in his gut. It whittled the shame away, but it hurt like hell all the same.

He placed the tip of his cane on the first stair and pushed himself up. No one had mentioned his cane. Everyone pretended not to notice that he limped, that he was no longer physically perfect. It wasn't vanity speaking—or perhaps it was—but he had once had a reputation as being a fine specimen of manhood. He had been a Corinthian of the highest order, and now once he finally managed to mount a horse, he could stay in the saddle only a fraction of the time he once could before his leg started throbbing. And he had given up fencing altogether due to his lack of grace.

At the top of the stairs he paused to give his leg a rest. These kinds of exertions didn't take the toll on him that they once had, but he had long ago accepted that he would never be as he was before the accident. He had made his peace with that knowledge. It was a small price to pay for being given a second chance to make something of himself. It was more than his father had been given.

Eleanor's jilting him hadn't been enough to wake him up. It should have been. It never should have taken his father's death and almost his own to make him realize what a mess he had become. How different things might be right now if only Eleanor's refusal had been enough.

But it hadn't. All it had done was drive him into a bottle

for a fortnight. For two blissful weeks he hadn't thought of her, and then he talked himself into believing he was better off without her. He believed it too—except for those odd occasions when soberness brought her memory with it, or he spotted her at a social function, such as that fateful night at Pennington's.

He managed to fool himself quite well until after the accident, when he started taking stock of the ruins of his life. The realization that he needed to change had brought with it an obsession with Eleanor Durbane, and the more people he confronted with his quest for forgiveness, the more he thought of her. She was second only to Wynthrope, and now that he and his brother had made amends, Eleanor was all there was left.

That's all it was. It wasn't as though he wanted a second chance at wooing her. God help him, that wasn't what he wanted at all.

"You are very thoughtful," a voice whispered near his ear.

Brahm jumped. How had she managed to sneak up on him like that? He took a quick step away, ignoring the twinge in his leg. "Forgive me. I did not mean to block the way."

Lydia watched him with amusement in her pale eyes. "There's no need of you being so polite and stiff with me, Brahm." She chuckled. "Well, perhaps 'stiff' was the wrong word."

His brows pulled together. "I am afraid I do not know what you mean." That was a lie, of course. He might be dim at times when it came to women, but he wasn't a complete idiot. She had obviously come looking for him.

She moved closer, the thin silk of her gown hugging her body in blatant invitation. Was the woman like this with every man, or was he one of the unfortunate few? Yes, he could take her, could plunge himself in her. It wouldn't take much effort to get hard and do just that, but if he was going to screw Lydia, he might as well go downstairs afterward and drink a whole bottle of brandy. Would she be so encouraging if she knew he thought sharing her bed would be a step down for him?

"Why are you here, Brahm?" Her expression was curious, her posture beckoning.

He shifted away from her, leaning on his cane when his injured leg refused to move fast enough. "I was invited."

She chuckled and pressed forward once more. "Obviously. But why did you accept?"

If she advanced any farther she was going to force him over the balustrade. Her question gave him pause. Answering her honestly might not be the best course of action, but lying might give the wrong impression. Did she know how much hurt their actions had dealt Eleanor? She couldn't, otherwise she wouldn't be there now, not if she loved Eleanor.

Obviously impatient with his silence, she tried again. "Are you here for me, or for Eleanor?"

"I am not here *for* anyone, madam." Politeness be damned, that was his last attempt at being gentlemanly with this woman. One more salacious remark from her and he was going to tell her to go straight to hell. He didn't have time for this. He didn't have *patience* for this.

Lydia ran a long, graceful hand along his lapel. "I have never forgotten our night together."

That was it. Staring at her and her pouty lips, Brahm was thoroughly disgusted with both of them. "And I have never *remembered* it. Excuse me."

He brushed past her and continued down the corridor to Lord Burrough's room. Her laughter followed him. She obviously was not a woman easily discouraged. Either that or she was simply having a laugh at his expense.

He was told to enter on the first knock, and he was all too glad to step inside. No matter what the old earl did to him, it was preferable to dealing with his lustful daughter.

The room was dark as he stepped inside, the light much dimmer than it had been in the corridor. A lamp burned on the table beside the bed where Lord Burrough reclined, a book beside his hip. He looked older than Brahm remembered, and tired, but other than that, he seemed surprisingly hale for a man reported to be in the twilight of his life.

Perhaps the gossips had exaggerated the earl's frailty.

"Well, if it isn't the Viscount Creed." His voice was strong as well. "Come in, boy, and let me have a look at you."

It never occurred to Brahm to disobey. He walked across the dark carpet until his shins were just inches from the earl's bed. The older man gazed up at him with pale eyes. "It's not polite to tower over me like that, young man. Sit."

There was a chair behind him, and Brahm pulled it up to the bed so he could sit, positioning himself so that his leg was stretched out at a comfortable angle. "It is good to see you again, my lord."

Burrough made a scoffing noise. "Don't 'my lord' me. I have known you all your life. Call me Burr, it's what your father used to call me."

Brahm nodded. "Very well." If a former friendship with

Brahm's father was to thank for this warm welcome, Brahm wasn't going to fight it.

The old man smiled and leaned back against his pillows. "I suppose you're wondering why I invited you here after what happened last time."

There was nothing like getting straight to the heart of the matter; Brahm appreciated that. "The question has crossed my mind."

Burrough guffawed, as if he knew just what an understatement that was, but his expression quickly grew thoughtful. "I invited you here because of Eleanor."

Brahm's heart gave a little leap at the mention of her. Had she told her father what happened?

"I do not know what happened between the two of you back then"—that answered that question—"but I do know that my daughter has never been the same since her disappointment."

Disappointment. That was an interesting way to put it. "And so you invited me here to do what exactly?"

"You have been an obsession with my daughter for years, and since you responded to my invitation, I can only assume that you share her affliction. I want you and Ellie to do whatever it is you need to do to set things right between you. I want her to get on with her life."

Brahm laughed and shook his head. "I do not think that is possible."

"Why?"

"Because Lady Eleanor does not want to set things right between us." Had she really been as obsessed with him as he was with her? That was a long time to carry so much hatred.

Burrough's eyes narrowed, but Brahm didn't feel threatened. "What did you do to my daughter, boy?"

Rubbing his hand over his face, Brahm sighed in resignation and leaned forward, resting his forearms on the black wool of his trousers. He forced himself to meet the older man's gaze. "Eleanor refused my offer of marriage because she caught me . . . in a very compromising situation with another woman."

The earl didn't even blink. "Lydia."

Damnation. Brahm's jaw dropped in a blatant display of surprise that was unlike anything he had experienced for quite some time. "How did you know?"

Burrough sighed. "Lydia married young, to a man I knew was no match for her, but she would not be dissuaded. It did not take long for her to start looking outside her marriage for a little joy."

If the old man wanted to call his daughter's affairs "joy," then Brahm wasn't going to correct him. "It is no excuse, but I was foxed. I do not remember it."

"I believe you." The old man's smile was kind, sympathetic even. "You were a hopeless drunk, but you were not dishonorable."

Brahm wasn't so sure of that, but he didn't have the inclination to argue if the old man wanted to believe it.

"If it is worth anything, I haven't had a drink in almost two years." Those months following his accident had been difficult and laudanum had proved to have its own appeal, but Brahm refused to hide in a stupor for the rest of his life, not when he had been given a fresh start. Now he was able to take laudanum for his leg and not worry that he might end up in one of the Oriental dens with a pipe in his hand.

The earl nodded. "It is worth a lot. Your father had similar demons, but that did not mean he wasn't a good man at heart. I have a strong suspicion that you are a good man as well."

Brahm swallowed. He didn't know what to say.

"I do not know if Ellie can forgive you for what you did, boy, but I do know this: if Eleanor does not make her peace with you, if she does not get what happened between the two of you out of her head, then she will never be able to find happiness, and above all else I want my daughter to be happy."

Brahm wanted that too. The realization came as a bit of a surprise, but if he was responsible for Eleanor's unhappiness, then he wanted to fix it.

"The two of you will end up either married or hating each other," the earl predicted. "To be honest, I don't much care which one, so long as Eleanor is happy."

Fair enough. "Why did you wait so long to force this confrontation?" So many years had passed. If the old man had been so concerned with Eleanor's well-being, why hadn't he done something long before this?

Burrough smiled, but there was more compassion in it than humor. "I had to wait till you sobered up."

True to his dictate, Eleanor's father refused to fling Brahm Ryland from their house. True to her own word, Eleanor gave Brahm little chance to prove his so-called change to her. She avoided him as often as possible over the course of the next two days. It wasn't easy. As hostess she was expected to chat with all the guests during meals and other activities. Somehow, though, she managed to make certain that Brahm wasn't one of those guests she spoke to.

Now as she sat underneath an airy canopy on the back lawn of her father's estate, waiting for lunch to be served alfresco, she began to wonder if perhaps her snub hadn't begun to work to her advantage. All but a few of the guests had already come outside for the meal, and Brahm Ryland was not among them. Perhaps he had decided to take refreshment in his chamber. Or perhaps he had finally come to his senses and decided to depart from the party.

Hmpf. That was unlikely. She ignored the disappointment that came with the thought of his leaving. Why would he leave when so many others seemed pleased by his company? Many of the guests treated him like some kind of delightful confection. His disgustingly scandalous past had made him something of a legend, it seemed, and that made him popular. Add that to the fact that there were several respected society matrons who went out of their way to support him, and the Viscount Creed was well on his way to being society's darling once more.

But his popularity aside, why would he leave when he knew his being there was bound to drive her to distraction? He took enjoyment from her discomfort, of that she was certain. And he had to know she was uncomfortable—even if their initial meeting hadn't gone as it had, her avoidance of him was a clear indication of what she thought of him.

No. Brahm Ryland had a reason to remain under her father's roof. What that reason was, Eleanor didn't know, and she wasn't particularly certain that she cared to, either.

Yet there was a part of her—that same part that made sure she wore a most flattering gown in a becoming shade of blue—that wanted to see him and have him see her. She wanted him to notice that she was in her best looks, and that though many years had passed, they had been kind to her. She knew she was aging well. In fact, she was more pleased by her own appearance now than she had been ten years ago. Of course, Brahm was weathering time well himself, but that was beside the point. She wanted him to see that her marriageless state was of her choosing, not because no one would have her. She wanted him to admire her, perhaps even try to renew his addresses just so she could have the pleasure of grinding his hopes beneath her heel.

God help her, after all these years she wanted at least some retribution for what he had done.

Thank God she hadn't been in love with him. What a mess that would have been! Her heart might never have recovered. As it was it took her pride—and yes, her heart—longer than it should have to repair the damage done. She had liked Brahm—liked him very much—and her disappointment had been keenly felt.

Much like the lurch of her heart when he stepped out into the afternoon sunshine and joined the rest of their party.

Even as Eleanor cursed her own body's reaction to the blasted man, her gaze fastened on him greedily, drinking in every detail of his appearance. How easy and composed he seemed—how uncaring. People stared at him, and he didn't seem the least bit bothered, but then he was probably used to stares by now, given some of his past exploits.

The sun brought out warm shades of gold and red in the waves of his too-long hair. Did the man not have a valet to tend to such things? Most men would have looked shabby with such locks, but not Brahm. He looked boyish and tousled, and more than a little rakish. The lines around his eyes and mouth should have made an old man of him, but they only added to his carefree appearance. He had the look of a man who laughed often.

Laughter. What amusement could life have possibly afforded Brahm Ryland? He had been disowned by society. He had earned a lame leg from the same accident that killed his father. Surely he found no laughter in such things?

She had more reason to smile than he did, and yet she knew her own face to be as smooth as a porcelain doll's. She could be just as cool and expressionless as a doll as well, though there was no explaining it. Despite the fullness of her life, she sometimes felt utterly empty inside. Somewhere along the way she had become so amazingly adept at concealing her emotions that she hid them even from herself.

Brahm smiled at someone who spoke to him, crinkling the skin around his russet eyes and revealing straight white teeth. With his impeccable buff trousers and chocolate jacket, polished boots and snowy cravat, he looked every inch the gentleman. The gold top of his cane flashed in the sun, adding to his elegant aspect. He had obviously taken pains with his appearance as well. But for whose benefit? Hers? Impossible.

"He is a fine-looking man, is he not?"

Despite the heat, a chill passed over Eleanor as she gazed upward. Lydia stood beside her, her gaze lingering on Brahm in what Eleanor suspected might be a hungry manner.

"Who?" How difficult it was to feign ignorance.

It seemed to take great effort for the younger woman to tear her gaze away from the man across the lawn, but when she did, she directed those pale blue eyes at her sister. "You know who. Take care not to stare, dearest. The gossips will say you still have feelings for him."

The words were said without a hint of malice or poison,

and yet Eleanor flushed at them. It was on the tip of her tongue to give Lydia a similar warning, but she held her silence. Her sister was only thinking of her best interests and did not deserve such vitriol in return.

"The gossips will say whatever they wish regardless," she responded coolly. "Do not concern yourself, Lydia. I am in no danger where Brahm Ryland is concerned."

The look her sister flashed her was hard to read, but there was an unmistakable air of amusement in it, as though Lydia thought her horribly naive.

"Any woman he sets his sights on is in danger from him, Eleanor. He is just that kind of man."

Eleanor looked away, swallowing hard. Did Lydia consider herself in danger as well? And why should that idea put such a sour taste in Eleanor's mouth? She didn't agree with dishonoring one's wedding vows, but a woman had a right to seize whatever happiness she could in this world dominated by men. Who was she to judge anyone's actions? Who was she to say she would not do the same in such a situation?

Or was she simply jealous because her younger sister had experienced what should have by rights been hers?

"I will take that under consideration." She kept her tone deliberately bland. "I believe Muriel is trying to capture your attention, dear."

Lydia sighed. "No doubt she wants me to rescue her from Lady Edwards. Excuse me."

In truth Eleanor was glad to see the back of her sister, even if her departure left her alone once more. How she wanted this luncheon over so she could escape to her room for some peace.

Feeling a gaze upon her, she looked up to find herself

staring into Brahm's eyes. Even from a distance his gaze affected her, making her heart jump in response. Had he seen her talking to Lydia? Did he wonder if perhaps they had been discussing him? Did he care?

Eleanor jerked her gaze away. It was foolish, but she didn't want to risk his reading anything in her eyes, and she didn't want him to think that she wanted anything to do with him, because she didn't.

The butler rang the bell that the meal was about to be served, signaling that guests not yet seated should do so. Luncheon was to be an informal affair, with several smaller tables rather than one large one set out underneath the canopy. Snow white lacy tablecloths swayed in the breeze, their tops decorated with simple displays of brightly colored flowers and glittering silverware. All had been done under Eleanor's supervision, and she took pride in seeing how lovely everything looked.

Her father joined her at the table, along with Arabella and her husband, Henry; one of her father's chosen bachelors; a respected society matron; and an older couple who were old friends of her father's. The chair next to Eleanor was empty until Brahm claimed it for himself.

How dare he! Eleanor's face flamed with indignation, but she fought to keep her reaction from showing. Other guests were watching their table with open interest, and she wasn't about to give them something to talk about over their pheasant and salmon.

Her father saved her from having to react at all.

"Creed, good of you to join us, boy!" he boomed, his voice stronger than Eleanor had heard it in weeks. "I trust you know everyone?"

Grinding her teeth, Eleanor snuck a glance out of the

corner of her eye as Brahm nodded. "Thank you, Lord Burrough. I bid you all a good day."

Everyone greeted him cordially save for the other bachelor—a Lord Taylor. Taylor was decidedly cool toward Brahm, and Eleanor sighed inside. Wonderful, she was going to be treated as a bone held above hungry dogs—a prize and nothing more.

Or perhaps Lord Taylor was simply being rude. Regardless, it didn't flatter him. Of course, if the poor man had been cordial, that wouldn't have painted him in a better light either.

Leaning to his right, Brahm slipped his cane between their chairs, letting it fall onto the grass. The movement brought his shoulder against hers, his sandalwood-scented hair dangerously close to brushing her face. Even as she froze, trying to shrink in her chair so as not to touch him, Eleanor inhaled a deep breath, drawing him into her lungs. Was she so starved for male companionship that she would react so basely to any man, or was Brahm Ryland special?

Please, God, let it be that I am simply starved for companionship.

He mumbled something as he straightened, something that sounded like "strawberry." She had used strawberry cream on her skin that morning, along with a dollop of specially made perfume of the same scent.

"Does my perfume offend you, Lord Creed?" she asked softly, haughtily. The others at their table were engaged in their own conversations as they waited to be served by the footmen carrying trays of food from the house.

He turned his head toward her. He truly was a handsome man. Too bad he was such a cad. She might have loved him if his insides had been as lovely as his outside.

"Not in the least," he replied in his low, smooth voice. "You smell exactly as I remember—like wild strawberries on a hot summer day."

It was an innocent enough description, but the sound of the words on his tongue brought a wave of heat washing over Eleanor. How could she despise him for humiliating her as he had and still find him so attractive? Was it some kind of weakness on her part, or was it simply an example of his seductive power over women?

She didn't know how to respond, so she didn't. She simply reached for her glass of lemonade and took a sip, hoping the tart drink would cool the flush under her skin.

He didn't speak to her again during the meal. In fact he didn't speak much at all, save when conversation was directed at him. Occasionally his knee bumped hers under the table, sending her heart into a cacophony of beats that surely could be heard in Scotland. What was wrong with her? It had to be her nerves. She didn't know his reasons for accepting her father's invitation. She didn't know what game he intended to play with her—if he played one at all.

Dessert was bowls of fresh, ripe berries covered in rich, sweet cream. It was then that Brahm broke his self-imposed silence. Dipping his spoon into the bowl, he retrieved a lush, red strawberry. Beads of cream dotted its shiny surface. Eleanor watched, unable to look away, as he lifted the spoon to his mouth. He popped the berry in whole, biting into its sweet flesh with such an expression of satisfaction that Eleanor was ashamed to look, but look she did. Her gaze was fixed on his lips, where a tiny drop of cream threatened to drip away until his tongue flicked out and caught it.

Eleanor shivered.

Returning his spoon to the bowl, Brahm cast her a slow

glance, accompanied by a smile that might have been apologetic if it hadn't looked so blasted mocking. "Strawberries are my favorite."

Eleanor's attention whipped back to her own bowl, where she intentionally avoided the strawberries. Tomorrow she would use the rose water instead of her berry scent.

It might be worth the experiment just to see if roses then became the viscount's favorite flower.

Perhaps she was being unfair, but he deserved no more from her—and it was far safer than imagining him devouring her as he devoured that strawberry, for that was the image his words conjured.

No doubt that was his intention.

When the meal was finally over, Eleanor was all too glad to be given the opportunity to finally escape. She was stiff from holding herself so far away from him during luncheon, and she was beginning to develop a pounding in her temples that had nothing to do with the heat.

Brahm followed her to her feet. Even with his cane for support, he was unsteady on the uneven ground. Eleanor reached out to assist him. It was either that or let him fall, and even she wasn't that cruel.

He moved his feet, seemingly shifting his weight to his good leg while stretching the other. No doubt his leg was balking at carrying him after resting for so long.

Brahm's face pinched a bit as he slowly levered some of his bulk onto the injured limb. The skin between his brows furrowed with the effort. Despite her better judgment, Eleanor couldn't help but feel for him. The pain must be unbearable at times.

A self-conscious chuckle escaped him as he slowly

pulled free of her hold. Reluctantly Eleanor let him go. If he fell, she didn't think she could catch him.

"We are in for rain, I believe," he remarked, taking a tentative step away from the table.

Eleanor raised a brow. So much for thanking her for her assistance. Had that much pride, did he? "You can predict the weather, can you?"

The grin he flashed her was meant to be careless, perhaps even roguish, but it was too uncertain to succeed. "Did you not know that about me?"

She could have walked away from him then, but she didn't. Instead she fell into step beside him, silently lending him whatever support she might offer until they reached the house. "I imagine there are a great many things I do not know about you."

"It is unfortunate that we never had the chance to rectify that."

She shrugged, her gaze fixed on the house rather than the man beside her. She had forgotten how tall he was. "Or fortunate, depending on how you look at it."

He was walking more easily now. "Yes, I suppose so."

Silence lingered until they were almost at the steps leading to the house. He stopped, and she didn't hesitate to come to a halt as well. Lifting her gaze to his, she waited for him to speak. How strangely calm she was now that he wasn't so close. She wasn't expecting the words that came so softly out of his mouth.

"I do not expect you to accept any apology I might make. I know I can never make right what happened, but I want you to know that I am truly sorry for any hurt I might have caused you. Injuring you was the last thing I wanted to do."

Was he jesting? He couldn't possibly be *that* dense, could he? "Surely you must have realized I would have been injured by . . . what you did."

His gaze was remorseful, but candid all the same. "I was beyond realization, Ellie, and far too foxed to separate reality from imagination."

It may not have been the prettiest of answers, but it certainly sounded honest. The familiar shortening of her name only added to her confusion.

"Reality from imagination?" She was certain she wanted the answer, as part of her already suspected what it would be, but she needed to hear it all the same.

His gaze was frank, without a hint of embarrassment. "Who was actually in my bed versus who I wanted it to be."

Eleanor flushed to the roots of her hair as she turned and began walking once more. Brahm followed silently, and Eleanor was glad he did not try to speak again. Her mind was already overwhelmed by what he had said to her that afternoon.

Did he mean for her to believe that he had pretended Lydia was she that night, or had he actually believed it to be so? Or was this confession simply scandalous words from a smooth-tongued devil who sought to toy with her affections once more?

And more importantly, which of the three did she wish was true?

Chapter 4

Brahm wasn't about to allow Eleanor to resume ignoring him—not after his minor victory at luncheon.

It wasn't much to crow over, but he saw a flicker of uncertainty in her gaze when he told her how drunk he had been the night he bedded her sister, and he saw the concern in her eyes when he almost stumbled because of his leg. Finally that damn injury had come in handy. Any embarrassment at having her see him weakened was a pittance when faced with the idea that she might actually soften toward him. He hadn't expected her to give him a chance quite so quickly, nor was he willing to give up said chance now that it had presented itself.

He had been seated too far away from her at dinner to talk to her, and now he was in the drawing room making small talk with those who would speak to him while he waited for the right time to approach her.

Perhaps "small talk" was not quite the right phrase. "Interrogation" might be a better term. It was an awful thing, being notorious. It gave people all kinds of strange thoughts as to one's character. Oddly enough, it seemed to give rise to the notion that he was some kind of exotic creature, rare and exciting. If they only knew just how utterly boring he was.

It also gave people the sense that they could ask whatever they pleased, tossing propriety to the wind.

"Is it true that you killed a man, Lord Creed?"

Brahm's heart stopped dead. For one split second he thought the man referred to his father. Rationally Brahm knew that he could not have prevented his father's death. If it hadn't happened that night while they were thoroughly foxed and wild, it would have happened some other night. Still, a voice persisted that surely he could have done *something* to prevent the accident.

"I beg your pardon?" The man asking was one of the bachelors invited to vie for Eleanor's hand—a dandyish sort whose name escaped Brahm. If the fool was trying to irk him, then Brahm wanted to force him into explaining himself. Explanations were so very wonderful for making people look as foolish as they deserved.

But the fop didn't look chastised at all. "I heard that you killed a dastardly criminal in defense of your brother. Is it true?"

Oh *that*. Yes, that was true. He had shot a man who threatened his brother North. "I believe the gossips to have greatly exaggerated my part in that intrigue." He could have boasted of his involvement, but his brothers were more deserving of a hero's laurels than he. He never aspired to such acclaim. Besides, all he had done was rid the world of one vermin. Aside from preventing any harm from befalling North, he hadn't done anything more special than killing a rat.

He was saved from any further questions by a footman offering refreshment. "Champagne, my lord?"

Brahm shook his head. "Thank you, no." It was easy enough to resist. He'd never cared much for champagne.

"Perhaps you would prefer something stronger?" the dandy suggested, craning his neck to glance toward a side-board near the back wall. "I've a mind for a whiskey. What say you?"

At the mere mention of the word, Brahm's mouth seemed to leap to life. He could almost taste the bitter smoothness on his tongue, the gentle burn as the whiskey slid down his throat. He could smell it, could feel the tension draining from his muscles as the liquor worked its potent magic.

Christ yes, he would prefer something stronger.

A tiny trace of moisture beaded along his hairline. He could do this. He was stronger than the craving.

"No," he said, sharper and louder than he intended. Many of the guests turned to see what had caused his outburst. "Thank you."

The fop obviously did not know when to stop. "Bourbon then?"

Brahm gritted his teeth. Bourbon would be delicious. "I appreciate the offer but I no longer imbibe."

It seemed that the second he finished speaking, the entire room fell silent. Gazes fell upon him like blossoms shaken from a tree. Some were surprised, some were pleased, and some were disbelieving. A few even voiced their support of the decision, congratulating him as though he had achieved some great feat.

He didn't care what the other guests thought of him, however. He didn't care what Eleanor's sisters thought. Praise was always appreciated, even if it was unwanted and unnecessary, but it wasn't as though he based his own sense of self on it. He cared for the reaction of one person and one person alone. His gaze found her easily, watching him from a short distance away, a glass of champagne in her hand.

Eleanor's normally smooth brow was puckered as she gazed at him with an expression he couldn't quite decipher before she looked away. Did she believe him? Was she now entertaining the idea that he might have indeed changed?

Why her opinion mattered so much was a mystery. Why he craved her forgiveness so badly he couldn't fathom. He didn't care if anyone else in this room believed that he was a changed man; only Eleanor's belief in him signified.

The dandy—Lord Faulkner was his name, now he remembered—was not to be satisfied. He gave a low chuckle, as though he thought Brahm had just told an amusing joke.

"Surely you can have one drink," he insisted. "One glass of bourbon never hurt anyone."

It was harmful enough to the man who had never been able to stop at just one.

Brahm shook his head. The stares were starting to weigh on him. "I cannot."

It was humiliating, admitting that he dared not have even one glass. Here he sat, among these people, many who knew just what a bastard he could be when deep in his cups, admitting that he was not strong enough to resist temptation. It was debasing to have so many see his weakness.

"Port then," Faulkner continued. "You must have something."

It sounded as if Faulkner was fishing for a drinking

partner—someone to get foxed with so he wouldn't be the only one drinking to excess. What a sad situation the dandy had gotten himself into. It would be so easy for Brahm to despise Faulkner for having placed him in this uncomfortable position, but he could not find anything but pity in his heart. He knew all too well the hold liquor could have on a man. The cravings ran deep, like the roots of an ancient oak, twisting around heart, soul, and mind until the sweet bliss of drunken oblivion blotted out all else. He would not risk becoming his former self just to save face with a fop too young and foolish to realize how deep a hole he was digging.

"Perhaps sherry if nothing else."

Faulkner would not give up. Just when Brahm thought he was going to have to take a firmer stance with the younger man, rescue came from the most unlikely of sources. The footman was gone, replaced by an angelic vision in a soft cream evening gown shot with shimmery golden threads. She offered him a delicate china cup on a saucer.

"Have some coffee, Lord Creed," Eleanor urged in a soft but determined tone. "I remember that you always did have a preference for it. You take it black with sugar, correct?"

Stunned, Brahm could manage little but a nod as he accepted the offered drink. What was she doing? Not only had she come to his rescue, but she had alluded to their past connection as well. Why would she come to his aid when he had betrayed her in such a deplorable manner? If nothing else, she should have been standing back enjoying his discomfort, not trying to assuage it by drawing attention to herself.

Finally composure returned. "Thank you, Lady Eleanor. You flatter me with your keen memory for such trivial details." Black with sugar indeed. It had been his standard remedy for a night of debauchery. The debauching he had given up, but the way he took his coffee remained. 🌶

"You are quite welcome." Her smile wasn't kind but it was sympathetic, and it gnawed at Brahm's gut. "There is a pot on the sideboard, should you care for more."

And then she turned her back on him and walked away as though nothing had happened. Had he imagined her swooping down to rescue him? Had it been a rescue at all? Or had it been Eleanor's subtle way of getting in her own dig at him? Whatever it was, he was pathetically grateful for it. Faulkner was off collecting his glass of bourbon, and Brahm was certain the young lord would not request he join him in drink again.

Lifting the cup to his lips, he took a sip, almost sighing in pleasure as the rich blend hit his tongue. It wasn't whiskey but it would do.

Conversation dwindled as the evening's entertainment began. There was to be music first, followed by a light supper and bit of cards before retiring. He would stay for the music as it would be rude not to, and he might even stay for the supper, depending on the demands of his stomach, but he would escape to his chamber before cards. Card playing was one of those activities that lent itself to drinking, and he had to be thoroughly inebriated to enjoy piquet or whist.

It seemed as though the years dropped away and he was young again when Eleanor took her seat at the pianoforte. Her lovely face was as smooth and unblemished as a cameo—no more lined than it had been when he first decided he wanted her for his own. Only the cool, quiet maturity of her features betrayed that years had passed and that they had not been transported back in time. She had been a beautiful girl, but she had become an exquisite woman. He watched as her neck bowed—a slender ivory arch that allowed her to direct her attention to the sheets of music spread before her.

Her fingers were deft and sure as she began to play. It was an unkind thought, but obviously all these years as an unmarried lady had improved her talent.

Had she been lonely? he wondered as the haunting melody she created filled the room. She played for the benefit of others now as she had the last time he'd sat and listened in this room. Last time he had been the one to lay claim to her and had sentenced her to being titled a jilt because she wouldn't reveal him for the bastard he was. Had she ever cursed him when she sat at her pianoforte and played to an empty room while each of her younger sisters left the house as a married woman?

He'd had liquor to amuse him, to keep him company. What amused and comforted Eleanor?

At least she'd make a better match this time around. Even as the thought crossed his mind, it brought a scowl with it. He hadn't given much thought to the fact that the purpose of this house party was to find Eleanor a husband, but that's why there were several very eligible bachelors present.

He no longer had any claim to Eleanor or her affections, but she had been his once, and he didn't much like the idea of anyone else having her.

He thought about the delicious flush that had crept up her cheeks earlier that day when he told her he had imagined it was she in his bed instead of Lydia. He couldn't be certain that she believed him, and he wouldn't fault her if she didn't, but for a second he had seen a flash of heat in her eyes.

Whatever else she thought of him, "unattractive" was not on the list, which led him to an interesting dilemma.

He had come here looking for her forgiveness and understanding. It hadn't truly occurred to him that his obsession with her might stem from the fact that he still had feelings for her. Perhaps that was the real reason for his attending this party. He didn't simply want to make amends, he wanted Eleanor.

It was folly to entertain such a fancy, but once it took hold of his brain, it refused to let go. If he could prove to Eleanor that he had changed, would she give him a second chance to win her heart? Would she give him a chance to see inside her, to know the woman she had become?

For the first time in a long, long time, Brahm felt as though there was hope for the future in his life. He had always known that he was expected to marry and produce an heir, but lately since all his brothers had found wedded bliss, he simply assumed one of their children would inherit the title. Now the idea of spending the rest of his days alone, playing Uncle Brahm, seemed less inviting than it once had.

It was all Eleanor's fault. She had burrowed her way under his skin, imbedding herself within him until she became as familiar as his hands. Years apart hadn't changed that. Perhaps it was guilt over how he had forsaken her, perhaps it was twisted obsession that would dwindle once he'd seized the prize, but he didn't think so.

His return to this house wasn't mere coincidence. This wasn't simply a means to soothe his guilty conscience by earning Eleanor's forgiveness. This was fate's way of handing him a second chance to have the happiness he had tossed away in a drunken rut more years ago than he cared to remember.

The whys didn't matter. He could question his good fortune all he wanted, but the one fact remained.

He had been given a chance to discover whether Eleanor was the woman for him and he the man who deserved her.

What kind of idiot would say no to a chance like that?

What had she been thinking, coming to Brahm's defense like that?

Alone in the darkness, Eleanor tipped her face upward and allowed the warm night breeze to caress her cheeks. She stood in the moonlit shadow of a statue of Diana the huntress, one hand resting on the goddess's cool marble foot, the other hanging loosely at her side as grass swayed against the hem of her skirts.

The relative quiet of the garden soothed her strangely irritated nerves. Water bubbled in the fountain; leaves rustled a balmy refrain. In the distance she could hear the gentle voices of night creatures and smell the delicate hint of jasmine in the air. It might be the perfect night if only she could forget the looks her family and even some of her acquaintances had shot her when she leaped to Brahm's aid. He had looked so very uncomfortable, and so very much in need of rescuing.

And she had always been the kind of woman who had an instinctive urge to look after the well-being of others.

The obvious surprise of her guests was easy enough to shoulder, but the concerned and—dare she think it?—censorious gazes of her sisters were more difficult to brush aside. Even Arabella had seemed concerned. What did they believe she was going to do? Run away with

Brahm Ryland simply because he claimed to have given up spirits? She was hardly ninny enough to do such a thing.

Did they believe her reputation, her very virtue, to be in danger now that Brahm had walked back into her life? How little they knew her if that were indeed the case. And who were they to cast judgment upon her? Only Arabella had succeeded in making a happy life for herself. Her other sisters were no strangers to secrecy and affairs. They should consider their own reputations and allow her to worry about her own. Perhaps they feared that so many years as a spinster was about to push her over the edge of reason and that she'd chase after Brahm like a hound, running him to ground and having her way with him.

The absurdity of the thought brought a smile with it.

"I hope I am not interrupting."

Eleanor's heart lurched at the sound of his voice. She had been so deep in her thoughts, she hadn't heard his approach. How long had he been standing there watching her?

He drew closer, grass bowing beneath his shoes. He was in evening dress, and the white of his cravat shone with a ghostly hue in the moonlight. How utterly lovely he was, especially when he smiled in that crooked manner.

"I am alone, Lord Creed. There is nothing for you to interrupt." As the words left her mouth, Eleanor cringed inwardly. How cold she sounded. Did she always sound so remote?

He stopped no more than a foot away from her, leaning on his cane for support. He wasn't fooling Eleanor. He could pounce in an instant if necessary.

"You do yourself a disservice, Eleanor. You were obviously deep within your own thoughts."

She shrugged. "My thoughts were nothing of consequence." She would never confess that he had been the subject of her wandering mind. "And I have not given you leave to call me by my Christian name." Pettiness, yes, but she needed all the defenses she had against this man. He had been under the same roof but a few days, and already she felt herself warming toward him once more.

He moved closer, mere inches between them now. Was that the humidity of the evening she felt pressing against her through the fabric of her gown, or was it the heat from his imposing frame?

"My dear girl, you gave me permission more than a decade ago. You cannot take it back."

When was the last time someone had called her "girl"? She raised her gaze to his. Impulse took over, and she allowed it to have its way. "I took back my consent to marry you. I can take back whatever I want."

He laughed then, a soft chuckle that sent a shiver down her spine. What did it take to wound this man? Something out of her power, obviously.

"Not if I refuse to give it," he replied with a rakish wink.

She frowned. No doubt he expected her to swoon. "What you are saying, then, is that it does not matter what I want, you will call me whatever pleases you."

He nodded. "When we are alone, yes."

"Then I shall have to endeavor to make certain we are not alone again." How very adept he was at flustering her. "Good evening."

He caught her arm as she moved to brush past him. Eleanor glanced down at the strong brown fingers gripping the soft flesh above her elbow where her glove ended. He was warm, his grip firm but not intimidating.

"We need to talk, Ellie."

Eleanor closed her eyes. If only she could blot out the

mesmerizing sound of his voice murmuring her name. If only the sight of him wasn't branded in her memory for all time. She wanted to believe the best of this man. She always had. If he told her now that she had imagined finding him and Lydia together, she would try to make it so, just because she didn't want to believe him capable of such deception. The fact that he was drunk when it happened only made her want to excuse him more.

"What could we possibly have to discuss, Brahm?" Saying his name felt so awkward but natural. Only in her mind had she referred to him by his Christian name since his betrayal. It was a mistake to do so now, she knew it.

"We can begin with you explaining to me why you did not tell why you rejected my proposal."

Her eyebrows arched, but he still did not release her arm. "I thought you knew."

Whiskey brown eyes were black in the darkness, but there was no hiding the hurt in them. "Was your opinion of me so low that you believed I would do something so awful if in my right senses?"

"Not of you," she confessed. "Of myself."

His fingers dropped away from her arm. Strange, but her skin missed his touch the second it was gone.

"You had to know I held you in the *highest* regard."

It was hardly a declaration of love, but what did she expect after all this time. She wasn't certain if she had loved him either.

"So high you bedded my sister mere hours after telling me you wanted me to be your bride." She choked on the words, all the old anger and betrayal rushing back. The scars on her heart protested as the old wound opened once more.

"I did not know what I was doing."

"Did you not?"

He didn't even flinch, as though he was accustomed to the rebuttal. Yes, he must have heard it often enough. "You have witnessed my behavior when I have been drinking, Eleanor. I am told it is as though another has taken possession of my body."

That was true. That night at Pennington's soiree when he had relieved himself in their punch bowl had been a nightmare. Eleanor had never seen anything so shocking, and the fact that he had smirked at her while doing it was something she would never forget. It had been like looking at another man. There had been nothing of *her* Brahm in that flat, malicious gaze.

"Ah, so then it was another man who took my sister to his bed. All is forgiven, obviously." Where was this sarcasm coming from? She'd never spoken to anyone like this in all her life, but he brought it out in her. As much as she wanted to forgive him, she wanted to strike out at him as well.

His smile was rueful. "If your forgiveness was that easily given, it would not be worth pursuing."

Now what the devil did that mean? Did he want her to be hard on him?

"I did not know what I was doing that night," he informed her. "If I had been in my right mind, it never would have happened. I would have known who it was coming to my bed."

There was that insinuation that he had mistaken Lydia for her again. Thank goodness for the darkness so he couldn't see the flush that was surely spreading up her cheeks—it made it so much easier to ignore his words.

"You said you were foxed. You do not need to explain to me how that weakened your resolve. I have heard spirits can have that effect on a man." Could he tell that she didn't believe it? She could not bring herself to accept that drunkenness could make someone act in a way he didn't at least contemplate when sober.

He shifted his weight. Was his leg bothering him? She fought the urge to lead him to a bench where he might sit. Let him be uncomfortable—Lord knew she was.

"Foxed is putting it mildly. Eleanor, I do not remember anything about that night except—except someone entering my room, and waking up with Lydia beside me."

Eleanor's eyes narrowed. Was it possible he was speaking the truth? And if so, why had he faltered? What wasn't he telling her?

"I am not quite certain I believe you, Lord Creed. Your hesitation tells me you have yet to confess all about that night, but do not mistake my words for curiosity. I do not care to take this discussion any further."

Even in the murky moonlight she could see his cheeks darken. He glanced away from her, suddenly uncertain, like a young boy. "I do." Then he turned to face her, his gaze boring into hers. "You see, Eleanor, the only other memory I have of that night is the thought that it was you who came to my bed."

Fire swept across Eleanor's flesh. He had admitted it. Of all the brazen, shameless things to say to her, he had taken his insinuations and forced her to consider them as fact.

"What a sterling opinion you must have had of me to believe I would play the seductress." It was impossible to keep the acrimony from her tone.

He didn't miss a beat. "Better than your own opinion if you thought I would so easily forsake you for another."

Damn him for throwing her own insecurities back at her

and using them in his own defense. He didn't stop there. "You accepted my proposal. I thought you wanted me as I wanted you. That was my opinion of you. Was I wrong in thinking you returned my feelings?"

What could she say in response to such an accusation? If she told him she had wanted him—that she had been on her way to falling in love with him—then she gave him power over her. If she told him he was wrong, then it would make her look as though she only sought to marry him for his title and his fortune. *She* was not the villain in this sordid tale.

"You were not wrong." God, how awful pride tasted— bitter and sharp in the back of her throat.

He raised his hand again, hesitating for a split second before brushing the knuckles so quickly across her cheek that she thought she might have imagined his touch.

"So can you understand how I might have allowed my cloudy mind to turn someone else into you?"

He wasn't asking outright for her forgiveness, only her understanding. Somehow Eleanor expected that to Brahm they were one and the same. If she understood him, then it would be easier for her to eventually forgive him. But how could she understand what it was like to completely lose oneself? The only time she had ever come close to that in the past was when he kissed her. Those feelings—lust, passion, desire, whatever one wanted to call them—had taken such a hold on her, she would have done anything for him, would have followed him anywhere.

"What do you want from me, Brahm?"

It was a simple enough question, but it gave him pause all the same. "It is not so much a want as it is a need. Does that make sense to you?"

"No. What is the difference?" There didn't seem to be much of one on the surface.

His brow wrinkled, then smoothed again. " 'Want' implies desire—that in itself suggests that the urge can be sated."

Was he deliberately using words like "desire" and "urge" to unsettle her?

"But a need is different. A person only needs things intrinsic to his survival." He met and held her gaze as the gravity of his words began to sink in. "I need you to understand what happens to me when I drink, Eleanor. I need you to know that it had nothing to do with you. I *need* you to know that I would do anything to take it back, to make it right. I need you to trust me again."

Eleanor's mouth was suddenly very dry. She licked her lips, unable to tear her gaze away from his. "I do not think you should say such things." God, what responsibility he was heaping on her! She didn't know if she could give him what he needed.

"Have you truly given up drinking spirits?" She had heard his words earlier when he announced them to the entire party, but she wanted—no, *needed*—him to say them to her now, while they were alone.

He nodded. "Yes."

"Has it been difficult?" If she was going to understand what happened to him when he drank, then she was going to require more information.

"Yes."

"Do you crave it?"

He chuckled; it was bitter and self-mocking. "God, yes."

That was a difficult thing for her to wrap her mind around. Certain times of the month she craved apple pie, and sometimes she believed she'd go mad if she didn't have it. Sometimes she ate a whole pie by herself. Was that how Brahm felt about spirits? She expected so, only on a much more dangerous scale.

This was too much for her to consider when he was standing so close, looking so hopeful.

"Why me?" The question burst forth before she could halt it. "Why do you need my trust?" Surely there were others he had disappointed. Had he gone to them with such requests as well?

She didn't have to think about it; she knew the answer was no. She was the only one to whom he had or would ever make this same request.

"I do not know," he replied, his tone starkly honest. "Perhaps because of all the awful things I have done, I regret injuring you the most."

Eleanor's heart leaped into her throat and began to pound there like a frantic knock on a locked door. "Even more than Lady Pennington's punch bowl?" Good Lord, how could she even ask such a thing? Hadn't she taught her sisters the importance of always giving the appearance of being a lady, even if one's thoughts were otherwise?

Brahm's answering chuckle was a soft brush of pure pleasure. Oh yes, she would do well not to give her trust over too quickly. This man was so very dangerous to her and her heart.

"Even more than that, yes."

She offered him her hand and he took it, holding her gloved fingers with the same elegance and certainty with which he held his cane, as though she were as much an extension of himself as it was.

"Everyone deserves a chance to atone for his past,

Brahm. It is the Christian way. I have regrets of my own as well. You have my word that I will endeavor to acquiesce to your request."

He smiled. "I would like that."

Eleanor smiled in return, but inside she trembled with trepidation. What was she doing? What was she entering into? It was all well and good that he wanted her forgiveness, and decent of her to give him the chance to earn it, but this bargain of theirs felt like so much more than that.

It was as though she was giving him another chance at her heart, and she didn't know if she could trust him with that again. She would do well to honestly forgive him for hurting her so.

Even more disconcerting than the fact that he wanted her forgiveness after all these years was the undeniable awareness that she *wanted* to forgive him.

In fact, for both their sakes, she hoped that she could.

Chapter 5

Giving Brahm a chance to prove himself took up more of her time than Eleanor expected. Oddly enough, she didn't mind spending time with him. In fact, if she didn't think about his betrayal, she enjoyed his company.

Of course, she did not allow herself to forget what he had done for long.

One of the changes she noted in him was the sense of age he seemed to have acquired over the years. Little shocked him, and he was slow to pass judgment. He seemed content to watch others in silent contemplation, joining conversations when asked, or if he had something of import to add. He rarely initiated topics on his own, although he had plenty to say the few times they were alone over the next day and a half. The realization finally dawned that he cared nothing about the other people at the party—not even her family, save her father. His attention was focused on her alone, and Eleanor was certain she wasn't the only one who noticed.

In fact, she was fairly certain that Brahm's attention to her was the reason her sisters were acting so strangely. Every one of them had been out of the house and out of Eleanor's charge for a number of years. They had families, and they arrived at the house with all the servants and baggage a family brought with them when traveling. Each sister had brought her own maid, but one would never know it from the amount of times they called at Eleanor's bedroom door since Brahm's arrival, wanting help with their hair or a gown. Eleanor knew their making these requests of her had nothing to do with vanity or a wish to look appealing and everything to do with nosiness. They wanted to know if Brahm had renewed his addresses to her, and more importantly, they wanted to know if Eleanor allowed it. It was a lovely compliment to her pride that they thought a man would want to marry her after but a few days' reunion.

She told them nothing, of course, save that he deserved the chance to prove if he had indeed changed. Arabella thought it a fair and honorable statement. Muriel, Phoebe, and Lydia weren't so convinced. Lydia seemed especially adamant in her insistence that Eleanor not believe in Brahm.

"Men never change," Lydia informed her with a bored expression. "They simply become more adept at lying."

Eleanor felt sorry for her sister then, because she knew Lydia honestly believed it.

Her sisters and their watchful eyes were the reason she was so grateful that today was her day to take food and supplies to the unfortunate in their little village. As the lady in one of the wealthiest houses in the area, it was not only her right but her duty to provide for those in need. She took her duties very seriously.

This morning she had listened patiently while Mrs. Rudd told her of her rheumatism and Miss Jones talked of Mr. Smith, a prosperous young farmer who had started calling on her as of late. These women had real concerns in their lives, real worries and obstacles to overcome. Wondering whether to trust in a former blackguard viscount was not something that would occur to either of them. Mrs. Rudd had no one to look after her and was often too sore and stiff to move. Miss Jones was from a family that had fallen on hard times. A good marriage would go a long way to ensuring her family's health and comfort.

The concerns of the villagers certainly put Eleanor's petty worries in perspective. She needn't worry about money or comfort. She would be well provided for whether she married or not. Her father had been her main concern, and she was beginning to suspect that there was little more wrong with his health than simply growing older. Her betrothal—if she found a suitable gentleman—would no doubt bring about a swift recovery.

She returned from her visiting with a clear mind and the resolution that no matter what happened between Brahm and her, her life would continue to be something she should be thankful for. Yes, she owed Brahm the chance to prove himself, but she also had to keep in mind that he was only human, and that she shouldn't let her expectations of him get out of hand.

And there was the fact that she had promised only to give him a chance to prove himself. That did not mean that she was duty-bound to forgive him when it was over. It really didn't matter. She would do whatever was necessary to rid herself of this preoccupation with him.

Upon entering the house she went up to her room, freshened her appearance, and changed into a more suitable gown for entertaining guests in the afternoon. She was expected to join her sisters and the female guests in the back parlor for tea while the men did whatever it was gentlemen did to keep themselves occupied.

Clad in a simple gown of dark blue muslin, Eleanor left her room and returned downstairs. When she entered the parlor, she discovered the rest of the ladies already in attendance.

A happy chorus of voices erupted at her entrance, bringing a smile to her lips. What a lovely welcome.

"Forgive my tardiness, ladies," she requested, taking a seat on the chair next to Arabella. "I had duties in the village to attend to."

"We only just poured the tea," Lydia informed her, offering her a cup. "Lady Dumont was about to tell us about a delightfully scandalous book she's discovered."

Lady Dumont, an attractive woman of middle age, colored ever so slightly. "I am not certain the unmarried ladies would appreciate such a text." She cast a hasty glance at Eleanor as she spoke.

It was meant to be considerate, but the remark was like a slap to Eleanor. She was not the only unmarried woman in the room, but she felt it. For her age and station in life, she was an oddity. Two-and-thirty and still a virgin.

She managed a smile. "I am hardly a green girl, Lady Dumont. Please do not worry about offending me. I am as in favor of naughty stories as any other woman." Actually, she hadn't much experience with risqué reading. She had read *Tom Jones*, and that was supposed to be unfit for single ladies. And when she was younger she had snuck a peek at a book of anatomy in her father's library.

"Although," she continued, "perhaps we should give the

younger ladies and their mamas the chance to leave the room if they wish?"

It was obvious that the girls wished to stay, but there wasn't a mama in the room who would allow her daughter to listen to something unsuitable for young ears. Several chairs were vacated, and when Eleanor was convinced she was the only untouched woman in the room, she spoke once more. "You may proceed, Lady Dumont."

Her words brought a smile to the buxom woman's lips as she reached underneath her chair and pulled out a slim volume. She held it up for all to see.

"The latest volume of Fanny Carson's memoirs," she announced with a smug expression.

Eleanor's exclamation joined with the others. Fanny Carson was of Harriet Wilson's set—a very popular member of the demimonde who had "entertained" some of the most powerful men in England and on the continent. Like Harriet Wilson, Fanny had decided there was more money to be made from her affairs and offered her memoirs to a publisher. Not only was she paid to write the books, but any gentleman who did not want his relationship with Fanny offered for public enjoyment had to pay to keep his name out of print.

However, while Harriet Wilson had at least kept a degree of decorum in her writings, it was said that Fanny Carson revealed an indecent amount of information about her lovers, giving intimate details about each liaison.

"Horace is in that book," Lady Merrott remarked dryly as she daintily lifted a cucumber sandwich from the tray before her. "I am eager to hear what Mrs. Carson has to say about my husband. I wonder if she found him as painfully dreadful in the bedroom as I did."

Her words were met with laughter. Even Eleanor, who was a bit embarrassed by the frank talk, had to chuckle. How could one not appreciate Lady Merrott's sense of humor? Lord knew, Eleanor would not be quite so glib if her husband's name appeared in such a work. It was well known that Lord Merrott had never been that kind to his wife, so no doubt few in the room had any sympathy for the man.

"Let us find out what Mrs. Carson has to say about dear Horace then," Lady Dumont chirped and began flipping through the pages. It was obvious she had several passages marked, whether for her own enjoyment or to read to the group was unclear.

By the time Lady Dumont was done reading—and she did so with much gusto and flair—about the unfortunate Horace, Eleanor was red to the roots of her hair. She laughed with the rest of the ladies at his expense, however. Mrs. Carson was not kind in her descriptions, and Lady Merrott had added her own comments throughout the reading.

The first reading was immediately followed by another concerning Lord Pennington, which was as equally scathing and amusing as the first.

"You should publish your memoirs," Lady Merrott told Lady Dumont coyly, drawing chuckles from some of the other women.

Lady Dumont adopted a look of patently false innocence. "Are you implying I have taken lovers?"

More chuckles. Eleanor glanced around the room. No one else seemed the least bit shocked or uncomfortable with this kind of talk. Was this what being married was like? Did a woman instantly become able to talk and joke about such intimate matters once her vows were said?

No, not once her vows were said. It was sexual experience that made these women able to talk so freely, experience that Eleanor didn't have and wasn't likely to at the rate she was going.

Lady Dumont lifted her blue eyes toward the ceiling, as though in contemplation. "I suppose I could give one or two gentlemen cause for alarm by publishing such a volume."

"One or two!" It was Lydia who made the incredulous outburst. "I believe there would be significantly more than that!"

Lady Dumont only giggled. "Name one."

Lady Dumont was enjoying this, Eleanor realized. She liked the attention. She liked their knowing she'd had a string of lovers—and she'd had many, even when her husband was alive. It made her feel powerful on some level. How odd. What kind of power was there in admitting that your marriage was so awful that you had to seek "companionship" elsewhere? She would think there was more to boast about in a faithful marriage than an unfaithful one.

"Wynthrope Ryland," Lydia crowed.

Eleanor's heart gave a little thump. Brahm's brother? Lady Dumont had an affair with him? But he was younger than she!

Lady Dumont shook her head. Her smile remained that of a cat who had just swallowed a whole nest of canaries, but now that self-satisfied curve turned rueful. "Wynthrope Ryland would not be the least bit uncomfortable by my revealing details of our affair."

"His wife might be," someone remarked. Eleanor couldn't tell who had spoken.

Lady Dumont's expression tightened for a split second. She obviously didn't like Wynthrope's wife. Why? Was she jealous?

"It is best not to interfere with happy marriages," Lady Dumont remarked with surprising sincerity. "It never goes well for the one who does the interfering. But there is one unattached Ryland left, and he is fair game."

Done with little thumps, Eleanor's heart gave a mighty leap as some of the other women murmured their appreciation. Brahm was the only unattached Ryland that she knew of.

"He's in there?" It was Lady Fairchild who asked.

Lady Dumont nodded. "He is."

"But he is here at the party," Phoebe remarked, casting the briefest of glances in Eleanor's direction. "It would not be right."

Lady Dumont didn't miss a beat. "Merrott is here as well, but no one minded hearing about him." She cast a more lingering gaze at Eleanor herself. "Unless you would prefer I not read it?"

Eleanor stared at the woman. Was she genuinely concerned, or merely trying to stir up gossip? It was obvious Lady Dumont was so eager to read about Brahm that she could scarcely contain herself.

And truth be told, part of Eleanor wanted to hear it. The other night Brahm had told her that he wasn't a libertine. What was he then? If he had affairs with notorious courtesans, then he was far from chaste. She wanted to hear what Fanny Carson had to say about his prowess as a lover. If it was bad, then perhaps she'd stop thinking about those few kisses they had shared a million and a half years ago. Maybe she'd stop wishing he'd kiss her again just so she might experience that same heart-pounding excitement once more.

Part of her wanted him to be a rotten lover so she would

stop wondering. Another part of her wanted to hear that he was everything she thought he was and more.

And if she told Lady Dumont she didn't want to hear it, then she would be admitting that she was bothered by it, and she'd rather jump off the roof than admit anything of the sort to this woman—or any of the rest of them.

"By all means," she replied with a slight smile. "I am as intrigued as everyone else."

Was that disappointment on Lady Dumont's pretty face? Good.

It seemed to take forever for Lady Dumont to find the page, but find it she did, and as she began reading, Eleanor's mouth became increasingly dry—not even tea could soothe it. Her throat tightened, her blood burned, and yet she sat as still and expressionless as she was capable of.

Fanny Carson praised Brahm for being a generous benefactor, for having a love of life and a quick wit. She also remarked on his ability as a dancer and a horseman, which indicated that their affair had begun prior to Brahm's accident. How much prior? Was he sleeping with her while he courted Eleanor? Or had he run to the courtesan after Eleanor rejected him? Or worse yet, did his going to Fanny Carson have nothing to do with Eleanor at all? Perhaps he had forgotten all about her at that time.

Fanny Carson also mentioned Brahm's predilection for strong spirits. It seemed that the "lady" shared his enthusiasm and they often drank together. No doubt that had been part of the attraction.

" 'As a lover,' " Lady Dumont read, " 'Brahm Ryland will forever be remembered by the author as a man without equal.' "

Several oohs and ahs heightened the fire in Eleanor's veins. *A man without equal.* Good God, what kind of man did a courtesan consider without equal as a lover? Certainly not a man who claimed *not* to be libertine.

Lady Dumont continued, " 'Always considerate, Brahm would often spend hours at a time tending to my pleasure without a thought to his own. He knew exactly how to reduce me to a heap of boneless flesh, sated and replete with sensual satisfaction. He is a virtuoso, and his instrument is a woman's form.' "

The band around Eleanor's throat tightened. Had she actually heard a sigh behind her?

" 'Not until he was certain I could take no more would he take his own fulfillment. Stretched and filled by his massive maleness, I thanked God that Eve tempted Adam, for being bedded by Brahm Ryland is paradise itself.' "

Lady Dumont looked up from pages and made a great show of fanning herself with her hand as titters echoed around the room. "Dear me. Such praise for Lord Creed." Her smile turned deviously coy. "I wonder if any one of us can testify to the validity of Mrs. Carson's claims?"

There were murmurs around the room, even a few giggles, but if there was one among them who had taken Brahm to her bed, she wasn't speaking. If Lydia spoke, Eleanor would personally wring her neck later.

Her sister kept her mouth shut, unlike Lady Dumont, who opened hers to read more. She was cut off, however, by Arabella, who mercifully announced that it was time for them to retire to their rooms to rest and change before dinner.

There were a few disappointed mutters, but the ladies filed out of the room like dutiful children. Several of them followed after Lady Dumont, no doubt wanting to hear more about Brahm and his "massive maleness." Did that mean what Eleanor thought it did? It had to. Innocent she might be, but she wasn't stupid.

"I am so sorry you had to hear that, dearest," Arabella said once the door closed and they were alone. Even their sisters had departed. Lydia had been one of the ladies following after Lady Dumont. Perhaps her sister wanted to compare notes.

"It is nothing, Belle. Brahm Ryland is a man like any other, with all the same flaws and weaknesses. At least Mrs. Carson was kinder to him than some of her other companions."

Her sister gifted her with a small, loving smile. "Always understanding. Always fair and unjudging. You are too good, Eleanor."

Too good? If Arabella only knew how patently *un*good she felt at this moment! She felt foolish and angry and humiliated—anything but good! As for unjudging, that was such a joke. She judged people all the time, especially Brahm.

She stood and gave her sister a hug before sending her on her way like a mother shooing a child. Dear Arabella, she always had been the sweetest of them. The sweetest and the best.

Alone in the parlor, Eleanor drifted toward one of the windows that overlooked the back lawn and garden. In the distance she could see the gentlemen's party returning from their ride. They were too far away for her to tell who was who, but a tall figure near the rear caught her attention. Was it Brahm? Did his leg ache from too much time in the saddle? Did he know that Fanny Carson had betrayed the bonds of intimacy between them?

Why did she care? Why did she feel so hollow inside?

Why was she so blasted angry at him, at herself, and most of all at Fanny Carson?

No, the person she was angry at most of all was Lydia. She had never truly admitted it, not even to herself until this moment, but she harbored such ill will toward her sister. Oh, it wasn't that she believed Lydia any more to blame than Brahm—it took two to do what they did. It was something deeper, something so much darker than simple hurt pride.

Lydia knew Brahm in a way that Eleanor didn't—a way that Eleanor should have. So did Fanny Carson. No doubt there were other women who held that distinction as well. No doubt Eleanor would feel this same anger toward them also.

She was jealous. There could be no denying it. She didn't like that other women had known Brahm in the biblical sense while she, who was supposed to have married him, whom he claimed to want most urgently, did not. Why had he never tried to bed her? That was where the anger stemmed. Why these other women and not her?

It didn't matter, she knew that rationally. It was all in the past. Even if Fanny Carson's memoirs damaged Brahm's claim that he was not a libertine, Eleanor could not allow the knowledge to affect her treatment of him now. He deserved the chance she had promised. If he hadn't changed, she would know it before the party was over, of that she was certain. If Lady Dumont didn't creep into his bed, then someone else would, and Eleanor would hear about it.

She could only hope that if she did hear about it, she wouldn't feel this same empty gnawing in her gut. Brahm Ryland did not belong to her, and she had no right to feel so possessive. But possessive she was. Despite his betrayal, despite everything, Eleanor had to face the fact that she retained feelings for Brahm. She reacted to him in a way she had never reacted to anyone else, and unless they set things right between them, there was a very good chance she never would react that way with another.

A man without equal, indeed.

Brahm returned from the afternoon's riding somewhat stiff and sore, but not as bad off as he had feared. It wasn't as though he hadn't been on horseback since the accident—he had been, just not for so long a time. It was difficult for him to mount a horse now as he never knew if his leg was going to support him or not. Having it stay in one position for so long was usually an invitation for pain.

Still, he had enjoyed the exercise and the chance to be social with some of his peers. It also gave him a chance to judge the other bachelors who had been invited. None of them was what he would consider serious competition. Perhaps old Burrough had planned it that way. Brahm wouldn't be the least bit surprised if inviting the other bachelors was part of an elaborate ruse, a ruse to reunite him and Eleanor.

That he was even thinking in terms of competition should have worried him but it didn't. His obsession with Eleanor was based on real feelings. Many years ago he'd taken quite a fancy to her. He still fancied her. He wanted her with an urgency he'd never felt before. She looked so cool, so remote, but he knew that she was passionate inside. It was that very passion that had him struggling to keep control when they'd first become involved. Time had not diminished her passion or his reaction to it. It had taken but a few days for him to resign himself to the truth.

He wanted to marry Eleanor, and he'd do just about

anything to make that happen. First he had to make things right between them. Then, if luck was with him, she would consent to be his. It didn't make sense, but that was the way of things.

He didn't deserve her, but he didn't care. She deserved better than a man with more scars and wounds inside than out. She deserved someone who didn't have to live with the knowledge that he had humiliated himself and his family more times than he could count. And she deserved better than a man who was convinced he could have saved his father's life if only he had been a better person. If only he hadn't been a helpless drunkard.

But there could be no changing the past, and he would do better not to dwell on what might have been. He could control only the now. He could try only to atone for the past and work toward making the future better. He had accepted so much already. He had accomplished so much already. Perhaps someday, after he had earned the forgiveness of those he'd wronged, after enough healing time had passed, then he'd forgive himself. He was closer to that goal now than he had been even six months ago.

Having his family around him had done more good than he ever would have thought possible. His brothers were everything to him, but they had their own lives now, and it was time for Brahm to take control of his own.

He was the last one to enter the house, as his leg prevented him from keeping up with the others. He didn't mind. Lord Brend—Lydia's husband—had fallen back and offered to keep him company, but Brahm sent him on his way. It wouldn't be right to make polite conversation with a man whose wife he had shagged.

Needless to say, Lord Brend had a little company on that account.

The peace of being alone was nice after the boisterous afternoon. Plus it made it easier for him to conceal how hard the day's exercise had been on him. Male pride, it was an awful thing.

Tension vibrated through his cane as he slowly dragged himself upstairs. It was a warm day, but the sweat on his brow had little to do with the temperature and everything to do with the exertion of the climb. There had to be rain coming for his leg to ache like this.

Of course there was rain coming. This was England.

By the time he entered his bedchamber, he was winded, damp, and in a hellish mood. Charles, his valet, was waiting. God love him, he had a hot bath and fresh clothes ready.

"Do you require my assistance, my lord?"

"Just with my boots, Charles. I believe I can manage the rest, thank you."

After the accident Brahm had depended on Charles for many things, and pride was not an issue where the valet was concerned, so it was not conceit that kept him from asking for help now. He just wanted to be alone. He wanted it badly enough that he'd wrestle himself in and out of the bath.

Charles didn't argue. He simply pulled off Brahm's dirty boots and took them with him to clean and polish. "I will check back in an hour," he promised.

Brahm smiled as the older man left the room. Sometimes Charles was very maternal toward him, clucking over him like a hen over her chick. It was nice. Normally Brahm was the one taking care of everything—it was his duty as viscount.

That responsibility was one of the reasons he found such solace in drink. Most of his life had been spent trying to be what was expected of him. When he drank, everything he kept bottled up inside came rushing out. After a while, it became a sort of obsession—letting the demons out. Now he was forced to recognize that there was no longer anything expected of him, by anyone, and the only thing left to do was to reconcile with those demons. He was beginning to think he had almost succeeded.

Alone in the cool, summer-fresh silence of his room, Brahm removed his clothes and tossed them on the bed for Charles to collect later to have laundered. Naked, he limped around the bed, using the mattress for support.

The copper tub had been placed close enough to the bed that he could hold one of the posters for support as he climbed in. It would be more helpful when he tried to climb out. He lifted one foot and eased it into the bath. The instant the hot water touched his lame leg, the ache in it began to subside. Slowly he slid down into the tub, wincing as his leg put up a last-minute fuss.

The water was hot—too hot for a summer's day. Sweat beaded behind his ears, but he leaned back and allowed the heat to work its magic. Soon the ache in his leg eased and tension leached from his body. He lay limp in the tub, dozing lightly until the bath began to lose its heat and his fingers were wrinkled.

He scrubbed with sandalwood soap and a soft cloth, covering himself in lather as he washed the dirt and sweat of the day from his skin. Then he rinsed, submersing himself fully in the tub before breaking the surface with a gusty gasp for breath.

He hauled himself from the cooling water with the help of the bed. The posters were sturdy and solid, easily taking his weight as he favored his leg as much as possible. The water lapped around his knees as he reached for the towel Charles had left for him. He was wrapped in it, surveying the clothing laid out for him, when his valet knocked.

"Perfect timing," Brahm told him as the older man entered the room. "I am in need of your magic."

Finally, a few hours after his return from riding, Brahm was fit to join the others downstairs for a drink before dinner—minus the drink, of course.

Cane in hand, he made his way down the wide stairs with lazy caution. There was no need to hurry, and he wasn't about to risk injuring himself just to watch other people imbibe when he couldn't.

It would be so easy to feel sorry for himself, not just for his inability to join others in something so commonplace as a before-dinner drink, but for the state of his leg as well. Some days he allowed himself to be sullen, but for the most part he put those feelings aside. What was the point to such thoughts? There was nothing he could do about his cravings except fight them. He could not have just one drink; it only made the need worse and more difficult to fight. There was nothing he could do about his leg except be glad the surgeon hadn't removed it. He had wanted to, but Devlin had stopped him. Thank God for his brother.

Thank God for the second chance he had been given. He could have been killed along with his father, but obviously fate still had plans for him. He was eager to discover what those were. If they were anything like the gifts he had already been given—his family, his friends—then he was one very lucky man indeed.

Almost immediately after entering the drawing room where Lord Burrough—Burr—and his family and their guests sat chatting and drinking, Brahm knew that something was different. That something had to do with him.

Gazes turned toward him as he entered. People smiled, some even chuckled. There were whispers, and the air suddenly seemed charged.

Good Lord, what had he done? His gaze immediately shot to Eleanor. She looked away, her cheeks flushing a becoming but worrisome pink. Just the other night she had agreed to give him a second chance, and now she couldn't even look him in the eye? This wasn't good. Had something happened with Lydia? Had Eleanor's sister said something about that night?

His gaze sought the younger blond woman and found her. She stood with a group of other ladies, including Wynthrope's former mistress, Lady Dumont. They were all watching him with expressions of barely veiled amusement—coy, sexual amusement that made him very nervous. Woman was the most effective of predators, and he didn't stand a chance against an entire pack. They looked as though they would dearly love to eat him—not in a cannibalistic manner but a very base sexual one.

Surely they wouldn't look at him that way if Lydia had revealed how he had betrayed Eleanor's trust? They would shun him, turn away from his gaze instead of meeting it with hungering glances of their own.

Was Lady Merrott looking at his crotch?

Shifting his weight, Brahm pivoted on his heel and turned away from their scrutiny. Lord Burrough gestured for Brahm to join him, and he did so. If Lydia had said something, he'd rather face her father than her.

But Burrough said nothing of any scandal. He wanted only to discuss the afternoon's ride.

The tension continued through dinner, with several guests making remarks that put a frown on Brahm's face. It wasn't until the ladies excused themselves and the port and cigars came out that he finally learned what the devil was going on.

"So, Creed," Merrott began, puffing on a fragrant cigar. "How is your 'massive maleness,' old man?"

Brahm's eyes widened as his companions' laughter filled the dining room. "I beg your pardon?"

"You are a virtuoso," Lord Birch, a bachelor of plain looks and large fortune, informed him. "And your instrument is a woman's body."

"Form," Merrott corrected.

Brahm glanced between the two of them. "What the hell are you two talking about?"

"Bunch of damn foolishness," Lord Burrough muttered. "Someone tell the boy. It is obvious he has no idea what is going on."

Birch took a small leather-bound book from his jacket and slid it across the table to Brahm. "Apparently you are a man without equal, Creed. You've made us all look like bumbling idiots."

Merrott snorted. "The whore was no more truthful in her details concerning Creed than she was with me. She was just angry I wouldn't pay her. No doubt Creed paid her to say what she did."

A book, a whore, and payments made? This did not bode well. A sense of unease filled him as Brahm lifted the book.

Memoirs of a Well-Loved Lady by Fanny Carson.

Sweet Jesus. He had gotten a note from Fanny revealing that she was writing her memoirs and asking if he would care to make a donation to keep his name out of them, but Brahm had ignored it and her request. It had seemed like a half-arsed blackmail attempt. Everyone who knew Fanny knew her skills did not lie with reading and writing.

He opened the book to the marked pages, his face heating as he read what was written there about him. Someone must have helped Fanny write this—someone with more vocabulary than sense.

Brahm closed the book. He had read enough.

"I did not pay her," he informed Merrott as he pushed the book toward Birch.

Merrott snorted, wrinkling his long nose. "You lie. No man treats a woman like that. Everyone knows women are incapable of sexual pleasure."

The rest of the men turned their gazes on the old lord.

"No wonder your wife has had more lovers than a dockside doxy," Lord Farnsworth, a Byron-esque man of charm and wit, remarked dryly. "You are clearly an idiot, Merrott."

Old lord turned on the young. "I could call you out for that, Farnsworth."

"But you won't," Lord Burrough informed him, "because he speaks the truth."

As the men around him raised their voices either defending or deriding Merrott and his views on women, Brahm slumped back in his chair and ignored them all.

No wonder the women looked at him as they had. "Massive maleness"? What the hell had Fanny been thinking? His "maleness" wasn't massive. Was it? It always seemed fairly ordinary to him—and over the years he had become well acquainted with it—more so than Fanny Carson had.

Good God, the things she had said about him! At least they'd been favorable. Apparently she hadn't been so kind to Merrott, not that the arse deserved it.

Frig. Had Eleanor seen it? She must have heard snippets at the very least. Snippets were often worse than the entire truth. No doubt she had heard only the scandalous bits, the bits that made him sound every inch the libertine he had professed not to be. No doubt she believed he had lied about that. All his adult life he had preferred long-term assignations to casual slap and tickles, although the latter had happened on more than one drunken occasion. He had kept Fanny for several years. Perhaps that was why she chose to be so . . . *kind* when she wrote of him.

He bit back a sigh and the urge to run his hand through his hair. He could not let his companions see how bothered he was. It wasn't that he had been outed as a courtesan's lover, many men in England held such a title at one time or another. What disturbed him was that Fanny's book might damage his chances with Eleanor. He didn't care how the ladies at this party looked at him. He didn't care what the men said about him, but he did care about Eleanor's opinion of him, and right now it didn't look as though that opinion was in his favor.

He was going to have to talk to her. He was going to have to try to make it right. Would she let him?

Fate, it seemed, had made a change of plans.

Chapter 6

"**A**re you looking for something, Lord Creed?"

Brahm had been in the library for a total of one and a half minutes before Eleanor's sisters descended upon him. After cigars he had accompanied the other men to the drawing room, only to discover that Eleanor had left. He played the part of contented guest for half an hour before going in search. Her sisters must have been watching him.

"Someone, actually," he answered Muriel honestly, pretending interest in a volume of Pepys on one of the numerous shelves.

"Not Eleanor, we hope."

He turned his head, his gaze going directly to Lydia. Who did she think she was pretending such hauteur with him?

He smiled coolly. "Then I am sorry to disappoint you. That is exactly who I am looking for."

Her hands fisted on her hips—no doubt because the action drew attention to her figure. "Have you not done enough damage where Eleanor is concerned?"

He feigned ignorance. "What damage would that be?"

It was Phoebe who answered, "Fanny Carson's memoirs for one."

Brahm turned his attention to the younger sister. How alike yet different they all were. They stood in the dying rays of sunshine filtering through the window like the Furies sent to avenge a wrong.

He could see a bit of Eleanor in each of them even though their hair colors were different shades of blond and brown, their eyes different shades of blue. Arabella had a touch more softness to her looks, a bit more kindness in her gaze.

"That was not of my doing." Why was he defending himself to these women who were so set on declaring him guilty? "I did not write the book and I certainly did not call Eleanor's attention to it."

Muriel stepped forward. "What about the damage you did when you broke her heart years ago?"

He had broken her heart, had he? Then he deserved to suffer for it, despite the perverse sense of joy it gave him. She had cared for him. Truly cared. "That is between Eleanor and myself."

"The point remains that you have a habit of hurting our sister, my lord." It was Lydia again.

"Do I?" He slipped the Pepys from the shelf. It would be good for helping him sleep later.

He ignored her for a count of five before meeting her gaze once more. Cold blue eyes bored into his. "We do not want to see her injured by your folly."

Brahm's lips curved upward in a mocking half smile. "It is not my folly you need worry about."

Lydia frowned. "I do not understand."

"You really do not want me to explain, my lady. Trust me."

She understood what he was saying; he could tell from the way the color drained from her face. If she thought for a moment that he was too much of a gentleman to reveal in front of her sisters that Eleanor had seen them together that night, then Lydia was too dull-witted to exist.

Arabella glanced from her sister to Brahm, curiosity plain in her pretty features. It was time to divert her. He didn't particularly care to have the rest of Eleanor's family know what had transpired between him and Lydia, and even if he did, it wasn't his place to reveal it.

"Ladies"—he gestured toward them with the book— "your concern for your sister does credit to each of you, but I have no intention of hurting Eleanor. I only want to try to make amends for the past." Even that admission was more information than he cared to reveal.

"That is very good of you, Lord Creed." Even Arabella's voice was soft. "You have brothers that you care for; surely you can sympathize with our situation?"

He nodded. He liked Arabella. She obviously got all the sense that the other three missed. "I do, just as I'm certain you can understand that Eleanor is a grown woman and capable of making her own decisions."

Arabella nodded. "Of course. And we will support her in whatever decision she makes."

Muriel tossed her an incredulous look. "You cannot be serious, Belle! What if he hurts her again?"

Brahm was so tired of this topic. It was going to put him to sleep far quicker than Pepys would. "What if I end up the injured party?"

The astounded gaze turned to him. "You?"

He nodded. "Eleanor might break my heart; you never know how these scenarios might play out."

Only Arabella caught the dry humor in his tone. She didn't smile, but amusement lit her pale eyes. The remaining sisters simply stared at him as though he was an attraction in a circus.

"Eleanor might break your heart?" Phoebe's tone was one of complete disbelief.

"What Eleanor does is no one's business but Eleanor's," came a voice from the door.

Brahm's heart recognized the sound of her voice before his ears did. A frantic pounding began behind his ribs, and despite the realization that he might never succeed in wooing her, he rejoiced in her presence all the same. God, he hoped that joy wasn't apparent for all to see.

Not that Eleanor could see it even if it was there. She didn't spare him so much as a glance. Her attention was centered on her sisters, and it was obvious that she was not impressed with any of them.

He couldn't help but smile as four grown women became children before his eyes. They were cowed in the face of their oldest sister's anger and avoided her disapproving gaze.

God, but she was lovely. Even with her looking so stern, he found himself completely enamored of her appearance. Her hair was still in the elegant knot she had worn to dinner. Little tendrils of bright gold curled around her ivory cheeks. Her gown was dark blue trimmed with silver, and the low neckline displayed a delicious amount of soft bosom. He remembered the feel of those breasts pressed against his chest. He remembered the taste of those full pink lips. He wanted to feel her again. He wanted to taste her again. He must have no pride at all where she was concerned if he could want a woman who no doubt thought the worst of him.

"Please leave Lord Creed and me," she instructed her sisters in a tone that brooked no refusal.

Without argument her sisters filed from the room as though they were being sent to bed without supper.

"You really are quite good at that," he praised her when they were alone.

Eleanor's expression didn't change as she closed the door behind her sisters. "They meant well."

He nodded. "They love you very much."

"I know."

Meaning she didn't need him to tell her that. Obviously she was not going to give him any quarter whatsoever.

There was no point in delaying it. "Eleanor, I know you have heard about Fanny Carson's book."

She laughed humorlessly. "Not merely about it, I've heard parts of it read aloud."

Brahm closed his eyes. *Frig*. "I can explain."

She held up her hand. "You do not owe me an explanation."

"I think I do. I want to give you one all the same."

"I do not need to hear any more, Brahm. I have heard enough."

She was persistent; he'd give her that. Stubborn too. Was she that determined to think the worst of him? And how much of the book had she been read? Just selected parts? No doubt they were the worst possible parts, such as the remark about his "maleness." At least she was still calling him by his Christian name. That was a good sign.

"Eleanor, you and I both know how malicious gossip can

be. I am not ashamed of my relationship with Fanny, and if you knew the truth of it, you would not want me to be."

"Do not presume to know what I would and would not want." Bright spots of crimson formed high on her cheeks. "You have no idea what I want!"

Brahm's temper rose as well—so much that he forgot to be pleased that he had managed to get some emotion out of her. "Forgive me for not being able to read your mind. Why do you not simply tell me what you want and save me the trouble of trying to guess?"

She blinked at his caustic tone. "I . . . honesty, for one thing."

The Pepys slapped against his palm. "I have been nothing but honest with you since my arrival."

She didn't look convinced, but she didn't argue. "Sincerity."

"Have I given you an impression of anything else?"

She thought for a moment. "Are you and Lydia still lovers?"

If he had twenty years to plan out this conversation, that question still wouldn't have occurred to him. It was absurd, really, but totally understandable that she would ask. He shook his head with a chuckle. This party had already provided in a few days more entertainment than he had enjoyed all year.

"I could tell you that is none of your business, but given the circumstances, I suppose it is. No. Our 'relationship' lasted the one drunken night that I cannot remember."

"There were no other nights you cannot remember?"

She wanted honesty; he would give it to her. "Not with her, no."

She paled. "With other women?"

Brahm sighed. Her interest, her apparent deflated pride

should have warmed him, should have given him hope, but it only made him weary. "Eleanor, do you know what too much drink does to a man?"

She made a face. "I have seen some of the effects, yes."

Again she referred to his indiscretion with Lydia. Or to the punch bowl. Damn, but the woman was like a wheel churning in a rut.

Swallowing a healthy amount of his pride, Brahm drew a breath. "It often renders a man unable to perform sexually."

Eleanor stared at him, her face perfectly blank.

Damn her to hell, she was going to make him come right out and say it. "There were many nights I could not have bedded a woman no matter how badly I wanted to."

She cocked a haughty golden brow, obviously doubting the validity of that statement. "Not even Lydia?"

"Not even you."

That drove the sarcasm out of her. She faltered, but only for a moment. "But you bedded Fanny Carson."

"On occasion." He had promised her honesty and he'd give it to her. "But there were just as many nights that both Fanny and myself were too foxed to do anything but pass out in our clothes."

She didn't understand such behavior; he could tell from her expression. Hell, he didn't understand it himself and he had lived it.

It was time to take control of the conversation and press his own suit. "You said you would give me a second chance."

"I gave you one."

"No you didn't." If she thought she was going to turn her back on him now and dismiss him because of a stupid book, she was in for a rude awakening. "You have not given me a chance at all. You admit to not reading for your-self what Fanny wrote about our affair, yet you judge me."

She recoiled in defiance. "I do not judge you."

He pointed the spine of the Pepys at her in accusation. "You took what little you heard and made me a villain."

Her arms folded across her chest. Brahm would have had to be much angrier than he was not to cast a glance at her cleavage as she did so. "I have not!"

"Then why are you avoiding me? Why have you be-come so cold?"

"Because—" She stopped, her expression changing to one of horror.

Brahm had never seen anything like it and it drained the anger and frustration from him. He almost felt sorry for her. "Because what?"

She looked away, the last vestiges of a sunset behind her haloed her profile. "Because I have resented you for so long, it is difficult for me to trust in you now. No mat-ter how badly I might want to believe you, a part of me in-sists I would be a fool for doing so. There, does that please you?"

"Of course not. In fact, quite the opposite." What did she expect, that he'd find her admission humorous?

But she wasn't done just yet. "When Lady Dumont read that woman's book to us today I was embarrassed for you, but then I began to wonder why you had not paid to be kept out of the book like any decent gentleman would have."

Now *that* statement was humorous. "Decent gentlemen do not often find themselves the victims of blackmail."

She nodded, her mouth tight. "Perhaps not. But you could have kept your affair private by parting with what

I'm sure would have been a pittance to a man such as yourself, but you did not. You deliberately allowed her to make public your relationship. Do you take some pleasure in knowing that people can read such awful things about you?"

Brahm scowled. "Awful? What, did she claim that I beat her, that I was cruel to her?"

"No."

"Then what was so awful? Surely not the bit about my 'massive maleness'? I rather liked that. Had I known she was going to be so verbose in her praise, I would have paid her to say more."

Her face contorted with distaste. "I cannot believe you find this amusing."

He shrugged. "Well, she could have been a lot less flattering."

"You are not embarrassed?"

Should he be? He supposed from her perspective he should. Women viewed intercourse in an entirely different manner than men. He had been taught that conquest was good. Eleanor, on the other hand, had been taught that to be such a conquest was bad.

"I'm not pleased, but there are a lot worse things that can happen to a man than to have his prowess publicly praised. I was a good protector to Fanny, and I will not be embarrassed or ashamed of having treated her decently." He had read more of her memories—Fanny had not spoken ill of his treatment of her.

She opened her mouth to speak, but he cut her off before she could issue a sound. "If you want to be offended on my behalf, you are welcome to it. But I do think you should read the entire chapter about me before you pass judgment. It is the Christian way." It was petty of him to throw her words from the other night back at her, but he was fighting for his chance of making amends with her— although at the moment he was having a hard time remembering why he wanted her forgiveness so badly.

Eleanor swallowed. He could see the slim column of her throat tighten. "I have to go," she whispered just before she bolted from the room.

Brahm watched her go. What the hell? There was obviously only one way to stop this idiocy once and for all. He had to make Eleanor see that he was not the shameless libertine she thought he was.

He had to find Birch and get Fanny Carson's damn book.

He thought she believed him a liar. He thought she was angry because she thought he bedded every woman he could get his hands on. And he in turn was angry because she didn't know all the facts.

Eleanor didn't want to know all the facts, and thank God the truth had never occurred to him. She had come so close to admitting her jealousy to him. She didn't judge him—not now, and she wasn't about to make him a villain. She had done that years ago.

How could he not be humiliated to have such private details of his life offered up for public scrutiny? He must truly not care what society thought of him. Or perhaps he knew from experience that scandals come and go, and eventually society would forget about Fanny Carson and her book and move on to something else.

He thought she was upset because she believed him to have been with many women. She was upset, but not in the way he thought. She was upset because she wasn't one of those women! What was wrong with her that she would have such shameful feelings? How could she admit to them, even to herself?

And how could she have them about a man who had betrayed her so terribly? And why was she beginning to feel sympathy for him? Drinking had been a sickness for him, and she would feel sorry for anyone who had been so terribly ill.

Modern doctors and essayists had begun to discuss the dilemma of alcohol consumption in England; that she knew from the books in her father's library. Through the years she had done a bit of reading on the subject in an effort to learn more about why Brahm lived the way he once had.

Profuse drinking was not an affliction limited to the wretched. Many of Eleanor's own set imbibed to excess such as Brahm had. It was only in the upper circles that drinking was considered a sport among gentlemen. In fact, there were those who believed excessive drunkenness to cause a kind of brain fever. Eleanor would not blame anyone for sins committed while in the grip of such an affliction. Should she not extend the same compassion to Brahm? He told her he had not known it was Lydia who came to him that night, and perhaps he truly had been too drunk to know better.

He'd also said that sometimes drink made him unable to perform sexually—just the thought brought a blush to her cheeks. Dare she hope that he had been struck by such a malady that night? No, there was no point. The image of Lydia beneath Brahm was enough to constrict her heart until it felt as though it was being ripped from her body. It burned in her mind, made her so very, very angry. But now that anger was directed more toward her sister than

Brahm. That would not do. Lydia hadn't known about Eleanor and Brahm; she was innocent in this.

Was she? How could Lydia have not known about Eleanor's infatuation? Everyone seemed to know that Brahm intended to ask for her. How could that have escaped Lydia's notice?

She would not think these things, not now. The first thing she had to do was further educate herself on the subject of excessive drinking.

Her father had books on the subject in the library, such as Thomas Trotter's essay on drunkenness and the effects it had on the human body. She would begin there. In fact, she was so determined to begin that she turned on her heel and headed back to the library. When she arrived she found the room empty. Brahm was gone. It was just as well. She did not want him to know what she was doing.

She found the book she was looking for, along with several others. She took just the Trotter for the time being. This time when she exited the library, it was with more of a purpose than simply escaping Brahm and her jealousy.

She hurried down the corridor and up the stairs. Before she could enter the quiet sanctuary of her bedroom, she was stopped by Arabella.

"Ellie." Her sister's soft voice held an element of pleading. "Might we talk for a moment?"

Arabella was still dressed in her evening clothes, and from downstairs Eleanor could hear faint laughter and music. The guests were still entertaining themselves. No doubt Phoebe, Muriel, and Lydia were assisting them. Had Arabella been waiting for her all this time?

Eleanor nodded. "Of course, would you care to come in?"

"Can we talk in my room? I need to lie down."

Eleanor frowned as she nodded. "I do not want you endangering yourself or the baby, Belle."

Her sister took her hand and squeezed it. "I am fine. Just tired."

They went to Arabella's chamber. "Is Henry with the others?"

Arabella nodded. "I told him I wished to have some private time with you. He respects that."

Henry was a good man—the best. Arabella deserved such a man. She believed her other sisters deserved good men as well, but Lydia would destroy a good man. Phoebe and Muriel had made good matches, but both were too strong-willed to have marriages that always ran as smoothly as Arabella's.

"What book are you reading?" Arabella inquired as she closed the door.

Eleanor's gaze drifted around the blue and cream interior. This had been Arabella's room since she left the nursery. Eleanor always loved this room—it was just as comforting and soothing as the woman who claimed it.

"It is a book on drunkenness." She admitted to Arabella what she would to no one else.

Her sister merely nodded as she removed her earrings and dropped them on the vanity. "You wish to better understand Lord Creed."

Even though it was not a question, Eleanor answered as such. "Yes."

Arabella removed her pearls. "Lydia seems to think he plans to injure you again."

Perhaps Lydia couldn't stand the fact that Brahm had come back for Eleanor and not her. Lord, how long was she going to jump back and forth between wanting to declare Lydia innocent and wanting to declare her guilty? "What do you, Phoebe, and Muriel believe?"

Arabella turned her back to her. "Come undo my hooks, will you, dear? We do not completely trust him, but we will respect any decision you make where he is concerned."

What did that mean? Eleanor began loosening the back of Arabella's yellow gown. "I appreciate that the four of you wish to protect me, but I do not need it." She didn't add that her sisters could not offer the kind of protection she did need against Brahm. No matter how much they might want to, her sisters could not protect her heart.

Arabella was silent until her gown was completely unfastened, then she turned to Eleanor with a gaze that shone with warmth and love. Her hands cupped Eleanor's shoulders as they stood eye to eye.

"I am sorry if we embarrassed or angered you earlier. We confronted Lord Creed because we love you."

Eleanor nodded, her throat tight. "I know."

"It is your own fault," Arbella chastised lightly. "If you had not been so wonderful to us while we were growing up, we would not love you half so much as we do."

Eleanor's eyes burned. Wonderful, now she was going to cry. "I love you too."

Her younger sister laughed and pushed her toward the door. "Go away before we both start to bawl. I am a highly emotional pregnant lady and I need to rest."

As Eleanor left the room, a smile touched her lips. There was such comfort to be found in her sisters, especially Arabella. They had always had the closest bond. It was one of the things in her life she was most thankful for.

She strode down the corridor, the sconces lighting her way. The sun was down, and night was finally upon them.

Soon the days would begin to shorten once more, and before long winter would come, trapping her here with her thoughts and books.

She didn't want to be spend another winter alone with her thoughts and books. As much as she loved her father, she wanted to share her long nights with someone else— someone who would share her thoughts and books as well. The odd thing was, she hadn't known she wanted this until this very moment.

Perhaps she would find a husband among her father's guests. Perhaps she would not be alone this winter.

Perhaps she and Brahm Ryland would get it right this time and end up husband and wife as they should have years ago. The thought shook her right down to her toes. An hour ago she had thought him the worst of men, and now she was thinking of him as a husband? It had finally happened. She had gone mad.

How lucky she was that they hadn't married then. She probably would have blamed herself for his drinking. She would not have known how to live with his behavior. She would not have been able to give him what he needed, nor would he have been able to see to her needs. But now . . .

Was it foolish of her to harbor such fantasies for him? Was it stupid and girlish to hope that he really had changed and that they might have their happy ending after all?

Lord, but it was so tiring questioning her feelings all the time! There was something about her that would not allow her to be impulsive, to give in and do exactly what she wanted. She was so reserved, so unsure of herself. It was terribly vexing.

Eleanor entered her room to find the lamp near the bed already lit. Her maid, of course, was absent, as the girl would not come until Eleanor called her. It was early yet, so Eleanor didn't bother ringing the bell. Instead she took her book and went to her bed to start reading.

But when she went to climb up onto the elegant four-poster bed, she discovered a book already waiting for her.

She picked it up with a small frown. What could it be? *Memoirs of a Well-Loved Lady* by Fanny Carson.

Oh dear Lord, where had this come from? There was a piece of paper sticking out from between the pages. Eleanor opened the book and lifted the paper to the light.

"Read it all. Then we will talk. B."

Brahm. Brahm had left this. Brahm had been in her room. He had let himself into her private sanctuary. Had he been the one to light the lamp as well? Such an invasion of her privacy should have angered her, but it didn't. It scared her and thrilled her at the same time. He had been here, where no other man ever had been.

She sat down on the bed and positioned the book near the lamp's glow so she could read. Part of her didn't want to discover the details of his affair with Mrs. Carson, but a stronger part of her demanded to know all.

She skimmed the parts that Lady Dumont had read aloud earlier. There was no need to read them again. It was the parts that she hadn't read that were the most enlightening. True, there were no more mentions of Brahm's "massive maleness," but there were other tidbits that were just as interesting.

Fanny Carson spent much time detailing Brahm's prowess, it was true, but she always went on to say that he demanded an exclusive relationship from her. She was his and he was hers for the duration of their time together, and neither was to take another lover. He was as faithful as a husband and more attentive, according to Mrs. Carson. He took her to the theater and the parks, bought her gifts and clothes. He was kind and considerate and treated her like a lady, something Fanny Carson had never experienced before and didn't expect to experience again. They spent much of their time together drinking, but they enjoyed each other immensely. They were friends as well as lovers—a friendship that Fanny claimed until this day.

If anything, Fanny Carson's admissions made Eleanor feel worse. If this was the way Brahm treated his mistress, how would he have treated his wife? Perhaps he would have resented that she wouldn't drink with him. Perhaps she would have resented his love of being foxed, but the consideration and kindness that he showed Fanny should have been hers. If only he had kept his wits about him. If only he had been strong enough not to drink.

But he was strong enough now. She had seen him consistently refuse spirits when they were offered. He didn't even drink wine with dinner. Not once since his arrival had she smelled liquor on him. He hadn't looked sideways at Lydia since his arrival. The situation was different. She was different. He was different. Surely that counted for something? Now if she only knew the full extent of his feelings and intentions. Did he simply want her forgiveness, or did he want her heart? Dare she hope that his feelings for her were as intact as hers for him?

There was really only one way to find out, and no sense in risking her heart until she knew the truth.

She set Fanny Carson's memoirs aside, no longer interested since she had read all that concerned Brahm.

Eleanor left her room and made her way down the corridor to the stairs. Down she went and on to the drawing room where the guests were. There was no sign of Brahm, but Arabella's husband, Henry, was there. Eleanor went to him rather than her sisters, whose attention she was very much aware of as she moved through the room.

"Henry," she asked softly, taking her brother-in-law's arm. "Have you seen Lord Creed?"

Henry's pleasant countenance and warm brown eyes were all kindness. "I believe he went out into the garden. Would you like me to fetch him for you?"

"Oh no. I only need to bother him for a moment. I will find him myself. Enjoy your evening."

She left then, not caring if anyone saw her go. This was her house, and she would come and go as she pleased. If people wanted to speculate about her movements, they were welcome to do so. She wasn't doing anything improper.

She opened the glass doors and slipped out into the night. The moon was rising and the night flowers were fragrant in the breeze. The stone path glowed in the dim light, and Eleanor took it deeper into the garden and its sheltering shrubs and bushes.

She found Brahm standing beside the goldfish pond. His leg must not be bothering him, as he wasn't leaning on his cane. The tip of it was between his feet, his hands resting lightly on the top. The moon illuminated his profile. He was so very handsome, and he looked so very lonely.

Eleanor cleared her throat. "I hope I am not intruding."

Brahm's head jerked up. He was surprised to see her. "No, not at all. I was not expecting to see you so soon."

That was understandable. She approached him. "I read the book."

He smiled. "That was fast."

She smiled back. "I only read the parts about you. It was very interesting."

He chuckled at that. "Do you want to discuss it?"

"There's no need. Mrs. Carson painted a very flattering picture of you. I am certain you will be despised by the men to whom she was not so kind."

"Do you believe me now that I am not a libertine?"

"I did not think you were."

He frowned. "But in the library—"

"In the library I was an idiot. I was angry and untruthful and I am sorry for it." There, she had said it.

"Untruthful?" He looked so fierce when he was perplexed. "About what?"

She didn't fear his scowl, but it was a little rude of him not to acknowledge her apology. "I told you I wanted honesty from you, but I did not offer you the same consideration. I was not angry because I thought you used and discarded women."

"Then why were you angry?"

Lord, but this was difficult. "I was jealous."

He stared at her, head twisted slightly to one side as though he hadn't heard her correctly. "Jealous?"

Eleanor nodded, twisting her fingers together as she moved closer to him. "This is very difficult for me to admit."

"Take your time."

She would have smiled at his tone were she not quite so nervous. She was standing directly in front of him now, as he had turned his body to hers at her approach. She could smell his soap, feel the heat of his body. She could not look away from the mesmerizing beauty of his gaze.

She drew breath, gathering her courage. "I hate the fact that you have been with other women—not because I believe you a rake, but because I was not one of them."

His eyes widened. "Of course you weren't. You were an innocent. I would have been a cad to take advantage of you, no matter how much I wanted to. I respected you too much to act as I wanted."

Some women might have been insulted that he admitted to having such sexual feelings for her, but not Eleanor. He had admitted as much several times since his arrival, but he'd never explained that he had felt them in the past, or why he hadn't acted on the feelings when he had a chance.

"That is why I was jealous," she explained. "You should have been mine and mine alone. I hate that those women knew you in a way I never had, even though you had claimed to want me as your wife."

"I did want you." His eyes were black in the darkness—black and bright. "I wanted you in every way I could possibly have you."

Eleanor flushed under the heat of his gaze and words. "I have no right to feel as I do, but I have never lost that possessive feeling where you are concerned. I once thought of you as mine, and as foolish as this all sounds, I cannot help but feel in my heart that you are mine still."

His hand came up to her face, cupping her cheek as his gaze drew her closer. "It does not sound foolish. Ever since we first met, you have had a hold on me that no one else has managed. I do not understand it, but I know it. All I ask is that you give me the chance to prove myself worthy of your claim."

Eleanor didn't know how she would have replied to that had Brahm given her the chance to speak. Any words she might have uttered were taken from her when he claimed her mouth with his own.

Firm and warm, his lips moved lazily against hers, as though all the years between their last kiss and this one simply hadn't happened. He tasted warm and spicy, and she opened her mouth to him, sighing in pleasure as his tongue slipped inside.

Never in her life had there ever been anything as sweet and right as this man's kisses. When she was younger she thought her reaction to him ordinary, the way she would react to any man, but now she knew the difference.

She clung to him, her fingers twisting in his lapels as she pressed herself against his length. How good he felt, how solid and strong. After so many years of being the one everyone depended on and leaned on, she felt that this was a man she could lean on if necessary.

And it was so wonderful not to have to pretend that she didn't care for him anymore. How freeing it was to admit the truth and to hear his own admission. So much time wasted between them. There were still obstacles for them to overcome, things to learn about each other before they could continue forward.

As if sensing the direction of her thoughts, he lifted his head, breaking their kiss. His breath was humid against her cheek.

"You realize, Eleanor, that by letting me hold you again you risk the chance that I might never want to let you go."

She smiled—impulsively. "I shall take that risk, my lord."

"Good," he growled, and covered her mouth with his once more.

Chapter 7

Underneath the shade of an ancient oak, Brahm leaned back on his forearm as he bit into a succulent strawberry. The day was warm enough that he had removed his coat and rolled up his shirtsleeves. The soft wool blanket beneath was sun-warmed and contributed to his sun-drunk state.

He shared his blanket with Birch, and another bachelor, Locke—both of whom were trying to entertain the ladies by holding blades of grass between their thumbs and using them to make whistling noises.

The picnic was a rousing success if the laughter and conversation buzzing about him was any indication. Set atop a hill not quite a mile from the Durbane estate, the party sat on blankets and dined on a meal of cold meats, salads, and bread, with fresh, ripe fruit for dessert.

Eleanor was several blankets away, sitting with her sisters, shading her peaches-and-cream complexion with a dainty white parasol. Her golden hair was up in a simple knot, leaving her lovely face open for his appraisal. She was trying to shelter Phoebe under her parasol as well, no doubt to prevent the younger woman from developing a burn. Where was Phoebe's own parasol? She wasn't an infant unable to look after herself.

Eleanor offered an apple to Arabella before taking one for herself. Did she ever notice that she put everyone else before herself? She even did it to him, and he was probably the least worthy of such condescension.

With every passing day she became more and more beautiful to him. And two nights ago, when she had admitted to being jealous, to feeling possessive of him, she became the most exquisite creature on the earth.

He could still taste her kiss, even though he hadn't had the chance to steal another. These last two days had been a sort of hell, having her so close but being unable to hold her as he wanted, or even talk to her as he wanted. He wanted to know everything about her—everything that had changed since their first attempt at courtship. He wanted to make her laugh, wanted to learn how she thought and what her secrets were. Those things were damn near impossible when she had to play hostess for her guests. And even more impossible because he had to share her attention with other bachelors.

He was so very tempted to tell her father to send the other single men home. No one else would have Eleanor but him. After spending so much time obsessing and longing for her, he was not about to give her up to someone who wouldn't worship her half so well as he would.

In such a short time this journey had become about so much more than Eleanor's forgiveness, or trying to put her behind him. He didn't want to forget her, and he wanted so much more than her forgiveness. He would not stop until he had her heart, because she was already in danger of claiming his.

She probably wasn't even aware of how mad he was for her. Just looking at her was enough to make his soul feel as light as a feather. Her smile was the reason God had given him a second chance at life. She was his salvation, his reward for having turned his life around. He would do all he could to endeavor to deserve her.

Why? Because despite the fact that she had every reason to hate him, she didn't. She was too good for that. She offered him understanding when most other people would turn their backs on him. And most of all, because she seemed as inexplicably drawn to him as he was to her, as though they were missing halves to the same piece.

"You look very pleased with yourself, sir."

Brahm looked up, past the dainty boots and muslin skirts to the woman who smiled down at him. It was Arabella. She looked harmless enough, but Brahm wouldn't be surprised if she had a knife hidden under her chemise.

He rose to his feet with the help of his cane. To remain on the ground while she stood would be remarkably rude.

"I am sorry," she told him, with what sounded like real remorse. "I do not wish to cause you discomfort."

Brahm stretched his leg. On a day such as this it hardly hurt at all. "No discomfort, my lady. I am simply an ungraceful lout nowadays. This is nothing a short walk won't remedy."

She smiled prettily, and for a moment she looked very much like Eleanor. "Perhaps you will allow me to accompany you in apology then?"

He arched a brow. She wanted to walk with him? Definitely a weapon hidden somewhere. Regardless of the potential danger to his person, he offered her his arm. "It would be an honor."

They strolled leisurely through the blanket of thick, green grass. Arabella shielded herself from the sun with a lacy pink parasol, the brim of which managed to shade Brahm's eyes as well. He did not speak, but simply enjoyed the day and waited for the woman next to him to make her attack.

They neared the edge of the hill, where they could see the entire valley laid out before them, including Lord Burrough's estate. Nestled in a bed of green, the stone mansion was the height of picturesque.

Arabella released his arm. "I wish to apologize for myself and my sisters, Lord Creed."

He turned his head to gaze at her. Her pale eyes were filled with oddly touching sincerity. "There is no need to apologize to me for wanting to protect your sister."

She smiled faintly as she turned her attention back to the vista before them. "That is very good of you, but no matter how noble our intentions, our methods definitely left something to be desired."

Brahm shrugged. "Decorum has no place where family is involved."

She regarded him thoughtfully, with a smile that seemed begrudgingly warm. "That is an interesting notion."

His lips lifted on the right side. "I find I am positively brimming with such notions lately."

She chuckled at that. A moment of comfortable silence passed between them, in which they both seemed to enjoy the sun, the view, and the company.

"I want to like you, Lord Creed." Her parasol twirled in her hands.

He nodded in acquiescence. "I would like that, my lady."

Her expression suddenly turned serious, almost plaintive. "Please do not hurt my sister."

Such a heartfelt plea deserved nothing but total reverent honesty. "I give you my word that I will do everything in my power to do as you ask."

She smiled—brightly enough to rival the sun. If only Eleanor would grace him with such a smile.

They turned back to the picnic then, walking arm in arm, just as slowly as they had when they left.

Ladies Dumont and Merrott watched their approach with barely concealed interest. "Oh my dear," Lady Dumont spoke. "We began to despair that you would never bring him back for the rest of us."

Brahm forced what he hoped was a charming smile. How could Wynthrope have had an affair with this woman? No doubt his former thief of a brother had robbed the woman while sharing her bed. Good Lord, he hoped whatever Wyn stole, it had made him a lot of blunt. Lady Dumont was about as subtle and attractive as a nest of vipers. True, her form was somewhat pleasing, but her personality ruined whatever charms she might possess rather quickly. There was nothing wrong with a woman playing the seducer, but there was a time and place for such behavior.

Arabella was all grace and ease. "Despair no longer, ladies. He is returned."

"Apple, Lord Creed?"

Brahm stared at the red fruit in Lady Dumont's hand. "No thank you, my lady. I have made it a habit to never accept fruit from beautiful women. It is the one lesson from the Bible I adhere to."

Lady Dumont giggled at his flattery of her appearance, his lack of sincerity unnoticed.

"I wonder if you would accept if Lady Eleanor was the one offering?" Lady Merrott's gaze was shrewd as she asked the question.

Eleanor, who sat only a few feet away on a blanket with her sisters, lifted her head at the sound of her name. Brahm smiled at her over the heads of the other ladies. Her gaze was questioning as it met his.

"Would you try to tempt me with an apple, Lady Eleanor?" he asked, letting her in on the absurd joke.

Eleanor waved a careless hand. "La, no."

Brahm covered his chest with a hand in a wounded gesture. Of course he wasn't truly offended by her dismissal. He could tell she wasn't any more serious than he. "See, Lady Merrott, Lady Eleanor has no desire to offer me fruit."

"If I remember correctly," Eleanor spoke again, drawing all their attention, "I would have better luck tempting you with cake, my lord."

Laughter erupted from Brahm's chest. Eleanor's bland expression had never once changed, nor had her disinterested tone, but her delivery of the remark was so wonderfully funny to him that she might as well have tickled his ribs as she said it. Even more pleasing than her well-placed jab at Lady Merrott's attempt to embarrass her was that Eleanor remembered how much he liked cake. It was a Ryland weakness.

"You have me at a disadvantage Lady Eleanor," he remarked with a grin, "remembering my deficiency so well."

"Oh, you have more than one weakness, do you not, Lord Creed?" It was Lady Dumont who spoke. Her tone was light, but her meaning was clear, as was the displeasure in her eyes. She did not like his favoring Eleanor over her.

"Of course he does," Eleanor responded loftily before he could. "He is a man. Were not you and Lady Merrott listing off the various weaknesses of that sex yesterday at tea?"

How innocently she asked the question, knowing full well that the gentlemen gathered nearby would jump on it. Suddenly, it was the ladies Dumont and Merrott who were the center of attention and not Brahm—and not Eleanor.

Brahm flashed his savior a grateful smile and was rewarded with a conspiratorial one in return. His heart rolled at the sight of it. He'd gladly brave Lady Dumont's barbs for the rest of his life if Eleanor would only continue to smile at him. Suddenly he didn't think her protective instincts were a flaw in her character at all. He rather liked them when they were directed at him.

He would have gone to her if he could have—if it wouldn't have caused tongues to wag, and if Lord Burrough hadn't chosen that moment to call out to him.

"Come play horseshoes," the old man commanded. "We need another."

Brahm did as he was bid. After all, the earl was going to be his father-in-law one day if things went as he wished.

For a man who seemed so ill when Brahm first arrived, Lord Burrough had taken part in a surprising number of activities. True, he wasn't the picture of health and haleness, being a little pale and tiring easily, but he was nowhere near death's door. No doubt he had used his "illness" to persuade Eleanor into allowing the party. There was no other way she would have agreed to being offered up like a broodmare at market.

Yet was that her father's intention? The more time

Brahm spent around the older man, the more he began to suspect that Burrough's motives were far more clandestine. The old man rarely bothered with any of the other bachelors, only him. Burrough only took part in the activities Brahm himself participated in.

The old man had set this whole thing up to reunite Brahm and Eleanor. The other bachelors were nothing more than a diversion to keep Eleanor from realizing the truth. Brahm wasn't certain how he knew this, but he knew in his heart he was correct. He knew it the instant his gaze met the old earl's and he saw the pleasure and acceptance there.

He joined the group of gentlemen and accepted the horseshoe Burrough offered him.

"It has been a long time since I played," he cautioned. "I will no doubt give you all something to chuckle at."

"You cannot be any worse than Birch," Lord Burrough remarked gruffly. "He spends most of his time trying to keep from getting his hands dirty."

There were chuckles all around, and Brahm took aim with the shoe in his hand. Leaning forward, he pitched the shoe toward the goal. It landed with a decided thud around the post.

Lord Burrough slapped him on the back. "You will do, my boy, you will do."

Brahm knew the praise was for so much more than his skill at the game.

They had only been playing for a few moments when Brahm was approached by two bachelors—Birch and Faulkner. They stood beside Locke, watching as Lord Burrough lined up his shot. Brahm watched them, his heart skipping uncomfortably at the sight of the silver flask in Locke's hand.

Unfortunately the men noticed him watching. Locke offered him the flask. "Drink, Creed?"

Brahm stared at the flask for a moment, his mouth moistening with longing. Was it politeness or malice that had prompted the offer? "No thank you."

Locke made a scoffing noise. "There's no one looking. No one will know."

That wasn't the point. "I will know."

The dark-haired man shook his head and took another swallow. " 'Tis a sad day when an Englishman is too cowardly to take a drink."

The men gathered around the horseshoe pit grew quiet, their attention now centered on the two men. Wonderful, this was going to be a repeat of the situation with Faulkner.

"Is it cowardly to avoid that which is harmful?" Brahm asked, forcing lightness into his tone.

The younger man scowled, turning his features from handsome to unpleasant. "What could be harmful in a drink?"

Was it Brahm's imagination, or was Locke terribly dim? Perhaps it was the liquor dulling his senses. "It is harmful because I will not wish to stop at one."

Birch tried to silence his friend, but Locke would not be denied his chance to speak. "Then it is weakness that stops you."

Sighing, Brahm turned to fully face the slighter man. This was obviously not going to stop any time soon. He was going to have to be a bit more forceful. "Locke, have you ever seen me foxed?"

Locke shook his dark head. "No."

No, of course he hadn't. He wouldn't be trying so hard if he had. "Have you heard any stories?"

Locke grinned. "A few."

Only the amusing ones, obviously. That was surprising. Normally the amusing ones were followed with an equal number of the unamusing ones, such as the time he had broken a man's jaw for insulting the color of his waistcoat.

"Then you probably have heard that me drunk is not a good thing."

Locke nodded, sipping from the flask. Yes, he was well on his way to tipsy himself. "I have heard that, yes."

"Good."

"But one drink won't get you foxed." He jabbed a finger into Brahm's arm with a raucous chuckle. "Unless you've the constitution of a woman."

The man wasn't listening at all. Brahm sighed and pinched the bridge of his nose between his thumb and forefinger. Maybe if he broke Locke's jaw that would put an end to this insanity.

"If I take a drink I'll drain that flask, and then if you continue to piss me off as you are doing now, I'll shove my cane so far up your arse, you'll be picking your teeth with it."

Silence followed his snarled announcement as he glared at Locke, who stared back in stupefied silence.

Suddenly the air was punctuated with Lord Burrough's booming laugh. Other guests turned to see what had transpired that deserved such a reaction, but all they saw was Eleanor's father slapping Brahm on the back as Lord Locke stomped away, his face flushed.

"Yes my boy," the old man chortled. "I believe you will do indeed."

Eleanor found but a few moments to share with Brahm that afternoon. Even then it was nothing more than a walk after his horseshoe match before heading back to the estate. They were with a larger party who wished to explore the area, but Brahm's leg prevented them from keeping pace with the others, giving them a modicum of privacy.

"I believe your father likes me," he told her, lowering the brim of his hat against the sun.

Eleanor smiled. "I believe Lady Dumont likes you."

"Yes, but thankfully your father's sentiments are of a different bent."

She laughed. It seemed to be so easy for him to amuse her. "Indeed. What happened between you and Lord Locke earlier?"

Brahm shrugged his wide shoulders. "He was trying to persuade me to have a drink from his flask. He could not seem to understand why I refused."

A neat frown knitted Eleanor's brow as her fingers tightened on the handle of her parasol. "Was it difficult for you to refuse?"

His laughter was harsh and abrupt. "Every damn time. Pardon my language."

Her smile deepened. "I have heard the word 'damn' before, Brahm."

He sighed ruefully. "And here I was trying not to corrupt you with my scandalous ways. Next thing you'll tell me is that you like bourbon and French cigars."

Eleanor shuddered. "Neither."

This time his laughter was far more pleasant. "Good."

They walked a few more steps in silence before Eleanor seized the moment. "I have been doing some reading on the subject of drunkenness."

He stopped, but just for a second, and then he began walking once more. "Have you?" His tone was careful, wary.

Twirling her parasol nervously, Eleanor nodded. "There are many who believe it to be a disease of the mind."

Brahm snorted, his gaze roaming everywhere but at her. "So I am mad, is that it?"

"No, not mad. But neither are you weak." Eleanor's lips compressed as she carefully considered what to say next. "It is an illness, like any other. Recurring and difficult to recover from."

He squinted as he looked up, fine lines creasing the flesh around his eyes. "You talk as though you believe recovery is possible."

"I think it is."

He smiled as though he pitied her. "So is relapse."

She nodded. "As it is with any disease, I suppose."

Suddenly he stopped, turning his body toward her. She stopped as well, held still more by his russet gaze than by the fact that he had stopped walking. "Would you nurse me if I fell 'ill' during my stay here, Eleanor? Or would you show me the door?"

It was a difficult question to answer, but Eleanor knew that answer it she must. It was one thing for her to talk so objectively about Brahm's illness when he was sober. It would be quite another to deal with if he were to have a relapse, as it were. She had seen him foxed before, and knew the kind of wild, destructive behavior he was capable of.

"I would nurse you," she answered honestly.

"Because it is the Christian way? Or because it is your nature to put anyone and everyone above yourself?" Was he mocking her, or himself? Or was he simply too embarrassed by her admission?

The truth sprang readily to her lips. "Because I care about you."

He looked away, but she could see the movement of his throat as he swallowed. He couldn't be that surprised by her confession, could he? He had to know that she wouldn't have kissed him as she did, wouldn't have researched his condition if she didn't harbor some degree of feeling for him. She had never stopped caring—her anger at him proved that, as did her willingness to believe the best of him once again.

"Thank you," he said finally after a lengthy silence. "Hopefully I will never be in need of your nursing capabilities."

She grinned, trying to lighten the mood. "I hope you never will either. I am not that good a nurse."

He laughed at her jest and they soon turned back toward the picnic area as the others were turning back as well. They talked about silly things as they walked, teasing each other and telling amusing stories about their families. The subject of his drinking never came up again. And Eleanor, despite the temptation, did not dare to ask whether he cared for her. He had kissed her. He seemed to enjoy their time together as much as she did. That would have to be answer enough.

When the party returned to the house after the picnic, Eleanor retired to her room. There was no rest to be found there, however, as her sisters decided that they needed to talk to her. And their subject was Brahm.

"Eleanor, surely you know people will talk." Phoebe folded her arms across her chest in a very chastising posture. "We all saw you walk off with him today."

Muriel joined in. "And when you came back your cheeks were flushed."

Eleanor rolled her eyes at the pair of them. "I had been walking in the sun. Of course I was flushed."

"Not that kind of flushed." Lydia's eyes were bright with something Eleanor didn't want to identify.

Drawing herself up to her full height, shoulders braced, Eleanor refused to be cowed. "I do not need to explain myself to my *younger* sisters."

"Perhaps not, but if you get yourself ruined it will reflect badly upon all of us."

Eleanor shot Lydia a furious glance. "I beg your pardon? Ruined?"

"People are already speculating, of that you can be certain." She sounded more peeved than concerned. "You cannot wander off with a man like Creed and not have people suspect the worst."

Eleanor's jaw was tight. "Of me, or of him?"

Arabella raised a hand. "I wandered off with him earlier. Do people suspect the worst of me?"

Dear Belle. Eleanor smiled thankfully at her sister. Lydia, however, was not done. "That Carson woman's book paints him as the kind of man who would seduce a woman."

How in the name of God did the book do that? "Lydia, if you had read what she wrote, you would know it does no such thing."

Her sisters gaped at her. "You read it?"

Grabbing the book from her nightstand, Eleanor held it up for them to see. "I read what it said about Brahm, and it does not make him out to be a seducer of women." Not unmarried virginal ones at any rate.

Lydia was not impressed. "The fact that you even read that filth shows how much he has already corrupted you."

What a hypocrite! "You did not seem to find it so filthy when Lady Dumont read from it the other day. In fact, I thought I heard you ask her if you might borrow her copy."

Lydia's expression hardened, and Eleanor braced herself for a fight. In fact, she welcomed the opportunity for one.

Arabella tried to smooth things over. "Ellie, we just do not want you to do something you will regret."

She could not bring herself to be angry at Arabella, yet frustration rang in her voice. "Why would I regret giving Lord Creed a chance to prove himself?"

It was Lydia who answered. "Because he hasn't changed, dearest."

"He no longer drinks." That ought to prove that he had changed indeed.

Lydia's expression was so pitying that it was tempting to slap it right off her face. "So he says. You do not know what he does when he is out of your sight."

No, but she believed in him. Didn't she? So why the shiver of dread at Lydia's words? Did her sister know something she didn't?

"Lydia," Arabella chastised. "If you have evidence that Lord Creed has lied about giving up drinking, then tell us."

Lydia shrugged and studied her nails. "I have nothing to tell."

"Then stop speculating." Arabella was obviously not impressed with their sister. "If Eleanor trusts in Lord Creed, then we must respect that."

Eleanor flashed Arabella a grateful smile.

Lydia's head jerked up, her gaze narrow. "And when he breaks her heart and she comes weeping to us, will I have to respect that as well?"

Sighing, Eleanor shook her head. "Rest assured Lydia, that if my heart is broken you will be the last person I come weeping to." Had she actually had a hand in raising this woman? If so, where had she gone wrong?

Lydia's expression was instantly contrite. "Dearest, I

meant no slight to you, but you are for all intents and purposes an innocent country maid, and Brahm Ryland is a worldly gentleman. Men such as he know exactly how to lie to make a woman believe in their attentions."

How did Lydia know these things? Had Brahm done such to her to woo her into his bed? No, she could not believe that. She had no reason to suspect him of such deception.

"He is not the man for you," Lydia continued. "He needs a woman just as worldly and experienced as he is."

Eleanor's gaze met her sister's squarely. There was something in Lydia's voice, in her expression that set off warning bells in Eleanor's head. "Someone like you, perhaps?"

Lydia had the grace to blush. "Heavens no!"

"Eleanor," Arabella chastised, "really, that was uncalled for."

If Arabella or Lydia thought she was going to apologize, they were going to be greatly disappointed. Poor Phoebe and Muriel were watching the goings-on with wide eyes and shocked expressions. They were unused to hearing Eleanor talk in such a blunt manner.

In fact, Eleanor never did talk in such a blunt manner—unless Brahm was involved. He seemed to bring out the boldness in her.

She seized the boldness while it lasted. "I think I would like to be alone for a while, if the four of you would not mind?"

The sisters glanced at one another, but no one argued. One of the advantages of having been a mother figure to her sisters was that they seldom argued when she told them to do something.

They filed out one by one, with Arabella bringing up the

rear. She turned in the door, her expression rueful. "I did not mean to upset you, Ellie."

Eleanor sighed and managed a strained smile. "*You* did not, Belle."

Her sister looked so relieved, it nearly broke Eleanor's heart. She closed the door with a heaviness weighing down on her chest. What was happening? She was rarely at odds with any of her sisters, even Lydia. The tension between them hadn't appeared until Brahm had. Could it be that Lydia had regrets about her tryst with Brahm, and she was trying to warn Eleanor away from him as a kind of penance? Did she think she was doing Eleanor a favor by doing so?

Rubbing her temples, Eleanor stretched out on her bed and closed her eyes. A little rest before dressing for dinner would do her good. The guests would just have to miss her at the afternoon's entertainments.

Slowly her body relaxed. She thought of Brahm and the kisses they had shared that afternoon. With those sweet images in her mind, she drifted off to sleep.

She awoke sometime later when her abigail, Mary, knocked on her door. It was time for her bath. Had she slept that long?

Eleanor rose, and after the footmen filled her tub with hot water, went into her dressing room, where her maid helped her disrobe. She climbed into the tub and scrubbed the last vestiges of sleep away. By the time she stepped out, she felt much better about everything, including Lydia's behavior.

She dried and dressed and allowed Mary to arrange her hair in a more suitable style for evening. She even agreed to having ringlets put in with the curling tongs, after which her maid pinned the elaborate coiffure up on top of her head so that ringlets tumbled down her back in the Grecian style.

Her gown was a warm, rich peach silk that accentuated her bosom and complemented her skin tone. Brussels lace edged the neck and made up the whole of the short, scalloped sleeves. Pearl earrings and choker completed the ensemble.

She could not wait for Brahm's reaction to her appearance. How silly and girlish of her to base so much on his opinion. Silly, perhaps, but she hurried downstairs all the same.

As she entered the drawing room, she spotted Brahm in the corner. His hair was slightly damp and fell over his brow in a boyish manner, softening the chiseled lines of his face. He was dressed in evening black, leaning on his cane as he talked with an elegantly clad blond woman.

Lydia.

What was her sister doing? Why was she talking to Brahm? Why was she standing so close? Eleanor watched with narrowed eyes as Lydia placed her hand on Brahm's arm. Brahm lifted his glass to his lips, forcing Lydia to remove her hand. Had he done it on purpose? And what was he drinking?

So many unanswered questions. At one time she might have withdrawn and thought the worst of Brahm. She had thought so little of herself that she would have naturally believed that Brahm preferred the sensual, worldly Lydia to her. Not now. Maybe it was because she was still angry with her sister for what she had said about Brahm earlier, but Eleanor wasn't about to turn away. Spite spurred her onward. She wanted to know what Lydia and Brahm were talking about.

As she approached, Brahm lifted his head. His gaze met

hers, and he gave her what she could only describe as a relieved yet apologetic smile. Then, as his gaze roamed the length of her, his expression changed. His eyes lit with an inner flame, and his smile became more possessive, more predatory.

"Lady Eleanor," he purred as she came up beside Lydia. "You look exceedingly lovely tonight."

Eleanor blushed at his words and resisted the urge to toss her sister a triumphant glance. "Thank you, Lord Creed. I hope I am not interrupting anything?" This time she did turn her attention to her sister.

Lydia's countenance was one of complete innocence. "Of course not. Lord Creed and I were merely chatting."

"Then you will not mind if I steal him for a moment," Eleanor remarked, linking her arm through Brahm's. "Lord Creed expressed an interest in seeing the orangery. I thought we might take a tour of it before dinner."

He was surprised by her boldness, that was obvious in the way he looked at her, but he went along with the ruse all the same. "I would like that very much, Lady Eleanor." He set his glass on a low table. It had nothing but water in it, of that Eleanor was certain.

"Do not be long," Lydia cautioned. "We will be going in to dinner soon."

Eleanor smiled tightly. Her missing dinner was not Lydia's true concern, but what was? Was she concerned about Eleanor's reputation, or did she merely wish to keep Eleanor and Brahm from having time alone?

Whatever her reason, it didn't matter. Eleanor would have time alone with Brahm, and they would be back in time for dinner. Despite her rather impudent behavior where Brahm was concerned, she knew better than to push the bounds of propriety.

They left the house arm in arm, through the French doors in the drawing room. Their leaving together would be noted, but provided they were not gone very long, there would be little speculation. She was supposed to be shopping for a husband, after all.

Through the garden they strode in silence, the tension between them mounting. Or at least it seemed to Eleanor that it was mounting. Did Brahm even notice?

The orangery was located in the back south corner of the garden. Eleanor breathed deep as she pushed open the door. The humid air was heavy with the smell of oranges and lemons—sweet yet sharp and wonderfully delicious.

"It is lovely," Brahm commented as she led him deeper into the leafy growth, so that they were obscured from outside view. "But I do not recall asking to see it."

"You did not," she answered, knowing full well that he was already aware of the fact. "I made it up."

He gasped in mock astonishment. "Made it up? Why, Lady Eleanor, are you saying you deliberately schemed to be alone with me?"

She turned to him, grinning at the mischievous light in his russet eyes. "Yes."

He chuckled. "Tired of sharing me, were you?"

"Yes," she answered honestly, wanting to shock him out of that mock arrogance.

His smile faded, but not the warmth in his eyes. "You truly are possessive."

She nodded. Why argue the truth?

"There is only one cure for a jealous woman," he informed her, his voice dangerously low and smooth.

A shiver rushed down Eleanor's spine. "What is that?"

Brahm's arms came around her, the tip of his cane brushing the back of her calf. He hauled her close so that their bodies were flush against each other. She could feel his heart against her breast.

"To give her what she wants," he murmured, and covered her mouth with his.

Chapter 8

Brahm didn't just kiss Eleanor, he feasted on her. His lips ravished hers; his tongue pillaged the hot, wet interior of her mouth. He held her tightly so she could not escape—not that she was trying. God help him, but she was matching the fervor of his kiss with an intensity of her own that was born purely of instinct. Eleanor might not have experience with men, but she knew exactly what to do to arouse him, simply because she was Eleanor.

What she wanted? Hell, he was giving her what *he* wanted. Her desire to have him to herself fueled his own. The more she yielded to him, the more pressure he applied to the small of her back. She was so soft, so pliant against him. Already he was hardening for her.

She should have fought him. If he were she, he would have. He was acting exactly as he claimed not to be—as a rake. But how could he not when she tempted him so? He'd kiss her in the middle of the drawing room with all the guests present if he thought that was her wish.

Her hands roamed his back and shoulders, their touch feather-light through his coat. They tangled in his hair, pulling and mussing as though she fought to hold him to her. If he was strong enough to break their kiss, he'd tell her she needn't fight. He wasn't going anywhere, but he didn't want to take his lips from hers, not even for a second.

She was so graceful in his arms, so supple and soft. Her eagerness for him was a heated flush, warming her perfumed skin and surrounding him with her scent. Sweet, wild strawberries. God, how he loved the smell of her, the taste of her, the feel of her.

Pliant breasts pressed against his chest. He moved one of his hands from her back to splay her side, then up, pushing between them until he claimed the prize. Firm, silk-covered flesh filled his palm. He stroked his thumb across the swell, groaning as he felt the hard poke of her erect nipple. Instinctively his thumb and forefinger closed around the small protrusion and gently squeezed.

Eleanor gasped against his mouth, her hips surging against his in reflex. Her reaction fired Brahm's blood. His hand slid over her breast, the neckline of her gown. Blessed be the man who designed these flimsy low bodices. One tug and the fabric would submit to his will, freeing the flesh he so dearly wanted to taste. And he wouldn't stop there. Once he had sated himself with her breasts, then he would move downward and bury his face between her pale thighs, where he would savor the succulence that was Eleanor. He would devour every inch of her if she would allow it.

And she would allow it, of that he was certain.

Of course, that would make them late for dinner.

Dinner. It would be ready soon. People would wonder where they were. There would be speculation, as everyone had seen them leave together.

God almighty. What was he doing? If he didn't stop now, he might very well ruin Eleanor. He wanted to woo her, not destroy her.

Reluctantly he eased himself away from her, lifting his mouth from hers. Her delicate eyelids fluttered. Confused, glazed blue eyes gazed up at him. Her lips were red and softly parted, inviting him to claim them once more.

He swore instead and released her. "Forgive me."

Eleanor smoothed her hands over the front of her gown. "Have you committed some offense?" Her tone was light, but he could hear the strain. Did she think he was rejecting her? One look at the front of his trousers should tell her just how badly he wanted her.

Raking his fingers through his hair in an effort to straighten it, Brahm drew breath. He was shaking. "It has been a long time since I have been with a woman. I was too exuberant."

Her expression was instantly shrewd. "How long?"

He chuckled. Were he thinking with the proper organ, he would have seen that question coming. Eleanor was different from anyone he had ever known, so good and pure, but she was still a woman, with all a woman's insecurities and odd behaviors.

And a woman's instinctive, inborn ability to seduce any man she set her sights on.

"More than a year," he replied honestly as he offered her his arm. "We should return to the house. They will be wondering where you are."

She nodded as her hand settled on his sleeve. "We would not want that."

Was it his imagination, or did she sound peeved? "No, we would not. I will not have anyone saying I took advantage of you."

Her gaze was earnest as it locked with his. "It would never occur to them to think I took advantage of you, would it?"

The very idea of it was so absurd, he laughed aloud. "You are a proper woman. Of course they would never entertain such a notion."

"A proper woman." She made a scoffing noise as they exited the orangery. "What good has propriety done me? I did my duty and helped raise my sisters, three of whom do not seem terribly happy with their lives."

"That has nothing to do with you. Your sisters made their own decisions, just as my brothers have made theirs." Devlin, North, and Wynthrope might sometimes do things that made Brahm want to shake them, but he supported them all the same.

"Perhaps if I had not been quite so proper, it would have been me in your bed that night and not Lydia."

What? Not paying attention to where he was going, Brahm stumbled as the tip of his cane rolled on a pebble on the path. Luckily for him, Eleanor helped him right himself before he could fall on his arse. Not quite so lucky was the pain that shot up his leg.

"Perhaps," he replied, his teeth clenched and his heart pounding not just from pain but from the idea of Eleanor in his bed. "But it hardly matters now, does it?"

She glanced away. "I suppose not."

They walked on in silence, Brahm fighting a grimace with every limping step. They were halfway back to the house before Eleanor spoke again. "Was Cassie your mistress?"

She truly was obsessed with women he had bedded. If she wasn't so honest and open about it, he might find it disturbing, but her jealousy was amusing in the fact that it told him that she wanted him. All that was left to discover was if that wanting extended to wanting to be his wife.

His affairs were none of her business, and in Brahm's experience it was never a good idea telling the woman you were interested in about past lovers, but he had promised her honesty and he would give it to her. "Briefly."

"Did you love her?"

Ah, how to answer? Honesty was not always the best route in such cases. If he lied and said yes, she might think him a better man—or she might get jealous. If he was honest and said no, she might think him a cad.

He chose the safest route. "I might have come to, but our association did not last that long."

Her expression was more curious than suspicious. "What happened?"

"She died." Poor Cassie. She hadn't just died, she had been murdered by a man out to destroy his brother North. Brahm had initiated their relationship in an attempt to keep her safe. It hadn't worked.

Eleanor's distraught expression broke Brahm's heart. "I am so sorry."

So was he. He was sorry he hadn't been able to keep his promise to Cassie. "Thank you, but you needn't feel badly. I have mourned her loss." And avenged her as well. The man who killed Cassie was the same man Brahm had shot defending North. Harker would never hurt anyone else again.

It was time to change the subject before he ended up telling her about killing Harker. That story was going to take a lot more time than they had right now. And with the throbbing in his leg, he would not tell the story with the delicacy it required.

"How is your reading coming along?" he asked. The

topic of drunkenness was preferable to murder, no matter how justifiable the killing was. "Do you still believe overindulging in spirits to be a disease?"

"Oh yes," she replied. "The more I read of Mr. Trotter's work, the more convinced I am of that very notion."

"So, Dr. Durbane," he asked teasingly, "what do you suggest as a cure?"

Her reply was quick. "Do not drink."

They chuckled together. If Brahm hadn't already resigned himself to the fact that he would have to fight his demons for the rest of his life, he might not have found her words so amusing.

"And you maintain your promise to nurse me if I ever suffer a relapse?"

"Absolutely."

He grinned. "That's almost reason to get foxed in itself."

Suddenly all the humor vanished from her face. She stopped on the path, just outside the doors leading into the drawing room, and turned to him. "I could not forgive myself if I knew I had driven you to find solace in a bottle."

Solace in a bottle. What a poetic way to describe what happened to him when he drank. There was very little solace involved.

She opened the doors and entered the house, leaving him to follow without responding to her proclamation. It was just as well, as he had no idea what to say.

"There you are!" Lord Burrough boomed when he spotted them. "Just in time."

No one seemed to pay particular attention to either of them, which was good as far as Brahm was concerned. No attention meant no one saw anything amiss with their appearance. It meant no one suspected that he had been about to shove his hand down Eleanor's bodice.

Unfortunately there was one person whose gaze lingered a tad bit longer than he was comfortable with, especially since that person was Lydia. As the guests and family paired off according to precedence to go in for dinner, Lydia raked him with a gaze so scathing, it could surely peel paint from walls. Her eyes narrowed as she turned her attention to her sister.

Could she see the faint pink shadow around Eleanor's mouth? Could she see wrinkles where his hand had crushed the front of Eleanor's gown? Had he left any telltale mark on Eleanor's beautiful pale skin? And if Lydia did see any such evidence, what would she do with it? Would she run to her father? The old earl might be pleased that Brahm and Eleanor were "friendly" once more—or he might toss Brahm out for taking liberties. Or perhaps Lydia would start malicious gossip, although Brahm couldn't see her doing something that would humiliate her sister in such a way.

What was he thinking? This was the woman who had climbed into his bed after he proposed to Eleanor. Even if she hadn't known about the proposal, she must have known Eleanor had set her cap for him. Lydia hadn't cared about hurting her sister then, and she might not care about that now. He would have to keep his eye on her. He wasn't going to allow her to destroy his chances with Eleanor this time. He would not give her the chance to prey upon his weaknesses.

He would have to be very careful then, because when it came to weaknesses, he had an abundance.

Later, when he had a chance to speak to Eleanor, he would tell her that she needn't worry about his drinking. He would rather die than give in to the devils that plagued him. There was no way she could drive him to such destructive behavior. He would also tell her that they needed to be more careful, that Lydia was suspicious. He couldn't very well tell Eleanor not to trust her sister, but he would do what he could to protect her.

Eleanor was right; Lydia was not a happy woman. In fact, she was very bitter and unhappy. That kind of woman liked to share her misery. He would not allow her to share it with Eleanor. She hadn't managed to do it years ago; she would not do it now.

Dinner passed much too slowly and the port and cigars afterward was a lesson in suffering. Brahm smoked, but he longed for a drink—not because he wanted one, but because he knew it would help numb the ache in his leg. Had he been exercising as he normally did, he wouldn't be in this condition, but the house party didn't allow for his normal schedule, and his pride wouldn't allow him to deviate from the planned activities. It was his own fault that he was in so much discomfort now.

He had laudanum in his room, but it would certainly put him to sleep. He took it only when the pain was to the point where he was like a wounded bear, ready to kill anyone who looked at him the wrong way. He was at that point now. In fact, Locke was looking like a very likely first victim. It took all Brahm's control not to tear the younger man apart with a few choice remarks. After that day at the picnic, his opinion of the man had dwindled further still. The only thing that kept him from giving in to temptation was the knowledge that Eleanor preferred him over Locke and every other bachelor in residence.

"Gentlemen, please forgive me, but I must retire." He slid back his chair and rose to his feet using both cane and table for support. There could be no disguising the grimace that twisted his features as he settled as much weight as he dared on his left leg. Damn it all to hell, but it hurt. If only he had been watching where he was walking, he wouldn't have stumbled.

Perhaps this was fate's way of telling him not to "stumble" again when it came to Eleanor. He would give her the respect she deserved and exercise more control in the future. It would be so much easier if he didn't want her so damn much.

Yes, it was definitely time to go to bed and put himself in a laudanum-induced slumber. If he was starting to feel annoyed with Eleanor, it was definitely time he separated himself from the rest of the party.

Lord Burrough quietly wished him a good night and advised him to rest up for the ball the next night. The thought of dancing made Brahm want to vomit. Sleeping on broken glass would be preferable to dancing at this moment. Regardless, he assured the older man that he had every intention of being in top form for the ball.

"Do not worry, Creed," Lord Taylor remarked in a loud voice. "The rest of us will tend to Lady Eleanor in your absence."

Brahm flashed his teeth—it was little more than a snarl, and Taylor knew it. "Do that. I am certain it will take the entire lot of you to make up for my truancy."

Chuckles followed him as he left the room.

By the time Brahm reached his bedchamber, he was sweating, panting, and in so much pain, his head swam. He paused long enough to shrug off his coat and toss it on a chair. Then he went to the bed and fell upon it with a hoarse cry.

The laudanum was on his bedside table. He uncorked the bottle and took a swallow. It wasn't the best-tasting stuff, but he'd had worse. He lay on top of the bed, still fully dressed, and waited.

Numbness came. It started slowly, seeping through his body from the outer edges, it seemed. Soon the pain in his leg lessened and the fog in his brain thickened. What a lovely feeling. Fortunately for him, opiates had never held the same fascination that spirits did, otherwise he'd be in a very rough spot.

His last thought before drifting off to sleep was of the ball the next night. He certainly hoped he would be able to dance with Eleanor at least once. He wanted to touch her again. Would anyone notice if touched her other breast?

He fell asleep with a smile on his face.

Brahm was not with the other gentlemen when they joined the ladies in the drawing room later that evening. Any pleasure Eleanor might have taken from the evening evaporated. How had she become so infatuated with him so quickly? How could she have forgiven him so easily for what he had done?

She didn't have the answers. She knew only that both had happened with relative ease, and that instead of enjoying this evening and the entertainments it might have brought, she would spend her time counting down the hours until she would see him again. Where was he?

"Lord Creed will not be joining us this evening," her father announced to his guests. "I extend regrets on his behalf."

"Poor Creed," Lord Locke commented with deceptive casualness. "I cannot imagine what it is to be only half a man."

Eleanor shot him a disapproving look. Why was he

looking at her that way? Surely he didn't think she'd be so easily swayed by such cruel remarks?

Lord Birch settled into a chair with a glass of brandy. "Of course you cannot imagine it, Locke, being but a quarter yourself."

A smile curved Eleanor's lips as she turned away from the flushing Lord Locke. Her estimation of Lord Birch rose several notches.

Unfortunately Lord Birch took note of her smile, and it wasn't long before he stood before her.

"Lady Eleanor, may I join you?"

There was room on the sofa beside her, and there was no way she could refuse his request without appearing rude. "Of course."

Lord Birch was simply the first. Soon Eleanor was surrounded by the bachelor guests, even Lord Locke. They vied for her attention, competed for her favor. Whatever had happened to make them act this way? Had Brahm's attention toward her whetted their interest? Or was it that with Brahm around they knew they could not hope to compete for her attention, and now that he was absent she was open game?

Or perhaps they had finally caught wind of the size of her dowry. Whatever their reasons, Eleanor was a bit overwhelmed by their attentions. She knew she was not unattractive, but she had never been such a beauty that she had more than one or two admirers at a time. What in the name of heaven was she to do with these half-dozen gentlemen clustered around her?

She smiled when it was appropriate, paid compliments when they were warranted, and refused to allow any of them to inflate her sense of self. Each of these men saw her as a prize to be won, and she would do well to remember that and not allow herself to be swayed by flattery that might not be totally sincere.

Their pretty words and vacuous conversation tired her. The bachelors imparted nothing of themselves to her, nor did they seem terribly concerned with becoming more acquainted with her beyond a superficial level.

Why on earth would any of them want to marry her based on how little they knew? They knew what she looked like and they knew the extent of her fortune, and that seemed to be all they were interested in knowing. Pity.

Escape came in the form of her father. Barely two hours had passed before he gave in to his weariness and decided to head to bed. He was not yet fully recovered, and Eleanor worried about his health, despite her conviction that much of his recent "illness" had been but a ruse to persuade her to agree to this party. She excused herself from her admirers and went to her father.

"I will help you upstairs, Papa."

One look at her face, and he obviously knew she needed an escape. Normally he would have dismissed her concern and told her not to worry about him, but tonight he took the arm she offered and allowed her to lead him from the room.

They climbed the stairs in silence. Upon entering her father's chamber, Eleanor helped him out of his coat, untied his cravat, and removed his shoes. He lay back on the bed, the lamplight softening his craggy features.

"Do you require assistance with anything else, Papa?"

He shook his head. "George will soon be here to attend to me." George was his valet, the son of the man who had been his valet before that.

Eleanor seated herself on the edge of the bed. "Are you certain there is nothing you need?"

"I am fine." He opened his eyes—a blue gaze with more clarity than Eleanor was comfortable with at times. "There is no need for you to stay with me, Ellie. Go back to the guests."

She pulled a face. "I would rather watch you sleep."

Her father chuckled. "The bachelors a tad exuberant for you, eh?"

"They were like roosters, all preening and clucking for the attention of one hen." She toyed with the signet ring on her finger. "They do not care to know me, only to own me."

Her father frowned, all traces of humor gone from his countenance. "Own you?"

Eleanor nodded. "They want a wealthy, connected wife and that is all."

"That is what most marriages of our set are based on. Wealth and connection are everything. They ensure the continuation of society."

His words made sense, but they were so very impersonal. "Am I not to wish for more?"

He patted her hand. "Of course you are. You deserve everything you wish for."

"You and Mama were happy, were you not?" She so desperately needed to hear that they were. So many unhappy marriages, so many affairs and deceits had reached her ears, she needed to know there was something else available.

He smiled at the mentioned of her mother. "We were. Ours was an arranged marriage, you know."

She hadn't known that. "Truly?"

His fingers closed around hers. His hand was strong and warm and comforting. "We were very fortunate that our temperaments suited one another. It didn't take long for us to fall in love—of course, your mama was already carrying you when that happened."

Eleanor's brows rose in surprise. She had always thought her parents were a love match.

"Marriage is not easy, Ellie, be it a love match or a business arrangement." His deep voice was rife with sincerity. "It is something that requires hard work if it is to be a pleasant match. Understanding, forgiveness, patience, those are but three virtues you must learn to cultivate if you are to be married. And trust. Trust will be a difficult one for you, I think."

"I beg your pardon?" Whatever did her father mean?

"Do not get yourself in knots now." He shifted against the pillows. "You need to trust in your own worth, my dear. You blame yourself for so much and think so little of yourself. Stop being so afraid of what might happen and enjoy what is. You will be much happier that way."

She opened her mouth to deny it, but quickly shut it again. There was nothing to deny. He was right. She did blame herself. She often blamed herself for her sisters' unhappiness. There were times when she didn't think much of herself, for example, thinking for so long that Brahm had chosen Lydia over her because Lydia was more worthy. And hadn't she compared herself earlier, asking Brahm questions about his former mistress, wondering if he loved her, wondering how she measured up to the dead woman.

"Marriages are partnerships," her father went on. "There are good times and bad. There will be times when you think the worst of each other, when you believe you will never get past whatever hurdle life has tossed in your path."

"Then why even try?" If it was so much work, so much pain, what was the point? She couldn't believe that love— true love—could be so difficult.

Her father fixed her with a surprised look. Had he expected her to know the answer?

"Because, my dear, love is worth the effort. Love is what makes you see the good again. Love is what lifts you over the hurdle. Do you think your mother and I never fought, never lied or distrusted one another?"

"I . . . I always assumed you were always happy."

"Bah." He reached for the glass of water beside his bed and took a sip, forcing her to wait until he had quenched his thirst before speaking again. "She almost left me once, you know. Took you and Arabella and was going to run back to her mother. I could have stopped her from taking the two of you, but what did I know of raising daughters?"

Eleanor stared at him. She had no memory of the event whatsoever. They often visited her grandparents, and no one visit stood out as being any different from the others. "What did you do?"

He shrugged. "I told her I was sorry—you do not need to know what I did, you are better off not knowing. But I meant what I told her. I regretted hurting her and I swore I would never do what I did ever again. I kept that promise, and she eventually learned to believe in me and trust me once again."

Her mouth slightly agape, Eleanor glanced away. Why was her father telling her this now?

"I see the way you and Creed look at one another."

Ah, so that was why he was telling her all this. "And?"

Her father smiled. "I hope you learn to believe and trust in him again. I know he regrets injuring you."

Eleanor sighed. "Papa, you do not know all the details."

"I know he bedded Lydia."

Heat rushed to Eleanor's face. Well then, perhaps he did know the details. How *did* he know? Had Lydia told him? Brahm? "I am fine as long as I do not think of them together, but when I do . . ."

His big fingers squeezed hers. "It hurts; it makes you angry."

She nodded. Even now, even when she knew Brahm had been in the clutches of a disease when it happened, the memory of them together was very painful.

"It will ease with time," he told her. "When you realize how much he cares for you, when you realize how much you care for him, the two of you will be able to conquer this. All you need to do is believe and trust—in yourselves as well as in each other."

Such sage advice, and from such an unlikely source. "I do care for Brahm," she confessed. "I do not believe I ever stopped. Perhaps that is why his betrayal hurt so much."

"But?" her father prodded.

Eleanor smiled ruefully. "But I am afraid to trust him. I am afraid that it is all a lie, even though I want to believe it is true. He has given me no reason to doubt his sincerity. I want to believe he cares for me, but it is so difficult."

"Why?"

Tears burned the backs of her eyes. "Because I am a bitter, remote old maid, and if I wasn't enough for him years ago, why would I be enough now?"

There, she had confessed the fear that she had confessed to no one else. She could scarcely confess it to herself.

Her father held his arms out to her, and she practically dived into his embrace. How long since she had felt his arms around her this way? His strength flowed into her, a balm against any and all injury.

"Oh my dear girl." He kissed the top of her head and stroked her back as if she were but a child. "Can you not see?"

She shook her head, her face buried in his shoulder. See what?

He pushed her up, so that she was forced to look at him rather than hide her face. "You have always been enough for that boy. You are what brought him to this party, even though he knew you would not want to see him at first. You are the reason he stays even though the temptation to drink dogs him at every moment. You are why he pushes himself to do things that make his leg ache so badly he has to retire early."

She was? And why was the fool risking injury to himself just to keep up with the rest of the guests? She didn't care if he could do all those things. Obviously he did, though.

"He did not come here simply for your forgiveness, Eleanor." Her father's gaze was kind, not the least bit patronizing. "He came here for *you*."

Straightening, Eleanor glanced away. For her. Her heart recognized it as truth even though her head insisted it couldn't be. Brahm's attraction to her now was not a new emotion, or one stemming from their previous attachment. He had never stopped wanting her. Surely that was more than just desire.

Surely that was more than what he had experienced with Lydia—or with Fanny Carson.

"I am no longer that girl," she whispered, voicing the new fear that pierced her heart. "What if he does not want the woman I am now?"

"Now you are being foolish." Her father scowled. "You think he would have stayed this long if he did not like who you are? Brahm Ryland is not some upstart digging for a rich wife. He is a man who has lost everything, who has pulled himself back from social ruin, and he has decided that you are his match. By God, girl, does that not tell you what he thinks of you—what you should think of yourself?"

Stunned, Eleanor could only stare at her father. He was right. It was so difficult for her to accept that a man so handsome, so strong and determined, and so sensuous could want her. It was far easier to believe that it had been her fault he went to Lydia, because then she didn't have to be so angry at the disease that made him stupid enough to believe Lydia was she. Lydia, the baby sister she had always adored, who must have seen her previous interest in Brahm, and who went after him anyway. It was easier to believe that Brahm preferred Lydia than entertain the idea that Lydia had taken advantage of Brahm's drunken state.

It was easier to think that Brahm wanted Lydia than to admit to herself that she had been afraid to marry him back then, that his drinking had frightened her, that his effect on her frightened her. When she had broken their engagement it had been almost a relief, because then she didn't have to face the fact that she believed she would be overpowered by Brahm.

And perhaps the girl she had been would have been overpowered by him. Perhaps his sickness would have come between them. But she was no longer that girl, and he had overcome his illness. The situation was different. They were different.

"Thank you, Papa," she said, rising to her feet. "You have given me much to think about."

Her father arched an interested brow as he lay back

against his pillows. "And are you going off to think about all these things now?"

Eleanor nodded. "I believe so. You will excuse me?"

He chuckled. "Of course. I excused you a quarter hour ago, remember?"

Eleanor smiled and bent down to kiss her father's cheek before leaving his room.

As she stepped out into the corridor, a flash of something caught her eye, and she looked up. A woman was walking down the corridor, her back to Eleanor. She wasn't that far away, but far enough that the muted lighting from the wall sconces made it difficult to ascertain her features.

There was enough light to clearly see her gown, however. The color, the cut, everything was discernible. It was Lydia.

What had her sister been doing up here? Her bedchamber was at the other end of the corridor, and Lydia had obviously come from this direction. The staircase was in the middle—there was no need for Lydia to have come this way.

Unless she had been listening outside their father's door.

Eleanor's blood turned to ice at the thought. It was so uncharitable, yet she could not escape the suspicion. If Lydia had been listening, how much had she heard?

And more importantly, what did she plan to do with the information?

Chapter 9

Tonight was the night Brahm planned to make his intentions toward Eleanor clear.

A fortnight had passed since his arrival at Burrough's estate, and this ball was to mark the beginning of the last half of the house party.

Two weeks, that was the amount of time he had spent with Eleanor. In that short amount of time he had convinced her to give him a chance, and in her usual way, she had given that effort her full attention. She knew he was not the man he once was, and she liked the man he had become. He never would have thought he could win her over at all, let alone so quickly. It was a prime example of her all too forgiving and understanding nature—not that he would want her any other way.

And he wanted her any way he could have her. The episode in the orangery had only made his longing for her worse. He thought about her body against his all the time. He fantasized about her breasts—and the rest of her—

naked before him. He could imagine touching her and how she would react to those touches, and it made him hard as a rock.

It was amusing and welcome, his attraction to her. For the longest time he worried that his excessive drinking had permanently destroyed his ability to lust for a woman. He and Cassie had had a physical relationship, of course, but he hadn't craved a woman the way he craved Eleanor in years. In the bath earlier the thought of her had given him such a raging erection that he would have gladly traded his entire estate for Eleanor's splayed thighs and the lushness between.

But no such offer was made, and so he ended up taking matters in hand—so to speak. When was the last time he had done *that*? He couldn't remember. That was what she reduced him to. Like a green boy, untutored and uncontrolled, he'd alleviated his arousal in an efficient yet unsatisfactory manner that only made him want Eleanor all the more.

So enough with the waiting. He was going to strike while everything appeared to be in his favor.

Charles had dressed him to perfection. Not a hair was out of place. Yes, it was a little long, but he preferred it to the fussy hairstyles many men wore as of late. He had even polished his cane so the rich, dark wood and the gold top gleamed. His snow white cravat was tied in the style referred to as l'Orientale—a simple yet elegant knot. His jacket and trousers were impeccable. It wasn't that he favored trousers over breeches, but rather that his injured leg didn't lend itself to stockings and whatnot. The leg was scarred and hadn't healed perfectly straight, and while it didn't bother him, others might find the sight vaguely disturbing. Would Eleanor? Probably not. She would probably fuss over him and blame herself for not being able to fix it.

He smiled at the thought of her. She was such a care-giver. She clucked over her father and her sisters, even the servants. All she wanted was to ensure everyone's comfort, but she rarely thought of her own. That was what his job would be. If Eleanor would have him, he'd spend the rest of his days tending to her comfort, her needs. It was nothing more than a pleasant boon that by doing so, he would be tending to his own comfort and needs at the same time.

He went downstairs at precisely ten o'clock, the announced time for the festivities to begin. Luck was with him, and his leg hardly hurt at all. He hoped Eleanor wouldn't mind that all he could manage was a slower version of the waltz. Anything else was asking for trouble, especially since some dances went on forever.

The ball was primarily for the house guests, but other families in the area had been invited to join the festivities. There was so little entertainment during this time of year that everyone invited came. Hence there were more than enough partners to go around, and hence Brahm was announced as he entered the ballroom.

Inclining his head in greeting to those who met his gaze as he walked in, Brahm was intent on finding Eleanor. Was she there yet? A blond in a green gown caught his eye. No, it was Arabella. He moved toward the other Durbane sister anyway. Chances were that Eleanor would find her sister as well.

Arabella welcomed him with a hesitant but kindly smile, which Brahm returned with a genuine one of his own. He liked Arabella. Of all Eleanor's sisters, she seemed the happiest, the most like Eleanor in her kindness and understanding. She was also the nicest and treated him with more courtesy than the other three.

Phoebe and Muriel were with the group as well, wearing gowns of apricot and pale blue, respectively. They did not smile as Arabella had, but they curtsied and bid him good evening in sincere tones. Why the effort to be nice to him? Had Eleanor said something to her siblings?

He would have asked, had he been able to find his voice, but it was at that exact moment that Eleanor was announced. He turned to look at her, and his ability to reason, speak, and move disappeared.

Eleanor wore a gown of raspberry satin beaded with tiny crystals that caught the light and glittered as she moved. She wore no jewelry save for a pair of diamond earrings that sparkled even more than her dress. Her rich blond hair was swept up on top of her head and pinned in a riot of curls that must have taken her maid hours to create. In short, she was devastatingly beautiful.

She smiled at everyone, dazzling the room with her brilliance as she glided across the floor like some kind of otherworldly creature. Brahm was not the only man caught in her spell. Locke and Birch stared at her with mouths agape as well. The other bachelors—Taylor, Faulkner, and one other whose name Brahm could not recall—were similarly affected. Damnation, he was really going to have competition now.

Eleanor nodded at her would-be suitors. She even graced them with a kind smile, but it was Brahm who received the sweetest gift. She joined her sisters, but her gaze remained fixed on him. Her smile wasn't hesitant, but it was . . . hopeful, as though she was uncertain of his reaction to her.

"Lady Eleanor." He bowed over her offered hand. "You are a vision of loveliness this evening." It wasn't quite what he wanted to tell her, but it would do for this audience. Later he would tell her just how beautiful she was.

Eleanor blushed prettily, despite his lukewarm compliment. "Thank you, Lord Creed."

Locke came up beside them, destroying what precious little intimacy had blossomed between them. "Lady Eleanor, might I claim the first dance?"

Eleanor's gaze flittered to Brahm, as if gauging his reaction. He made certain to give none, even though he would have dearly loved to stuff his cane down Locke's throat. Eleanor didn't look very pleased by his intrusion either.

Then again, she didn't look impressed with him either, but he was not going to tell her how to act. "I would be honored, Lord Locke. Thank you."

"And the second dance for me, Lady Eleanor?" It was Birch who asked.

Eleanor smiled kindly. "Certainly, Lord Birch."

For God's sake, was he going to have to stand in line to spend time with her? Inwardly he sighed. This was not the way he wanted to ask, barking for her attention like a rambunctious puppy. "Perhaps now would be a good time, then, for me to request the first waltz?"

Did Birch and Locke notice how bright the smile she flashed him was? Did they notice that she blushed at his request? Her feelings for him were fathoms deeper than what she felt for either Birch or Locke, and it was all Brahm could do not to crow about it.

"The first waltz is yours, Lord Creed."

He bowed and took his leave so he would not have to watch her accompany Locke to the center of the ballroom for the first set. He could accept that she had to adhere to social niceties. He could accept that as hostess certain things were expected of her. That did not mean he had to watch another man put his hands on her.

He had not gone far when Lady Dumont intercepted him.

"Lord Creed, how delightful of you to join us this evening."

Brahm arched a brow. "Was there any question of my attendance?"

The older woman fanned the generous cleavage revealed by the neckline of her pink gown with a delicate matching fan. She was a little old for such a girlish color, but somehow it suited her. "Why, yes. We all assumed that since you were indisposed last evening, you would be tonight as well." Her gaze dropped pointedly to his leg when she spoke. Or was it his groin that she seemed to find so fascinating? Ever since Fanny Carson's damn book, the women at this party had spent more time looking at his crotch than his face.

"A little stiffness was my only ailment last evening," he informed her. "I do appreciate your concern, however."

Her blue eyes brightened. Hell, he should have known better than to use the word "stiffness" in her presence.

"Well, if you are struck by a similar affliction tonight, please let me know if I might offer my assistance in bringing you relief."

God deliver him from randy dowagers. "I do not believe that will be necessary, but thank you."

Lady Dumont raked him with another predatory gaze. "Pity. You know where to find me if you change your mind. Enjoy the evening, my lord."

And with that she sashayed toward another group, leaving Brahm feeling slightly dazed in her wake. What a strange woman. He was really going to have to ask Wynthrope about her sometime. Perhaps it was strangeness that had brought her and his brother together. Lord knew Wyn was odd enough.

He made his way to the upper corner of the room where the orchestra was hidden beneath a strategically placed folding screen. Hiding the musicians gave the impression of magic, he supposed, as the music appeared to come from nowhere. He waited there for what felt like an eternity. As they were about to begin playing the second dance, he requested a waltz for the third. He was not waiting any longer than he had to for Eleanor's attention. Neither his patience nor his leg was going to last the entire night.

By the time the second dance had ended, he was standing almost exactly where he had been when he had left her, waiting for Birch to return her to her sisters. Birch did just that, but the fair lord seemed reluctant to leave the lady's side so that another partner might claim her. Brahm counted to ten and then made his move.

The first strains of the waltz were just starting as he made his presence known. "Birch, my good man. Thank you for watching over Lady Eleanor for me; now do be a good boy and hold this."

The shock on Birch's face as Brahm shoved his cane into his hand might have been laughable if he hadn't managed to awaken a very jealous side of Brahm's personality. Eleanor was *his*. If Locke and Birch and the others wanted to make fools of themselves trying to win her, they were welcome to do it, but not when it was Brahm's turn to have her for a few moments.

He didn't wait for Birch's reaction, but took hold of Eleanor's arm and led her out onto the floor as she stared at him in stunned silence. When they were where he wanted to be, he turned and opened his arms to her. "Forgive me if I am not as graceful as I once was."

Warily she stepped into his arms, placing one hand in his and the other on his shoulder. His free hand settled on the small of her back. He wanted to haul her flush against him, but that would not do, not at all. He would have to content himself with the scent of her, the sight of her pulse fluttering at the base of her throat.

"You're holding me closer than is proper," she informed him as he slowly drew her through the first turn. Forget graceful, he wasn't as quick on his feet as he used to be either. He had to be careful. One wrong step and he would end up on his arse—with Eleanor on top of him.

That just might be worth the humiliation of falling.

"I'm not proper." He turned her again. She followed him effortlessly, already attuned to the pattern of his steps, the way he compensated for his leg. It was just one more thing that convinced him they were perfect for each other.

"So I noticed." Her gaze locked with his, blue eyes rife with censure. "It was rude of you to chase Lord Birch off like that."

How motherly she sounded. That might work on her sisters, but not with him. He shrugged. "It was rude of him to monopolize you as he was."

"Monopolize?" Her tone was incredulous as they turned again. "We were having a perfectly innocent conversation."

Innocent, eh? "About what?"

Her lips pursed. "None of your business."

He pulled her closer, causing her to stiffen in alarm.

Her gaze darted around them, horrified that someone might be watching. He stepped back once more. "About what?"

She wasn't pleased with him at all. "About cattle."

"Cattle?" Surely he hadn't heard correctly. What kind of man was foolish enough to use time with Eleanor—even if other dancers were present—to discuss livestock?

The wild flush that spread up her neck and cheeks told him that his hearing was impeccable. "Yes. He wanted to know if I like horses. He breeds them, you know."

Brahm could not fight the grin that spread across his face. "I know."

Her eyes narrowed. "You needn't look so smug. You have never asked me if I like horses."

He shrugged. "I do not have to. I know that you do not."

Ah, he had startled her with that tidbit. "I know more about you than you think I do, Eleanor. I know it because I pay attention, because I want to know everything about you. You might do well to remember that."

She fell silent, and he knew she was wondering what else he had discovered about her. Not as much as he wanted. One hundred years would not be enough time to learn all he wanted to know about Eleanor.

When the waltz ended he led Eleanor back to her sisters and requested the next waltz. Once Eleanor agreed, he took his cane from Birch, who was waiting to request another dance as well, and walked away. He wanted nothing more than to stay with her, but he didn't want to seem too eager. He would not have the other guests refer to him as Eleanor's lapdog. Let Locke and Birch earn that title.

He left her with her sisters after the second waltz as well, and he gave her plenty of room during supper. He didn't need to crowd her to have an effect on her. More than once he caught her watching him, or searching the crowd for someone, only to look so relieved when her gaze settled on him. He knew she compared the other bachelors to him, it was only natural. She compared them all to one another. He also knew that for whatever reason, she preferred him over the others. He didn't question why, he simply gave thanks for it.

He also gave thanks for the narrowing of her bright eyes every time she saw him talking to another woman. That was what she got for flitting off with her bachelors and leaving him alone.

During a later set he watched as she crept out onto the patio for a breath of air, and he followed after her. It wasn't proper behavior, but as he had told her earlier, he wasn't proper.

He found her leaning against the granite balustrade, her face lifted to the gentle evening breeze. A colorful lantern hung from a post beside her, illuminating her delightful features. Such an unusual beauty was hers.

"You should not be out here alone," he chastised as he approached. His leg was beginning to ache again. He was fortunate to have made it this far. All he asked was that it held out a little while longer.

She glanced over her shoulder at him, her smile one of amusement. "You should not be out here alone with me."

He grinned as he propped his arm on the railing beside her. "True. What do you suggest we do about it?"

Eleanor sighed. "I suppose one of us should return inside."

Brahm raised his hand to her face, cupping her cheek in

his palm. Her skin was so amazingly soft. "We could stay out here."

Her eyelids fluttered, thick dark lashes like delicate wings. "Brahm, you shouldn't. If anyone sees us—"

"Shh." He stroked her temple with his thumb. "Just let me touch you for a moment."

Their gazes locked as she acquiesced. She was as still as a frightened doe, and just as hesitant, but she was his—at least for the moment.

"You are so beautiful," he whispered, his fingers trailing down her cheek to brush the petal-soft curve of her upper lip. "The ache in my leg is nothing compared to the ache in my heart when I look at you."

She gasped, her mouth parting softly. Her breath was warm and moist against his fingers, a humid temptation he could not resist. He lowered his head and brushed his lips across hers. She tasted of her own special sweetness and wine. The latter he didn't notice until his mouth was firmly clamped to hers, tongue stroking hers. He shivered at the taste, but it wasn't the wine that had his heart pounding and his body demanding more. It was Eleanor—only Eleanor.

He pulled back, gasping. He had promised her nothing more than a touch. This was not the time or the place for anything more, not when any number of people could happen upon them at any moment.

They stared at each other, mere inches separating their bodies. Heat engulfed them both. Eleanor's eyes were heavy lidded and slightly glazed. She hadn't wanted him to stop kissing her any more than he had wanted it. Good Lord, when the two of them finally made it to a bedroom, he was going to combust with need.

"I'm sorry," he rasped. "I should have had more control."

She licked her lips as she nodded. He wanted to lick them as well. "It is all right."

From inside, the familiar notes signaled the beginning of yet another waltz. This was the opening he had been waiting for. After this his leg could give out completely for all he cared.

"Dance with me." Taking her hand in his, he tugged gently.

She didn't budge, but shook her head. "I cannot."

Another tug. "Why?"

"You know why." Her expression told him not to be so foolish, as did her tone. "What will people say?"

"Do you care?"

Her eyes snapped with indignation as she pulled her fingers free of his. "Of course!"

Brahm was not put off. He leaned closer, brushing the delicate rim of her ear with his mouth as he whispered, "Liar."

She pulled away, but not before a shudder raced through her. "I beg your pardon?"

The smile that tilted his mouth on one side was smug. "If you truly cared what people would say you would have made certain your father didn't permit me to stay at this party."

She wasn't impressed with his amusement at her expense. "I tried to make him force you to leave, but he wouldn't budge."

Brahm laughed. Of course she had tried. But she obviously hadn't tried hard enough, a fact that warmed him. "Come dance with me, and ignore whatever people say. This is your house, you can dance with whomever you want."

He tried to tug her away from the balustrade, but she dug in her heels. "It will be our third dance. You have danced with few others. It will look as though you have laid claim to me."

He met her gaze squarely, honestly. "I have danced with no others, and declaring my intentions is exactly what I wish to do." How could she not have seen where this was leading? How could she not have known what he wanted? Unless he had been wrong in thinking she wanted it too?

Her eyes were as wide as saucers, bright as aquamarines in the night. "I . . ."

He held up his cane. "You do not have to say a word." In fact, he wasn't certain he wanted to hear what she had to say. "Just this once, throw propriety to the wind and indulge me. It has been so long since I have been able to dance this much." No, he was not above using guilt to get his way.

Ultimately he did get his way. He had known he would. She could have walked away from him, but she didn't want to do that any more than he did. Eleanor allowed him to escort her into the ballroom and onto the floor. She was going to give him his third dance. It had to mean something, because she knew as well as he did that, come the morning, everyone would be talking about it. Everyone would know that he wanted to marry her, and that Eleanor had as good as given her consent.

Long after the ball ended, Eleanor lay in her bed, staring at the ceiling, reliving parts of the evening in her mind—all the parts that had to do with Brahm.

The windows nearest her bed were open, allowing the gentle breeze inside. It would be dawn in a few hours, but for now it was cool and quiet, and so dark she could see little more than shadowy shapes in her room. She should be asleep, but her mind was too busy to relax.

It pleased her that her sisters had made an effort to be nice to Brahm, even if they did it only because she told them it was what she wanted in payment for their shoddy treatment of him since his arrival. That wasn't what had made the evening so special, though.

Brahm had singled her out. He had danced with her more times than considered proper for a mere acquaintance. He had not only announced his intentions to her, he had announced them to the entire party..He had let everyone know that he planned to have her, body and soul. He planned to have her as his wife.

As his wife. How was it possible? If he hadn't indicated so much to her himself, she wouldn't believe it. He had yet to propose, but Eleanor was certain that he meant to. Perhaps he meant to make her wait since she had refused his proposal when last it was offered. No, that was cruel and Brahm was not cruel. Perhaps he wanted to be certain she would accept before he offered. Were her kisses, her free behavior with him not enough indication that she would acquiesce?

Or maybe he treated her so very properly because he thought it was what she deserved. He had mentioned that before—that the reason he hadn't tried to seduce her years before was that she was a proper young woman. He was treating her the way a gentleman ought to treat the lady he sought to marry. What Eleanor wanted, however, was for him to treat her as a man treated the woman he wanted in his bed. She was two-and-thirty years old, she was familiar with sexual need, and she was tired of feeling frustrated and unsatisfied.

According to Fanny Carson, Brahm was very good at

providing feminine satisfaction. Lucky for Eleanor, she planned to be the last woman Brahm Ryland satisfied.

Yes, she wanted his fidelity. She wanted his heart. She wasn't certain that what she felt for him was love—if it was, it had come on rather quickly. Or perhaps it had simply been slumbering these past years, waiting for the right time to resurface. Regardless of her feelings for him, she wanted Brahm to love her. What woman wouldn't want the love of such a man? His past disregarded, he was a man loyal to his friends and family. He loved fiercely and with all his being. If he put his mind to something he achieved it.

She remembered hearing about the accident that had claimed his father's life. Brahm's leg had been broken in more than one place. The physician hadn't expected him to live, but Brahm had recovered not only from the accident, but from a tremendous fever. A feat like that required a will of iron, and there was no doubt in her mind that Brahm could move mountains if he so wished.

She could sneak to his room right now if she wanted. No one would know. Would she find him asleep, or was he lying awake as she was, wishing they'd had more time in the orangery the other day? If it hadn't been for dinner, would he have made love to her there? Would she now know what it was like to join with him instead of wondering about it?

There was a soft tap upon her door, interrupting her scandalous thoughts. Who could it be at this hour? Brahm? Heart tripping in anticipation, Eleanor slipped out of bed and quietly whisked across the carpet to let her visitor in.

It wasn't Brahm. It was Lydia. She held a wrap around her shoulders with one hand, a candle in the other.

"You needn't look so disappointed, Ellie." The shorter

woman brushed past her to enter the room. "You were expecting someone else?"

"It is late," Eleanor informed her, closing the door. "I was not expecting anyone." Expecting, no. Hoping, yes.

Standing in the middle of the carpet, Lydia turned to face her. Everything about her posture and expression screamed of agitation. Eleanor frowned. Lydia had never been what she considered a serene person, but she was acting a little intense, even for her.

"What is it?" Had something happened to their father? Had Lydia fought with her husband?

"There is something I need to tell you," Lydia blurted. "Something I should have told you a long time ago."

Oh dear. There was only one thing that Eleanor could think of that deserved this kind of gravity. Did she tell Lydia she already knew and risk a major blunder if bedding Brahm was not what her sister was there to confess? Or did she pretend ignorance?

Ignorance. It was better that way. What good would it do to let Lydia realize how much she had hurt Eleanor in the past? There was nothing to be done for it now, and Lydia hadn't realized that Eleanor and Brahm had made an attachment. Had she?

"Perhaps we should sit," Eleanor suggested, returning to her bed. It felt as though they were children again, both of them in their nightgowns, Lydia coming to Eleanor for guidance late at night. But they were not children anymore, and neither of them was so innocent either.

Lydia shook her head, pacing the carpet in her bare feet. "I would rather stand, thank you."

"Lyddie, you're going to wear a hole in the floor. Whatever has gotten into you?" Perhaps that was a bad choice of words given the assumed subject matter. Eleanor already knew "who" had gotten into her sister.

Lydia stopped pacing and whirled around to face her. She looked so distraught. Her body was tense, her shoulders high. Her expression was tight, and yet . . . and yet there was something in her eyes that made Eleanor wonder how much of this had been rehearsed. Was Lydia simply pretending this turmoil? It was such an unfair suspicion, but it would not go away.

"It is about Lord Creed," Lydia replied in a low voice.

Eleanor forced a blink. So she had been right. Why had Lydia chosen now to confess? Why had she kept her silence all these years? Perhaps she thought it for the best, given the fact that Eleanor and Brahm had parted ways. Perhaps she doubted Brahm's sincerity now and wanted to put her sister on guard.

Or perhaps Lydia was jealous and wanted to keep Eleanor from having the man Lydia wanted but hadn't managed to hold on to. As much as it had pained Eleanor to see her sister and her almost-fiancé together, it must be a real thorn in Lydia's side to see the man she had seduced return for her sister.

"What about Lord Creed?" How calm and cautious she sounded.

"Oh Eleanor!" Lydia's face became a mask of anguish as she rushed forward, falling to her knees at her sister's feet. "I am so sorry!"

Eleanor's brows rose as her mouth narrowed to a tiny O. This was not what she had been expecting. This was overdoing it, even for Lydia. Either the girl truly was devastated about this, or she belonged in a farce.

Gingerly she patted Lydia on the head. "Sorry for what,

dearest?" No matter how strange this situation was, Eleanor planned to see it through. Perhaps it was cruel of her, but she had waited more than a decade for Lydia's confession, and she planned to have it.

Lydia lifted her chin, her face a contortion of pain. "You have to believe me that at the time I did not know that he had proposed."

"What time? What happened?" Oh, she was going to burn in hell for this.

Lydia shook her head, averting her gaze. "You will hate me."

"I could never hate you." That was a lie. She could hate her, but it wouldn't last. Lydia was her sister; Eleanor would love her no matter what.

"You must understand. I was very unhappy in my marriage at the time."

And she wasn't now? Eleanor kept the question to herself.

"Brahm was very attentive, very charming."

Eleanor nodded, not liking where this was going. "You do not need to explain yourself, Lydia. What happened?"

"I'm only telling you this so you will know what kind of man he is."

Oh, she already had a pretty good idea. "Go on."

Her sister's face crumpled as she choked on a sob. "Oh Eleanor, he seduced me!"

Eleanor looked away from the girl sobbing in her lap. She stroked Lydia's hair as she gazed out the window. How difficult this was. Lydia seemed so sincere, and yet there was just enough falseness to her disclosure that Eleanor doubted the validity of her words. Perhaps Lydia was sorry. Perhaps she did think of herself as the victim, but it wasn't as bad as she tried to make it sound. What was Lydia's motive?

Suddenly an idea occurred to Eleanor. It wasn't a nice idea, but it wasn't going to hurt anyone either, and if this was a ploy on Lydia's part, it would let her younger sister know that Eleanor wasn't going to fall for it. Even if Brahm did seduce her, Eleanor had seen enough to know Lydia liked it.

Perhaps Lydia just didn't want to look bad in Eleanor's eyes. Perhaps she was scared that Eleanor would be angry with her. If Eleanor was angry, it was because Lydia did not respect her more.

She shhed Lydia's sobs. "Dearest, do not distress yourself. I know what happened."

Lydia's head jerked up. Her eyes were red but there were no tears on her face. "You do?"

Eleanor nodded, fixing what she knew to be her best motherly, nurturing smile on her face. "Brahm told me."

Lydia straightened, all traces of guilt gone from her expression. "He did?"

Another nod. Eleanor bit the inside of her mouth to keep from laughing. How horrible she was! She should not be enjoying Lydia's confusion, but she was. Oh, how she was!

She ran a gentle hand over Lydia's pale hair. "He confessed all shortly after we began to become friends again. I knew he had been with someone; that's why I refused him years ago. He didn't want it to continue to be an issue between us, so he confessed the truth to me. It is awful what drink will do to a man, is it not?"

Lydia was on her feet. "Drink?"

Oh-oh. Perhaps she had taken this a bit too far, but there

was no going back now. Eleanor tilted her head in what she hoped was a sympathetic manner. "He told me he was very drunk that night and was not in his right mind. Of course, he was often drunk back then. I know it is of small consolation, dearest, but believe me when I tell you that Brahm never would have done what he did had he been in possession of all his senses."

Lydia looked dazed, as though someone had slapped her with no warning. Eleanor's heart twisted with something very much like guilt, but she pushed it aside. If Lydia was sincere, then her explanation would make her feel better and help her forgive Brahm. If she was lying, then she would know that Eleanor believed Brahm's side of the story.

Did she believe Brahm over her sister? Yes. God help her, but she did. And she did not know if she was right to do so.

Eleanor rose to her feet. "It means so much to me that you found the courage to confess this to me, but you may ease your mind now. It is in the past where it belongs. If you need to make peace with someone, let it be with Brahm."

There was no mistaking the anger in Lydia's gaze as she whipped her head up to stare at Eleanor. So intense was the emotion that Eleanor took a step back from it. It was gone in an instant, however, and Lydia looked once more the sorrowful lady.

"You are right. Thank you, Eleanor. I feel much better now."

Placing an arm around her shoulders, Eleanor led her sister to the door. "I'm glad. Now go back to bed and do not trouble yourself with this again, all right?"

The last thing Eleanor saw before she closed the door

was Lydia's nod. Shaking her head, she padded to her bed and fell on it with a gusty sigh. She didn't know what to think, what to believe. Her mind was in such turmoil. In fact, the only part of her that seemed perfectly at ease was her heart.

And her heart told her not to believe in her sister, but to believe in the man who had once broken it.

Chapter 10

The morning after the ball Brahm rose and dressed for breakfast feeling happier than he had for some time. He went downstairs smiling and freshly shaven, dressed in buff trousers and dark blue coat. His leg ached a bit from last night's dancing, but he barely noticed. It was an overcast morning, but it was beautiful regardless.

There weren't many up and about as he entered the dining room. Many guests would no doubt sleep into the afternoon, as the dancing had gone on until nearly five. It was half past eleven now.

Birch was present—he shot Brahm a look that could be only described as one of resigned rivalry, as though he knew Brahm was going to win, but he had to compete against him anyway.

Arabella and her husband, Henry, were at the table as well, dining on a delicious-smelling breakfast of coddled eggs, ham, sausages, bread, and coffee. Brahm's stomach growled.

After bidding his three companions a good morning, Brahm went to the sideboard and loaded a plate for himself. There were even kippers. He added three to the side of his plate.

"Coffee, Creed?" Henry asked when he was seated.

Brahm nodded. "Please." Even the coffee smelled more delicious than usual. He was enjoying his second cup, having cleaned his plate, when Eleanor entered the room. The second Brahm's gaze fell upon her, his good mood faded.

She looked tired, drawn and pale, as though she hadn't slept the night. Obviously whatever had kept her awake had not been a pleasant thing. He could only hope it had nothing to do with him.

Had one—or all—of her sisters chastised her for dancing those three times with him? Had one of the guests said something to offend her? Perhaps she had decided on her own that it had been a mistake? That didn't make sense. She wanted him, he knew that. Most decent women were not in the habit of trysting with men they would not marry if given the choice.

Of course, there was no way he could ask her what was wrong with the others present. He would have to wait. Her behavior would be his only indication.

She made an attempt at cheeriness when she bid them all good morning, and when she came to the table, her plate was almost as heaped as Brahm's had been. Either she had a healthy appetite or she was the kind who ate when she was upset.

Eleanor seated herself across from her sister, which also ended up being the chair on Brahm's immediate right. Did she realize what she was doing? The three dances last night would have practically sealed their fate, but her sitting next to him would only strengthen the gossip. Either she was telling him that she wanted him as well, or she simply felt too awful to care what people thought of where she sat.

"Did you sleep well, Lady Eleanor?" he asked, sipping his coffee.

She turned her head to meet his gaze. She looked so tired, so sad. "Thank you for asking, Lord Creed. No, I did not sleep well. I am afraid the excitement of the evening kept me awake for many hours after the house fell quiet."

It was a simple enough answer, and Lord Birch offered his sympathies. Apparently it had taken him some time to drift off as well. Brahm didn't give a damn about Birch. There had been something in Eleanor's tone when she referred to the "excitement" of the evening that made him wary. Something *had* happened that had nothing to do with their three dances, but involved him all the same. Since there was nothing he could do about it now, he sipped his coffee and felt the patience slowly drain out of him as the minutes ticked by.

More guests joined them as the morning waned. Finally Eleanor excused herself to go for a walk. Brahm waited a few moments before following her. If his suspicion that she wanted to talk to him was correct, then he knew exactly where her walk would lead her.

She was waiting in the orangery.

"What happened?" he demanded.

Eleanor rubbed a hand over the back of her neck. Her expression was distraught. "Tell me that you did not seduce my sister."

Not quite what he'd been expecting, but not totally a surprise either. "What happened?" He wasn't telling her anything until she answered his question.

"Lydia came to my room last night."

Christ. He should have known that Lydia would try to cause trouble. Women that unhappy always had to try bringing others down with them. "And said that I seduced her?"

Eleanor nodded.

Of course Eleanor believed her sister. Were the situation reversed and it was Devlin who told him such nonsense, he'd believe it as well. He wouldn't want to, but why would a sibling lie? "When did this alleged seduction take place?"

"That night."

"That night?" Frowning, his chin tilted downward. "You mean over a decade ago?"

Another nod. She looked so very torn. She wanted to believe them both and knew there was no way both of them could be telling the truth. For a moment he was tempted to allow her to believe her sister, just to spare her the pain of the truth.

But what was the truth? He didn't want to believe himself capable of seducing Lydia any more than she did, but he had been drunk and remembered practically nothing of that night.

"I already told you that I believed Lydia to be you. I might have been capable of seduction, but what I remember equates to a few moments and then nothing."

It was impossible to tell whether that answer satisfied her or not.

Her arms folded across her chest, an age-old gesture of self-protection. "She said you were attentive to her during your visit."

Ah. So Lydia led her sister to believe that there had been more than just that one night. "I had no interest in Lydia whatsoever. Not then, and certainly not now."

Her countenance was so hopeful, it was heartbreaking. "So you did not have an affair, then?"

She already knew the answer to that. He had told her. "What do you think?"

She shook her head. "I do not want to believe it."

She didn't quite trust him, and that was all right. She didn't quite trust Lydia either. Once she saw the truth for herself, it would be easier for her to know where to put her belief. It was a difficult thing realizing that a sibling had lied. Wynthrope used to lie to him on a regular basis. He had lied to them all by hiding his past, but that didn't stop Brahm from loving him. Eleanor wouldn't stop loving Lydia either, even though the wench deserved a good thrashing. "What does your heart tell you?"

"She is my sister." She raised pain-filled eyes to his, her tone plaintive. "And my heart tells me to believe you. Is my heart wrong?"

"Eleanor—"

"Please!" She held up a hand to cut him off. "I do not care if you have been dishonest or not. I beg you, tell me now the honest truth and I will never ask again."

She truly had herself worked into a state over this.

Brahm set his palms on her shoulders and gave her a gentle squeeze. If he could take this away from her he would. "I did not have an affair with your sister. Any relationship we might have had was restricted to that one night. I do not know what happened, but Lydia came to me, a fact which you unfortunately already know. She was not invited, nor was she welcome. Had I been sober nothing would have happened between us, but I was not sober, and that is something I have to live with."

There was nothing more he could say. He had nothing else with which to defend himself, nor was he prepared to continue defending himself. Either Eleanor believed him or she didn't.

She turned her face away, the shadows highlighting the mauve shadows beneath her normally bright blue eyes. She looked so fragile.

"Lydia lied to me," she realized aloud, her voice a soft whisper. "Why would she do that?"

A number of reasons occurred to Brahm, none of them overly charitable. "I do not know."

Again her expression was heartbreakingly hopeful. "Perhaps she truly believes herself the injured party. Perhaps she believes you will break my heart and only wants to protect me."

Brahm nodded, biting his tongue to keep from blurting what he thought. "Perhaps."

Eleanor's shoulders sagged beneath his hands. "Or perhaps she is so very unhappy in her own life that she cannot bear to see anyone else happy."

That was more like it. He kept his tone carefully neutral. "Perhaps."

Her gaze was sharp as it locked with his. "Has my sister tried to renew your . . . acquaintance?"

Did he lie or tell her the truth? He had promised her honesty, but this honesty would only hurt her more. "Do you suspect her of being jealous?"

"I do not know what I suspect," she admitted on a sigh. "I do not want to suspect her of anything, but to believe her I must doubt you, and my heart tells me that you are truthful."

Well, at least he had that. Poor Eleanor, she had not seen much of the harshness of life, save for his betrayal. Until now it had been his betrayal alone. Now she had to face the fact that her sister had betrayed her as well—and might be trying to betray her once more. It was not a lesson anyone should have to face.

"I am sorry."

She looked up with a quizzical gaze. "For what?"

"For my part in this debacle." He smoothed a hand over his jaw. "Had I been in control of myself that night, none of this would have happened."

Many people would have tried to comfort him, or ease his guilt by telling him it wasn't his fault, but that would be a lie and they both knew it.

She smiled. It was sad, but it was sincere. "Thank you."

Silence fell between them. He removed his hands from her shoulders, and she took a step backward, then another, until there was several feet of space between them.

Was this it? Had Lydia's interference destroyed whatever chances he had of winning Eleanor's heart? No, he refused to believe that.

"You asked me to be honest with you," he reminded her. "Now I ask the same of you."

Her arms were no longer across her chest, but loose at her sides. She was no longer on the defense. "Of course."

Brahm took a step toward her. This distance between them was unbearable. It was stupid and senseless. "Do I have any chance of winning you? Or should I give up now and return to London?"

A becoming flush blossomed along her cheeks, doing much to erase the pallor of fatigue there. She even went so far as to shy away from him. Certainly after all the kisses, conversations, and caresses they had shared, she wasn't about to go missish on him?

"No," she replied, and his heart faltered as she turned around to face him once more. "Do not return to London."

Elation replaced dread. For a moment he had thought

she was rejecting him, but now he could see her acceptance of him in her eyes. She had not decided against him.

As though she wanted to prove to him just how good his chances of winning her were, Eleanor came to him, stepping into his welcoming arms without hesitation. She laid her cheek against his shoulder like an infant seeking solace. Brahm cradled her to him, closing his eyes in silent thanks to the Almighty for giving him such a gift.

"Why do you want me, Brahm?"

"I do not know. I only know that you make me feel as though I have found a part of me that is missing."

"But we have only been reacquainted for a fortnight. Surely that is not enough time for either of us to feel this way?"

He smiled down at her upturned face. Did she always have to question everything? Why could she not just accept what felt right?

"Perhaps *you* are what I have been missing these past years. Perhaps you have been missing me as well. I do not know the whys, Eleanor. I only know that I go outside for a breath of air and I smell you on the breeze. I try to sleep and you haunt my dreams. And it has been this way for quite some time. My heart has never forgotten you."

She stared at him, her eyes wide and damp. Perhaps he shouldn't have made such a flowery admission to her, but it was how he felt. Her hand came up to touch his cheek, the softest brush of heavenly fingers. "Nor mine you."

He kissed her then, pressing his lips against the soft sweetness of hers, his heart pounding with desire and joy. Eleanor was his, and she would be his forever if he had his way. He would continue to court her, to make his claim public, and when he was certain marriage was what she wanted, then he would go to her father. He would do things the right way. He would not have his chances ruined as before. The only person who would keep him from marrying Eleanor this time was Eleanor herself.

When Eleanor and Brahm returned from the orangery, Eleanor went up to her room to rest. It was amazing what simply talking about things had done for her state of mind. She was no longer plagued by confusing thoughts or doubts. She knew the truth. She believed Brahm.

That didn't mean she wholly disbelieved Lydia. Perhaps Brahm was right and her sister had actually convinced herself that her own version of events years ago was the truth. Or perhaps *she* was right and Lydia simply sought to protect her from a man she believed to be the lowest kind.

It hardly mattered what Lydia's motives were. Eleanor and Brahm understood each other. He cared about her, and she about him. Feelings from years before had lingered, masked on her side by hurt and anger, but even she had to admit that she had often thought of him over the years, and held every man she met up against the impression he had made. It had been easy for those feelings to return because neither of them had ever let them truly leave.

How odd it was to realize that those feelings for him had remained alive inside her for so long. Cloistered and sheltered she might have been as an unattached lady, but she was still the daughter of an earl, and she had met many gentlemen over the years. She'd never wanted one of them the way she wanted Brahm.

He was so flawed, so imperfect, and yet that was what made him so perfect as far as she was concerned. He was a man who would not expect her to mother him. He was strong and independent. He was someone she could lean on when she needed support. He knew the truth was not always pretty and yet he preferred it, both to say and to hear.

He also had fought a tremendous battle and won. Her reading taught her just how difficult it could be for someone caught in the clutches of strong drink to break free. Oftentimes their minds and bodies would rebel against them. They would see things that weren't there, shake and tremble violently. The idea of Brahm suffering such awful things in the course of shucking off the demon that drove him broke her heart. And he had been all alone when he did it. His brothers had no doubt helped him, but they could not be there for him all the time.

She should have been there for him. If things had gone as they should have years ago, she would have been the one to help him through such a difficult time. But that hardly signified now. All that mattered now was that he had won his personal battle. He had come out of it a better and wiser man.

And to think she had been so prepared to toss him out of her house when he arrived a fortnight ago! Eleanor had to shake her head when she thought of it. He had come there determined to prove to her that he had changed. Had he not done that? Two weeks in his presence should have provided ample proof that he was not the same man he had once been, and it had. She had watched him struggle to resist the temptation to drink, and she had seen him triumph. He had not paid a worrisome amount of attention to any other woman at the party—even though a few of them tried to win his favor—and that included Lydia.

In fact, Lydia's story—and lack of sincerity—only seemed to enforce Brahm's explanation that he thought it was Eleanor in his room that night. He thought he was seducing his betrothed. Somehow, that made the whole situation a little more understandable. It still hurt her to remember. It still hurt to think about it, but the hurt was less now. The wound, so raw and open for so many years, was healing.

But that was the past, and she needed to concentrate on the future. For so much of her life she had thought only of her father and her sisters. She tended to their needs and wants as her mother would have. Now it was time to think of herself, and it was proving much easier than she'd ever thought it would be. Now that she had all the world available to her, what did she want from it?

She wanted Brahm. She wanted his kisses, his touches. She wanted his companionship. She wanted to experience life with him. Did she love him? If she didn't, she was certainly on her way. And the thought of his sharing the rest of his years with another woman filled her with an emotion very much like rage—a feeling so intense, her jaw tightened with it.

No. No one would have Brahm but she. She knew what she must do, if she could only summon the courage to do it. She would do the one thing that would prove to him that she wanted him and force him to admit his own feelings for her. If he was waiting for a sign from her, this would certainly be it.

But it was still early. Her plan would have to wait until that evening. She rolled over onto her side on her bed and closed her eyes. She was asleep within minutes, secure in the knowledge that she was going to ensure that by the end of the week she was betrothed to Brahm Ryland.

"Ellie, might we talk?"

Eleanor glanced at Arabella. She looked concerned, not

her usual jovial self. Whatever she wanted to discuss was of some gravity.

Eleanor hoped Arabella wasn't going to inform her that she had been seduced by Brahm several years ago.

"Of course."

They were in the drawing room following dinner. The gentlemen had just joined them, and conversation buzzed throughout the room. In one corner Lady Dumont was arranging a game of whist. In another corner Lord Merrott entertained guests with tales of his hunting prowess. A chess game began in another. Ladies took a turn about the room on each other's arms, chatting to everyone who would listen. Lord Locke sullenly drank by himself. Stories were read aloud to eager audiences, bawdy jokes were shared and met with raucous laughter. It was the perfect after-dinner soiree.

Because of all this gaiety, no one noticed when Eleanor and her sister slipped from the room. It was raining, so they were forced to make their escape into the house rather than out of it. Arabella led the way to their mother's parlor—a room in which they were certain not to be interrupted, unless it was by one of their sisters.

"What is it, Belle?" Eleanor said once the door was closed and she felt it safe to ask.

Arabella twisted her fingers together as she seated herself on a small dark pink sofa. "You will think me meddlesome."

Eleanor smiled. "You are my sister. I always think you meddlesome."

Normally Arabella would have smiled, perhaps even giggled at that. Tonight Eleanor's humor was met with nothing more than an apprehensive gaze.

Eleanor sank into a nearby chair. Good Lord, Arabella was going to tell her she'd had an affair with Brahm as well. As forgiving as she was, even she could not forgive that.

"Belle, I think you had better tell me what this is all about."

"I had a disturbing conversation with Lydia last night," her sister confessed.

"About Lord Creed?"

Arabella looked surprised. "Why, yes."

Eleanor nodded, already knowing where this was going. "She spoke to me as well."

Arabella raised her brows, her expression beyond surprise now. "Truly?"

"Obviously that surprises you."

"Well, yes."

If Lydia had started a dialogue with Arabella, then Eleanor saw no harm in continuing it. This whole situation was beginning to leave a bad taste in her mouth. She had kept silent all these years out of respect for her sister. Obviously Lydia was not going to offer the same.

"Did she tell you that he seduced her?"

Arabella colored. "Yes."

"That is what she told me as well." Eleanor's tone was carefully neutral. "Obviously you believed her."

Her sister's blue eyes widened. "Of course I did. She is my sister."

"She is my sister as well, but I do not believe she and Brahm had an affair."

Arabella sighed. "He has blinded you to the truth."

"No, Belle. Lydia has blinded you." Of this she was certain. How clever of Lydia to send Arabella after her. She knew Eleanor would be more tempted to believe Arabella.

"Dearest, I know this is hard for you to accept—"

Eleanor cut her off with a lift of her hand. "There is nothing to accept. Brahm told me his side of what happened and I believe him."

"But Lydia is family. Why would she lie?"

"I'm not sure. You would need to ask her."

Arabella was not impressed. "Eleanor, why would you believe this man? A month ago you thought him no better than dirt."

"A month ago I thought as you do."

Frowning, Arabella shook her head as though to clear it. "What do you mean? I thought Lydia confessed to you last night."

"She did. Only she did not know—and does not still—that I already knew about her and Brahm."

Understanding lit her sister's gaze. "That was why you refused to marry him."

Eleanor nodded. "Yes. I walked in on him and Lydia."

"Oh, Ellie! How awful!"

"It was."

"Then how can you believe him when you saw the truth with your own eyes?" The anguish and bewilderment in Arabella's expression was painful to look upon.

"Because what I saw was very different from what Lydia told us both. Brahm admitted to me that he was foxed when Lydia came to him. It was the night he proposed to me. Belle, he thought she was I."

Arabella shook her head. "It cannot be. He's lying."

"His story makes more sense and is more truthful than Lydia's. At the time she did not know he and I had an understanding. She was simply an unhappy woman looking for something she believed he could give her."

"No. I cannot believe it."

"She waited ten years to confess the truth, Arabella. She

could have told me a long time ago but she waited until Brahm came back into my life. She has done nothing but try to keep me from forgiving him from the moment he entered this house. Why? Why did she wait until Brahm made a public declaration of his intentions by asking me to dance three times?"

"Because she didn't want to hurt you. Because she does not want to see you marry a man who will treat you badly."

"What about Brahm and Lydia sharing a bed makes you think he will treat me badly?"

"He betrayed the promise he made to you!"

"He believed her to be me. He was drunk. He has very little memory of what happened."

"That is very convenient, do you not think?"

"I think that if he thought that little of me then, he would not be here now. And he would not be trying so very hard to prove to me that he is not that man anymore."

For a moment Arabella looked uncertain. Then she sighed. "You will not be dissuaded, will you?"

Eleanor shook her head, her jaw set with conviction. "I will not."

"I cannot believe you would believe him over your own sister. You read that Carson woman's book! You know what he is capable of."

"Yes, I do. I also know that Lydia confided in you so you and I would have this exact conversation. I would not doubt it if she went to you directly after leaving me."

"That is an awful thing to accuse her of."

"It was a quarter to six when she came to my room. What time did she come to you?"

Arabella swallowed. "Quarter past."

Eleanor was silent. There was really no need to say anything. "Brahm has been very open with me, Belle. I believe he regrets what happened. I have no reason to doubt him—unless Lydia gave you reason to believe that their 'affair' is still going on?"

"No. Oh, Ellie. I do not like to think that Lydia would try to cause trouble for you."

"Neither do I. I can only think that she believes that Brahm is not worthy of me and seeks to keep me from making a poor choice. Anything else is too awful to consider."

They talked for a few more moments before leaving the parlor and returning to the other guests. Lydia, Eleanor noticed, was absent.

Across the drawing room, Brahm met her gaze. The warmth in his eyes sent a shiver through her so acute, the bottoms of her feet tingled. In just a few more hours she would go through with her plan.

Brahm would be hers before morning.

The corridor was quiet as Eleanor slipped from her room. The wall sconces were lit so guests still awake could find their way through the house, but were dim enough not to disturb those trying to sleep. It wouldn't matter if the corridor was pitch black, Eleanor would be able to find her way.

Brahm's room was at the far end of the east wing where all the nonfamily guests had been put. The family rooms were in the west. Eleanor crept on sure feet, avoiding every creak and groan the floor held within.

She didn't dare knock on his door. Didn't dare risk alerting other, curious ears to her presence. Her heart pounded violently in her chest. If she was caught now, she would be ruined for certain. Brahm would feel duty-bound to marry her, and she would never know if he did it because he loved her or because he had no choice.

The click of the door catch releasing was no more significant than the tap of a fingernail upon a table, but it seemed to echo through the dark house like the dropping of a pianoforte lid. Eleanor winced, pulse thumping in her ears. Quickly she shoved the door open and dived inside, lest anyone decide to investigate the noise.

Inside the darkened bedchamber, she closed the door and leaned against the heavy oak, desperately trying to calm her heart and lungs. There were no sounds from the corridor, no opening doors, no questing footfalls. The only sound inside the room was the gentle breathing—and occasional snore—of the man in the bed.

There was little light in the room, despite the open draperies. Only the shadowy outlines of furniture were discernible. Eleanor tiptoed toward the bed, her gaze fastened on the dark lump beneath the covers. It was Brahm. He was alone.

Of course he was alone. Dear God, did she actually just have that thought? Why wouldn't he be alone?

It was her apprehension, that was all. She was so scared of discovery, so nervous of what might happen once Brahm woke up, that she suspected being found at every turn.

Gingerly she lowered herself to the bed. Her eyes had adjusted to the murky light enough that she could just barely make out the features of the man before her. He slept on his side, one bare arm over the blankets. She laid her hand on that arm—near the muscled slope of his shoulder. How warm his flesh was, how surprisingly soft. Her fingers explored in fascination.

The bones in his shoulder were hard, almost sharp. His muscles were firm, only slightly yielding, even in sleep. It wasn't until her fingers slid past his slightly stubbled jaw into his hair that he began to stir.

Startled, Eleanor jerked her hand away, only to have it seized in a strong grip that set her heart pounding even faster.

"What the—Eleanor?"

"Yes," she croaked.

He pushed himself up on an elbow. "What the devil are you doing here?"

Eleanor shivered. His voice was so low and scratchy, thick with slumber. She never would have thought a man's voice could be so . . . arousing.

"Is it not obvious?" She tried to lower her voice, to make it as seductive as his. "I plan to seduce you."

Chapter 11

Brahm blinked, his expression endearingly sleepy and boyish in the lamplight. "You plan to do *what*?"

"Seduce you," Eleanor replied, her confidence waning. This wasn't going quite as she expected. He wasn't supposed to question her. He was supposed to ravish her. Now.

He sat up, the blankets pooling around his hips, baring him from the waist up. He ran a palm over his face. "You should not be here. You will be ruined if we are caught."

Eleanor wasn't listening. She was staring at his chest. Years ago when she had seen him naked, she had been too hurt and shocked to enjoy it. Now she was so close, the moonlight so gloriously generous, that she could see every delicious inch of his upper body.

He was rich bronze, the muscles in his chest and arms heavy and defined. The fine dark hair on his torso seemed a natural contour to the hills and valleys of his trunk and stomach. What would he feel like beneath her hand?

He looked down at his bare chest before flashing her a

look that was almost apologetic. "I have the body of a laborer, I know. I have had to compensate in many ways for my injury."

"You are beautiful," she whispered, her tone as awed as her gaze as it met his—briefly. "Michelangelo would weep at the sight of you."

A soft chuckle escaped him. "I doubt it, but thank you. Eleanor, you must stop looking at me like that."

"Why?" Her fingers reached out to touch his stomach.

Brahm caught her hand before it reached its goal. "Because I am already using all my control not to kiss you."

Brazenly, she raised her gaze to his. "I grow weary of your control, Brahm. I want you to kiss me. I want you to touch me. Now release my hand and let me touch you as I want to."

He didn't release her as she demanded, but leaned forward until she could feel the heat and smell the warm sandalwood scent of his skin. He braced one strong arm beside her knee, the muscles taut and shadowed in the lamplight.

"I do not want to take advantage of you, Eleanor."

Eleanor shivered as his warm breath caressed her cheek. "You are not. You are a guest in my house. If anything, I am taking advantage of you, or I would if you would only allow it."

He did not chuckle at her teasing. His expression was serious—gravely so. "If you touch me I will not be satisfied until I make love to you."

She smiled, her other hand coming up to caress the stubbled plane of his cheek. "My darling Brahm. *I* will not be satisfied until you make love to me."

He kissed her then, his wide lips firm and hot against her. Eleanor opened her mouth for him, moaning softly as his tongue slid inside. He tasted her. She tasted him. His tongue stroked hers, teased and tantalized. Her heart thudded noisily against her ribs as a wave of shivering longing swept over her.

Brahm's arms encircled her, drawing her closer as he lay back on the bed. Eleanor had no choice but to follow, her lips still locked to his. She was draped over him like a blanket, her hips nestled in the hollow of his pelvis. He was hard and solid beneath her. Instinctively she pushed against that hardness, sending a ripple of pleasure darting through her. An ache awakened between her legs, deep inside her. It was a familiar ache—one she knew only Brahm could relieve to her ultimate satisfaction.

Through the thin material of her wrapper and nightrail, she could feel the heat of his hands. His fingers were gentle but firm, the strength there obvious as he gripped the curve of her bottom. His hips arched, and she could fully feel the hard length of him through the layers of fabric that separated them. This was the "massive maleness" that Fanny Carson had spoken of, that Eleanor had felt pushing against her before. Such an exotic organ should frighten her, should make her reluctant to leave her innocence behind, but it didn't. Eleanor undulated against it, shoving herself against him until she was sure her tender flesh would bruise.

His hands came around to her front, deftly dealing with the tie of her robe. He pushed the flimsy garment aside. Eleanor lifted herself so he could slide it down her arms. What he did with it after that, she didn't know and didn't care.

Her gown rode up her thighs as she moved against him. His fingers found the backs of her legs and slid upward, taking the gown with them until the cool night air brushed the bare skin of her backside.

Brahm sat up suddenly, taking her with him. She straddled his hips as he hauled her nightgown upward. Without question, Eleanor raised her arms so that he might remove it completely. Then she faced him, naked and vulnerable and trembling with need.

She could cringe under his appraisal. She could list her flaws and insecurities, but there was no point. Brahm looked at her as though she was a goddess, and his obvious appreciation of her body made her feel like such a divine creature. Whatever her flaws, tonight they were nonexistent, at least in this man's eyes.

"I imagined this moment so many times," he admitted in a raspy voice. "I am not certain if you are real or a dream."

His words caught at her heart. Slowly Eleanor lifted her hands to her hair, tugging at the ribbon there. The heavy tresses fell free, tumbling down her back like a waterfall of hair. She wanted Brahm's hands in it. Wanted to see it against his skin.

"Touch me," she whispered. "See for yourself that I am indeed real." His appreciation gave her a kind of shameless confidence.

His hands slid up her arms to her shoulders and neck. His caress was feather-light and just as tender, as his hands came up to cup her jaw.

He kissed her again, his lips lazy against hers. There was great restraint in his kiss, and Eleanor railed against it. She didn't want restraint. She wanted passion. She wanted the full force of his desire for her, because she intended to give him the full extent of hers for him. Desperately she caught at his shoulders, the bones there sharp against her palms. She tried to pull him closer, but he wouldn't budge. She slid her tongue along his, trying to coax him into a more insistent kiss. He resisted. He was in control, and she could either accept or rebel.

"Please," she begged against his lips. "Please."

He did not deny her. The pads of his fingers were velvet-rough as they slowly trailed down her chest. Gently, lightly they circled her nipple with a touch so acute it was little more than a sharp tickle. Eleanor's breasts tightened at his touch, the peaks puckering into tight, wanting pebbles. When his fingers finally squeezed the aching bud, she whimpered against his mouth. He rolled the nipple between his fingers as his tongue stroked hers, inhaling her moans.

His mouth drifted away from hers, trailing along her jaw and neck. He pressed a soft kiss to the pulse at the base of her throat before continuing downward. He leaned forward, forcing her spine into a lithe arch. Her breasts jutted forward, longing for his mouth. His lips branded a path along one curve until the wet heat of his mouth finally closed over her nipple. Eleanor's breath caught in her throat, trapped somewhere between a cry and a sigh.

Brahm's mouth tugged at her flesh, suckling until the ache between her legs grew to a fevered pitch. Eleanor pressed her hips down, wantonly seeking the pressure of his body.

Without taking his mouth from her breast, Brahm lifted her and rolled at the same time until Eleanor was on her back on the bed and he was hovering over her, laving her nipple with his tongue as he shoved at the blankets that separated them.

Bracing himself on one forearm, his other hand slid down past her ribs, down her belly to the valley between her thighs. Her legs fell apart as his fingers parted the moist curls, easing into the slick furrow. Slowly he began to stroke her, his questing fingers easily finding that part of her that was coiled into a tight bud of tension.

"Oh!" Eleanor's hips lifted at the first pass of his fingers. He replaced his fingers with his thumb, sliding his fingers downward to the entrance to her body. One slipped inside her, easily parting her eager flesh. She gasped at the intrusion, her muscles clenching at him. She never knew it would feel like this. Her entire body was on fire for him, and they were far from over, that she knew.

His teeth nipped at her breast, drawing a cry from her. Lifting his head, he gazed down at her, his fingers still ruthlessly stroking the wetness between her legs until she writhed and gasped for more. She met his gaze with a boldness she never knew she possessed. Did it arouse him to watch her? Did her reaction to his touch make him hard, pulsing with the need to be inside her?

"You are so tight," he told her as his finger eased in and out of her body.

Eleanor gasped as the coil of pleasure wound even tighter. "Is that good?"

He chuckled. "Very good." Lifting himself up on his hand, he loomed over her. "I want to watch you shudder. I want to be buried inside you when you come. I want to shove myself inside you until you sob with pleasure."

Her body reacted to his words, warming and melting inside. She wasn't so innocent that she didn't know what he was talking about, and God help her, she wanted it too.

Brahm leaned down, brushing her cheek with his lips. He kissed her mouth again, tasting her as though he had never tasted her before, and then he began moving downward. He was so slow, so exquisitely languid with this sumptuous exploration of her body. His lips moved with deliberate slowness from her jaw down her neck to her shoulder, as though he wanted to savor every taste of her flesh. The fingers of her right hand combed through the thick silk of his hair while the left caressed the satiny expanse of his shoulders and upper back.

Still he stoked the fire between her legs. He seemed to know exactly how to touch her so that the ache continued to build but was careful not to send her tumbling over the edge. Just when she thought he was going to give her the release she so desperately craved, he changed tempo so that orgasm eluded her.

His mouth teased her sensitive breasts, sucking and tugging until the line between pleasure and pain blurred, until she gasped at the slightest touch. The tip of his tongue flicked, tickled, and alternately applied firm, delicious pleasure that brought her to the pinnacle of sexual pleasure.

Brahm lifted his head, moving his body up over hers as he moved between her legs, positioning the blunt head of his sex against the eager entrance of hers. She stiffened just for a moment as she remembered Fanny Carson's description of this mysterious creature.

He rubbed the head of it against her cleft, spreading the moisture there while his fingers continued their divine stroking.

"Easy." His voice was low and throaty, easing the tension that gripped her. "We will fit, Eleanor. We will fit perfectly."

She believed him, and relaxed beneath him. How could she do anything else when his touch felt so good?

This time he did not change the tempo of his hand when the pressure became deliciously intense. The coil within her gave with a force that had her arching her hips and crying out in the ecstasy of it. And as the waves ripped through her, Brahm shoved his hips forward, pushing himself inside her.

Even as pleasure rippled outward from the spot where they were joined, Eleanor winced as the length of him—it felt so thick and blunt—pierced the only resistance her body offered against his. It hurt, but not as badly as she had heard it could—as she had feared it might. Discomfort mingled with rapture, until she was uncertain if having him within her hurt or was the most wonderful thing she had ever felt.

Once he was fully inside—and she knew he was fully inside her because she could feel his pelvis against hers—he stilled. Eleanor drew several slow, deep breaths. When the discomfort began to subside, when her body became restless for the movement of his, she opened her eyes once more.

Brahm was watching her, so still that his only movement was the gentle rhythm of his chest against hers. His gaze was tender, dark, and intense as he loomed above her.

"This," he told her softly in a voice like warm chocolate, "is the only pain I ever wished to cause you, and even so I would take it away from you if I could."

Tears burned the backs of Eleanor's eyes and she fought to blink them away. His words broke her heart, pierced something deep inside her. Her soul, perhaps?

"I would not wish it," she confessed, her voice embarrassingly throaty. "I would not have you change a thing."

He did not reply, but his eyes seemed to brighten as they gazed upon her. With his arms braced on either side of her head, he began to move his hips. Eleanor's hands slid down his back so she could feel his muscles undulating beneath her palms as he thrust within her. He began slowly, withdrawing only a fraction before filling her completely once more. Her inner flesh was sensitive, but it did not hurt, and soon she was moving her hips in rhythm with his, grinding her pelvis against his as the tension built within her once more.

With every thrust, every roll of his hips, his pubic bone pressed against hers, heightening the growing ache. Eleanor arched, shoving herself forward so that he filled her as fully as he could, moving closer to a second climax.

Brahm quickened his pace, deepened his strokes. His gaze never left hers, even as his breathing turned to husky gasps and pants that thrilled her more than any touch. At that moment, Eleanor knew that her body was the sweetest place he had ever been, that she was not the only one experiencing the most incredible pleasure. It filled her with a sense of incredible power to know that she could make him feel this way.

Hers. He was hers.

She came again, a sharp moan escaping her as an orgasm more intense than the last burst within her. Above her, Brahm stiffened, plunging within her one last time as a groan tore free from his throat.

They remained locked together for some time, until Eleanor's hips began to ache and Brahm's arms trembled from supporting his own weight. He withdrew from her—his warm presence replaced by a cool, damp stickiness—and rolled to his side.

What happened now? Did they talk? Should she leave? Should she at least dress? Brahm saved her from having to decide by drawing her into his arms once more. She snuggled against him, craving his heat even though they were both sweaty.

His gaze was intense as he smoothed her hair back from her face. What a tangled mess it must be. She surely had a rat's nest in the back from all that writhing. Oh, but she'd suffer a thousand tangles for what she and Brahm had just shared.

Snuggling against him, she forgot all about tangles and what she should do and gave herself over to the complete and utter contentment that overwhelmed her. There would be time for talk and decisions when she woke up.

For the first time in his life, Brahm did not fall asleep immediately after achieving climax.

He lay in bed, tucked around Eleanor's slumbering form. She was soft and warm in his arms, her hair fragrant and silky against his jaw. Silence cocooned them, broken every once in a while by a gentle snore that made him smile.

This was contentment, this emotion that overwhelmed him. He could stay like this forever, with Eleanor beside him, the night keeping them secret and safe. Realistically he knew that could never happen, but that didn't stop him from wanting it all the same.

She had felt so good wrapped around him, the wet heat of her body sweeter than anything he had ever known. He fit within her as though she had been made for him and he for her.

He should wake her up and send her back to her own room, but he couldn't do it. It felt too good, holding her like this, as he had wanted to for so long.

Everything he wanted was coming true, and it was as frightening as it was exciting. Eleanor was with him. Eleanor believed in him and wanted him. She had given him her innocence. Would she give him her heart as well?

She stirred against him, the swell of her buttocks push-ing against his groin. Just that one touch was enough to grab the attention of his John Thomas. With a mind of its own, it thickened, insistently probing the warm cleft cradling it. Brahm sighed. Not only was he wide awake, but he was ready to make love again. It had been a long time since that had happened.

He could ignore it. In fact, he should ignore it. Eleanor was sound asleep and probably sore from their previous session. Never having deflowered a virgin before, he had no idea how long these things took to heal. Causing her lasting discomfort was not something he wanted laid upon his shoulders.

But Eleanor, it seemed, had other plans. Her backside shifted, so that his sex was hugged by her soft cheeks, which flexed around him. Brahm bit back a groan as he pulsed in response.

"Is that what I think it is?" she asked in a sleepy voice.

His hand splayed across her stomach, Brahm stroked the soft flesh there. "I am afraid so. Ignore it, it will go away."

Her buttocks moved against him. "You want me to give it the cut direct? How rude."

Brahm winced. "Do not use the word 'cut' in anyway when discussing my 'massive maleness,' please."

Eleanor chuckled. "My apologies, my lord."

"You are forgiven." His hips pressed against her. Damn, but this wasn't helping.

"Tell me the truth," she said as she rolled to face him. "Is it really massive?"

The organ in question was now poking itself against her stomach. "You tell me."

In the pale night, he could almost fancy he saw her roll her eyes. "I would not know large from small, having no experience in these matters before tonight."

"In that case I am indeed massive. I am so large, in fact, that you are now ruined for other men and can only be satisfied by me for the rest of your life."

Her laughter was husky, sending a shiver down his spine that then twisted and ended up as a swirling tension in his sac. "I suspected as much."

All humor faded from him. Here he was joking about the size of his cock when he should be inquiring after her. "I did not hurt you, did I?"

Her fingers stroked his face with a tenderness that pulled at his heart. How generous she was with her caring and affection. She would make a wonderful mother someday—better than his own had been—not that he had known her that well. Most of his young life had been spent learning what was expected of him as the future viscount.

"It hurt but for a moment," she assured him. "And then it was the most wonderful experience of my life."

She was only saying that to placate his ego, was she not? "The next time will be better."

Her breasts pressed against his chest. "Will it?"

Was this seductress rubbing herself against him his Eleanor? It seemed too much to hope that she would suit him so totally in so many ways, but he was through questioning it for the time being. Right now he was going to enjoy her.

She rolled with him, falling to her back without hesitation. She trusted him with her body, trusted that he would not do anything to hurt her. If only it was so easy to determine whether she trusted him with her heart. She had so many reasons not to trust him, and yet she seemed hellbent on trying.

He braced himself above her, allowing himself the luxury of roaming her body with his gaze. The moon was not bright, but it was enough to paint her flesh an ethereal hue. Her nipples were almost violet, the downy hair between her thighs a dark silver. She was like an angel, or a goddess fallen to earth.

His fingers skimmed the tops of her shoulders, traced the faint ridge of her collarbone and her neck. Her skin was so delicate, so fragile beneath his hand. Everything about her was so doll-like, and yet she had a strength that baffled him. A waif with a spine of steel. Only her mouth disagreed with the porcelain image. That wide, curved upper lip lent a seductive quality to her features, hinting at the passion below the surface. How he loved that lip.

Her blue gaze, dark in the soft light, locked with his as his hands slid slowly along the indent of her waist and drifted across her ribs. She was exactly as a woman should be—not stick sharp, but not too soft—if there was such a thing as a woman being *too* soft.

"You are beautiful," he whispered. "Everything about you is perfect."

Her smile was sweet, lazy, and so seductive, he could scarcely stand it. "No one is perfect, Lord Creed, although I am tempted to say that you are as close as I have ever seen."

Brahm's heart gave a painful thump at her words. She had yet to see his leg, but somehow he knew she wouldn't be the least put off by the sight. She would probably weep for the pain it had cause him, but she would not be repulsed by it. "You are perfect to me."

Her smile faded as his fingers stroked the tightening rose of her right nipple. "Do you suppose that makes us perfect for each other?"

Dear God, she was killing him. Did she know how wistful she sounded? How sweetly, tenderly hopeful her tone was? His chest constricted as though a mighty arm was wrapped around it, crushing him with its strength.

"Yes," he rasped in response. "I suppose it does."

He lowered his head to hers, his heart unable to stand any more of this talk. Her mouth was eager as he possessed it with his own, her tongue warm and inviting as she parted her lips.

Velvety softness closed around his hips as he slipped between her thighs. The flesh there was warm and humid, and oh so inviting as he probed it with the head of his sex. He knew that it was too soon for him to take her as he wanted. Tomorrow perhaps—or the next day—he could have her as he desired, but for this second time he would have to be as gentle as, if not more so than, the first time.

Brahm's hand slid down the gentle curve of her abdomen to her feathery mound. His fingers parted the damply matted curls, easily finding the slickness within. She was wet and wanting, the hooded ridge that housed the center of her pleasure hard and eager for his touch.

"You're ready for me," he murmured against her lips.

She smiled against his mouth. "I have been ready for you for a long time."

He stroked her wetness. He was hard and ready, his cock impatient. "Put me inside you."

Her body gave a little jerk. Whether it was from his touch or his command, he didn't know. "I do not know how."

"Yes you do." He gave her another stroke with his finger, drawing a shaky gasp from her lips.

Eleanor's fingers were tentative as they reached between them and closed around the hard length of him. Brahm shuddered at her touch, his hips reflexively arching, pushing himself into her hand. Curiosity got the better of her, and she explored the length and head with questing fingers that made him tremble like a sapling in the wind.

"Take me inside," he demanded between clenched teeth. He would not humiliate himself by coming in her hand. He would not.

She did as he commanded, drawing him closer to the sultry heat between her thighs. He withdrew his finger, allowing her to guide him to the entrance of her body. She might never have done such a thing before, but her body knew exactly what to do.

The tip eased inside her, parting her tight, honeyed flesh. He entered her slowly, inch by inch, every muscle in his body tense and ready to withdraw if the slightest discomfort flickered across her features.

Her gaze locked with his, her lips parting as he filled her at last.

"Are you all right?" he asked, his voice hoarse with passion and emotion as he stared down at her flushed, beautiful face.

"I'm fine." Her hips moved against his. "Stop talking."

Wrapping an arm beneath her, Brahm rolled onto his back, taking her with him so that she was now the one on top. He wanted to watch her ride him until she exploded with pleasure.

Eleanor gasped at the motion, staring down at him with wide eyes. "What are you doing?"

"I'm not doing anything," he murmured, lifting his hips into her. "*You,* however, are going to do something— to me."

Her brows rose. What a delicious mess she was with her hair hanging around her shoulders in thick, tangled clumps. Just the sight of her astride him brought him to the brink.

"Why?"

"Because this way I do not have to worry about hurting you, and because I want to watch you ride me."

A moment of hot, sizzling silence passed as their gazes locked.

"Tell me what to do." Her voice was a hoarse whisper.

There were so many things he could demand, could beg her for, but they would have to wait. Right now he wanted her to discover the delight of being the one in control. He wanted to show her that he had no wish to keep her under him, subservient and dominated. "Do what feels right."

Eleanor did just that. She shifted her hips and experimented with different motions until she found one that suited her. Slowly sliding her body up and down on his, she drove him to the brink of ecstasy time and time again, until sweat beaded on his brow and his entire body was tight with tension.

She engulfed him, drenched him with her juices, her body clenching at him like a wet silken vise. Their moans mingled as she writhed on top of him. He didn't care if someone heard them. He didn't care if they were caught. All he wanted was to explode inside her.

She was close as well; he could hear it in her gasps, see it in her heavy-lidded gaze as she took him as deep inside her as he could go. Her thighs widened, lowering her even further, so that she took him completely inside her and the lips of her sex rubbed against his pelvis with maddeningly sweet friction.

Tight, aching pressure coiled low inside him. He wanted to seize her by the hips and hold her still while he pounded himself within her, but he gritted his teeth as sweat trickled down his forehead and dug his fingers into her thighs instead. This was torture—delicious, acute torture.

Eleanor's moans quickened with her movements. Her hips rotated faster as she lifted herself up and down upon him. The muscles of her thighs flexed beneath his palms, stiffening as her back arched. Her neck bowed, her hair brushing his legs as she tossed her head back, crying out loud as her climax shook her.

Her orgasm sent Brahm over the edge. He arched his hips, his fingers biting into her thighs as ripple after ripple of intense pleasure shuddered through his body. He emptied himself within her, his body twitching as the shocks seemed to go on forever. Eleanor collapsed on top of him, and he slid his hands up around to cup her buttocks, holding her tight against him lest she try to leave.

He knew it was wrong of him to come inside her without a sheath. In all honesty, he hadn't even thought to bring one with him. The thought of bedding Eleanor had seemed too far-fetched for him to entertain. Oddly enough, the realization that a child could result from this night didn't bother him in the least. In fact, the idea of having a family of his own, of Eleanor being the mother of his children, filled him with an emotion he could not name, but he liked the feel of it all the same. He also knew that if Birch, Locke, or those other four even looked at Eleanor after this, he'd kill them without so much as a flinch. She was his, and would always be his.

It was sometime later before either of them could find the strength to speak. Pinned beneath the soft weight of her body, Brahm drew what blankets he could reach over them as their flesh began to cool, leaving them slightly damp and chill with lingering perspiration. Eleanor's head nestled between his jaw and shoulder, and he stroked the velvety surface of her hair. He would have to help her get those tangles out.

"Mmm." She stirred against him, her legs sliding down his. "I think I have a cramp in my backside. Is that possible?"

Brahm chuckled. It was her hip no doubt, aching from their exertions. He was reluctant to let her go, but he didn't want to cause her any more discomfort. Gently he caught her about the waist and rolled to his side, slipping from the heated confines of her body. He massaged her hip to ease the ache before climbing out of bed. They both needed to be washed after two sessions of lovemaking.

He brought the washbasin and a cloth to the bed and washed Eleanor first. She fussed over his attentions, but he rolled his eyes and bathed her anyway, wiping the residue of their lovemaking from between her thighs with gentle strokes. Then he washed himself and dropped the cloth in the water. The basin he set on the floor to tend to later.

"I have to go back to my room soon," she reminded him as he slid into bed and drew her into his arms once more.

"I know." He didn't want her to go, but it was inevitable. The alternative would result in others finding out about their tryst, and as much he wanted the world to know that Eleanor was his, he didn't want to make her the object of petty gossip.

"Can we do this again tomorrow night?"

The coy lightness of her tone made him chuckle. "On one condition."

Eleanor raised her gaze to his, smiling warmly. "Anything."

Brahm's smile faded as his heart reacted to her vow. "Marry me."

Chapter 12

Marry him? Had she truly heard correctly? Her heart was pounding so loudly that she thought for a moment that she might have imagined his question.

"Did you just ask me to marry you?"

He nodded, a slight smile curving one corner of his mouth. "I did. Would you like me to ask again?"

Eleanor shook her head. "No, that will not be necessary." She stared at him. Marry him. He wanted them to spend the remainder of their lives together. He wanted her to have his children and help him raise them. Her plan had worked; she had seduced him into asking the very question she longed to hear. True, he had made no declaration of love, but it was almost as good. He would not have made love to her if he did not have some degree of emotion for her, and he wouldn't have proposed if that emotion didn't run to the true and lasting kind. There was more than just desire between them.

"Would you care to give me an answer?" His smile had

waned. Surely he wasn't doubting himself?

She opened her mouth to do just that, but the answer was stolen by a sudden and awful thought.

"My family will not approve." That was putting it mildly. Until recently Arabella had been on her side and in a position to help her convince the other girls, but thanks to Lydia, Arabella didn't trust Brahm, and she wouldn't go out of her way to convince their sisters to trust him either.

"Hang your family." His scowl spoke volumes as to what he thought of her sisters' approval. "I want to marry you, not your sisters."

That might be acceptable were there not another member of her family to consider. "But my father—"

He cut her off. "Your father likes me."

That was true, and she was of an age when she did not necessarily need her father's permission to marry.

"He knows about my . . . mistake with Lydia."

Eleanor nodded. "I know."

Raising himself up on a elbow, Brahm propped his head up with his hand. "He told you?"

"Yes. You confessed to him, didn't you?" She would have thought a man like her father would kill Brahm for such an affront.

"Indeed." He smiled crookedly. "I do not believe he was particularly impressed, but he knows I was drunk, and that I regret it. All he wants is for you to be happy, and he seems to believe I am the one to make that happen."

So her father was fine with her marrying Brahm. Her sisters would accept him eventually, once they got to know him. Once they realized what a wonderful man he was.

"He said you were obsessed with me." He stroked her

cheek with the pad of his index finger as he teased her. "That you had been obsessed for years."

Eleanor made a scoffing noise as she fought a smile. "Do not flatter yourself. He only told you that to play matchmaker."

"Hmm. He seemed to think that my acceptance of his invitation was indication that I returned your fascination. Perhaps he was mistaken in that regard as well."

Her gaze snapped to his. "You were fascinated by me?"

How she longed to stay in the warmth of his arms and bed, even though she knew time was against her. "I did not say that."

"Yes you did."

"I said your father suspected as much. I did not say it was true."

She grinned at him. "But here you are."

He grinned back. "Yes, and so are you."

As he lowered his head to hers, Eleanor's heart began to pound in anticipation of his kiss. This was too perfect, too wonderful for words. His lips were soft yet insistent, drawing a sigh of contented pleasure from her.

All too soon it was over, and he was lifting his head to gaze down at her once more. "So," he prompted, "will you marry me?

"Yes," she whispered, her throat tight as she said the word. "Yes, please."

He kissed her again, this time a long, leisurely kiss that robbed her of her breath as well as reason.

"I just ask one thing," she told him, when they were snuggled together once more.

"I've always thought that a rather ominous request coming from a woman," he joked. "What is it you wish?"

"I do not want anyone to know of our engagement until

I've had a chance to tell my family. Will you agree to that?"

"Of course." His tone was hesitant, but it pleased her all the same. "Who would I tell?" ❧

Eleanor crept from Brahm's room just before dawn. She was sated and a little sore from their lovemaking, and terribly reluctant to leave him, but elation caused her feet to practically dance all the way back to her own chamber.

She was finally going to be Lady Creed. She was going to leave her father's house and become mistress of her own.

Her father. The thought of him gave her pause as she tiptoed up the stairs to the family wing. She knew now that he had capitalized on his ill health to coax her into agreeing to this party in the first place, but that didn't change the fact that his health was not good. Who would look after him when she was gone? Perhaps she could talk him into coming to live with her and Brahm? He would dig in his heels at that suggestion. He hated feeling like a burden.

There was always the house in London. He was forever saying he wanted to spend more time there. She would feel so much better knowing he was close to Lydia and Phoebe, who kept London as their main residence. No doubt she and Brahm would spend a great deal of time there as well, and London had physicians and apothecaries galore in case Papa required medical attention. She would broach the subject with her father as soon as possible.

But first she had to announce her betrothal to her family. She would not wait as she had years ago. It wasn't that she expected anything awful to happen, but there was no harm in taking preventive measures. And, a little voice in her head whispered, she didn't want to give Brahm the chance to change his mind.

With these two decisions made, it was as though a huge weight had been lifted from her. By the time she made it safely back to her room without being seen, she was positively giddy from all the change taking place in her life. After more than a decade of standing still, she was dancing so fast, she was dizzy.

Yet despite this excitement—or perhaps because of it—she fell into bed and was asleep within minutes. By the time she awoke, it was nine o'clock—time for her to get up and meet with her family before all the guests were up and about.

She rang for her maid and the housekeeper. The two of them exchanged brief, curious glances when Eleanor asked Mrs. Blynn to deliver her summons to the rest of the family. Eleanor was not the least bit bothered by their behavior. Of course they were curious. They knew the true nature of this house party just as well as she did. They expected that she had finally found herself a husband. No doubt the entire staff would be speculating as to who it was within the hour. It was for that very reason that she intended to request Brahm's attendance on her own. Servants talked, and the last thing she wanted was her maid telling Lady Merrott's maid that Brahm looked to be Eleanor's choice of mate. She and Brahm would publicly announce their betrothal when they saw fit.

Within that same hour that the household staff was speculating as to Eleanor's choice, she and her father and her sisters and Brahm were in her mother's parlor, where they would be least likely to be set upon by guests or inquisitive servants trying to ferret out what information they could.

Per her request, her sisters came alone. This kind of announcement did not need to be made in front of their husbands—partly because Eleanor didn't like three out of four of them, and because there was a very good chance her sisters would react badly, and the fewer people who saw that, the better.

As they were all seated, their gazes hopped from Eleanor to Brahm and then to one another. The air in the room thickened with tension, tension that Eleanor thought best quickly dispelled because her nerves couldn't take any more of it. It was like a black cloud hanging over her happy news, and she was uncertain enough of what the future held for her and Brahm. Would she be enough woman for him? He was so experienced, what if she bored him? Would she truly be able to help him if he fell to temptation and drank? These things that she had been so certain of when she wanted him to propose made her very anxious now that he had.

"I will not keep you for long, I know we all have personal duties to attend to because of the party."

"I should much prefer to listen to anything you have to say rather than gossip," Arabella informed her with a smile. Her gaze was anxious, however, as it drifted toward Brahm.

Eleanor returned the smile with a bright one of her own. She kept her attention focused on her father, the one person whom she knew would be delighted for her. "Lord Creed has asked me to marry him and I have accepted."

Her father beamed. Her sisters exchanged startled glances. Lydia especially looked less than enthusiastic about the news. They wanted to voice their opposition, but wouldn't. They were too well mannered to make such an outburst in front of Brahm—although Eleanor expected they'd have overcome their manners had Papa not been present.

"Excellent news!" her father boomed as he rose from his chair. His rugged face creased with a grin and he came to

Eleanor with his arms outstretched. Eleanor went eagerly to his embrace, laughing at his happiness and her own.

"I am very pleased that the two of you worked things out," he murmured against her ear before releasing her. He went to Brahm next, catching the younger man's hand in his own fierce grip.

Eleanor turned to her sisters. Their downcast faces annoyed her. "Are my sisters not going to congratulate me?" It was the same tone she had used with them as children when she wanted them to know that she was on the verge of being terribly disappointed in them—not to mention angry. It worked as well now as it had back then.

Arabella came forward first. She always had and always would be the first to acknowledge that Eleanor knew what she was doing. Eleanor's younger sister might be fearful of Brahm and his motives, but she would support Eleanor no matter what.

Arabella hugged her. "I *am* happy for you, Ellie," she whispered. "Honestly."

Eleanor's smile was tight with unexpected tears. "Thank you."

Arabella moved on to Brahm. "Eleanor deserves the best of everything. I expect you to see she gets just that."

Eleanor's eyes widened at Arabella's protective demeanor. Eleanor was the one who always played mother to her siblings, protecting them as best she could. When they sought to protect her, it was always a surprise. It was doubly odd to see gentle Belle practically threaten a man such as Brahm.

To his credit, her betrothed smiled warmly at his future sister-in-law. "I will do my best to ensure just that."

That seemed to appease Arabella, who gave him a quick hug and returned to her chair.

Muriel and Phoebe were next, following Arabella as they always did. Lydia was last.

She was stiff as Eleanor returned her hug. "I am so very happy for you, Ellie."

Eleanor fought a frown. Her sister's words sounded sincere, but everything else about her demeanor rang false. Her embrace was cold, her smile just a touch too bright to be true, and in no way reaching her eyes. It filled Eleanor's heart with cold dread. Their relationship would be forever changed by this. Whatever Lydia's reasons, she would never forgive Eleanor for accepting Brahm's proposal, she was that set against him.

When Lydia moved on to Brahm, her entire countenance changed. A strange, predatory gleam entered her eyes, but it wasn't sexual. It was almost as though she despised him, as if he had done her some great wrong, and she wanted to make him pay for it.

"How lovely it will be to have you in our family, Lord Creed." Her voice was a purr. Eleanor suppressed a shudder at the low, throaty tone. This was an unfamiliar side of Lydia, and she didn't like it at all. Fortunately no one else in the family could see her face. To them she no doubt sounded warm and sisterly, but Eleanor knew better.

Brahm, however, seemed unaffected by such open hostility and sensuality. He bowed over Lydia's hand—she was the only one not to offer him an embrace—and smiled. Only his eyes held a degree of wariness. "Thank you. I look forward to calling you my sister."

Lydia's jaw tightened at his words. Obviously the last thing she wanted was to be Brahm's "sister."

What then, Eleanor wondered, an invisible band cinching around her chest, did her sister want?

* * *

The afternoon's riding was canceled due to rain, and so the gentlemen were forced to find other ways to amuse themselves. Some played billiards, others played cards or talked near the fire over a glass of port in the games room. Still others played chess or chatted with some of the ladies in the drawing room.

Brahm sat at one end of the room, enjoying a cup of coffee with the other bachelors. Eleanor was at the other end, working on some kind of needlework with Arabella and two other ladies.

"How goes the pursuit of Lady Eleanor, Creed old man?" It was Lord Merrott who asked, joining the group with a drink decidedly stronger than coffee, unless Brahm's nose deceived him.

The other single men watched him with open interest, waiting like vultures for his answer. Idiots. He was tempted to tell them all to go home now, Eleanor was his.

He shrugged. "It goes."

The sixth bachelor, a man named Stevenson, snorted. "She favors you above the rest of us. You would think at her age she wouldn't be so quick to narrow her chances."

"Perhaps she is simply demonstrating her good taste," Brahm replied with a smile.

"Good taste!" Locke sneered. "She's a frigging ice queen. Burrough is trying to sell her off like a mare for stud, but none of us can get close enough to mount her."

Birch replied before Brahm could, "She's a *lady*, Locke, not one of your doxies."

Locke shrugged. "They are all doxies underneath. Lady Eleanor is no different. She just thinks to entice us by playing the demure miss. Five minutes alone with her is all I need to prove otherwise."

The end of Brahm's cane came up, pinning Locke to the back of the sofa by his throat. One good push and he could make certain Locke never spoke again. "Touch her and no one will ever find your remains."

Locke stared at him in wide-eyed terror. His nod was the slightest movement, so afraid was he of what Brahm might do to him. Of course Locke, like everyone else, had heard the rumors about Brahm's involvement with Harker's death. Locke knew Brahm had no compunction when it came to killing for someone he cared for.

It was Birch who intervened. Everyone else seemed content to watch the goings-on. Fortunately for Brahm, none of the other guests seemed to notice the altercation at all, so involved were they in their own activities.

"It is all right, Creed. Locke was just being an ass as usual. He would never harm Lady Eleanor."

"Quite right," Locke croaked. "Never."

Slowly, Brahm withdrew his cane. Perhaps Locke had simply been talking out his arse, but Brahm would not tolerate such talk about Eleanor. The idea of any other man touching her, let alone in such a vulgar manner, made his blood boil. He meant his threat. He would kill Locke or any other man who hurt Eleanor, and take his damn sweet time about it.

"Excuse me." He rose to his feet with the help of his cane. Inside, rage still bubbled and popped. He needed to be far away from Locke right now, because he wasn't so certain he wouldn't do him further harm if the man remained in his sight.

He left Locke rubbing his throat and the rest of them watching him. Their gazes ranged from aversion to respect and covered all manner of opinion in between. One thing was for certain, they all knew now that his feelings for Eleanor were a fair bit deeper than their own.

He left the drawing room and made for the library. It was the safest room in the house for him right now. A book was just what he needed to distract him and help him pass the hours. If he spent any more time with the other guests, he would either blurt out the truth or murder one of them.

He had been there perhaps a quarter hour when the door opened. He looked up from his copy of *Gulliver's Travels* hoping to see Eleanor and found her sister instead. Dear God, this was not good. He was all alone in a room with Lydia, and she was blocking his only exit. There were always the windows.

"I hope I am not disturbing you." Her voice was like velvet, but her back was as stiff as steel.

His first thought was to tell her that disturbing him had been *exactly* what she hoped, but he kept that thought to himself. There was no need to antagonize Eleanor's family before the marriage license could be procured.

"Just rereading Swift," he informed her, setting the book aside. "Nothing of significance. What can I do for you?"

That might not have been the best choice of words for talking to Lydia, but there could be no taking them back now.

Everything about her was hostile, her stance, her expression, even her voice. "I suppose you are feeling pretty proud of yourself right now."

"For?" As if he didn't know.

She rolled her eyes. She knew he was playing dumb. "For convincing my sister to accept your suit."

"Yes. I am very pleased."

Her eyes were downcast. "At least she told us, not like

before." He might have laughed at her feigned expression of guilt had her actions of years ago not caused both him and Eleanor so much pain and trouble.

"Nothing is like before." He was sober. He was older. Everything was different. He would not end up in bed with Lydia. Eleanor would not find a reason not to trust him.

Her gaze lifted to his. "Sobriety does not change a man, Brahm. It only makes him craftier."

What kind of idiot was she married to? He didn't know the man personally, but he had to be a real piece of work to have turned Lydia into such a bitter woman.

"Many things have changed me. Your sister sees that. I am sorry that you cannot." Actually he wasn't sorry at all, although he did harbor a degree of pity for her.

Lydia snorted, distorting her once pretty face into a mask of contempt. "When you tire of Eleanor and want something new, do not come sniffing around my door. You will not be welcome."

Bitter she might be, but Lydia certainly thought a lot of her own power as a woman. "I do not expect to ever tire of Eleanor, and trust me, if I ever do tire of your sister, your door will not be the one I come 'sniffing' at."

She stiffened. "I was good enough for you years ago."

What a mess she was. Clinging to one night in the past that meant nothing to him but obviously meant something to her. "We had one night that I do not even remember."

"Well I remember it!" She took a lurching step toward him. "You told me you cared for me! You told me you loved me."

It took a great deal of fortitude not to step back from her. He wasn't intimidated by her fervor, nor did he feel particularly threatened. He didn't feel particularly comfortable either. "I was foxed." It was difficult to be angry with her when she sounded so bloody pathetic. "I am sorry if I misled you, but I never harbored any feelings of the kind for you."

"Only Eleanor." Was that a sneer or a sigh?

"Yes."

"You are not good enough for her, you know." She was as petulant and pouty as a child. "We all believe it."

Yes, he knew it. But if she hoped to turn him away with mere words she would have to try much, much harder. "Then it is fortunate for me that Eleanor believes otherwise."

Lydia's expression was ugly and accusatory. "You will hurt her."

"Not if I can help it."

"You cannot help it. It is your nature."

This time her words pierced his armor and struck home. Was it his nature to hurt Eleanor? Would he be unable to help himself and one day injure her in a way that could not be repaired?

No, he would not. He could not. "This conversation grows tedious." He drew on his haughtiest voice, his most commanding manner. "You will have to excuse me, my lady, but I have more important things to attend to than listening to your accusations."

Lydia flashed him a mocking smile. "Running to Eleanor, Lord Creed?"

That was exactly what he was about to do, and it needled him that she knew it. "Actually, I thought I might have a word with your husband first."

He brushed past her to the door. Much to his satisfaction, she paled. It was a cruel gesture on his part, but necessary to his pride.

"Be careful what you start with me, my lady." He

paused briefly as he opened the door. "Do not fool your-self into thinking I will not finish it for you."

Unfortunately it was late into the evening before Brahm had the chance to speak to Eleanor. Fortunately they were alone in her mother's parlor, the door locked, the drapes drawn, and but one lamp lighted. It was an intimate set-ting, the two of them sitting on the sofa, Brahm with his arm around Eleanor's shoulders.

As much as he hated to disturb this contentment, he knew he had to. "I had a confrontation with Lydia today."

Eleanor sat up, turning worried eyes to his. "About what?"

He told her, repeating word for word everything that had been said between them. He left nothing out, even if he thought it might make him look less than good in Eleanor's eyes.

When he had finished, Eleanor sighed and shook her head. "She is so protective."

Protective? It was all he could do not to snort. "She's jealous."

Eleanor nodded, her expression sad. "That too. How awful her own marriage must be that she wants mine to be so as well."

"You are far too forgiving and understanding with her."

She smiled sweetly at his gruff tone. "She is my sister."

That was supposed to explain everything, was it? Oddly enough, it did. Brahm sighed. "Fine, but I do not trust her."

Again she nodded, settling once more into his embrace.

They sat in silence, listening to the rain fall outside and the distant rumble of thunder.

"I have been thinking," she murmured a short while later.

"About?" he prompted when she didn't immediately continue.

Gentle fingers trailed along his thigh, awakening the nerves there through the wool of his trousers. "About the last time we were alone together."

In his room. Naked. In bed. One thought of it was enough to have his trousers suddenly feel very tight in the crotch. "Are you trying to seduce me?"

Her head tilted back, and her laughing blue gaze met his. "Would I be successful if I were?"

"Hell yes." His voice was a delighted growl. "But here?"

Eleanor glanced around them. "It seems as good a place as any."

How practical his little seductress was. In fact, she was proving to be many things that amazed and pleased him. She was intelligent and amusing and so very open with her feelings and desires. The only thing she was not open with was her heart. He knew she liked him. He knew she wanted and desired him, but he did not know if she loved him.

For now wanting and liking would do, but his ultimate goal was Eleanor's heart and he meant to have it, as surely as he meant to give her his.

But at this moment his betrothed wanted to seduce him, and he planned to let her. "Straddle me," he instructed in a low tone. "Have your way with me."

She did as he bid. Her cheeks were flushed and her movements were a little awkward, but Brahm had never seen anything so erotic in his life as Eleanor hiking her skirts up around her pale thighs so that he could see her stockings and garters, and straddling his lap.

He was hard as a rock already.

She kissed him, her lips sweet and demanding, coaxing

his tongue into mating with hers. Instinctively she knew how to arouse him. Once she gained more confidence and experience as his lover, she would be able to turn him into a quivering mass in seconds.

God, how he looked forward to helping her gain that experience and confidence.

Without his telling her to, she reached down beneath her skirts, her hands brushing the bulge in the front of his trousers. His hips jerked at the contact. Quivering mass indeed.

Her fingers fumbled with his falls, every second making him harder and harder and more and more eager. Were it anyone else, he would suspect this maidenly awkwardness was a ruse, but not with Eleanor.

Finally she freed his aching erection, stroking the length of it with anxious, inquisitive fingers—fingers that threatened to undo him.

"If you want me, stop playing with me and take me," he growled.

Eleanor only laughed at his desire. She rose up on her knees and positioned herself over him, lowering her body until he felt moist curls brush the tip of his cock. He groaned, his eyes closing as she placed the sensitive head at the slick entrance to her body and slowly allowed him to ease inside her. A shudder racked her frame as her muscles embraced him. Gritting his teeth, Brahm arched his hips, trying to shove himself deeper within her tightness. She would have none of it. She kept herself lifted just enough that he could do nothing but sit there and let her have her way with him. It was his own fault; he had told her to do it.

Eleanor's cheek brushed his temple as she slowly flexed her thighs, lifting herself until he was in danger of slipping out of her. Then, suddenly, she dropped back down, taking him so quickly he groaned aloud.

With excruciating slowness, she undulated atop him. Her hips set a maddeningly docile pace as she lifted her hands to the neckline of her gown. Her movements perfectly controlled, her fingers amazingly steady, she shoved the sleeves of her evening gown lower on her arms before tugging the neckline down and baring her pink, round, pert breasts to his gaze.

Beneath her skirts, his fingers dug into the soft flesh of her buttocks. He tried to control her movements, tried to set the rhythm of her hips. The sight of her nipples hardening under his gaze was enough to make him want to thrust inside her until they both came with abandon. Her thighs trembled with exertion, but she maintained her control of their lovemaking.

Her fingers slid around to the back of his head, tangling in his hair as she pulled him forward, silently demanding that he worship her breasts with his mouth.

"All I can think about," she whispered in a voice so throaty he ached just from hearing it, "is how it felt to have your mouth on me."

She didn't have to say any more. Leaning closer, Brahm took one nipple into his mouth and gently bit at the puckered flesh. Eleanor gasped hotly, and the satiny nub in his mouth hardened further.

"Oh!" She shoved down on him hard, her buttocks brushing the front of his thighs. "I never knew it would feel like this, that it would feel so good. It's like we were made to fit together."

Had he not thought the very thing himself?

"We were," he rasped against her skin as he moved his

mouth to her other breast. His sex pulsed within hers. "You are mine and I am yours."

His words must have had the same effect on her as hers had on him, because she ground her body down on his like a wild woman, pumping him so fiercely, with such tight, slick strokes that he thought he might expire from pleasure.

Grasping her hips, Brahm held her as she rode him. His tongue circled her nipple, flicking it with teasing strokes even though he wanted to suck it until she cried out in pleasure and pain. He wanted to make her feel as acutely as she made him feel.

Tension coiled in Eleanor's body as she moved. Her thighs trembled; her internal muscles gripped him like a vise. Her little moans rang in his ears as her buttocks flexed in his palms. His own body reveled in it, tightening in response.

Her release struck first. Her spine arched, thrusting her breast into his mouth. He sucked hard as she shuddered around him. Her head thrown back, she cried out as climax rolled over her. She soaked him with her juices, clenched at him with her sex as her body continued to move with his. Her orgasm was so incredible that it triggered his own. His breath rushed out of him in one wild gasp. He couldn't see; he couldn't think. The world ceased to exist as his release pumped out of him into her welcoming body.

Their foreheads resting together, they both gasped for breath. Neither of them made any move to separate their bodies. They held each other as their bodies cooled.

"I believe I am going to enjoy being married to you," Eleanor informed him, her breath warm against his cheek. They were still joined, still one.

Brahm chuckled as he gathered her closer. "I *know* I am going to enjoy being married to you." And then he kissed her, his heart soaring. They were simply perfect for each other. Nothing could ever tear them apart now.

Nothing.

Chapter 13

Eleanor could not wait to be married.

It wasn't just the pain in her toe—throbbing and making her want to curse in a most unladylike fashion—that made her wish that either.

Once she and Brahm were married there would be no more of this sneaking about at night, no more worries about being caught together. And no more stubbed toes or other injured extremities. It was a mistake to keep their engagement secret. They should have made the announcement already, then she would not feel like an intruder in her own house, sneaking down corridors in the dark, dead of night.

She sighed as she silently hobbled closer to his door. It was half-past two in the morning. All the guests were abed—she hoped. Only she and Brahm knew of their plans to meet, but that didn't keep her heart from pounding a little too fast. There would be so much gossip were she caught. It did not matter that this was her house and she should be able to come and go as she pleased. Even if she and Brahm announced their engagement immediately after, there would still be those who speculated and wondered if Brahm had proposed simply because he had compromised her.

Too bad she couldn't be more like Brahm and not care what people thought, but she did care, especially when those thoughts might have an adverse effect on her family.

Finally she reached his room. Soon she would be inside where no one could see them, no one would find them. And then she needn't worry about gossips or anything else until she left him again.

She did not knock—someone might hear. Instead she hastily turned the handle and slipped inside on quick, silent feet. Besides, they had planned this meeting earlier. She had the note to prove it.

A lamp burned low on the bedside table, illuminating the blue and white interior. Like all the guest rooms, this was neither too feminine nor too masculine, pleasing to both sexes, with a view that overlooked the garden and lake beyond.

However, the view from the window was the last thing on Eleanor's mind—a good thing too, as the drapes were drawn.

She turned her attention to the bed and gingerly moved toward the figure beneath the blankets. Slowly she came out of the darkness into the dim light, her gaze never leaving the bed. Was Brahm asleep?

She frowned. The body in the bed looked too small to be Brahm's.

It was too small. It was also too voluptuous. And too blond.

Eleanor froze, staring in horrified disbelief at what she saw. There was a *woman* in Brahm's bed.

Not just any woman, but Lady Dumont. Brahm was nowhere to be found, but there was Lady Dumont, obviously naked, and obviously as surprised to see Eleanor as Eleanor was to see her.

"Lady Eleanor!" Lady Dumont sat up, hugged the coverlet to her bosom, her expression so horrified, it could not be false. "What are you doing here?"

Heat swept over Eleanor, followed by cold and then followed by nothing at all. Odd how something that should have crushed her made her feel so . . . empty. "I might ask you the same question," Eleanor remarked hoarsely, "but the answer is fairly obvious."

The older woman looked far more curious than Eleanor was comfortable with. "I suppose so. The answer to why you are here, however, is not so obvious."

It was next to impossible to speak with her throat so tight. Had Lady Dumont slipped a dagger between her ribs when she wasn't looking? It would explain the sudden, sharp pain there that broke though the haze of nothing. "I needed to talk to Lord Creed."

Lady Dumont tugged the blanket up further, casting a needless glance about the dimly lit room. "He's not here."

That was fairly obvious, unless the blackguard was hiding beneath the bed. How dare he do this to her—again! "Yes, I can see that. I would wait, but the room is a little crowded. Good night." She had to get out of there before the tears came. She could hold this façade for but a few more minutes, and then she was going to completely fall apart.

Lady Dumont and Brahm. At least it wasn't Lydia in his bed. She could be happy about that, but she wasn't. How could he do this? Had he no self-control? Or had he replaced his craving for alcohol with a craving for women?

It had to be the former, because there was a bottle of wine and two half-full goblets beside the lamp.

Wine. He was drinking wine? Was this all some kind of nightmare, or had Brahm Ryland been lying to her ever since his arrival at the party? He told her he was not a rake, that he no longer drank, and yet here was evidence to the contrary.

Evidence that Eleanor did not want to believe, and no longer wanted to look at. It simply hurt far too much.

"Please tell the viscount I was here," she asked, pivoting on her heel. Yes, let the bastard know that she knew what he was up to.

But escape eluded her. She had taken only three steps when Lady Dumont said, "You are in love with him." The softly spoken accusation clung to Eleanor's skin like oil.

She turned, shoulders slumping under an invisible weight. "I beg your pardon?" Was this the part where Lady Dumont crowed about her conquest? Perhaps she would inform Eleanor why a man like Brahm would never be satisfied with one woman, especially one as provincial and plain as she.

But Lady Dumont didn't looked pleased with herself at all. In fact, Lady Dumont looked very, very sorry. "Lady Eleanor, I think perhaps I owe you an explanation."

"You owe me nothing, I assure you." How much more of this humiliation was she expected to take? This woman was in Brahm's bed—the very bed she had shared with him herself. It was a profanity against everything she had hoped for and dreamed of. When Brahm was gone, she would have the bed burned.

"It is not what you believe." Lady Dumont looked very

young sitting there, her hair about her shoulders. Eleanor could see why Brahm would find her so attractive. He was obviously partial to blonds.

Eleanor snorted. "Oh, I think it is exactly as I believe. Now do excuse me, Lady Dumont. Your lover will no doubt return soon." And she did not wish to be there when that happened, else she would not be responsible for her actions.

Lady Dumont raised up in the bed, as though she thought to give chase. She hesitated, obviously remembering her nakedness. "Please, let me explain."

No. She'd had all she could take, all she would suffer through. Eleanor left the room without acknowledging the older woman's pleas. Without thought to her own reputation, or anything else for that matter, she hiked up her skirts and ran down the corridor, all the way to the end and then over to the family wing. The pain in her stubbed toe spiked through her foot and up her leg, blessedly distracting her from the pain in her chest. She did not stop running until she reached her own room, her lungs near bursting from her exertions.

Her own room was quiet, a gold and cream sanctuary for her broken heart. She could throw herself on the bed and weep, but she was too angry for that right now. Pacing. Pacing was good. She would do that instead. Despite her sore foot, she needed to keep moving, else she just might lie down and never get back up.

Her strides were muffled by the thick beige rug as she paced. Her movements were jerky and stilted at best, as though both her legs had fallen asleep. In fact, her entire body seemed to have fallen asleep.

How could she have been so stupid to trust that man?

How could she be stupider still in wanting to find some excuse for his actions. Was he foxed?

Eleanor's lip curled. Had he mistaken Lady Dumont for her? Would that be his convenient excuse for having another woman in his bed when he was supposed to be with her?

He was supposed to be with her.

Eleanor stopped. This was just too bizarre to be true. Why would Brahm make an assignation with Lady Dumont in his room when he was supposed to meet her there? And why was Lady Dumont in his bed alone? Lady Dumont had looked so stricken to see Eleanor standing there. She said she could explain. Explain what exactly? What she was doing in Brahm's bed?

Had they been carrying on an affair since his arrival, and Lady Dumont planned a surprise visit? No. She would have heard gossip if they had been. Lady Dumont was far from discreet; she herself would have been the first to let it slip that Brahm was warming her bed—or vice versa.

No, it didn't make any sense at all. Brahm was not a stupid man. He would not have arranged an assignation with Lady Dumont when he was supposed to be with her. And knowing Eleanor as he did, he would not be foolish enough to let any other woman come to his room. He would go to his lover, not have her come to him. He knew Eleanor was just impulsive enough to sneak off to his room; after all, she had done it once before.

How could she marry Brahm when she had such doubts? She knew now that there had to be some kind of explanation for Lady Dumont being in Brahm's bed. Most likely she had gone there of her own accord, hoping to seduce him. Brahm probably didn't even know she was there.

But where was he? He was supposed to have been waiting there for her.

She didn't trust him.

No, that wasn't entirely so. As long as she held Brahm's interest, she knew he would be faithful to her. It was herself that she did not trust. She did not believe she was capable of holding his interest; she believed that he would find someone better than she. Even though she had forgiven him for that night with Lydia, she couldn't help but feel that some part of him had known it wasn't Eleanor in his bed. He had never tried to seduce her back then, and yet it had been so easy for Lydia.

If she did not trust him, it was in the fact that she did not trust his feelings for her were lasting. How unfair of her. She had faith in her own feelings, but not in his. Of course she had feelings for him, she had shared his bed, given him her innocence. Men were not the same in that regard. Hadn't Brahm himself told her that he hadn't loved Fanny Carson or his late mistress?

She wanted to be more than a companion, more than a bed partner. She wanted to be loved. She deserved no less, and neither did Brahm. And both of them deserved to be honored and treated with respect and trust.

Rushing out of his room as she had and thinking the worst proved that she obviously didn't have much respect for him either. How had Lady Dumont gotten into his room? How long had she been there?

And why? As morally lax as Lady Dumont might be, she was not the kind of woman to simply hop into a man's bed without some kind of invitation. So who had invited her? It did not make sense for Brahm to have done so and then not be there.

Unless he had wanted Eleanor to find Lady Dumont. Perhaps he was testing her—testing her trust. No, that was absurd. No one in his right mind would do something so ridiculous.

Perhaps he had changed his mind about wanting to marry her? Perhaps this was his way of breaking their engagement?

That was almost as ridiculous as her "testing" theory. There had to be a good and rational explanation for this situation. Lady Dumont had tried to offer her one, but Eleanor had been too upset to listen. Blast! Why could she not have better hidden her emotions? She had always prided herself on being able to put on the perfect serene face, but tonight that ability had deserted her. If only she had stayed, Lady Dumont would have told her what she was doing in Brahm's room.

She had so many questions that needed answers. So much of this evening did not add up in her mind. Every theory she formed seemed more far-fetched than the last. She should go back to Brahm's room. Lady Dumont had some of the answers she sought, and when Brahm returned—if he hadn't already—he would have the rest.

The challenge then would be believing anything either of them said.

She couldn't go back, she just couldn't. Even if Brahm was still absent, her reappearance in his room would do nothing more than convince Lady Dumont that she was correct in thinking Eleanor in love with him. That was the last thing Eleanor wanted at this point. To be sure, Lady Dumont had looked sincerely concerned, but Eleanor had been privy to gossip told by that woman, and she did not want to have herself talked about in the same manner— not if she could help it.

No, the only person who could tell her the truth was Brahm, although there was the very strong chance that by the time he got around to telling her, it would already be too late.

Something was not right.

Cautious in the darkness, Brahm slowly looked around at his surroundings. The cottage was musty and dusty, the furniture covered. The air was thick and warm, indicating that it had been a long time since the building had been used. His own tracks were the only ones that disturbed the dust on the floor.

This was where Eleanor wanted to meet him? Where she wanted them to spend their precious few hours alone that night? Impossible. But the directions and instructions in her note were clear. This cottage was the spot she had chosen.

At first he had thought something had detained her from making the place presentable, but now he wasn't so sure. Not having the time to tidy the cottage was one thing. Perhaps she hadn't wanted to send a servant to do it, and perhaps her duties as party hostess had interfered, but he'd been waiting for almost a half hour now, and still no Eleanor. It was unlike her to be late. However unlikely that she would find this dirty cottage romantic, it was even more unlikely that she would keep him waiting this long.

It worried him, but not to a great extent. No doubt there was a reasonable explanation for her not joining him. There might even be a note waiting in his room. There was no point in waiting here any longer. Eleanor was not coming.

Using his cane to search out obstacles before him, he slowly moved toward the exit. Had he been the man he once was, this cottage wouldn't have held any trial for him at all, but broken as he was, every unknown inch held potential danger. Of course, if he was the man he used to be he'd be passed out somewhere right now and not engaged to Eleanor.

The walk back to the house would not have been much of a trial in the daylight, but at night, with clouds covering the moon, it was much like the cottage—riddled with obstacles for a man with a cane. The path was reasonably well kept, but there were still ruts and roots to contend with. One misstep might land him in the burrow of an animal, leading to injury, a rebreak in his leg, or God forbid, a break in the other. The last thing he wanted was to try and explain what he was doing this far from the house this late at night, never mind that he'd either have to wait to be found or attempt to drag himself back to civilization.

So he picked his way along, cursing his leg and the lack of willpower that had led to its being lame in the first place. Finally he entered the garden, his footsteps crunching on the familiar gravel of the whitewashed path.

By the time he entered the house, Brahm's leg was aching around the knee. It had been a long walk to the cottage and back, plus he had remained standing the entire time he was there. He did not blame Eleanor for his discomfort, but, damn, the woman had better have a good reason for not joining him.

Making his way through the darkened house was not an easy affair either. Twice his cane snagged on an unseen piece of furniture and almost toppled both Brahm and the item that had snagged it. Neither of these close calls did anything to improve his mood or the burgeoning ache in his leg. If there wasn't a note from Eleanor awaiting him in his room, he would just have to assume she had been called away by something more pressing and get her explanation in the morning. Once he made it to his chamber, he was going to stay there.

His room was not empty.

Lady Dumont sat on his bed—his *unmade* bed—in a nightgown and wrapper, her golden blond hair spilling down her back in disarray. For many men it might have been a seductive sight—were the man anyone but Brahm and if Lady Dumont didn't look like Joan of Arc on her way to the stake.

Brahm was cautious as he closed the door. This would not look good were they caught together. He would never be able to explain this to Eleanor. She would no doubt think the worst, and how could he blame her when Lady Dumont looked as though she had just crawled out of his bed?

"Please explain why you are in my room in your night-clothes." It wasn't terribly polite, but it was the best he could manage under the circumstances. She was, after all, in his room, uninvited and scantily clad.

Lady Dumont looked at him with remorseful eyes—an expression he had never seen on her face prior to this night. "You invited me."

Brahm blinked, not just at the words but at the plaintive manner in which they were spoken. "I beg your pardon? I believe I would remember issuing such an invitation, and I assure you I do not."

She nodded. "I would have thought receiving such correspondence from you a strange thing as well, had I not been told just yesterday that you had confessed your regard for me to another."

Were this but a few years ago, he would automatically

assume he had been drunk at the time of uttering said sentiment. However, that was impossible in this case.

"My dear lady, while I believe you to be of fine character"—he was going to hell for his—"I have never had the urge nor the opportunity to confess such to anyone. I must ask you who it was that so misguided you."

Lady Dumont glanced away, clutching her wrapper tightly around her. He never would have believed her capable of such modesty. "You must think me a fool."

Why did women do that? Why did they say such things in a manner that required the man to answer? Why not simply say, "I feel like a fool" or "I am such a bloody idiot." Why bring the poor man into the equation? No matter what his answer, it wouldn't be the right one. If he said yes, then he was cruel. If he said no, then he was giving her license to behave similarly in the future.

"I believe there might be something foul afoot." That was putting it mildly in a theatrical turn of phrase. "Please, who told you I had voiced my regard?"

For a moment he thought she might not answer. "Lady Brend."

Brahm's shoulders tingled as a shudder tried to force its way down his spine. He should have known that Lydia was behind this. He wouldn't be surprised if she was the one who had sent him the note supposedly from Eleanor.

He ran a hand over his face. This went beyond the excusable as far as he was concerned. He tried to maintain some degree of belief that there was goodness in Lydia for Eleanor's sake, but now he was convinced that the woman was evil through and through. "Do you have the note I allegedly sent you on your person?"

She held out a hand—there was a crumpled sheet of paper in it. Had she abused it out of spite when he did not come as she expected? Or had she twisted it so much in anxious fingers waiting for him to come so she could explain?

Brahm took the paper and opened it. Not surprisingly, the hand that wrote this note had also written his. It was definitely a feminine hand. Had Lady Dumont not noticed that?

"I thought the script a little fancy," she remarked, as though reading his thoughts. "But your brother Wynthrope has very fine penmanship, and I thought perhaps it was a family trait."

He handed the paper back to her, ignoring her remark about Wyn. There were no clues in the note, only a few brief lines asking Lady Dumont to come to his chamber that night if she so "desired." However, the time given was the same time that had been given in the note he received.

He hoped Lydia's timing had been ill-conceived enough that only Brahm and Lady Dumont need know of this fiasco—at least until Brahm could tell Eleanor. He would not keep it from her, that would be as good as lying.

"It seems we are victims of a well-planned ruse, Lady Dumont. And for that, you have my sympathy."

She shook her head ruefully. "How humiliating."

Brahm actually did feel bad for her. "Please, do not berate yourself. I was duped as well by a similar note. We will keep it our little secret."

Something in her expression made his heart skip a beat. It *was* their little secret, was it not? "Does anyone else know of this?"

Again she looked away. She seemed to have a deuced hard time looking him in the eye. Perhaps she wasn't as innocent in this as she claimed. "That is why I waited for you."

There was that shudder again; cold insistent bastard. "Why?"

"I was in . . ." She glanced toward the bed. "Waiting for you when a visitor came to your room."

Good God, no. No, this could not be. "Who?"

"Lady Eleanor."

Hell and damnation. Lydia's timing was better than he hoped. So much better that he had to wonder if she had sent Eleanor to his room at an appointed time. Had Eleanor confided in one of her sisters? Or had Lydia somehow gotten her hands on the note he had slipped under Eleanor's door earlier confirming the time of their meeting?

What the hell did it matter now? She no doubt thought him the worst kind of cad. "When was she here?"

"No more than forty minutes ago."

While he had been cooling his heels at the filthy little cottage, Eleanor had kept their scheduled rendezvous and come to his room, only to find another woman in his bed. Wonderful. He pinched the bridge of his nose. This could not be happening. It could not.

"She loves you."

Brahm's head jerked as though Gentleman Jackson himself had landed his fist on it. He scowled, his expression as fierce as his tone. "What?"

Lady Dumont rose to her feet, an expression of envy on her lovely face. "Oh, she did not confess as such, but she did not have to. It was there in her eyes. She looked so very distraught."

His heart twisted. Of course she had. She no doubt believed him to be a lying bastard.

"I tried to explain, but she would not listen." As though adding some credence to her story, Lady Dumont pointed at the door. Did she expect the heavy oak to support her claims? "She practically ran from the room. Poor girl."

Poor girl indeed.

"I am very sorry, Lord Creed. Had I known of your relationship with Lady Eleanor, I would never have accepted the invitation, no matter how real I thought it was. I would never intentionally cause either you or Lady Eleanor such pain."

She was truly sincere in her regret, for which Brahm found himself surprisingly grateful. "Thank you."

She merely nodded and moved toward him, then past toward the door. "I will retire to my own chamber now. I know you have not asked my counsel, but were I you, I would take those notes to Lady Eleanor immediately."

That was sound advice. "I shall. Good night."

Her smile was sorrowful. "There has been little good in it thus far, my lord, but I thank you all the same."

Lady Dumont slipped from his room as quiet as a cat. No doubt she had a lot of experience tiptoeing around at house parties. He wasn't being malicious toward her, quite the opposite. He was very thankful for her skill at skulking at the moment.

He waited but a few moments—long enough for Lady Dumont to make it back to her own room—before exiting himself. The darkened corridor welcomed him once more. He traversed it as quietly as he could with a stiff leg and a cane, and picked his way down the short flight of stairs, across the landing and up the other stairs to the family wing with excruciating speed. He hadn't wanted to disturb the other guests because the gossip was sure to spread, but he did not have such qualms about the family. In fact, he would like to show these notes to Lydia's father and husband and see what they had to say about them.

But Lydia's father and husband would have to wait. Right now his main concern was Lydia's sister. What would her reaction be to the notes? Would she absolve him of any wrongdoing? Christ, he hoped so.

He rapped on her door with his knuckle, the sound more muffled than if he had used his cane. Perhaps he didn't want to confront the entire family after all.

Silence followed. No sounds issued from behind the heavy wood. Was she asleep? Or worse, was she off somewhere weeping or cursing his name? He could search for her for the remainder of the night and never find her. The only other hiding spots he could think of were the library, the parlor, and the orangery, and she would be sure to avoid those, as she would no doubt realize he would search those locations first.

He was just about to turn away and start the search when the door opened, giving him full entrance.

He entered cautiously, half suspecting an ambush to be waiting—all five Durbane sisters waiting to draw and quarter him.

Instead there was only a lonely lamp and a woman who looked at him as though her world had fallen apart.

"I thought you might come," she admitted, her voice as disheartened as her expression.

What did he do now? Did he go to her and take her in his arms as he so badly desired, or did he try to explain? Or did he shove the notes at her and let her figure it out on her own?

"I am not having an affair with Lady Dumont," he blurted as he moved toward her. "I have *never* had an affair with her."

She nodded, but the sorrowful expression did not leave her face. "I know. I am not certain what she was doing in your room . . . Well no, actually I am certain of *why* she was there, I just do not know *how* it happened that she thought she would be welcomed."

"She was tricked. I was tricked as well. That is why I was not in my room when you arrived."

She nodded, her head seemingly too heavy on her delicate neck. "I had wondered at that."

So she hadn't totally believed him a bounder then. "Is there any chance that someone could have seen the note I sent you earlier?"

Her gaze drifted slowly—painfully so—to her vanity. Following her gaze, Brahm spotted a folded piece of paper. "I suppose. My room was not locked. Lady Dumont could have been in here. I do not know."

Should he tell her now or later that it was not Lady Dumont who saw the note? "Eleanor, this whole debacle was engineered. It is nothing more than a grand error that never should have happened."

Another nod. Her lips compressed, trying to still her quivering chin. "I reasoned as much, but it did happen, and in a way I am glad it did."

His brows jumped in unison with his heart. "You are? Why?"

Her throat worked on a swallow. It took a few seconds. "Because it forced me to face a few facts that before this I had allowed myself to ignore, and for that I owe you an apology."

This conversation was not going as he had hoped. It hadn't gone the way he had feared either, but something in her tone told him this night was not going to end favorably. He wanted to be wrong about that.

Her eyes were wet as her gaze locked with his. "I am so very sorry, Brahm."

His blood turned to solid ice, seizing his heart as well as his lungs. There was so very much unspoken in that statement. "Eleanor, what are you saying?"

A single tear trickled down her cheek. "I cannot marry you."

Chapter 14

~~~~~ ◯◯ ~~~~~

She couldn't marry him? "Why the hell not?"

Eleanor flinched at his harsh tone but Brahm couldn't bring himself to regret it. She should flinch. This was the second time she had refused his proposal, and this time she was damn well going to explain herself. He was not walking away so easily this time, not when he had worked so hard to win her heart.

Perhaps he hadn't won her heart at all.

"It would be wrong for us to marry," she told him quietly. "It would be unfair to you."

Unfair to him to marry? What the devil did she think refusing him was? Fair? "I believe you owe me more of an explanation than that, Eleanor."

She drew a breath and squared her shoulders as though she was the one being attacked, being so brutally wounded. He was the one with his hopes and dreams being destroyed here. He was the one who had worked so hard to change, only to discover that apparently it was not enough.

"After finding Lady Dumont in your room—"

He didn't let her finish. "I told you I did not invite her. You said you believed me."

She nodded, her fingers twisting together over her stomach. "I did. I do."

"Then you know that was a mistake. It has nothing to do with us. It should have nothing to do with your decision to marry me." And she would marry him if he had anything to do with it. The idea of living without her now that he'd had a taste of what their life together might be like was unbearable.

A rueful sigh escaped her lips. "It has everything to do with my decision to *not* marry you, Brahm."

She knew exactly what to say to twist that knife in his chest just a little harder, dig it in just a little farther. His jaw clenched. "How?" By God, she had better make this good. He was deliberately holding back telling her about Lydia to save her further grief, and she seemed to be doing everything in her power to do the opposite to him.

"I did not trust in you. I thought you had bedded another woman. I believed you were having an affair with Lady Dumont." She looked so stricken, he was torn between wanting to go to her and comfort her and wanting to shake her for being so damnably foolish.

"Of course you did, you found her in my bed." He couldn't blame her for suspecting the worst at first. Such a surprise would catch anyone off guard and wreak havoc on her ability to think rationally. "I would have wondered the same thing were the situation reversed."

"No you would not." Tears filled her eyes, causing his heart to crack even further. It would shatter into a thousand pieces soon. "You would not doubt me at all, not because I came to you a virgin, but because you trust me."

She was right. He would be mad, but his first impulse would be to pound the bounder in her room senseless. Demanding to know what that same bounder had been doing there in the first place would be his second. "Ellie—"

Eleanor swiped at her eyes with the back of one hand, the other held up to silence him. "I even wondered if you might have been drunk. I almost wanted you to be drunk, then I could forgive you for Lady Dumont like I forgave you for Lydia."

Brahm stared at her. Good Lord.

"I'm not certain I have forgiven you for Lydia, Brahm." She sniffed, obviously fighting more tears, but she held his gaze regardless, her eyes glistening in the lamplight. "Perhaps that is why I was so quick to jump to conclusions."

"But you realized they were just that, conclusions." How quickly the words spilled out of his mouth, as if getting them out faster was going to help him keep her. He couldn't tell her the truth about Lydia now—not at this moment—she wouldn't believe it. Would she?

She raised her chin. "And if it happens again, how long will it take me to realize?"

He couldn't help but chuckle at the absurdity of that question. "You are not likely to ever find a woman in our bed." Damn unlikely.

"Perhaps not, but when you go to your clubs and do not come home when I expect you to, will I wonder if you are with another woman? Will I wonder if you are drunk?"

A bitter taste filled his mouth. He couldn't fight this. He should have known it would not be this easy to atone for his past. It was coming back to taunt him once again. "I do not know. Will you?"

Eleanor shook her head. "I would love to say no, but I

think I would, yes. I think I would be very afraid that you had found some diversion to keep you from me."

"You do not trust me." Or she didn't trust herself. It hardly mattered. She didn't trust in the two of them, and there was nothing he could do to repair that. It was something she had to do on her own.

"I do not." She was uncertain, he could see it in her eyes. What was she hiding from him? "You deserve to be trusted, Brahm. You deserve someone who will not doubt you."

He took advantage of her reluctance. "You did not doubt me, not really."

"I did." She did not sound totally convinced, but she was working on it. "And I will again."

"You cannot be certain." Perhaps if he kept insisting, she would finally agree with him. She would forget this nonsense and give them a chance.

"You cannot spend the rest of your life trying to prove yourself worthy to me."

It was time for a new tactic. Time to remind her what this was all about, why they were having this discussion in the first place—not because she didn't trust him, but because someone had conspired against them. "Eleanor, you are missing the real crime in this. Neither you nor I is to blame."

"Then who is?"

He drew a breath. It was time. He had promised her honesty, and he would keep his promise, even if it was likely to hurt her even more. "Lady Dumont and I both received notes written by the same person. A woman. I suspect it was Lydia."

"Lydia!" Her face was totally white save for two red splotches on her cheeks. "Oh, Brahm, no!"

Of course she didn't want to think so low of her sister.

"Eleanor, Lydia was very angry with me for proposing to you. She was jealous. She also told Lady Dumont that I had been overheard expressing feelings for her. This whole debacle reeks of her interference."

"No. I refuse to think that my own sister would do such a thing. Someone else wrote the notes."

He offered both letters to her. "Will you not look for yourself."

She stared at the papers in his hand as though they were writhing snakes. "I will not. There is no need. It will not change anything."

She was afraid. She had this whole thing worked out in her bizarre little mind and couldn't bear to think that her own sister might have conspired against her. She would rather think ill of herself, blame herself rather than Lydia.

"It will change everything, Eleanor. It is not me or yourself you should mistrust, but your sister."

"I will not have you make such accusations against her, Brahm. I know she has done some rather regretful things in the past, but Lydia would never do something so devious, not after learning that we were betrothed."

So if Lydia had done this before their announcement to the family, it would have been excusable?

"Did you do this the night you found her and me together?" The question tumbled out before he could stop it. "Did you find a way to blame yourself rather than the drunk and the whore who caused you so much pain?"

She recoiled as though he had spit on her. "You will not talk of my sister in such a vulgar manner."

This was where she and he were different. Brahm would defend his brothers to the end of the earth, but he was at least able to recognize their faults.

"Forgive me." He wouldn't take the words back because he believed them, but he didn't wish to cause Eleanor pain. "You must admit, however, that all roads lead to her in this matter."

"The only thing I must realize is that you seem to want me to distrust my sister, when I see no reason. *She* was not the woman in your room."

Her jealousy was showing, as was her loyalty to her sister. She had been willing enough to believe that Lydia might have lied about his "seduction" of her years ago, but not that she might have been involved in this latest farce. Why? "Only because she knew even you would not be gullible enough to believe she and I fell into bed a second time."

She blanched. "I beg your pardon?"

Brahm winced. "Gullible" had not been a good choice. "Eleanor, she knew exactly how you would react."

She shook her head, denying until the end. "Lydia would never do this to me. Never."

Obviously there would be no persuading her. She refused to see the truth. He could strangle Lydia at that moment. How he was going to spend the rest of his life with that vicious harpy as his sister-in-law was a question he did not have the answer to.

But he wouldn't be spending the rest of his life with her as his sister-in-law—not unless Eleanor changed her mind and carried through with their engagement.

"Will you look at these letters?" He offered them once more. "You would know your sister's hand."

Her chin came up stubbornly. "No. I do not have to look to know my sister did not write those notes. I do not know who did, but does it really matter now?"

Brahm's patience was at an end. "Hell yes, it matters! Someone has deliberately tried to set us apart from one another—and it appears as though they have succeeded."

Shaking her head, Eleanor sank wearily onto the trunk at the foot of her bed. "It does not matter who is to blame for the instigation of this, Brahm. What matters is that it has made me realize some things about myself. I do not like feeling this way. I do not like knowing that I can be so small and petty, but it is there and I cannot ask you to live your life with a woman who will question everything you do."

"You will not question *everything*. And your insecurity will fade with time."

"Or it will get worse and drive us apart."

"That is a possibility," he conceded. "But it is a remote one. Eleanor, you only need to trust in us."

She wanted to believe him; he could see it in the tortured depths of her wide blue eyes. He could also see the determination there.

"But I do not trust in us, Brahm." Her voice was so hoarse and low he would not have recognized it as hers were he not standing before her, hearing it with his own ears. "You said yourself that I distrust you, and a part of me thinks you are right. But I also distrust myself. You do not deserve to be doubted by your wife."

She was right, he did not deserve that. "What about what you deserve?"

Her smile was sad. "I deserve to marry a man I do not doubt."

There it was, the final crack. In his chest, Brahm's heart fell away in shards that cut him from the inside out.

"You are right," he murmured. He could not argue with her on that point. She did deserve a man she didn't doubt, and as much as it was killing him to admit it, he knew he was not that man. He might never be that man. It didn't matter that he was mad about her, or even if she was equally as mad for him. Christ, it wouldn't even matter if they were in love. It wasn't going to work between them, not like this. And Brahm had no idea how to fix *this*.

"Promise me something." He made it an order, not a request.

She jerked her head in a semblance of a nod. "Of course you will know if I change my mind."

"Thank you." That was good to hear, but it wasn't something he expected to happen. "That is not what I want you to promise me, however."

She looked surprised. Did her pride sting a little? Did she hope he would try a little harder, just once more to change her mind? He wasn't going to do it. He had his pride as well, and it was almost completely shredded to ribbons at the moment. It was all he could do not to let it dissolve completely and fling himself to his knees, begging for her to marry him.

"Promise me that if there is a child you will come to me."

If at all possible, she blanched even whiter. "I will."

He didn't need to add that she would have no other choice but to marry him in the event of a child. His heir would not be a bastard. He had seen what that kind of stigma had done to his brother North. He would raise his child and Eleanor could doubt him all she wanted, but she would be his wife regardless.

Satisfied with her promise, Brahm gave a stiff bow. "I will leave immediately."

Her mouth opened, her eyes widening as well. "You do not have to leave—"

He laughed then—bitterly, loudly, not caring if anyone heard. "Oh yes, I do. I cannot remain under this roof seeing you every day and know that you have refused me—

again. Do not ask it of me Eleanor, for I will not torture myself, not even for you."

She bit her bottom lip as tears brimmed on her bottom lashes. "I am sorry."

He nodded, his own throat tightening with repressed emotion. "I am sorry too." He tossed the crumpled letters on the vanity and left her then, without taking his leave. He didn't care if it was rude. He was walking away from the only woman he had ever wanted totally and completely in his life. He had allowed her to reject him. He didn't mind saying he was sorry, because he was very, very sorry.

He'd be damned if he'd say good-bye.

He left at dawn. Eleanor watched from her window as his carriage was brought 'round and his belongings loaded on. Men were so fortunate that they didn't have to pack gowns and corsets and stockings and beauty aids. All they had were their clothes and a few toiletries.

That she was thinking of toiletries when her life was in ruins did not surprise her. She was numb from head to toe, inside and out. What else was there to think about? She was an old maid once more.

No, not a maid, though no one but she and Brahm would ever know that.

How could she stand there watching and not feel anything? She had given him her body, had offered him her heart but obviously not her trust—the very thing she should have offered first. She'd done everything backward, acting on impulse rather than rational thought. She thought she had forgiven him. Bah. She'd lied to herself as surely as she had lied to him. Forgiveness. What did she know of that?

The man had come to her trying to prove that he had changed, and she wanted to believe it so badly she talked herself into it, but she hadn't believed it, had she?

What did it matter that she realized the truth later? She could not spend the rest of her life doubting him. It would destroy their relationship, their friendship, their marriage. He deserved someone who wouldn't look at every woman as a potential threat. Someone who didn't think so little of herself that she automatically thought lowly of everyone else as well.

A soft rap fell upon her door. "Who is it?" She didn't bother to look away from the window.

"Arabella." The door opened, finally drawing Eleanor's attention. She met her sister's worried gaze. "Dearest, are you all right?"

Obviously Arabella knew Brahm was leaving, and now, looking at Eleanor, she would know that Eleanor was the reason. Of course she would want to talk. But Eleanor didn't want to talk—not now.

"I'm fine, Belle. I just need to be alone."

She'd hurt Arabella with her rejection, that was obvious, but Eleanor couldn't bring herself to feel badly about it. She would have, if she had been capable of feeling, but there was nothing in her heart.

"Later, dear," she added as a concession, knowing full well that she would desperately need her sister when the ability to feel returned.

Arabella nodded. She was obviously not pleased, but did not push.

When she was gone, Eleanor turned back to her window. A man in a greatcoat and hat left the house. It was Brahm. Even if she hadn't caught a glimpse of his cane she would have known it was he. Despite the watery light of an overcast dawn, she knew him. She would recognize him from any distance until the day she died, of that she was certain.

A footman opened the door to his carriage and held it for him. Doffing his hat, Brahm made to enter. He paused on the step and turned, looking over his shoulder and up.

Their gazes locked. She stared at him helplessly. He was leaving. She did not want him to leave. She opened her mouth to call out, to say something—anything that would keep him with her.

He turned away, but not before she saw the coldness in his eyes. He climbed inside the carriage, the door shutting after him. A few moments later the horses were spurred into motion and the coach rolled down the drive.

It seemed her heart went with it.

Was he thinking of her as the distance between them slowly grew? Did he despise her now? No, not yet. Right now he was disappointed and hurt, but he still cared for her. It would take a while—not too long, a few weeks perhaps—and then he would start to resent her. His regard for her would fade long before hers did for him. She would go back to living her sheltered, quiet life and he would go back to town where so many diversions would keep him from dwelling on thoughts of her.

She would have nothing to think of but him. Not unless she accepted the suit of one of the bachelors still slumbering in the north wing. The thought of marrying anyone but Brahm caused every part of her to rebel, but she would not be marrying Brahm. She would never marry Brahm. No matter what happened in the future, he would never renew his address, he would be a fool to propose to her three times in his life. If she were Brahm, she would never speak to her again.

Yes, her only chance at happiness now, her only chance

at any kind of life, was to marry someone else and hope for the best.

At least by marrying one of these bachelors she had no hopes, no expectations. She would not care if he drank or if he took lovers. No doubt the less time they spent together, the happier she would be. She would end up like Phoebe or Muriel, or poor Lydia.

Poor Lydia. Her gaze drifted from the window, and the spot in the drive where Brahm's carriage had stood, to the wrinkled paper on her vanity. The letters Brahm had left her, the ones he claimed were written by Lydia. He had no proof, only his own suspicions. Eleanor could prove her sister's innocence simply by looking at the handwriting.

The handwriting might also prove Lydia guilty.

Eleanor turned back to the window. She caught another glimpse of the carriage as it continued down the very long lane that connected the estate to the main road.

She did not want to believe Lydia would hurt her so. She did not believe Lydia would hurt her so. There was no "want" about it. Lydia was her sister. They had suffered through their mother's death together. They had played together, leaned on each other. They would do anything for each other. They would never hurt each other, not intentionally.

No, Brahm was mistaken. He was wrong. Someone else had sent the notes. Perhaps even Lady Dumont herself had fabricated them, or Lady Merrott. Maybe one of the gentlemen had thought to play a joke—not that it was very amusing.

It did not matter who sent the notes. The notes did not matter. All that mattered was she had hurt Brahm and lied to herself. Realizing that she doubted him, that she doubted herself, was crushing, but at least she had realized it before it had a chance to ruin their marriage. Living without him would be hell, but living with him and slowly earning his disdain would be even worse.

Dear God in heaven, please let there be no child. She would keep her promise to him if there was, but it would be so awful to marry for that reason, to have the poor child grow up in a house where there was no love. Brahm, she knew, had been raised in an environment much like that. Surely he would not wish the same for his child.

There could have been love between them. In fact, Eleanor suspected it might have been there already, but love soured quickly with no trust behind it. Better that she regretted Brahm for the rest of her life than grow to hate him. She had harbored enough contemptuous feelings for him in the past. It was time to accept the blame herself.

There was another knock at her door. Eleanor glanced toward it. God love her sister. "I am tired, Arabella."

"It is Lady Dumont," came the muffled voice from the other side.

A great thud echoed inside Eleanor's ribs. Lady Dumont?

It was tempting to tell her to go away as she had Arabella, but she truly wanted to hear whatever it was the other woman had to say. It obviously wouldn't do any good where her relationship with Brahm was concerned, but still, she wanted to listen.

"Come in."

The door opened and Lady Dumont entered, as timid as a chambermaid. Her gaze was downcast, flickering every so often to Eleanor's and then away again.

The older woman was dressed in a fashionable morning gown of green sarcenet, her hair artfully arranged. She looked tired, however, as though she had not slept. No doubt her maid hadn't either, not if the lady looked this well turned out at such an ungodly hour.

Eleanor herself was still in her nightgown, her hair spilling down her back in a wild tangle. She hadn't slept much either.

"Good morning, Lady Dumont. To what do I owe this pleasure?" As if she didn't know. As if Lady Dumont didn't know.

Her gaze was met and held. "I came in hopes of explaining what you would not allow me to explain last night."

"There is nothing to explain."

"I beg your pardon Lady Eleanor, but given Lord Creed's hasty departure this morning, I believe there is."

Eleanor arched a brow. Unable to argue with that logic, she waited silently for Lady Dumont to do her explaining.

"Lord Creed and I have not been conducting any sort of affair."

"I am aware of that."

Lady Dumont seemed surprised, but she continued. "I went to his room last night because I was led to believe he wished it. I was told that he had expressed interest in me and then I received an invitation to his chamber, which I believed to have been written by him."

Eleanor's gaze jumped to the notes on her vanity and then back again. "He maintains that it was not."

"No." Lady Dumont flushed a little. "He told me my note had been written by the same person who wrote the note inviting him to a cottage on the estate." The tone of her voice and the expression on her face told Eleanor exactly who Lady Dumont believed Brahm thought the note was from. Eleanor was so dead inside, she couldn't even blush in embarrassment.

"Obviously I did not write the notes, Lady Dumont."

"No. Your shock at seeing me in his bed was proof of that. I believe the person who wrote the notes might very well be the same person who told me that Lord Creed was supposedly interested in bettering our acquaintance."

What a polite way of saying that she believed Brahm had wanted to bed her. "Might I ask just who this person was?" Even though it would serve no benefit now, she still wanted to know who had taken such pains to help her ruin her future.

Lady Dumont grew even more uncomfortable. "It was your sister Lydia."

Eleanor closed her eyes. She could finally feel once more, and oh it hurt! Brahm was right.

Or had he put Lady Dumont up to spinning lies about her sister?

No, even Eleanor knew when it was time to stop pretending. Lydia was not the innocent victim Eleanor wanted her to be. She might have been such at one time, but not anymore.

"Thank you for your candor, Lady Dumont. I trust I have your confidence in this matter?"

Lady Dumont nodded her acquiescence. "He cares about you very much. I hope this unfortunate incident does not keep the two of you from finding happiness together."

Eleanor might have laughed at that if she weren't trying so hard to keep from losing her mind. "Thank you."

Once Lady Dumont took her leave and she was alone again, Eleanor crossed to her vanity and picked up the crumpled papers there. Smoothing them open, she read the elegant script. The first one was to Brahm, asking him to meet in the gardener's cottage on the estate at two. It was signed with her name, but the handwriting wasn't hers.

Brahm was right that the penmanship on the notes matched. The second was a simple request for Lady Dumont's company in Brahm's chamber—at two. A coincidence that the time and handwriting were the same on both? Not a chance. A mistake that the writing looked so much like Lydia's? Even less of a chance.

Her sister had conspired against her, plotted to hurt not only her, but Brahm and Lady Dumont as well. Why? What was the purpose of such deceit? To keep Eleanor and Brahm from marrying?

She rang the bell for the housekeeper. When the woman arrived a few minutes later, Eleanor asked her to relay a message to Lydia that Eleanor wished to see her immediately. Eleanor then rang for her own maid and a cup of coffee. She wanted to be alert and ready when her confrontation with Lydia took place.

And take place it did, within the hour.

Lydia swept into the room, a fashionable, lavender-scented vision in lemon muslin. "Eleanor, dearest, you look awful! I heard about that awful Lord Creed deserting you. Are you quite all right?" She made as though to embrace her, but Eleanor took a step backward.

Her sister froze, bewilderment lighting her features—it was as false as everything else about Lydia. "Dearest, whatever is the matter?"

Eleanor offered her the notes. "You wrote these. Why? Why did you try so hard to make it look as though Brahm was being untrue?"

Lydia didn't try to deny it. She cast a quick glance at the letters and shrugged. "He would have been untrue eventually."

Frowning, Eleanor shook her head. "What the devil kind of logic is that?"

Her sister's demeanor turned haughty, and defensive, as though she was the one who had been wronged. "I did you a great service, Eleanor."

Eleanor gaped at her sister. "A service? By sending another woman to his bed to trick me? How was that a service?"

"My actions forced you to realize that you do not trust Brahm." Lydia practically crowed the words.

She was right, of course, in a twisted way. "It was not your place to do so."

"I did it for you."

"You did it because you cannot stand the fact that I was going to marry him. Was it because you wanted him for yourself or because you want everyone else to be as miserable as you are?"

An expression of deep hurt crossed Lydia's face. "I cannot believe you would ask me such awful questions. I sent those notes because I love you. I could not allow my own sister to marry a man she would never be able to trust, who would never love her as she deserved."

That last remark struck a little too close to home. "What of Lady Dumont, what did she deserve?"

Lydia dismissed the question with the wave of her hand. "Lady Dumont will be fine. You were my main concern. I had been trying to think of a way to make you see the truth."

"You will forgive me if I find that difficult to thank you for."

Lydia, it seemed, did not like her lack of appreciation. "If you had married Creed you would have eventually grown to despise him for your lack of trust. Yes, I did you a service. I wish someone had done the same for me before I married."

At one time Eleanor would have felt sorry for her sister, but all she felt now was revulsion—at Lydia for being so malicious, and at herself for being so stupid and weak.

"I wish someone had warned me of you, Lydia. But make no mistake, I will not make the error of trusting *you* ever again. Please leave my room."

"He called me by your name that night." If Lydia had dropped a bag of rocks on her head it wouldn't have surprised—or hurt—any more than her words.

Eleanor trembled with barely restrained anger. Lydia sounded so self-satisfied, as though she was the victor in a game. Perhaps she was; she had made Eleanor doubt Brahm, had made her reject him once again. This time, for good.

"Get. Out."

To her surprise, Lydia complied instantly, as though she had no idea just how angry Eleanor was with her, or perhaps she simply didn't care how upset Eleanor was.

"You will thank me for this one day," she predicted with a smug glance as she opened the door. "You know it as well as I. Marriage to Brahm Ryland would have made you miserable."

Eleanor did not reply. She simply stood there, her arms tight across her chest as her sister made her grand exit. Marriage to Brahm might very well have made her miserable, but she wasn't about to admit that to Lydia. And she'd be damned if she thanked her for it.

Nor was she about to admit to anyone but herself that marriage to Brahm might just have easily made her the happiest woman on earth. It didn't matter what marriage to Brahm might have made her.

She was never going to find out.

Chapter 15

London held none of the pleasure it once did. The city was dark and gray upon his return, the weather damp and chill, much like the feeling in his heart.

Brahm ordered his driver to take him to his club on St. James and told the driver not to wait. He would find his own way home.

His leg was stiff and uncooperative as he climbed the few steps to the club entrance. A doorman greeted him. "Good day, Lord Creed. May I take your coat and hat?"

Brahm removed his outerwear and passed the clothing to the man with a mumbled thanks. Inside, the club was warm and inviting, the air scented with beefsteak and cigars. Chatter, incoherent but lively, filled the main room. The club was not full, but many tables were taken by gentlemen drinking and talking. Some dined on beef, some drank coffee. In another room there would be games of chance and wages made in a betting book.

Yes, this was a good place for him to wallow in his self-pity.

And pity himself he did. When he didn't pity himself he was angry—angry at himself, at Eleanor, at Lydia, at anyone he could possibly think of who might be connected in any way, no matter how remote, to this debacle.

How could he have been so stupid as to think that he could make her believe he had changed? How could he have believed it had been so easy to win her? He hadn't won her. His claim had been tenuous at best.

All that rubbish she had spouted. He deserved better, what a load of horse shite. How could she say that and then claim she couldn't trust that he had changed? It was contradiction at its finest. If he hadn't changed, then he wouldn't have deserved less than her, let alone better. The man he had been hadn't deserved much more than a kick in the arse.

The most pathetic part was that he had actually started to believe that he did deserve her, that he was worthy of her and all her goodness and fucking propriety. Propriety. That was a laugh. She had been the one to come to his bed, not the other way around. She had wanted him and taken what she wanted from him. She had used him and then stomped on the heart so freely offered to her. She had treated him in a manner that no one else ever had. He knew men who had treated women in such a fashion, but he had never been guilty of such a crime himself—not even when horribly drunk. Lydia had been the only mistake he'd ever made. He was glad that he had generally been above such behavior now that he knew what a debasing thing it was to have happen.

Damn her, even after the hurt she had done, after the insult she had leveled upon him, he wanted her still. His heart ached from his loss. For a brief time she had made him think that life might have more to offer him, that there was lightness and good in his future. She had made him believe that he could be a better man, and that others might see it.

For one short, blissfully tragic moment, he had cared what someone else thought of him, and it rent him to the bone.

At least here he might find some kind of diversion from the pain.

He approached a table of gentlemen, one of whom he recognized as Lord Mitchley, an old friend of his father's. It would be rude not to stop and say hello, even though he didn't feel much like talking.

Lord Mitchley's eyes were slightly unfocused and his cheeks a tad too ruddy, but his smile was genuine as he looked up at Brahm. "Good day to you, Creed. Care to join us for a brandy?"

He didn't even think. "Don't mind if I do."

The men exchanged startled glances, but no one raised an objection as he slid into the only vacant chair at the table. A snifter of brandy was placed in front of him, so extremely innocent and tempting.

Brahm stared at it for a moment. He shouldn't do this. He knew it was wrong, but what damn difference did it make? Everyone expected him to give in and go back to his old ways eventually. No one believed he had actually changed. Eleanor didn't believe. His own brothers didn't even believe. Had not Wyn expressed his doubts before Brahm left for Burrough's estate? Perhaps he hadn't come right out and said it, but it had been obvious that his brother suspected the trip would not go well.

Did Brahm care what the gossips might say? Yes and no. He didn't care what they thought of him, but he definitely cared about not being given a chance. What was the point in trying if no one was willing to give him the chance to try?

Eleanor had promised him a chance and then taken it away.

The snifter was familiar and comforting in his hand. He lifted it to his lips and opened his mouth against the rim. Brandy rushed over his tongue, flooding him with flavor so rich, he shivered as it rushed down his throat.

Sweet God, it was good!

He drank deeper, draining the snifter. His companions chuckled as he lowered his arm. It was an appreciative sound, not a malicious one.

"You drink like a man who has something he wants to forget," one of the gentlemen commented.

Brahm nodded as his snifter was refilled. "I do."

"Then let us aid you in your quest," Lord Mitchley boomed. He raised his own brandy, and the others followed suit. "To forgetting."

Brahm drank as well. Yes, to forgetting. It seemed to be working. He had already forgotten that he no longer drank.

During the week after Brahm's departure, Eleanor did everything she could to make herself forget him, to get on with her life, but to no avail.

She threw herself into her remaining duties as hostess. The party would be over soon—by the end of next week most, if not all, of the guests would be gone. By that time she was expected to have found herself a husband. No one had ever voiced this expectation, but that had been the whole point to this party, and people assumed it would happen.

No one outside her family—not even Lady Dumont, who knew more than Eleanor was comfortable with— knew that Eleanor had already found the man she wanted to marry, and that she had lost him as well.

So she tried to find something to love in each of the remaining bachelors. Lord Locke had absolutely nothing to recommend him, and so he wasn't a consideration at all. Lord Birch was much more likable, but he didn't stir her interest either. Lord Faulkner was too short, Lord Taylor talked too much, and Lord Eakes didn't talk enough. Minor, petty grievances to be sure, but they were there all the same.

None of these men, however rich or handsome he might be, came close to making her feel as Brahm did. Brahm made her laugh. Brahm knew when to speak and when not to. Brahm had never treated her like a delicate or irrational creature, even though she had no doubt given him reason to. He had never treated her as though she was somehow less than him, or as though he would be doing her a favor by marrying her. And even though she knew he had come there with the intention of atoning for their past and then wooing her, she never once felt as though he saw her merely as a prize to be won.

He was everything she wanted, and she had pushed him away. At the time it had seemed the right course of action, but now she'd be deuced if she could remember why.

Oh yes, she couldn't trust him. Or rather she couldn't trust in herself enough to trust in him, some such rubbish. Why couldn't she? It was an answer she'd never thought to look for when her emotions ran away with her and made her refuse him. Now she thought about it all the time. Why couldn't she trust in them? It was a relatively simple thing to do, was it not? So why did it fill her with terror? Why, after being so certain that he was what she wanted, had she turned him away?

"What are you thinking?"

Eleanor raised her head. She and Arabella were in her room, sitting on the bed in their nightgowns. It was late, very late, but Arabella had made a habit this past week of coming to check on her older sister every night before going to bed. In truth, Eleanor looked forward to her visits and had come to look at them as the only thing keeping her sane.

"I am trying to determine whom I should marry."

Arabella made a great show of twisting the end of her thick braid, her gaze flitting everywhere but to Eleanor's own. "You have already made that decision."

Eleanor's throat tightened. Her sister hadn't even said his name and her heart was pounding like the hooves of a runaway horse. "We have already discussed this, Belle. You know I cannot marry him, and even if I did change my mind, he would not have me now." The realization hurt more than she would admit, for it forced her to consider just what an enormous mistake she might have made.

Brahm might have harbored great feelings for her, but he was a proud man, and no man would give a woman who had rejected him twice a third chance. It did not matter that she'd had good reason the first time, she had handled that situation almost as badly as she had handled the current one.

A gusty sigh escaped her sister's lips. "I know you claim to have some idiotic reason for not being able to marry him, but I still do not understand why you cannot."

Not this again! Eleanor threw her hands up in the air. It was either that or tear her hair out. "Because I doubted him! I believed he betrayed me. I can never trust him."

Arabella rolled her pale eyes. "Oh for pity's sake, Eleanor! I doubt Henry at times!"

"You do?" This was a new addition to the conversation. Actually, they usually never made it this far. Arabella would try to talk to her about things and Eleanor would tell her she didn't want to discuss them. Apparently she had changed her mind. It seemed she was making a habit of that.

Her sister made a face that said, *Do not be so foolish.* "Of course I do. It is only human to doubt. I worry that when I'm fat with child he'll find someone prettier or more mild-mannered than I." Arabella's hands settled on the gentle swell of her belly. Eleanor hadn't noticed just how much her sister was beginning to show signs of her pregnancy. "He tells me that I am silly and I tend to believe him, but every once in a while I am struck by the same fears."

Arabella was unsure of her marriage? How could that be possible? She and Henry seemed so perfectly . . . *perfect* for each other. "How do you cope?"

"Because, my dear idiot sister, they have the same fears!" Arabella chuckled as though the answer should have been obvious.

It was not so obvious to Eleanor. "Who?"

"Men, of course!" Arabella's fingers still stroked her own stomach. "They worry that their wives might find a younger lover, that their hair will fall out and they will grow fat. They worry about us falling out of love with them just as we do about them. All you can do is trust in one another."

Had her sister not been listening to her when she did talk about her and Brahm? "But I do not trust in Brahm, that is the problem."

"No," Arabella insisted with a knowing smile. Just which one of them was the elder sister? Wasn't Eleanor supposed to be the one who had all the answers? "You trust in Brahm. You would never have given him a chance to prove himself if you did not."

Eleanor lowered her gaze. "I thought I had given him a chance, but I know now that I did not."

Her sister made a *hmpf* sound. "How long did it take you to realize you were being irrational?"

Eleanor shrugged, her own fingers toying with the lace on the edge of her sleeves. "A few moments, maybe less. As soon as the shock wore off I began to think more clearly."

"There, see?" The other woman's smile was bright with confidence. "Anyone would have been shocked by what you saw. If I found a woman in Henry's bed, I would want to know what the hell she was doing there. Of course, we share a bed, so that would truly be a strange occurrence."

Eleanor couldn't even summon a grin at her sister's cursing, despite how strange it sounded coming out of Arabella's mouth. Instead she sank deeper into the well of despair and self-loathing she had fashioned for herself. "I should not have doubted him."

"Poppycock." Arabella lightly slapped Eleanor on the leg as though to chastise her for such thoughts. "You do not doubt him, you doubt yourself, and now you are punishing him because you are afraid to leave the safety of Papa's house and finally have a life of your own."

"I am not!" Was she? Was that why she had reacted as she had? Out of fear? It had occurred to her that while

Brahm found it so easy to dismiss what others thought of him, she did not. Did part of her worry that society might think her a fool for giving him another chance when he had so wonderfully alienated himself from most good *ton*?

No, she refused to think that she could be so shallow. Foolish she might be, but she was not a snob.

Arabella shot her a knowing glance. "You are so afraid. You've spent the entirety of your life making certain your sisters were well looked after, and during that time you built a nice little cocoon for yourself. Tell me, what is the worst that could happen if you marry Brahm?"

God, she didn't want to think of the worst thing. He could die. No, that would be awful, but it wouldn't be the worst. "He could find someone else to replace me." Yes, that was the absolute worst thing that could happen, especially if Eleanor continued to love him after his feelings for her had died.

Did that mean she loved him now? Arabella prevented her from pondering the question. "So could you."

A vehement shake of her head answered that question. "No, never." She knew herself well enough to know that when she loved, it would be forever.

"You do not know that any more than you know he might do the same to you." Arabella's words were so calm and logical, Eleanor had no choice but to consider them despite her own resistance. "Why are you not worried about you betraying him then?"

"Because I would never do such a thing!" How could she even ask? Did her sister honestly think so little of her? She would never be so disrespectful to her husband, no matter how awful their marriage became.

Arabella fiddled with her braid again, one hand still on

her stomach. "You know, Lydia said the same thing to me once."

Eleanor froze, an odd icy heat prickling her flesh. "I beg your pardon?"

Arabella shrugged, as though she had said nothing of import, rather than something that stopped Eleanor's heart. "Lydia once told me that she would never betray her marriage vows."

Anger took root in her chest. How dare Arabella make such a comparison. She knew that Lydia had been involved. Eleanor had not kept that from her. That first day after Brahm left and she had talked to Lady Dumont, Eleanor had been too vacant from herself to know better than to confide everything to the sister closest to her. "I am nothing like Lydia."

"No, you are not." At least Arabella wasn't going to argue it. Eleanor might have had to kill her if she did. "And Brahm is nothing like the man he was ten years ago. Who knows what either of you will be like in another ten years, but are you willing to throw away the chance of a good and happy life just because you are afraid?"

"I—" She had no answer. No words would come. Arabella was right. Was she willing to do that? Which would be better, a few short years of happiness with Brahm or a lifetime of nothing but the same thing she'd been living for the last ten? Or worse, marriage to another man whom she would always compare to Brahm, knowing that he would never measure up?

The answer came to her with such clarity, she wondered why it had taken her this long to realize it.

It was time to stop living her life like a hermit. She had finally been given a chance to have a wonderful, eventful life. She could be a wife, a mother. She could be her own woman and do all the things allowed to a married lady. She could go out in society and make friends—London had always held an appeal for her.

And she could spend her nights in Brahm's arms, spend her days getting to know everything about him, growing old with him.

Yes, there was a chance it would not work between them, but there were hard times in every relationship; hadn't her father and Arabella both told her that? There was an even better chance that she and Brahm could have a beautiful life. If their mutual fascination with each other hadn't faded after ten years apart and an eternity of bad feelings, surely it could only grow with the proper care and nurturing?

Her father had also told her to stop being afraid of what might happen and enjoy what she had. She and Brahm might make a mess of things, but they might make a beautiful life together. She would never know unless she took the chance and followed her heart.

She shot Arabella a hopeful gaze. "Do you think he might return if I asked him to?"

Her sister's expression changed then, taking on an edge of anxiety and uncertainty that caused Eleanor's heart to give a painful leap. Arabella knew something that she didn't.

"I think it would be best for you to go to London, dearest. The sooner the better."

Eleanor pressed a hand to her chest. Dear heaven, had something happened to Brahm? Please God, no. "What do you know?"

Arabella shifted uncomfortably. "There have been reports from London—"

"Gossip, you mean." It was impossible to keep the sneer from her voice.

"Perhaps. There is talk that he has been seen at several clubs and parties about town."

With another woman? "And?"

Arabella drew a deep breath and pursed her lips. "He was foxed."

Oh. Did she laugh in relief or cry in despair? Brahm was drinking again. Because of her? She didn't doubt for a minute that she was the cause. Her rejection no doubt made him think there was no point in trying to prove that he was a changed man.

Or perhaps he missed her so much, it was the only way he could numb his pain. Yes, she preferred that reason. But she would much rather hear that he was sober and melancholy than drunk on her account.

There was only one thing to do. He was miserable. She was miserable, and there was no need of it. It was foolishness that kept them apart, and she was tired of being foolish.

She jumped to her feet. "Help me pack, Belle. I will leave in the morning."

Her sister offered no argument, but also rose to her feet and went straight for the chest of drawers where Eleanor kept her stockings and shifts. "What are you going to do when you get there?"

What was she going to do? Keep her promise to look after him, to help him heal? She didn't know, but she had to go. Her heart would not allow her to stay away and be this ungodly miserable any longer. If she had a chance to be happy with Brahm, then she owed it to the both of them to fight for it.

Pulling her trunk from the wardrobe, Eleanor set her

jaw determinedly. "I am going to find out if he is the man I believe he is. The man he told me he could be."

The man she was very much afraid she had lost for good.

His eyes were burning, rough and dry as a desert. His throat was parched, his tongue was thick, and his head was splitting. Worst of all, he was sobering up.

Brahm's stomach churned as he shifted on the bed. He kept his eyes shut against the motion of the mattress. The room was not turning, it was just his head. He knew this, still, it felt as though he were spinning in circles.

He moved his feet, at least they still worked. He hadn't broken his other leg in a drunken stupor.

He was still wearing his boots. Ah, he was wearing trousers and a shirt as well. He had obviously managed to shuck his waistcoat and cravat before passing out. Was that smell him? Christ, he needed a drink before he came completely to his senses.

His eyes closed, he groped for the bottle beside his bed. He knew it was there because that was where he always put it.

His hand met nothing but air. He groped some more. There was nothing but carpet beneath his hand—no bottles to be found.

Damnation. He was going to have to go get one. He'd ring for a servant and have him bring him one, yes, that was the answer. Better that than the alternative, which was sobriety. It might have been a long time since he felt this utterly rotten, but it would be a longer time still before he forgot what it was like to become sober again.

He was raising his hand to the pull cord when a blinding light pierced his brain, bringing with it a pain that felt very much like his skull being cleaved in two. His eyes, he realized, were not closed, they were open. The drapes had been closed, leaving the room black as pitch, but now a set of those drapes was open—opened by, he could only guess, Satan herself. She stood by the window, her arms folded beneath her breasts. She had only a shadow where her face should be and an angelic halo around her head.

Oh yes, it was Satan all right.

"Hello, Brahm."

His heart lurched. His stomach churned. Pride demanded that he leap to his feet and pitch her from the room, but he could do nothing but lie there and pray for death. Death was the best he could hope for now that she had found him.

Eleanor. It was Eleanor who was trying to kill him. Beautiful, delicate, funny Eleanor, who had ripped out his heart and stomped on it. She was in his room.

He tried to scowl at her, but it felt more like a half-arsed squint. "What the hell are you doing here?"

She came closer. Now that she was no longer backlit by the window, he could see the disappointment on her beautiful face. "What kind of question is that for your betrothed?"

"Go back to the window," he ordered. "You are not my betrothed."

She came closer, arching a fine brow in obvious defiance of both his request and his statement. "Am I not? Are you reneging?"

"You did, remember?" He'd lift his head if it didn't weigh ten stone.

"Ah yes." She made a show of pondering that for a moment. "Then I suppose you will have to consider me your nurse."

"My nurse! What the hell are you talking about?" Oh God, it hurt to raise his voice.

She was near enough now that she bent down to talk to him, bringing her face so close to his that he could see the striations of blue in her eyes.

"I promised you I would nurse you should you ever fall ill again." Her haughty nose wrinkled. "I can see that you have indeed fallen ill."

"I am not ill, I am hung over. Nothing a glass of Scotch will not cure." He reached again for the bellpull. Damn her for being here. Damn her for seeing him this way. Damn *him* for not being too drunk to care. He stank like the very devil of brandy, whiskey, scotch, sweat, dirt, and God only knew what else. Actually, *he* knew what else, but Brahm didn't want to think of that right now, not with his stomach in such a delicate condition.

"You needn't bother the servants," she said quickly.

His hand stilled around the cord. She'd let him go through all this exertion only to stop him now that he had reached his goal? She was of a cruel nature, this one. "What do you mean?"

Her spine was as straight as a nun's, her expression just as pious and righteous. What had she done now? "Only that there is no Scotch, whiskey, or anything else of that nature for them to bring you."

He would have yelled every expletive he knew if he didn't think it would kill him. "What do you mean?" There had been a whole case two nights ago. Even he couldn't have drunk it all that fast.

Was it his imagination, or had she taken a step back now that he had moved away from the bell cord? "I had it thrown out—all the whiskey and bourbon, port and brandy. Actually, I think some of your footmen plan to sell it to a dockside tavern, but I'm not supposed to know that."

The wench had thrown out his drink. She had destroyed his chances of getting blissfully drunk. Hadn't destroying his chance at happiness been enough? Christ almighty, he never would have thought her capable of such unwarranted fiendishness. Well, he hoped she was prepared for the consequences of her rash actions. Once all the alcohol was out of his system—and it wouldn't be long now—he was not going to be a pretty sight, and the only thing that would take the edge off was a drink. He'd start shaking then, and God knew what else. The brain fever would come. But before that, he'd be retching his guts up all over the place.

He'd be damned if he'd let her witness that.

"Get out of my house."

She took another step back, but the steel was still in her spine. "No."

He lurched upward. "I said, get the hell out of my house!" Damn, damn, damn. He fell back on the bed, his skull pulsing in agony.

"Brahm?" Eleanor was by his side, her hands cool on his face and forehead. "Brahm, are you all right?"

"No," he croaked. "Chamber pot . . . under bed . . . hurry."

He kept his eyes closed to ease the pain and the spinning, but he could hear her as she looked under the bed and withdrew the porcelain pot there. He hoped it was empty.

"Where do you want it?"

Obviously it was clean or she would have expressed her disgust. He opened his eyes as wide as he dared—it wasn't much, but he could make out her fuzzy outline. "Give it to me."

She did so without hesitation. Snatching it from her

hands, Brahm sat up once more and tore the cover from the pot. Yes, it was empty, but he was too far gone to care at this point as he finally gave up fighting his stomach and allowed the muscles there to do their worst. He retched once, twice. Bitter, acrid. His stomach emptied itself, yet refused to stop heaving. It was as though the damn thing was trying to turn itself inside out.

He had forgotten this part, forgotten how awful it was. He could add humiliating to the list as well. It had been a long time since he'd had someone watching when he puked.

He wiped his mouth on his sleeve when he was done. Eleanor took the pot from him, and he was too drained to argue. His hand trembled ever so slightly as it released the cool porcelain.

It was starting already.

"Eleanor, please go."

She shook her head. "I cannot leave you like this."

How he wished he could do something to wipe that stricken expression off her face. No doubt she'd find some way to blame herself for this as well. Let her. She'd leave when it got bad, and he was low enough that he didn't mind admitting he'd enjoy knowing she felt some guilt over his current state.

He was tempted to tell her that, but the minute he opened his mouth, bile rushed from the back of his throat, and he dived for the chamber pot, seizing it just in time.

She couldn't leave him, eh? He'd give her an hour at the most before she broke that promise as well.

Chapter 16

Brahm was dying.

Eleanor had expected him to be less than pleased to see her. She had expected that his condition would be unpleasant, to say the least. She did not expect it to worsen after her arrival. Wasn't he supposed to get better now that he wasn't drinking?

He'd been ill—violently so—and then his foul mood worsened. He became mean and belligerent, agitated and easily set off. Then came the tremors that eventually grew into shivers that would not stop.

Just a few moments ago, shortly before dawn the morning after her arrival; he had begun to shake so fervently that Eleanor thought he must be having a fit. And still he told her to leave. He said many things, none of them pleasant. A few of them Eleanor hadn't quite understood, and she didn't want to. His belligerence had come very close to making her want to leave, he had been so mean, but his physical symptoms were so awful, she could not leave him.

This latest development was what had her running down the stairs, wearing the same clothes she had been wearing the entire night sitting by his bed. It was the first time she had left his room since her arrival. She took her meals there, and used his dressing room for more private necessities.

What was she going to do? She had to get help for Brahm, but it had been so long since she had spent any significant time in London that she didn't know where the best physicians were. She certainly didn't know who Brahm's personal physician was. Surely one of his servants would know. His valet at least.

Luck was with her when she hurried into the great hall. The housekeeper and a man she took for the butler were standing in the middle of the floor, talking. They were talking about her no doubt—the strange woman who hastily introduced herself, asked for tea, then spent the night in the master's apartments.

Normally she would have been moved to stop and admire her surroundings—the cool, lustrous marble, the chessboard floor—but not this morning. Later, if Brahm allowed her to stay, if he married her as she wanted him to, then she would take the time to appreciate the house of which she was mistress.

"Quickly," she snapped as she approached the pair. "Lord Creed needs a physician. Immediately."

The two of them stared at her as though she had spoken Javanese rather than English. "Did you not hear me? I said Lord Creed needs medical attention."

"We heard you, ma'am," the man replied in a tone not totally disrespectful.

Where had Brahm found this man, Covent Garden? "Then why are you not sending for the physician?"

He exchanged an uncomfortable glance with the woman. "No offense, ma'am, but Lord Creed does not take kindly to our interfering when his condition is such as it is. And since you are not known to us, we must bow to his wishes."

Not known to them! Had Brahm's valet not informed the other servants of her identity? Surely he would know her. Come to think of it, she hadn't seen the man since her arrival. Brahm had either dismissed him or told him he had no need of his services at present.

"I," she informed them in her haughtiest tone, "am Lady Eleanor Durbane, daughter of the Earl Burrough and future Viscountess Creed, a title I may never get a chance to hold if one of you does not send for a physician. *Now,* please."

The housekeeper jumped to do her bidding, but not before bobbing a quick curtsy. The butler flushed and bowed, but stayed where he was.

"Shall I send for His Lordship's brothers, my lady? They have some experience in these matters."

Eleanor nodded, rubbing her forehead with the tips of her fingers. She was so tired and frightened. "Yes, do that." She'd appreciate all the help she could get at this point. "And what is your name?"

"Jeffers, my lady. I will also instruct Cook to make a light broth. It tends to work best at such times."

Another nod, distracted this time. "These matters." "Such times." Brahm's staff were used to this. They knew exactly what was going on and what to do. The racing of her heart eased somewhat.

Jeffers wasn't done with her yet. "And if I might be so bold, my lady, I will also have Cook make you some breakfast. You have a bit of a battle ahead of you, and you will want to keep your strength."

Eleanor raised her head. "Battle? Whatever do you mean?" This wasn't the worst of it?

The elderly man's expression was sympathetic. "I must be candid, my lady, though you may find it impertinent."

"Please, anything you can tell me will be most appreciated."

The butler nodded. "Very well. His Lordship will be . . . difficult for the next few days, and if you intend to help him through this ordeal, you may find it very tiring."

Eleanor stared at him. The next few days? She was going to have to suffer through this fear for *days*? Impossible!

"If there is nothing else you require, Lady Eleanor, I will send for Lord Wynthrope and Mr. North."

"Yes, yes, of course." She would be glad to have his brothers with her. They could tell her what to expect, whether she should fear for Brahm's life.

After Jeffers left her to take care of matters, Eleanor raced back upstairs to Brahm's room. He was as she had left him, quaking and perspiring in his bed.

Should she cover him with another quilt? He seemed cold, his skin clammy to the touch, but he was sweating as though he was far too warm. Was this a fever or something else? God, how she hated being so helpless! She was a capable woman, everyone said so. She should know what to do.

It was so frightening to see him like this, so awful to watch him suffer so and not know how to ease it.

His head tossed on the pillow, his dark hair clinging damply to his forehead. The lines around his mouth seemed deeper, his eyes underscored with dark smudges. Several days' growth of stubble decorated his jaw and upper lip. He bore little resemblance to the man who had left her little more than a week ago.

Had he done this to himself because of her? Stupid, idiot man. Did he not realize she was not worth his own health? No one was.

"Eleanor."

He had spoken! Eleanor rushed to the side of the bed. "Brahm?"

But he didn't hear her—or at least didn't acknowledge her. His head moved from side to side, his brow puckering as a dream or some kind of delusion took hold.

"Eleanor," he repeated, his voice hoarse and low. "Does not trust me . . . does not believe . . . changed. Have not . . . changed."

Tears stung the back of Eleanor's eyes. This *was* because of her. All because of her. Reaching down, she brushed a lock of hair back from his warm brow. "I do trust you, Brahm, I really do." In her heart, she knew it to be true.

At least she trusted him when it came to other women. She trusted him with her heart. It might take a little time for her to trust him not to get drunk every time things became tense between them, but she would get there eventually, of that she was certain. Brahm would see to it.

It would take some time for him to learn to trust her again as well. She had wounded his pride with her rejection. She would have to prove her sincerity and her loyalty. It might be quite a while before he renewed his desire to marry her, if he did at all. She wasn't going to think of that right now. All that mattered at this moment was getting him through this ordeal. Everything else could wait.

But if Brahm thought he was getting rid of her once he was himself again, he was in for a disappointment. She wasn't going anywhere—not without a fight.

He talked more as she hovered over him, but she didn't

understand any of it. She didn't try to speak to him or wake him, she merely watched, her forehead aching with the strain of her frown. She mopped his brow with her handkerchief, too afraid to do anything else for fear of making matters worse.

Finally the physician—Griggs was his name—arrived. He had a friendly face and a kindly manner that instantly put Eleanor at ease. He told her he had seen Brahm's symptoms before and had attended to both Brahm and his father in the past.

"Go get some rest," he urged with a smile. "Have some breakfast, and do whatever it is you ladies do in the morning. I will look after Lord Creed. I promise."

Eleanor believed him. He was certainly more qualified to help Brahm than she was. She left him once he had promised to find her before taking his leave—and if anything should happen to Brahm—and went to the room the servants had prepared for her. She rang for her maid and hot water. Surely she must look and smell a fright.

One look in the mirror confirmed her suspicion. She did look a fright. Ugh. She smelled awful as well.

She bathed quickly in a hip bath, resolving to take a more leisurely soak later when she was sure Brahm was going to be fine. Mary helped her into a morning gown of summer blue muslin and brushed out her hair, only to restyle it in a very simple knot at her nape. Eleanor didn't have time for frivolities. She had to get downstairs and have something to eat before Brahm's brothers arrived and Griggs left.

Once Brahm was back in her care, she knew food would be the last thing on her mind. And she certainly wouldn't be able to eat with his brothers around. What if they blamed her for the lapse in Brahm's behavior as well?

Earlier she had thought they would be well-appreciated support, but they might just as easily despise her.

She was seated alone at the long, highly polished table, sipping a cup of tea and somehow managing to enjoy eggs, sausage, and buttered toast, when two gentlemen entered the dining room. Wynthrope and North, if she was not mistaken. Her appetite vanished at the sight of them.

They were handsome men, as one might expect from a Ryland. Both were tall and blue-eyed, though the shade of blue varied vastly from one to the other. Wynthrope was the slighter of the two, with dark hair and a self-possessed air. North was the more powerfully built, his wavy hair touched with auburn. He offered her a slight smile.

"You must be the famous Lady Eleanor," he said as he approached the table.

"More like *infamous* if our brother's rantings are to be believed." Wynthrope smiled as well, taking the sting from his words. "It is a pleasure to meet you at last."

Eleanor couldn't prevent her shock from showing. "Please, sit. A pleasure?"

"Indeed." Wynthrope's grin widened as he pulled out a chair. "Anyone who can vex my brother as thoroughly as you have has my utmost respect."

Respect. She had his respect for what she had done to Brahm. Was this man mad? No, he was joking with her. She could see the amusement in his eyes. A reluctant smile lifted the corners of her mouth.

But then she remembered Brahm and her smile faded. "Your brother is very ill."

The two men now sitting across from her were suddenly very serious as well. "Vomiting, shaking?" Wynthrope inquired.

Eleanor nodded.

North exchanged a glance with his brother. "The delusions will start next."

"I believe they already have," Eleanor informed them, strangely comforted that they seemed to be familiar with all the symptoms. Perhaps Brahm was going to recover after all.

The brothers nodded, almost in unison. "He will be belligerent as well," North cautioned her. "He may say some very mean things to you."

"Try to ignore it," Wynthrope advised. "It is not him but the poison inside coming out."

That was a very interesting way to think of it. She didn't tell them that Brahm had already said awful things to her, and she didn't want to think that it might get worse.

"Mr. Griggs is with him now," she informed them. "He should be down soon. I asked him for a meeting before he leaves."

"Then we will wait with you." North helped himself to a cup of coffee from the silver pot. When he was finished, Wynthrope did the same.

Eleanor could avoid it no longer. If they were going to remain silent on the topic, then she would have to broach it. "I am very sorry."

Both men looked at her over their cups, their expressions curious and nearly identical. "For what?"

Was it not obvious? Her own cup returned to its saucer with a rattle. Perhaps Brahm's shaking was contagious. "I am to blame for your brother's relapse."

Wynthrope's gaze was mildly teasing. "Held the bottle to his lips, did you?"

This man had the strangest sense of humor. "Of course

not, but had it not been for my refusal of his proposal, this wouldn't have happened."

"So that is what happened." North took a swallow of coffee. "I had wondered."

His brother shot him a smug look. "I knew it."

They hadn't known? Brahm hadn't told them? Now that they did know, how could they not despise her? Eleanor could not believe it. "I feel terrible about it."

Wynthrope shook his head. "You shouldn't. It really is not your fault."

How could he say that? Obviously the question was plain on her face because North answered it. "Brahm had a choice, Lady Eleanor. No one made him take a drink. He chose to do it. What is happening to him now is his own fault, not yours."

The arrival of Mr. Griggs prevented Eleanor from arguing. The trio around the table stood. How she wished she could look as calm as North and Wynthrope did, but even she could not hide her emotions that well.

"How is he?" Eleanor inquired softly.

Mr. Griggs offered her a slight smile. "Sick as a dog and not likely to feel much better for at least another day."

Oh dear heaven! "What can I do for him?"

The physician handed her a folded slip of paper. "I have made a list. He will need plenty of fluids, although it will be difficult for him to keep them down. No solid food for at least another forty-eight hours. Just broth, tea, and water."

"That is it?" No medicine, no poultices or treatments?

Mr. Griggs's countenance turned sympathetic. "Patience is the only medicine you can give him, my lady. The ill humors must work their way out and his body introduced to food slowly. Once the brain fever has subsided, he will begin to return to himself and there will be more you can do for him."

Eleanor thanked the physician and offered to see him to the door, but he insisted that wasn't necessary.

"Have you emptied the house of all liquor?" Wynthrope asked once there were just the three of them once more.

Eleanor nodded. "Yes. All that I know of is gone."

He turned to North. "I will check all the usual hiding spots." He flashed Eleanor a sincere smile. "There will be more stashed throughout the house. Better to be rid of it before he comes to his senses and is strong enough to go looking for it."

North set his empty cup on the table. "I will send for Charles, Brahm's valet. He is no doubt beside himself waiting for news."

This was normal then? "What should I do?"

"Sit with him," North suggested. "Once Charles returns we will bathe him, but for now you can take him some water."

And that was it. She was the one who was supposed to look after him, to make everything right again, and she couldn't. "I feel so useless." Eleanor froze, realizing she had said the words aloud.

The brothers came to her then, each laying a reassuring hand on her shoulders. How comforting their presence was, despite her anger at her own ineptitude. North spoke, "Your job will come soon enough, and it won't be an easy one."

"What is that?" she asked, her gaze drifting from one to the other.

Their smiles were grim, and it was Wynthrope who answered. "Convincing him to stay sober."

* * *

"I thought I told you to get the hell out of my house."

They were in Brahm's bedroom. He had just woken up—too damn early at that—to find Eleanor in his room. She had a tray in her hands, and he could smell the hot buttered eggs, freshly brewed coffee, and toast from the bed. His stomach growled in welcome, despite his malcontent.

"You did." Eleanor set the tray across his lap, seemingly unbothered by the scowl on his face. "Several times, in fact."

"Then why are you still here?" Yes, dear God, why was she?

She flipped open a napkin and laid the snowy white linen over his bare chest. "I chose to ignore your request."

Brahm looked down at her handiwork. The napkin looked ridiculous against his hairy skin. "I do not require a damn bib!"

She continued on as though she hadn't heard, arranging everything on the tray so that it was within easy reach.

Four days. Four days she had been in his house, harping at him, hovering over him like a hen with her chick. No matter what he did, how vilely he behaved, or how disgusting the symptoms of his recovery, she would not leave.

Why? Why did she stay? Did she blame herself for the state he had gotten himself into? Probably. Eleanor was a wonderful, nurturing person, but she was also a first-class martyr when she wanted to be. Was it that ridiculous promise to nurse him? She should know he wouldn't hold her to that.

She had taken all his liquor. He knew because in a moment of weakness two days ago he'd had a footman look for some, as he was still too shaky to get out of bed, even with his cane. Not only had she found the obvious stock, but the secret stashes as well, which meant she'd had help from his brothers. Damn Wynthrope and North. They'd been around often the last four days as well. They never lectured or talked down, but he could see how disappointed they were with him. Thank God he didn't have to deal with Devlin as well. He was in the country with Blythe and their son. He was in no mood to suffer all three of his brothers.

He should be thankful that she had done away with all temptation, but he wasn't. A sip of something a couple of days ago would have eased the shaking. And at least if he was drunk he wouldn't have to suffer through her presence. Did she not realize that she was more tempting than any bottle of whiskey or brandy? Eleanor, with her golden hair and spring-scented skin. Every time he saw her he wanted her, craved her. Not just her touch, but her laughter, her smiles, and her companionship.

Guilt had to be what kept her there because she certainly wasn't acting as though it was anything else. North claimed she had been beside herself with worry for him when the brain fever started, but he wouldn't know it from the cool way she treated him. Perhaps she'd simply been concerned that people might think she had killed him.

'Course, if she was that concerned what people thought, she wouldn't be there at all. It was highly improper for her, an unmarried woman, to be in the house of an unmarried man. They had no chaperone, save for her maid, and for all her effectiveness, the girl might as well not even be there.

She had to realize she was ruining herself by staying with him. Perhaps she hoped he would propose to her again. She could keep on hoping. The thought brought a sharp ache to his chest. It didn't matter that he still wanted her. It didn't matter that he wanted nothing more than to get down on his knees and beg her to have him. He would be damned—heartily so—before he made himself so vulnerable to her again. Twice she had broken his heart and made a fool of him. She would not do so again.

No, he would not propose, not unless he heard from her lips that she wanted to be his wife. And if he knew Eleanor, it would snow in Hades before she swallowed enough of her pride to do that. It would be taking too great a risk for her. If there was one thing he had learned about her, it was that Eleanor did not take risks unless she was almost positive of the outcome.

He watched her, his brow knitted. Why did she have to be so frigging lovely? That flawless skin, those bright eyes. There were dark circles beneath her eyes and a pallor to her complexion that he had never seen before, and yet he still thought her the most beautiful woman alive. The circles and the pallor were because of him. Too bad he could not bring himself to feel any guilt for them. No one forced her to stay. She chose to witness the full horror of his compulsion. What she had seen surely must have repulsed her, and yet here she was, still trying to "fix" him.

"Would you like me to help you eat?" she asked serenely.

Brahm scowled at her. What did she think he was, an invalid? Granted he was still weak from his ordeal, but he would recover. He would much rather be drunk than faced with her and her damn good intentions. "I want you out."

"Fine." She started for the door. "I will check in on you later."

Damn her to hell for being so bloody obstinate. She

knew full well what he meant, but she was going to make him say it. "I do not mean simply out of my room, I want you out of my house."

She stopped, turning to face him with her arms folded beneath her lovely breasts. He remembered the weight of them in his hands, the taste on his tongue . . . "No."

Heat suffused his cheeks, part desire, part anger. This was *his* house. She had forsaken the right to act as mistress there. "I will have Jeffers toss you out."

"Jeffers would never do that," she replied saucily. "And neither would you."

That was true. She knew him too well. "What kind of perverse punishment is this that you stay here?"

Her eyes widened. "You think I am punishing you?"

What a beautiful idiot. She looked so hurt, so *wronged*. What did she expect from him? What did she want? "You are punishing yourself. You cannot possibly ruin my reputation any more than I have already done myself. But you were above reproach before this. Why risk your future?"

She looked at him as though there were so many reasons. "Because I owe it to you. I am trying to make amends, surely you of all people must understand that."

Ah, so she was being a martyr. Wench. "You could have sent me a note."

She tried again. "Because I promised I would nurse you should you suffer a relapse."

So it *was* that damn promise. "That was simple flirtation." Surely she knew the difference. And damn her for bringing it up and reminding him of how sweet things had been with them for that brief time. When he had asked her for that promise, he'd had no intention of ever drinking again.

No. He had to be honest, at least with himself. He had gone to the club that day looking to get foxed. He had wanted to numb himself to the pain her rejection caused. His pride had needed the numbness.

She shrugged, the gesture causing the arms beneath her breasts to rise, lifting the soft, firm flesh against the demure dip of her neckline. "It was a promise."

"So was agreeing to be my wife. Why keep one and not the other?"

She flushed, humiliation filled her eyes, and Brahm was instantly contrite, but he would not say it. He would not apologize. He wanted to hear her answer. She owed him that at the very least.

She said nothing, just stared at him as though he had shoved a shard of glass into her heart.

"Do not look at me like that," he commanded. "Do not act as though you are the wounded party. I do not care how much you martyr yourself, you were the one who rejected me."

"I know." She looked bloody awful about it too.

"Then *why*"—his teeth ground together—"are you here?"

"Because I want to be."

"Surely you do not regret your decision not to marry me?" He said it with so much mockery, she would be a fool to admit otherwise, and he knew it. He didn't want her to admit anything. Regardless of what she said, it was going to hurt.

She said nothing.

If she was going to be silent, then he would go on. Anger, hurt, and humiliation spurred him onward. "You were right about me, Eleanor. I cannot be trusted. The minute things did not go my way, I ran to the nearest bottle. How could you ever be certain I would not do it again?"

The color slowly seeped from her cheeks.

"God only knows what else I did before you arrived." He sneered in self-loathing, but it was true. He had but vague memories of the days between taking that first drink and waking up with her hovering over him. "Perhaps you will be able to read about it in some other courtesan's book in the near future."

That was a cheap shot and he knew it, but he couldn't seem to stop himself. He wanted to hurt her. The wound in his heart was too raw and fresh. Being near her and knowing she was not his—that she didn't want to be his—was more than he could stand.

"I just want to help you, Brahm," she whispered.

His laughter was harsh. "Having you here is not helping me, Eleanor. Knowing that you are here because you feel you owe me something is not helpful. Seeing you and not being able to touch you is not helpful. In fact, the only thing your being here is good for is showing me just how stupid I was to think I could change."

"You did change." She held out both hands, as though holding within them all the proof of her words. "You are nothing like the man you once were. You showed that to me."

Why? Because he hadn't pissed in a punch bowl at her party? Because he hadn't bedded her sister again, despite the availability of Lydia's bed? Or because this time he had been stupid enough to truly give her his heart?

"Do not humor me." The fact that he was lying in this bed, recovering from his debauchery, was proof enough how wrong she was. "We both know you do not believe that, any more than I do. When it comes to you, I do not think I will ever change, and I can never make you the kind of promises you need me to make in order for me to have you, because I cannot even make those promises to myself. And I cannot make those promises to myself because I do not know if I have the strength to never drink again. Obviously, I do not."

"Brahm . . ." Her expression was so plaintive, begging him to let her say or do whatever it was she needed to assuage her own guilt. He didn't want her guilt. He wanted things she wasn't prepared to give him, and anything else was an insult, no matter how good her motives. She was not there because she loved him. She was there because she felt beholden to him, and no man with any pride would allow that.

"Please, just go. If you want to help me so much, then give me some peace and go."

The hurt expression on her face filled him with self-disgust, but even that was far preferable to the pain of having her just a few feet away physically, but miles away emotionally. Did she not realize that having her in his house was doing him more harm than good?

Her arms fell limply to her sides as she straightened her spine. He was in for a battle with her, he knew that. "I will be downstairs in the green parlor if you need me."

"I won't."

He watched her leave. Long after she was gone, her face haunted him. He shoved his untouched breakfast aside and slumped back against the pillows. God help him, he was such a rotten liar.

Would she come if he called for her? Because he needed her. He needed her so very, very badly.

Chapter 17

❦❦❦

"**P**ardon me, Lady Eleanor, but there is a Mrs. Carson awaiting you in the great hall."

Sitting at the little writing desk in the green parlor, Eleanor raised her head from the letter she was composing to Arabella to gaze at Jeffers in surprise. Would that be Mrs. *Fanny* Carson by any chance?

"Are you certain she is here to see me?" It would make more sense if the woman was there to call on Brahm. It would also give Eleanor good reason to rip Mrs. Carson's hair out by the roots.

The butler nodded. "She asked for you specifically."

This was an interesting turn of events. Stacking her papers into a neat pile and satisfied that the ink was set, Eleanor brushed the sand from her hands and placed the shaker back in the drawer. "Then you had better show her in."

Jeffers looked positively mortified. "No disrespect meant, my lady, but Mrs. Carson is a woman of ill repute."

Eleanor wiped her quill on a stained piece of cloth and place it back in its holder. "So I am aware, which makes me all the more curious as to why she would come to call on me." Yes, her reputation was bound to suffer greatly for her staying in Brahm's house without the proper chaperone, but Eleanor didn't think she had sunk quite so low yet that women such as Fanny Carson might consider her their equal. She didn't care how uncharitable a thought that was. Fanny Carson had tried to blackmail men for her own gain—that was what made her low, not the fact that she'd had many lovers.

"As you wish, my lady." But it was apparent that Jeffers didn't approve at all. It seemed both he and Mrs. Stubbins the housekeeper had warmed to her—so much so that they had adopted an almost protective stance where she was concerned. She appreciated their sudden loyalty, but it was not necessary.

While she waited, Eleanor stood and smoothed any wrinkles from her gown. It was suddenly very imperative that she look her best when Fanny Carson saw her. It was impossible to look good given the past few days, however, so she would simply have to do what best she could. She chewed her lips and pinched her cheeks for color, and positioned herself in front of a window so the light behind would halo her and, she hoped, conceal the smudges beneath her eyes. It wasn't that she wanted to impress Fanny Carson, but she didn't want the woman to find her lacking all the same.

The woman who entered the parlor and made Eleanor's heart leap with ridiculous anxiety was not what Eleanor had expected. A woman like Fanny Carson should be beautiful, worldly, and sophisticated.

Perhaps this wasn't *the* Mrs. Carson after all.

The woman standing in the doorway was tall—amazingly so—and of a generous figure. Her face, while in no way ugly, was not classically beautiful, but unforget-table all the same. Her hair was an impossible shade of red, yet Eleanor did not doubt it was natural, given the woman's coloring. There was nothing remarkable about her dress. Her olive velvet spencer would have looked drab on any other woman. The gown beneath was a plain cream-colored muslin, hardly the height of fashion, but stylish all the same. This woman would look foolish in anything too busy.

No, this woman was not the petite, curvy blond that Eleanor had expected. This woman was something more, and Eleanor didn't like it.

"Lady Eleanor," she began in a voice low and husky. "Thank you for seeing me."

Coming around the desk, Eleanor gestured to the sitting area. "I must admit to being curious as to the nature of your call, Mrs. Carson. Please have a seat. Tea?"

Mrs. Carson seated herself on one of the chairs with embroidered cushions and began removing her gloves. "Thank you. Tea would be lovely, but only if you will join me. The nature of my visit is twofold."

This was interesting. Eleanor rang the bell, and when the maid came, requested a pot of tea and a plate of sweets. Then she seated herself in the chair directly across from her guest—another with embroidered cushions. They were not as comfortable as they looked.

"Twofold?"

Mrs. Carson placed her hands over the gloves in her lap. "Lady Eleanor, forgive my impertinence, but do you know who I am?"

The question was asked with genuine feeling, no false

hauteur or defiance. Mrs. Carson, whatever else she might be, was no game player. Eleanor would have to be careful or she just might wind up feeling sympathetic toward this woman, and that wouldn't do at all.

"You are Fanny Carson, author of *Memoirs of a Well-Loved Lady*."

Fanny actually seemed surprised. "Why, yes. Have you actually read my book?"

No one else would dare ask such a question of an unmarried lady—not anyone proper. Of course, Fanny Carson was far from proper. For that matter, Eleanor herself had lost much of the right to call herself such as well. She had engaged in fornication with a man who was not her husband, and now she was living in his house. What, besides birth, made her and Fanny Carson all that different?

Eleanor smiled. "Just the parts about Brahm."

The older woman—and Eleanor could see that she was indeed older—laughed. Like the rest of her, her laugh was unrestrained and voluptuous. "I was right about him, was I not?"

"Perhaps in some respects."

Fanny leaned forward, a conspiratorial gleam in her green eyes. "In *all* respects?"

Eleanor couldn't help but chuckle as well. If the woman thought she was going to comment on Brahm's "massive maleness," she was mad. "Now you are being impertinent, Mrs. Carson."

The redhead sobered, but a smile remained. "Call me Fanny."

Normally she wouldn't dream of such an intimacy with such a woman, but it felt right to agree. "All right."

"And might I call you Eleanor?"

She supposed there was no harm in it. It wasn't as

though they would ever meet again socially. If Brahm rejected Eleanor, she would return to the country and no doubt never set foot in London again. But that was the future and not worth the anxiety it caused at the moment. "Of course."

The maid arrived with the tea, and Eleanor poured for both of them. Fanny drank her tea black. Eleanor had never known anyone who didn't at least take milk in her tea. The redhead helped herself to a small, heavily iced cake and balanced it on the edge of her saucer.

"Now that we have that business about names out of the way, how is dear Brahm?"

So Fanny knew, then. No doubt all of London knew that Brahm had had a relapse. He wasn't exactly what one might term a discreet drinker. When deep in his cups Brahm had a tendency to flaunt himself in the face of all things proper.

"He is recovering," Eleanor replied honestly, after taking a sip of hot tea. "He is much better. Would you care to see him?" The invitation surprised even her. She must be mad to invite Brahm's former mistress to his room!

Not that she had any reason for concern, she realized somewhat dazedly. Brahm would not engage in any kind of romance while she was under his roof. Besides, he didn't want anyone but her, unless his feelings had changed suddenly.

Odd that she could see that now and not when he had proposed. Time must have cleared her mind.

Fanny dismissed the invite with a wave of her hand. "Thank you, but no. I would imagine I am not someone he wishes to see just yet, given my recent publication. Give him my best, will you? I will inquire after him in a few days when he is back on his feet."

She spoke as though she knew exactly what Brahm was going through. Everyone seemed to know but Eleanor. This was all so new and awful and strange to her. And everyone else treated it as commonplace. It angered her. How could they be so nonchalant about his health? How could they treat something so frightening as though it were nothing at all? She had been afraid for his very life, and no one else seemed to care!

"Have I said something to anger you, Eleanor?"

Fanny looked truly concerned, bringing a rush of guilt to Eleanor's conscience. "Not you alone, per se. I simply find it so very hard to comprehend how everyone around him can treat Brahm's condition as normal."

The other woman's expression turned to one of bewilderment. "Because we have all seen it before, my dear. Many times." Fanny spoke as though it was something she might have experienced herself, but Eleanor wasn't going to pry into the other woman's life. And she certainly wasn't going to inquire after the times Fanny had watched Brahm go through it. She was jealous enough of this woman as it was—not because she thought her a threat now, but because she had known Brahm so very well in the past.

"I haven't. Not this aspect of it." She would never forget the night at Pennington's soiree when Brahm relieved himself in the punch bowl. Never. Although now the incident almost made her want to smile. What the devil was wrong with her?

"You say it as though you regret never having seen it before." Fanny shook her head. "Perhaps it is for the best that you have not."

"Why do you say that?"

The other woman licked a spot of icing off her finger.

"Because he will know that it has affected you, and that will make him less eager to repeat the process. When they know that you have seen it and accepted it, they stop caring if you see it again."

How right she hoped Fanny was. She never planned to "accept" Brahm's drinking. She would help him fight it and she would support him, but she would do everything in her power to keep from becoming complacent.

But she didn't want to discuss that now, not with a woman who was still very much a stranger, no matter how much she might want to open up. She wasn't going to discuss Brahm with a woman who had no qualms about revealing her own personal life to the public.

"You said your visit was twofold?" Perhaps it was time to get this conversation back onto its original course.

Fanny smiled and took another cake. "You are very direct, Eleanor. I like that."

Most people would have found her curt or rude. Fanny liked it. Eleanor might have known the courtesan would go against convention.

With more patience than she knew she possessed, Eleanor waited as Fanny finished her second cake.

The redhead wiped her mouth on her napkin, leaving a faint carmine stain behind. She was wearing cosmetics. "I am here because I wanted to get a glimpse of you."

"Of me?" Why in the world would this painted, exotic creative give a flying fig about her?

"Yes. I wanted to see the woman who rejected my dear Brahm."

Not just once but twice, but then Fanny didn't know that. Did she? Oh Lord, had Brahm revealed their relationship while in a drunken stupor? It would be humiliating, but at least it might do something to save her reputation if people thought she was there to renew their engagement.

Her dear Brahm? The other woman's words finally sank in. Brahm was not Fanny's. He hadn't been for some time. He was Eleanor's; did the woman not see that?

"I had to see for myself the woman so incredible that she had Brahm Ryland obsessed with her for more than a decade." Fanny leaned back in her chair, giving her a frank but unthreatening appraisal. Eleanor wondered what she thought of her. "He spoke often of you, you know."

Eleanor shook her head. Obviously Fanny realized just whom Brahm belonged to after all. No, not belonged to. Belonged *with*. "I did not know that."

Dark green eyes narrowed. "Rumor has it that his recent sojourn to your father's estate might be the cause behind this latest escapade."

If Brahm had said anything, he had said it to someone thankfully close-lipped. There would be no speculating at all if society knew she had refused his proposal.

"And now that you've seen me?" Eleanor asked, lifting her chin. She would not acknowledge the remark about Brahm's trip to her house and his drinking.

Fanny smiled once more. "Such spirit. You make me feel quite old. Now that I have seen you, I begin to realize why he never got you out of his system. You intrigue me, Eleanor."

"I do?" This call was becoming increasingly surreal.

Setting her cup and saucer on the tray, Fanny rose to her feet. "Yes, you do. And now I must go."

Dazed, Eleanor stood as well, leaving her own cup on the table. "Thank you for stopping by." It seemed bizarre to thank her when the visit had been so odd—and unasked for.

The redhead tugged on her gloves. "Take care of my boy. He is more delicate than he looks."

The idea of Brahm as delicate made Eleanor want to laugh. "I will try."

Fanny paused, fixing her with a look that was void of any humor or warmth. It was such a contrast to her earlier behavior that Eleanor's heart stopped at the sight of it.

"Do more than try, my lady. You are obviously here because you care for Brahm, and that does you credit. But I can see that you are also here because of guilt, which makes me believe that you very well might have had something to do with Brahm's latest debacle. He swore on his father's grave he would do everything in his power never to drink again. If he broke that vow because of you, then you have real power over him, and if you abuse it, I will personally see you pay. Good day."

Eleanor watched the statuesque courtesan stride from the room with her mouth gaping and her heart pounding. What had just happened? Had Fanny Carson threatened her? She had. But she had also made it sound like a compliment, saying that Eleanor had real power over Brahm. Why, Fanny had sounded almost envious of that! How could anyone envy the fact that she had been the one to drive Brahm to break a vow made on the memory of his father?

She felt awful about the whole thing. It was more than just guilt. She truly felt horrible. She had let her fears guide her. She had allowed her own insecurities to make her hurt Brahm. She had behaved in a most cowardly manner. She could only hope it wasn't too late to make things right. She was there for so many reasons other than a promise—and too afraid to admit them, even to herself.

A knock on the door drew her attention. Mrs. Stubbins

stood there. "Begging you pardon, my lady, but Lord Creed needs you."

Yes he did. Setting her mouth grimly as she left to answer his summons, Eleanor vowed she would find a way to make him realize it.

While Eleanor had been downstairs, plotting his demise or crying, whichever his jackass behavior had driven her to do, Brahm had been visited by North and Wynthrope, who informed him that Devlin and Blythe were traveling up from Devonshire.

Normally such news would have been welcome, especially since Brahm would be able to see his nephew, but the knowledge that they were coming because he had been stupid enough to drink himself senseless, and they were worried for him, robbed him of any joy their imminent arrival might afford.

Wynthrope and North also informed him that gossip was not being kind to Eleanor—or him for that matter, but he didn't give a rat's arse about that. Gossip about him had never been good—and it was usually truth, not speculation.

"It does not help that she followed you here from the country," North had remarked, folding his arms across his broad chest, pulling the shoulders of his gray coat taut. "It looks as though she was chasing you—and that she caught you, which of course paints her as a fallen women in society's eyes."

"Society needs spectacles," Wynthrope retorted. "Everyone knows that when she arrived here he was so drunk, he couldn't even lift his eyelids let alone his pecker."

Wynthrope certainly had a way with words. He was also—unfortunately—right in this case. Brahm would be damned if he'd admit that publicly though. All it would do was add to his own humiliation. Society already had Eleanor ruined. He could not change that unless he married her.

North turned clear eyes on him, pinning him with a gaze that had made him very intimidating as a former Bow Street Runner. "Do you plan to marry her?

"I want to, yes." There was no point in lying to his brothers.

Those unnerving eyes narrowed. "Then why have you not proposed?"

"Because she's already refused me twice." Was that not reason enough?

"But surely now that her reputation is destroyed . . ." North shook his head as realization sank in. "Ah yes, hardly the kind of thing you want to base your marriage on, is it? Don't want her saying yes because she had no other choice."

Oh, she would have a choice. She could take ruination over him, which was what Brahm was afraid of. "I would never know if she married me because she loves me or because she felt she had to."

"You could always ask," Wynthrope suggested after an amazingly long silence, as he picked a hair off the arm of his dark blue coat. "No, forget it, that is too simple."

Brahm threw a pillow at his brother, which Wynthrope easily ducked, being light on his feet and possessed of cat-like reflexes. Brahm had been that sure of foot once. Now he'd topple like a house of cards. "She would not admit to it, you idiot. Besides, she has given me no indication that she even wants to marry me. She has been too busy blaming herself for my drinking."

"Women." Wynthrope shook his head. "They will

blame themselves for the most foolish of things. Honestly, it's not as though you gave her reason to blame herself. It's not as though you went directly from her father's estate to a club and got foxed." He snapped his fingers. "Oh wait, that is exactly what happened."

Brahm's jaw tightened. "Get out."

His younger brother shrugged carelessly. He obviously wasn't about to leave, and Brahm was in no condition to remove him physically. "I'm only saying what is true, and you know it."

Wynthrope had him there, damn it. If only Brahm had his strength back, he'd get out of bed and plant a good solid facer on Wynthrope, but he was still too weak for that.

"You have to tell her it is not her fault, Brahm." It was North who spoke—North, ever the voice of reason.

Brahm sighed and laid his head back. "Yes, I know."

"And you have to marry her before society rejects her altogether."

Wynthrope made a scoffing sound. "What difference does that make? It's not as though marrying *him* will improve her social standing."

"I will marry her because she loves me and wants to marry me," Brahm informed them, annoyed that his brother was right once again. "She will not agree to it for less." Which was one more reason he was terrified to ask.

North pursed his lips. "Do you love her?"

Was this hollow feeling in his gut love, or was it hunger? Was the ache he felt inside love, or the results of his drunken debaucheries? Could he love her? He was obsessed with her, to be sure. But was it love?

"He must love her," Wynthrope remarked.

North frowned at him. "He hasn't said anything."

"I know. It is taking him too long."

Brahm's head moved back and forth on the pillow as he watched the two of them discuss him as though he wasn't even there.

"How does that mean he loves her then?" North scowled.

Wynthrope threw open his hands. "Because he is trying to think of something to prove that he *isn't* in love with her and he cannot."

Brahm and Wynthrope might not always get along, but it was eerie how well his brother knew him at times.

"It is time for us to go." North took Wynthrope by the arm, obviously unimpressed with his brother. "Come on, you."

Wynthrope allowed himself to be pulled along. "Beg for forgiveness," he advised Brahm as he neared the door. "Nothing will make a woman realize she loves you more than casting yourself at her feet. I know this for a fact."

Brahm chuckled as North yanked Wynthrope's arm, practically pulling their brother off his feet. Wynthrope was an ass at times, but he was also good for a laugh when needed. And he had a very concise way of putting things in perspective.

Would begging for Eleanor's forgiveness work? What if he begged for her heart?

He reached for the bellpull. When Mrs. Stubbins arrived, he asked her to have Eleanor come to his room. After his behavior a few hours earlier, he'd be lucky if she didn't keep him waiting. Hell, he'd be lucky if she came at all.

Luck, it seemed, was on his side after all. Just a few moments after he sent Mrs. Stubbins after her, Eleanor appeared in his door.

"You rang?" Her tone was so droll, so caustic that

Brahm smiled. Still smarting from their argument earlier, eh? He didn't blame her. He had been an ass.

"Come in, please." He pushed himself up in the bed, not bothering to haul the covers up with him. She was far from immune to the sight of his bare chest, and he was prepared to use any weapon in his arsenal.

She did as he asked, her gaze lighting on his naked torso and then flitting away like a butterfly on the breeze.

"Wynthrope and North were just here," he informed her.

"Oh?" She looked disappointed that she had not seen them. Or was that relief? It was hard to tell. "I had a visitor myself."

"Who?" If it had been a man, he'd kill him. He might have had to deal with other men under Eleanor's roof, but when she was in his house, there would be no other man but him attending her.

She shot him a gaze much like the one North had pinned him with earlier. "Fanny Carson. She asked me to give you her regards."

If she had told him Christ Himself had come down from heaven to take tea with her, he could not have been more surprised. "Fanny? Came to see you?"

Eleanor nodded. "She said she wanted to see the woman whom you had been obsessed with for so many years."

Brahm's mouth went dry. Damn Fanny. The next time he saw her, he was going to throttle her. Hadn't she done enough damage with that frigging book of hers?

"That was nice of her." Lord, but that was the most stupid thing he had ever said while sober.

Eleanor actually chuckled, and Brahm's heart warmed at the sound. "Your expression looks very much as mine must have during her visit. She is not what I expected."

Brahm folded his arms behind his head, giving her an unabashed view of his upper body. He was not above exploiting her attraction to him to get what he wanted. "Were you disappointed?"

She tried not to look, but he could see her peeking from the corner of her eye. "I liked her better than I thought I would."

Ah, so jealousy reared its disfigured head. "Did you?"

"Yes. I can see how the two of you would have been friends."

She was comparing herself—negatively so—to Fanny Carson? Fanny had been a lot of fun, but she could never hold a candle to Eleanor. No one could. "We were friends, but I never thought of her as anything more than that."

She merely nodded, her lips compressed and silent, officially putting an end to the topic. Obviously she did not want to discuss Fanny anymore, which suited Brahm just fine.

"My brothers told me something that gave me cause for concern while they were here."

"Oh?" She straightened, apparently grateful for the change in topic.

"Apparently the gossips and scandalmongers are wagging their tongues about us."

She blushed—a very pretty pink. "Yes. I have heard similar accounts myself."

"You do not have to ruin your reputation because of a promise—especially one so foolish." He rolled to his side, embarrassed by how much effort it took. His arm actually trembled as he propped his head up with his hand. "I do not like to think that your association with me would harm you."

"I know that," she replied with a lift of her chin. "It's

not just that promise. You were right—I feel some responsibility for your relapse. I know I didn't *have* to come. I could have sent you a note, as you so kindly pointed out."

Heat actually rushed to his cheeks. He had been a complete ass to her. "Yes."

"Or I could have paid a simple visit, I could have sent flowers. There are no doubt one hundred different ways I could have expressed my regret without staying here with you." Why did she sound as though she was becoming increasingly annoyed with him? "What does that tell you, Brahm?"

He flashed what he hoped was a charming grin. "That you are a martyr of the first order?" Honestly, he didn't want to answer her question, because he might voice a hope that had no chance of ever being true.

She shook her head with a sigh. "It should tell you that regret is not the reason I am here."

He stilled. "Then what is?"

Eleanor bowed her head, then raised it again, her face a perfectly sculpted mask, lacking emotion. "I thought you might have need of me."

That wasn't what she was initially going to say, but Brahm didn't care. Need of her? Need was only scratching the surface.

He picked at the coverlet, carefully mulling over his words before raising his gaze to hers. "I owe you an apology."

She was perplexed now. "For what?"

"For my remark earlier about your promise to marry me. I should not have said it."

"It was true."

Brahm would have shrugged were it not for the position he was in. "Perhaps, but it was said to hurt you, and for that I am sorry. I seem to be rather good at hurting you. I am sorry for that as well."

"We both seem to be rather adept at hurting each other." A sad smile curved her wonderful lips. "I am sorry for that as well."

He held her gaze with an earnest one, trying to will his sincerity into his eyes. "You really should not continue to stay here without a chaperone, Ellie."

"Bah." How easily she dismissed his concern, as though he had no idea what he was talking about. As if she didn't care. "If I'm ruined, then Papa will have no choice but to cease his efforts to marry me off."

Brahm smiled, but it felt tight on his face. "That was your evil plan all along, was it not?"

Her own attempt at a smile failed miserably. "You found me out."

"I am sorry I am not enough for you, Eleanor."

She went white. "Brahm—"

"Stop." He cut her off before she could try to explain, before she could say something stupid like the fault was with her and not him. He couldn't stand to listen to such rubbish again. And this theory of Wyn's had his palms sweating like a boy's. It might not have been begging exactly, but it felt like it. "You do not have to say anything. I just wanted you to know that I am sorry—for everything."

She nodded, her face ravaged by some mixture of emotions he couldn't begin to fathom.

"I would like to rest now," he told her, not allowing her the chance to respond. He didn't want her to respond.

Another nod. "I will leave you then."

Yes. She would leave him. That was exactly what he thought she might do.

Chapter 18

Was he completely senseless, or simply playing with her?

As she dressed for dinner, Eleanor pondered the question for what must be the—she had lost count—hundredth time that week.

Brahm had to recognize by now that she stayed with him because she realized what an awful mistake she had made—she had as good as told him such. But didn't he also realize how much more there was to it? He had to know she risked her reputation for more than an apology. Did he not understand that she cared for him? She wanted him to renew his addresses. She wanted to marry him. She wanted him to touch her the way he had before, but he hadn't so much as held her hand.

Most of all, she wanted him to love her, because she could finally admit that she was desperately in love with him. In truth, she suspected she had loved him for years. At the very least she knew that the emotion had reawakened while he was at her father's house. His leaving had made her feel as though she had lost a part of herself.

Only since coming to London had she come to know just how much she adored and loved him. She had been so worried when she first found him, terrified of losing him. Now that he was better, she thanked God for it every day.

She watched with a pleased eye as her maid put the last pin in her hair. It was an elaborate coiffure of glistening curls, bouncing tendrils, and so many pins that Eleanor's scalp tingled all over. It would be worth it if it made Brahm look at her in appreciation. She even wore that strawberry scent he seemed to like so much.

His opinion was all that mattered. All her life she had been taught to live within society's dictates, and she had thrown all of that to the wind for Brahm. She had read a book no single lady should see. She had engaged in an illicit affair with a man under her father's roof. She had cast caution aside and followed that same man to London, placing herself in his house without a decent chaperone, inviting rumor and speculation. Surprisingly, she cared not for what society might think of her. And for once in her life, she didn't care about her family either. If they suffered for her actions it would be awful and wrong, but the most important thing to Eleanor right now was convincing Brahm that they were meant to be together.

Being with him this week, helping him recover, had taught her so many things. The sight of him drunk didn't bother her as she thought it might. She felt pity for him that something could bring him to his knees as alcohol did, and she realized it was indeed a sickness that he would battle for the rest of his days. She also knew that he had the strength to fight it, and this relapse had been caused by Brahm's own self-pity. Yes, perhaps her refusal of him had begun it, but she wasn't the one who made him take that first drink.

They were past all that now. She would do whatever was necessary to spend the rest of her life with him. His compulsion to drink was something they could overcome together. The fact that he was still considered a social pariah in some circles didn't matter. Did he love her? That was the question. And if so, did he love her enough to forgive her for being such a frightened idiot?

And did she have the strength to ask for his forgiveness? For his love?

She fastened diamond drops to her ears. There was a matching choker, but it obscured most of her throat, and she knew how Brahm liked to kiss her neck. She wasn't above revealing the line of her throat to its best advantage for that reason.

Finally Eleanor rose from her vanity, twisting and turning before the cheval glass in grim study of her appearance. Her hair was perfect. Her skin glowed with dewy softness, thanks to Mary's creams and potions. Her blue satin gown flattered her figure from every angle, displaying a generous—but not vulgar—amount of bosom. She hoped Brahm would appreciate her cleavage as well. She intended to make it as difficult as she could for him to continue avoiding physical contact with her. She had seduced him once, surely she could do it again.

But first she was going to have to confess her feelings for him, because it was apparent that he was going to hold out as long as he could. His pride was like that. The fact that he had swallowed enough of it to come looking for her forgiveness in the first place should tell her just how high his regard for her was. Or at least how high it had

been. It would be that high again. She would make certain
of it.

"You look beautiful, my lady." Her maid beamed at her.

Eleanor returned the smile. "And it is all due to you."
She might be vain enough to realize that she had pleasant
features, but it was Mary's adornment that made her look
as good as she did this night.

By the time Eleanor reached the drawing room, the rest
of the Ryland family were already gathered. Brahm's
brother Devlin and his wife, Blythe, had come up from the
country with their young son, who was already showing
signs of being as tall as his parents. Blythe and Devlin reminded Eleanor of some great warrior king and queen,
and they were so in love, it was almost embarrassing to
witness—as though one was intruding on a private moment between the two of them.

North and Octavia were there, as well as Moira and Wynthrope. Octavia was so very pregnant, and Moira, though
not visibly showing yet, was very openly excited about her
impending motherhood. How Eleanor envied them.

As she caught sight of them, she was very glad she had
chosen to dress as she had. The three of them were dressed
in elegant but rich gowns in varying colors of silk and
satin. Blythe wore a lush green that set off the deep red of
her hair. Octavia wore a pale gold that brought out the gold
in her strawberry hair, and Moira wore an intense plum that
complemented her fair skin and dark hair. Jewels twinkled
in the lamplight, their quality apparent but not gaudy.

The men rose as she entered the room. "Forgive me,"
she said, coming fully into the room. "I hope I have not
kept you waiting long."

"Not at all," North replied with a bow. His brothers
bowed as well.

Eleanor's attention went to Brahm. Could he see how hopeful she was as she stood under his inspection?

His well-shaped mouth curved into a crooked smile. Yes, he appreciated her appearance all right. In fact, his appreciation made her mouth suddenly very dry. "A woman as lovely as you need never apologize, Lady Eleanor."

Lady Eleanor. Her heart drooped a bit. Yes, it was proper etiquette for him to use her title, but it felt like a slight all the same. "You are too kind, Lord Creed."

"Allow me to introduce the members of my family you have not had the pleasure of meeting."

Within minutes of the introductions, Eleanor felt as though she was part of the family. The Ryland wives wasted no time getting to know her. Blythe was the most talkative, Moira the most reserved, but all three of them were kind and open, instantly relieving her of any apprehension she might have had over meeting them.

She felt the strongest kinship with Moira, which was odd given that Brahm and Wynthrope got along the least well of all the brothers. Maybe because they were too much alike in some ways.

The nanny brought Devlin and Blythe's son to visit just before the infant's bedtime. Everyone swarmed around as Blythe took the baby in her arms, glowing as only a new mother could.

"Hand him over," Brahm demanded with a grin.

Eleanor was surprised that Blythe obeyed so easily. She obviously trusted Brahm implicitly. Cradling her son's head, she placed him in the crook of Brahm's arm. He held the baby with one arm as though he had been doing it his whole life. His other hand, of course, held his cane.

A lump caught in Eleanor's throat at the sight of him. There should be a law against virile, handsome men holding babies in front of vulnerable, single women, especially when they looked as marvelous doing it as Brahm did.

"You, my little man, are my only heir," Brahm told the cooing infant, who waved his arms in response. "How do you like the sound of that?"

The words spilled out before Eleanor could stop them. "You may have a child of your own one day."

The look Brahm shot her scorched her right down to the soles of her feet. She could almost smell the smoke.

"You are right, Lady Eleanor, I just might." His voice was so low, so full of meaning that she shivered. Could anyone else see the energy passing between them?

No, no one else was paying the least bit of attention to them. They were all talking among themselves—or doing a good job of pretending to do just that.

Yes, she was going to have to seduce this man, or at least coerce him into admitting his feelings for her. She couldn't take much more of this. She wanted him so badly, her body itched in places she didn't know it was possible to itch—and proved even more impossible to scratch.

Brahm passed his nephew on to North, who then turned to Wynthrope. How odd that the men got to hold the baby before the women. It must be some kind of Ryland tradition. Finally Octavia and Moira took a turn, and then the bundle was offered to Eleanor.

"Do you mind?" She directed the question at Blythe. She had always been a pushover where babies were concerned, and this adorable little person was no different.

Blythe shook her head. "Of course not."

A look passed between the family that Eleanor couldn't decipher as she took the baby in her arms. It felt almost as though she had been given a secret seal of approval.

Little Aidan was warm in her arms. His fingers twined together as he kicked his feet against each other. He stared up at Eleanor with big brown eyes that were wide at the sight of a new person, but not the least bit fearful. How lovely and new everything must look through those eyes.

"Perhaps you too will have one of your own someday," murmured a voice near her ear.

Another shiver raced down her spine. Blast the man and the effect he had on her! Eleanor raised her gaze to meet his smoldering one. "Perhaps." Did he find her voice as full of meaning and promise as she had found his?

If the darkening of his eyes meant anything, then yes he did. "I would think the two of us would have had enough of raising children, having as many siblings as we do."

Eleanor shrugged, tearing her attention away from him long enough to smile at the infant in her arms. "It is different, I believe, when the child is actually your own."

"You will make a good mother, Eleanor." His tone was full of conviction, and to someone such as Eleanor, who prided herself on her ability to care for and look after those dear to her, it was the highest of compliments.

"Thank you. Hopefully I would do better by my own children then I did by my own sisters." Excluding Arabella, of course. Phoebe, Muriel, and Lydia seemed so malcontent in their lives. Eleanor couldn't help but wonder if she might have been able to do something differently. If she had been a better sister and surrogate mother, then perhaps her sisters would have ended up happier.

Although she didn't think there was anything she could have done for Lydia. Lydia made her own unhappiness, and sought happiness in all the wrong places. The poor thing. It would be a long time before Eleanor forgave her sister, but she felt for her all the same.

"I am certain any child of yours will never lack for love and support."

Her gaze locked with his again. She swallowed hard against the tightness in her throat. There could be no mistaking the regard in his eyes. She had vowed to seduce him before the evening was over, and he was the one doing all the seducing, talking about these things that were so personally dear to her.

"I could say the same for you, my lord."

There was that hint of a smile he was so good at. "Then it would be a waste for either of us to remain childless."

Eleanor's heart slammed against her ribs. "Indeed," she whispered hoarsely.

Brahm's brow puckered thoughtfully as he watched her. Could he see the love in her eyes? Could he tell how badly she wanted those loved and supported children of hers to be his as well?

"Eleanor—" He took a step toward her, but was cut off by Devlin.

"Time for this little fellow to go to bed." The youngest Ryland brother scooped the baby out of Eleanor's arms with a proud grin. How tiny the child looked next to his father. *Everything* looked tiny next to Devlin Ryland.

Eleanor returned the smile and watched him walk away. When she turned her attention to Brahm, she found him gone, and with him he had taken whatever he had been about to tell her. Her heart plummeted, but she rallied once more. He would not escape her so easily next time, she vowed to herself as they went in for dinner.

Next time he was not going anywhere until she was done with him.

* * *

Brahm couldn't hold out much longer. He was going to propose again if he wasn't careful.

More than a week had passed since Eleanor's arrival at his house. He was almost totally himself again. All that was left was to try to get himself under control again, get to the point where the cravings weren't so strong.

That and figure out what to do with Eleanor.

All through dinner he watched her interact with his family, charming them all and being charmed in return. She cooed over Devlin's son in the drawing room, damn near breaking Brahm's heart with the serenity of her expression. She expressed sympathy over Moira's morning sickness and joined in when the topic turned to naming North and Octavia's child. Octavia was convinced it was going to be a girl. North maintained it would be a son. Wynthrope told them it didn't matter what it was, *his* child would be superior in every way to North's.

And of course, there was the conversation she and he had concerning children. Was he foolish to suspect that she wanted to be the mother of his children as badly as he wanted to be the father of hers? If so, what had changed in her mind since rejecting his proposal a fortnight before?

Lord, he was getting so tired of trying to guess what was going on in that head of hers. It would be easier in the long run if he didn't try to figure it out. It would make it that much easier to say good-bye.

If everything had gone as Brahm had originally planned, this dinner might be in honor of his engagement. His family might be teasing him and Eleanor about soon starting their own family. But it wasn't a celebration. It was a thinly veiled investigation by his brothers and their wives. They wanted to investigate Eleanor. They wanted to add their own assumptions to what her reasons were for staying. They wanted to interfere in his life and see for themselves whether he could be trusted near a bottle of wine, such as the one on the table.

Oddly enough, he didn't care about the wine. All he wanted was Eleanor—the one thing he could not have.

Growing up, he had seen how his mother had looked at his father. He had seen the disgust in her eyes when his father would come home foxed. The last thing he wanted was for Eleanor to look at him that way. She deserved better than that.

As hard as it was, he was finally beginning to accept that they were a poor match, no matter how much his heart railed against the idea. He would rather die a bachelor than live his life slowly watching her regard for him turn to hate when he did not live up to expectations.

And he wouldn't live up to expectations, even if she had lowered them. His was a hard battle. There would always be doors closed to him because of things he had done. There would always be those who thought the worst. Eleanor did not need such stigmas placed on her as well. And there would always be the chance that he might fall off his high horse once again and get stone-faced drunk. Asking her to live with that was too unfair.

At least now with Blythe and Devlin in residence, Eleanor's reputation might yet be salvaged. Brahm had already dropped a few subtle remarks to the servants—and anyone else who would listen—about Eleanor's generosity in nursing him, and how it was very good of her to stay and risk her reputation when Devlin and Blythe's arrival had been so delayed. Whether it would do any good was beyond him, but he was certain that a woman like Eleanor would have no trouble finding herself a husband regardless of reputation.

A husband. The mere thought soured his stomach. No other man should be her husband but he. But he wasn't the right choice for her. He told himself that, even though her continued presence in his house, her support, and every gaze told him otherwise.

He was beginning to suspect that she might love him—and that hurt most of all. He would surely die if that was the case. If she loved him, it would make letting her go all the harder.

And he would let her go, because he was beginning to suspect that he loved her as well.

North and Octavia took their leave shortly after dinner. Octavia was tired, and North was anxious to get her home to rest. Wynthrope and Moira followed, and it wasn't long before Blythe was yawning as well.

"We are on country hours," the Junoesque redhead quipped as she took her husband by one large hand. "Please excuse us."

Grinning, Devlin rose to his full height of six and one-half feet and followed her from the room like a puppy. Sleep was obviously the last thing on his brother's mind.

That left Brahm and Eleanor alone in the drawing room. A fire crackled in the hearth to ward off the rainy evening's chill. The crackling warmth lulled Brahm into a sense of contentment, even though he had every reason to feel ill at ease.

She was starting to look too damn tempting in her low-cut blue gown. Her breasts lifted against the neckline with every breath. The ivory swells beckoned, made his fingers itch to touch them, his mouth water to taste them. He wanted her legs wrapped around his back, her husky voice crying out her love for him over and over as he plunged within her.

He wanted to drain himself into her. He wanted to kiss her and love her and demand that she marry him.

"I should go to bed as well," he announced, rising to his feet so quickly that his lame leg almost didn't support him. Fortunately he had his cane.

"Don't go." Eleanor rose as well, her face filled with anxiety. How could he explain to her that to stay would drive him insane? That he couldn't look at her without wanting her? He was so weak where she was concerned. She was more tempting, more sweet than any wine or spirit could ever be.

"I have to." But he only made it one step before she intercepted him, placing herself between him and the door.

"We need to talk," she informed him.

Standing this close, Brahm could smell her perfume. Her scent, heightened by the warmth of her flesh, filled him, made his head swim. She was spicy yet sweet, subtle yet bold. And every fretful breath made him ache to bury his face in her warm cleavage.

"If I stay," he warned her in a low voice, "talking will be the last thing we do."

She gasped, a welcoming, arousing sound. He had not made one improper advance toward her during this entire week. To be honest, he had been too sick for the first few days, but now his health had returned, and with it, his hunger for her.

Her gaze met his, wide and oh so inviting. "We can talk later."

For a second he thought she meant that he could go, but then she moved forward, closing the scant distance between them until her breasts were flush against his chest. Her hips brushed against his upper thighs. Lowering his head, Brahm breathed the sweet fragrance of her hair deep into his lungs. She shivered, and he hadn't even touched her.

She wanted him. Wanted him enough to instigate this encounter. Were he a strong man he might resist, but he was not strong.

He pressed his lips to the gentle indent of her temple. Her skin was petal soft and warm against his mouth. He did not stop there. His moved his lips lower, groaning in satisfaction when she tilted her head, offering her throat to him. He kissed the warm, delicate flesh there, breathing in her scent as though she was air itself.

She jumped when he tossed his cane to the floor, and her breathing quickened as he brought his hands to the supple arch of her back. Brahm did not lift his head, but instead, continued to nuzzle her neck. He gave in to the urge to run his tongue along her salty sweetness as he slid his palms around to splay her ribs. His fingers moved of their own volition as her hands clutched at his arms, squeezing his biceps. A wave of gratification washed over him as he cupped the gentle mounds of her breasts in his hands. Her breath hitched, warm and moist against his ear. He shuddered.

Her neck was not enough. Lifting his head, he gazed down at her. Wide blue eyes stared at him, dazed with desire. They were in such terrible danger, the two of them. He should let her go, order her to run to her room and lock the door, but there was no lock in this house that he didn't have the key for. She would not be safe from him while this need ran through his veins. *This* would not be denied by either of them.

Pink crept up her chest, washing over her neck. Brahm followed the flush with his thumbs, bring them up beneath the jut of her chin. His fingers splayed across her jaw and throat as he committed to memory every minute detail of her exquisite face.

She didn't move as she ought to have, didn't run or fight him as his mouth claimed hers. A low growl rumbled in his throat. She was so soft, so sweet and yielding. Her lips parted without resistance as he probed with his impatient tongue. She tasted of wine, sharp and tangy. The growl became a groan. Yes, the wine was sweet and tempting, but Eleanor was sweeter, headier, and far more dangerous to his well-being.

Her fingers gripped the lapels of his jacket, her knuckles pressing against the wool. The tension in her body reverberated through his. Could she feel the pounding of his heart against her breast? He could feel hers, the frantic rhythm that made him think of the way their bodies moved together.

God help him, this wasn't supposed to happen, but it was happening. His hands slid down and around to cup her buttocks, pulling her hard against him so she could feel just how badly he wanted her, burned for her. She pressed back, arching her hips so that the soft V between her legs met the hardness between his. Slowly she rubbed against him, making every nerve in his body tingle with the urge to possess her.

He lowered them both to the floor. The descent was far less graceful than he would have liked, the landing even less so, but Brahm didn't care. He fell onto his back on the rug. Eleanor sprawled on top of him, her skirt riding up around her knees, her thighs parted beneath the silk to embrace his. Her heat permeated the wool of his trousers, and his cock throbbed in response.

Their gazes locked. Her eyes were bright with need; her lips were red and moist. Her breasts, shoved over her gown and flattened against his chest, were dangerously close to slipping out of her bodice. She arched her back, shoving her pelvis down onto his, and her neckline deepened, revealing the soft baby pink crescents of her aureolas to his hungry gaze.

Mindless, Brahm raised a hand to that neckline as his other hand cupped her bottom, forcing her down on him as he lifted up. One demanding tug and her breasts were free. One impatient grab and her skirts were yanked up over her thighs, his hand eager to caress the flesh beneath.

Eleanor did not try to stop him, even though he was being rough. The smooth cheeks of her bottom rose against his hand, then fell again as she writhed against him, her panting breaths hot and sweet to his ears. Her back remained arched, thrusting her breasts toward his face. Her gaze was dark and hooded, and there was no mistaking what she wanted. He wanted it too.

His mouth captured one of her nipples, his tongue swirling against the puckered peak. She was hard and tight, and she shoved her torso against his mouth as her lower body undulated against his. He was so hard for her, harder than he had ever been before. He ached with the need to plunge into her. It terrified him, this need to have her, and yet it felt so natural, so right. He was powerless against it.

Brahm rolled them so that he lay on top of her. Bracing himself on one arm, he lowered the other so that his hand could slide beneath the bunched fabric of her skirts, eager to claim the delicate heat waiting there. His mouth returned to her breast, his tongue laving her pebbled, blood-hot flesh.

His hands found the ties of her garters as his teeth grazed the hard sweetness of her nipple. Eleanor moaned, bending to his caress. The thigh beneath his hand flexed as she dug her heels into the carpet, parting and tilting her hips in welcome. Her hands were in his hair, pulling at the strands, pushing at his skull as he sucked her. The more intense his attentions, the more fierce her tugs and whimpers became until she cried out in pleasure-pain.

The valley of her thighs radiated humid heat. Beneath her skirts, his fingers left the frilly lace of her garter to climb upward, finding the eager dampness on her soft inner thigh. His body leaped at the discovery, his cock aching to sink itself into the searing moisture his fingers now parted and stroked. Easily he parted her, his fingers drenched by her juices. He found the hooded hardness he wanted and stroked it lightly, teasing her with his touch.

Eleanor's thighs fell apart. Her skirts were up around her waist now, and she didn't seem to care. Her hips moved under his hand, shoving herself upward against his fingers. Under his thumb, the tiny crest of flesh grew tauter and slicker with every caress.

Releasing her breast from his mouth, he pulled back, lifting himself above her. He continued to stroke her, his gaze moving from her breasts, wet with his saliva, up to the beautiful flush of her face, and then down to where his hand and her body were joined. Glistening pink flesh beckoned. Her scent filled his nostrils, enticing him closer. Shifting his body, Brahm moved downward, until his head was level with her hips.

"What are you doing?" Her voice was low and slightly anxious.

Raising his eyes, Brahm met her gaze over her rumpled skirts. She looked so wanton lying there with her breasts free, the taut nipples distended and flushed. "Something I have wanted to do for quite some time."

Lowering his head, he nuzzled his mouth against her damp curls. Her hips jumped at the contact, and he smiled. He parted the succulent lips with his fingers, easing his tongue into the waiting folds.

Eleanor moaned as he licked the little nub that was so hard and slick beneath his tongue. Her thighs clenched at his shoulders as Brahm dined on her like an exotic dish that he could not get enough of. She shoved herself against him, soaking his face with her essence, her cries urging him onward even though he could scarce draw breath.

In his trousers he pulsed with need, and the urge to grind himself against the carpet until he found release was tempting, but he resisted. Instead he concentrated all his need and desire on Eleanor. He thrust his tongue inside her, licked her honeyed flesh until she was writhing and panting beneath him. Finally her thighs clamped hard on his arms and her cries of release filled the room as she shuddered around him.

He lifted his head and drew a deep breath, inhaling her fragrance once more before wiping the dampness away with her chemise. He sat up, turning himself ever so slightly away from her in an effort to cool the fire raging through his body. His head spun, intoxicated on her juices.

His body didn't want to cool, and the only thing that could quench this heat was the wetness between Eleanor's splayed thighs. Closing his eyes, Brahm prayed for strength. If he made love to her as he wanted to, he would expect it to mean that she had changed her mind about marrying him. He would leap to all kinds of conclusions—conclusions that might very well result in his heart being broken again.

"Brahm?"

He jerked his head around to meet her stare. She looked so fragile, lying there on the floor, like a discarded rag doll.

He smiled. "Yes?"

"Aren't you going to . . ." She made a gesture with her hand near her abdomen.

God, she was so naive still, so sweet and innocent despite her delicious sensual nature. He shook his head. "No."

She looked so shocked. "Why?" There was no denying the want—or the disappointment in her tone.

"I forgot myself," he replied, his voice harsh in his own ears as he drew her skirts down over her thighs. "In the future, we should take care that this kind of situation doesn't arise again." He wanted to take the words back as soon as he said them. He wanted to gather her into his arms and hold her forever and beg her not to go. He wanted to promise her everything that would make her stay. And God help him, he wanted to be the kind of man who could keep every promise.

"Yes," she whispered, averting her gaze as she sat up. Her hands shook as she righted her bodice. "I suppose we should."

Brahm swallowed. "I cannot be this close to you and not react to you, Eleanor."

Her gaze was unashamed as it met his. "I know. Neither can I."

He watched as she rose to her feet. "I'm sorry."

Her smile was so very sad as she glanced down at him. "I know. So am I. Good night, Brahm."

He watched her leave with her shoulders braced and her spine straight. How much had this night cost her dignity? He should have known better than to touch her. He should have had more strength, but as he had realized earlier, he wasn't a strong man.

If he had been, Eleanor would have married him years ago.

Chapter 19

So much for Brahm being at her mercy.

Eleanor watched him with his brothers, laughing and chatting as the group of them sat out in the back garden eating luncheon alfresco. It was one of those fine, late summer days in which the sun wrought just the right amount of warmth and the breeze just the right amount of cool.

She was thankful for the cool. Memories of last night in the drawing room kept her skin at an infuriatingly scorching temperature. She had been the one to find release and yet she burned as though unfulfilled. What was Brahm suffering?

She cast a glance at him as she chewed thoughtfully on a grape. He looked calm and collected, not like a man driven by lust. Was it possible that his ardor for her had cooled? Had she ruined any chances of making things right between them?

No. She refused to believe that. He was simply not going to make it easy for her.

"He will come around."

At first Eleanor thought she had imagined the voice, but then she realized it came from outside her head. She also realized that Brahm's sisters-in-law were watching her.

"He will," Blythe assured her. It had been her voice Eleanor had heard before. "You only need to be patient."

Octavia snorted. "Patient, while he wreaks havoc with her reputation?"

"It was my decision to take that risk," Eleanor reminded her, knowing there was no point in playing dumb with these women. She didn't want to play dumb. She wanted friends, and she wanted women who had experience with the Ryland pride and stupidity to guide her. And since the men were too far away to hear what they were saying, there was no harm in speaking candidly.

Moira smiled at her, a gentle madonna. "Of course it was. You love the fool. You would not be here if you did not."

Was it that obvious? Eleanor must have looked horrified, because Blythe laid a comforting hand on top of hers. "It is only obvious to those of us who have been through it with a Ryland of our own."

"I think I have ruined everything," she confessed, her voice embarrassingly tight.

Octavia shook her head, her pale cheeks flushed with color. "No, you have not. Brahm believes he is doing you a service by resisting you."

"How do you know that?" Eleanor was practically breathless. Had Brahm said something?

Octavia's expression was droll. "North did the same thing to me."

"Devlin too," Blythe chimed in with a nod.

Moira held up a delicate hand. "Wynthrope as well."

The three women shared a chuckle while Eleanor watched with a sense of something that was as hopeful as it was fearful. "What should I do?"

Blythe raised her teacup to her full lips. "Make him realize he's doing the both of you a disservice."

"It is quite easy actually," Octavia continued. "Once you know what to do, that is."

When she didn't immediately elaborate, Eleanor raised her brows. "And that is?"

The three of them laughed. It wasn't a mean sound, but rather made Eleanor feel as though she had finally been accepted into a kind of sisterhood.

"You give him what he thinks he wants," Moira explained with a bright smile. "Make him think he has succeeded in convincing you that you would be better off without him."

How was she supposed to do that? After last night, he had to know that he was the only man she wanted.

The question must have been plain on her face, because Octavia handed her the answer. "Tell him you are leaving."

Leaving! But what if he let her? What if he held the bloody door for her? What then?

Moira calmed the pounding of her heart. "He won't let you go, dear."

"No," Blythe agreed. "In fact, he'll probably seduce you into staying."

There was a collective sigh. "I love that part," Octavia murmured.

Eleanor's laugh was full of disbelief. "That's it?"

Moira shook her dark head. "No. Afterward he'll have a fleeting moment of stubbornness, and you'll have to tell him to stop being so ridiculous."

"The important thing to remember," Octavia told her, "is that you must take control of the situation."

Blythe spoke her agreement. "Make him realize that it is hopeless to fight. You know he loves you and you will not let him go."

"But I do not know that he loves me."

There was that laughter again, as though they knew so much that she didn't.

"You would not be here if he did not," Octavia told her. "He would have tossed you out."

"He tried."

"No." Blythe shook her head, indicating that Eleanor didn't understand. "He would have succeeded if he truly wanted you gone."

"He loves you, Eleanor." It was Moira who spoke this time. "We all know it, even if Brahm hasn't admitted it to himself. He has always loved you. Why do you think he accepted the invitation to your house party?"

"He said he wanted to make amends." Her gaze flitted between the three of them. "He wanted to prove to me that he had changed."

Octavia tilted her head in contemplation. "I wonder why it meant so much that he prove that to you when he's never given a flying fig what anyone else thought of him?"

"His brothers and you," Blythe remarked. "The only opinions that ever mattered to him."

Then why had he waited so long to come for her? Why so long before he decided to try wooing her once again?

He hadn't believe he was ready. The answer was as clear as day. He had waited for his courage, and for his faith in himself. Unfortunately her own courage had failed. No wonder he was so reluctant now. Octavia was right, she would have to take full control of the situation. She would have to force him to admit that he wanted her as much as she wanted him.

"Pardon me, I hope I am not intruding."

Eleanor looked up at the familiar voice. "Belle!" Leaping out of her chair, she seized her sister in a fierce embrace. "Oh, it is so good to see you!"

"I hope you do not mind. I was in the area and thought I would pay a call."

"Of course not!" Releasing her sister, Eleanor bade her to sit and introduced Arabella to her three companions. They had caught glimpses of each other at social functions before, but had never been properly introduced.

"We will give the two of you some privacy," Blythe announced ten minutes later, after Arabella had been made to feel welcome.

"Please do not leave on my account," Arabella insisted.

Blythe dismissed her anxious frown with a gentle smile. "We are not, I assure you. I need to go check on my son."

"And I need to lie down." Octavia stretched, sticking her round belly out even farther. "I cannot believe how much energy this child takes just to carry."

"I am going to see if Cook has any pie," Moira mused. "I have a sudden craving for apple."

"Oh," Arabella agreed. "That sounds delicious."

Moira's gaze dipped to Arabella's own gently rounded belly before lifting back to her face. She flashed a conspiratorial grin. "If I find any I will have her send a piece out to you."

Eleanor and her sister watched the three of them go with amused smiles.

"They seem very nice," Arabella remarked once they were alone.

"They are," Eleanor agreed. She took another glass from the tray and poured her sister some lemonade.

Arabella flashed her a grateful smile as her hand closed around the cool glass. "They will make you good sisters."

Eleanor sighed and took a sip from her own drink. "If I can convince Brahm to marry me."

Arabella looked surprised. "He hasn't proposed again?"

"No."

"Dearest, this is not good." Arabella's brow wrinkled as her voice filled with trepidation. "Your reputation . . ."

"I know." Eleanor silenced her with a firm tone. "Do not worry about me, dearest. I will do all I can to protect you and the other girls from the taint of scandal."

"Hang scandal! I am concerned about you."

"I will be fine." She smiled assuredly. "Trust me. I am not finished with Brahm just yet. Now, we will not discuss any more of that. You must tell me all the news."

"The party ended very smoothly, although I think Lord Locke was very upset by your departure."

Eleanor rolled her eyes. "As though Lord Locke ever stood a chance of marrying me, the arrogant swine."

Arabella wrinkled her nose. "No, he is not much of a catch is he? His connections might be good, but the rest of him is terribly unfortunate."

Enough of Lord Locke. "How is Papa?"

"Wonderful." Arabella sipped her lemonade. "You know, your decision to come after Lord Creed seemed to do wonders for his health." She frowned. "One would expect it to have quite the opposite effect."

Eleanor chuckled. "But I'm only doing what Papa wanted. He has always wished that Brahm and I would reunite."

Arabella didn't look completely comforted. Eleanor

knew her sister wanted nothing more than her happiness, but she was worried about Eleanor's reputation, and found it odd that their father wasn't equally so.

Of course, their father had much more confidence in Eleanor than she or Arabella had.

"How is Lydia?" As much as she hated to ask, she knew she must.

Arabella's gaze fell to the table. "She did not take your leaving well. In fact, she demanded that Papa go after you. When he refused she threw a fit. The next morning she packed up and left."

Sadness crept over Eleanor. Would things ever be good or comfortable between her and Lydia again? Somehow she doubted it. Lydia was so unhappy, she couldn't stand the thought of Eleanor's achieving something she had sought and lost. Why her jealousy chose Eleanor as its target and not Arabella, who had already achieved a happy marriage, Eleanor did not know. Perhaps it was because Lydia had thought Brahm the answer to her sorrow, and blamed Eleanor for that not being the case.

"Don't you dare put Lydia before your own happiness." Arabella's tone was strong—stronger than Eleanor had ever heard before.

She smiled at her sister, though it was a little sad given the topic of discussion. "I shan't. I promise."

As they chatted about other things, Eleanor's gaze drifted every once in a while to the man standing in the sunshine, ribbing his brothers as they played at lawn bowling. The breeze carried his laughter to her ears. How keenly she felt that laughter. How she wished she had been the reason for it. She wanted him to smile at her like that, to show such unrestrained joy in her presence.

As though sensing her stare, his gaze turned to hers. His

smile faded a little—just enough to twist at her heart, but he did not look away. Eleanor smiled and raised her hand in a wave. Brahm hesitated, then waved back.

Did he love her? Moira claimed that he did, that they all were aware of his feelings even if Eleanor herself wasn't.

Well, she was certain of her own. She might have been foolish enough to let Brahm slip through her fingers once—twice—but she would not be so foolish again.

Yes, it was time she took control of the situation.

"I will be leaving in the morning."

Brahm's heart froze as he stared at Eleanor. In the golden lamplight of the drawing room, she looked like a mythical goddess wrapped in a shimmering halo. She looked so beautiful that he hadn't expected her announcement to be so awful.

"What?" He didn't care that the others exchanged glances at his agitated tone.

Was that amusement he saw so briefly flicker in her blue eyes? "I am leaving. Tomorrow."

This was what he wanted, he told himself, but that didn't change the fact that he wanted to demand that she stay exactly where she was. And if that didn't work, a part of him was prepared to beg.

"You should send word to your father first," he suggested.

"Oh, there is no need," she informed him blithely. "I am staying with Arabella and Henry for a few days before returning to the country."

London. She was going to be staying in London for a few days. So close and yet so far. It would be a worse torment than having her under his roof. At least while she was under his roof he knew where she was and that no other men were sniffing around her. Now, with her reputation injured as it was, she would be considered fair game for every lowlife and libertine in London. She might even fall prey to one. After all, she had succumbed to him.

"I am so glad you will be in town a few more days, Eleanor," Moira remarked. "You will have to come dine with Wynthrope and me."

"Yes," Wyn chimed in, casting a bright glance at Brahm. "Of course, we'll have to invite another gentleman for a fourth."

Bastard.

Moira laid a hand on her husband's arm. "How about Nathaniel?"

Wynthrope grinned. "An excellent choice."

Brahm gritted his teeth. Nathaniel Caylan was blond and handsome, wealthy and damnably easy to like. In fact, women seemed to adore him. He did *not* want Eleanor to be one of those women.

He did not want her to leave either, even though he had decided the night before that he had to let her go. Letting her go running to another man—a man who could dance properly, no less—was not what he had in mind. How could he stop her? Even if he made an ass of himself by admitting his feelings, there was no guarantee she'd stay. In fact, she looked very happy about going.

Of course she was happy. He'd treated her abominably ever since her arrival. And then there was that fiasco last night. She'd tasted like heaven on his tongue. His heart rolled over in his chest and his groin tightened at the mere thought of it. There could be no denying that she had wanted him as much as he wanted her, and then he'd left her. That must have seemed odd to her, even if he had given her pleasure and denied his own before leaving.

"Excuse me," he said, rising to his feet awkwardly even with the aid of his cane. No doubt Nathaniel Caylan would have done a more graceful job of it. "I think I will retire."

"Retire?" Wynthrope's tone was incredulous. "But it is still early."

Brahm fixed him with what he hoped looked like a smile, but felt like a snarl. "I am tired."

He said his farewells and left the room, cursing his leg and every other inadequacy as he limped down the corridor. His anger grew as he walked. As he climbed the stairs to his room, his cane thumped heavily on each and every stair. By the time he reached his room, he was practically smoking under his cravat and in terrible want of a drink. A good stiff one.

He wasn't tired. He simply didn't want to sit there and listen to Eleanor make happy plans of all the things she would do once she left his house. Damaged reputation or not, it appeared that she was going to embrace life and all it offered. Meanwhile, he would go back to life as it always was. He would look after his properties and his tenants, and survey the few husband-hunting misses tossed in his path with the same disinterest.

He wanted no other woman but Eleanor, and for the life of him he did not know why. What was it about her that made her so very special? He could not narrow it down to one thing. He only knew that when she was near he felt whole and content. He had a reason. Without her, he was an automaton, going through life but never truly living.

Stripping off his jacket and cravat, he seated himself in the chair by the window and tried to pass the time by reading. He sat there for what felt like hours, reading but a few pages. His mind kept wandering, kept drifting to thoughts of Eleanor.

When the knock sounded on his door, it was hardly a surprise. It was Devlin, no doubt coming to check up on him. "Come in."

It wasn't Devlin. It was Eleanor.

He didn't bother to stand. "You should not be here." Damn, but the woman had no compunctions about coming to his room regardless of the hour.

"I know." She closed the door behind her. "I thought we should talk."

Sighing, he closed his book and set it on the table before him. He forced his expression to remain impassive. "Is there something we need to discuss?"

She smiled at his attempt at ignorance. "Many things, but mostly I want to apologize."

Apologize? "For what?" Yes, what now? Perhaps she blamed herself for there not being enough salt on the fish at dinner. Or perhaps the moon wasn't high enough in the sky. Lord only knew what the woman had found to blame herself for this time.

She came closer, finally settling into the chair opposite his. The lamp there lit her face. If he lived to be one hundred, he would always remember her features by lamplight. "For not trusting in you, or myself for that matter. I am sorry for everything I said that night at my father's house."

Not quite what he was expecting, and much more appreciated. "What did you say that wasn't true? You would have a difficult time trusting me. Anyone would. There are times when I do not trust me either."

She hung her head. "You asked only that I give you the chance to prove yourself, and I took back my promise after granting you that one boon. I reacted out of fear and foolishness, and I hurt you. For that I am truly sorry."

Brahm stared at her, swallowing hard. She was sorry.

But did she love him? "You do not have to apologize, though I appreciate it. Perhaps it was your heart's way of making you realize that you did not want to marry me after all."

"No. That wasn't it." There was conviction in her voice. Strong conviction.

Good God, he had been holding his breath. It rushed out through his flared nostrils. He wanted to speak, but was too bloody scared to ask what he wanted to know.

Leaning forward, she placed one long hand on his lame leg. The warmth of her touch radiated throughout the damaged tissue and bone. If he was of a more religious bent, he'd think she had just healed him. "I am sorry that the situation drove you to drink."

He shook his head at the remorse in her voice. "You should not blame yourself for that either. It was my decision."

"I know, but I helped you make it, I think." Her gaze was clear and honest as it met his. She straightened again, leaving his leg cool and aching where her touch had been.

This was the least martyrish she'd been since her arrival at his house. It both pleased and wounded him. Pleased because she wasn't blaming herself for things that weren't her fault, and wounded because she was accepting responsibility for things that were.

"Do not do this to yourself," he advised. "Do not blame yourself for someone else's actions. You did nothing. Nothing. Trust me, I know a thing or two about carrying around needless guilt. It never goes away and you can never assuage it. You simply have to release it."

She leaned forward once more, but didn't touch him. This time she rested her forearms on her thighs as her fingers twined together. "You are talking about your father's death, aren't you?"

He nodded. They had never talked about it. Usually he avoided the subject altogether, unless he was forced to discuss it with his brothers. Odd that now he felt like telling her everything.

He leaned forward himself, copying her posture. Their faces were no more than six inches apart. His gaze locked with hers, wanting her to see the truth in his eyes. "I have blamed myself for my father's death ever since I was sober enough to take responsibility."

Eleanor blinked. "But it was an accident."

"Yes." He could admit that without hesitation. "An accident that I have often told myself I could have prevented if I had been a thousand things other than what I was at the time."

She tilted her head. "Such as?"

He ran a hand through his hair. "Oh, sober, a better son, a better man. Mostly sober."

A smile curved her amazing lips. "What could you have done if you were sober?"

Wasn't it obvious? "I could have stopped him."

"But if you were sober you probably would not have been with him."

She had a point. "Perhaps not."

She eyed him intently. "Maybe instead of blaming yourself for something you could not control you should just be thankful that you and your father were so close, and that you were there with him his last night on earth."

He blinked. "I never thought of it that way."

Her smile grew. "I know. You do not think of many things the way I do."

Wasn't that the truth. It was also something he didn't

want to think about at the moment. He just wanted to enjoy what time they had left together, not make it worse by getting maudlin. "I never got to say good-bye."

"Few of us do."

She spoke like someone with experience. "Did you get to say good-bye to your mother?"

"No. I knew she was dying, but I wasn't with her when she died. I often wish I had been. I would have liked for her to know I was there."

"What would you have done?"

"I do not know. Told her I loved her, perhaps?"

"She knew that."

She frowned. "People always say that. When you die, do you think you will realize who loves you and who does not?"

Yes, she certainly thought about things differently than he did. "Perhaps when we die we take stock of those we love and are simply thankful to have had them love us in return."

She was not done with her philosophical debate. "What about those who loved you without the sentiment being returned?"

Brahm's throat dried. "I suppose we should be even more thankful for those people."

"And those whom you loved but did not love you in return?"

Was she asking about herself? "With any luck I will never know who they were."

Her expression grew soft. "I do not think it is something you will ever have to worry about, Brahm. You are the kind of man who knows where he stands with people."

"Not with you." The words tumbled out before he could stop them.

Again her head tilted. "Do you not?"

"You never told me why you stayed, despite the risk to your reputation." Nor had she told him why she was leaving now that the damage had already been done.

"I thought perhaps you would have figured that out by now. You are not a dumb man."

"I only look intelligent."

She laughed.

Grinning despite himself, he continued, "I could offer a few reasons why you would persevere through my moods and shaking and charming disposition, but I want to hear it from you. Will you tell me? Before you leave, tell me why you stayed."

"All right."

He held his breath.

"I stayed for the same reason that I am leaving tomorrow—because I love you."

She loved him. All the breath rushed from Brahm's lungs as his heart imploded.

"I have loved you forever, I believe," she added. "And that is why I'm leaving. You want me to go, so I will go."

He didn't want her to go, but it was for the best; he knew that. As much as his heart screamed for him not to let it happen, he could not ask her to stay when he could not trust himself to be good enough for her.

"But before I leave, I have a question for you."

His heart leaped into a gallop. If she asked if he loved her, what would he say? If he told her yes, then she might cling to some hope for the two of them, but if he told her no, it would be a lie—a lie that would hurt her. "Fine."

"Will you marry me?"

Chapter 20

Marry *her?*

Brahm shook his head, trying to clear the confusion there. He fell back in his chair, staring at her as he slumped in disbelief. "Did you just propose?"

Eleanor nodded, her smile unsure. "I did. Will you answer?"

He would, but not in the way she wanted him to. "Eleanor, you know as well as I do that we cannot marry."

She looked so crushed, he could have bitten his tongue clean off. "Why?"

He rose to his feet. In his haste he forgot his cane, and his steps were uncertain and jerky without it. "Because I'm a drunk and you deserve better than that. You deserve someone who you can trust, who you do not have to wonder about when he is at his club or with friends. You said as much yourself." He shouldn't have to explain, she knew all of this already. It had been she who made him see it.

"I will never doubt you again, Brahm." She stood as

361

well, as though afraid he might take flight. "I might doubt myself, but never you."

How idealistic she sounded. Could she hear herself? Doubt herself? Did that mean that every time he made a mess of things, she would blame herself? That wasn't right. She would grow to hate him as his mother had his father.

Both of his hands raked through his hair. "This isn't a sickness I will ever recover from, Ellie." It damn near killed him to say it. He had fooled himself for so long thinking that he could be cured if he was strong and patient, but there was no cure, he knew that now. "I am going to try my damnedest to make certain I never drink again, but it is not a promise I can give you. Do you understand?"

"Yes." Her expression was resolute, her spine straight and sure.

"You saw what happens to me when I drink to excess. You saw how low I can fall."

Her smile was serene and gently amused. "I saw you at your worst years ago, Brahm."

He nodded. "With Lydia."

"With Lady Pennington's punch bowl." Yes, she was definitely amused, but that night she had been as appalled as the other guests. He never wanted her to look at him like that again. "I do not think you could ever sink much lower than that."

She had him there. Of all the things he had done, that was probably the most humiliating and damaging. If she could find humor in it, if she could forgive it, then perhaps there was a chance for them after all.

God, he was starting to sound as idealistic and foolishly hopeful as she was. He was actually starting to believe her. "Are you willing to spend the rest of your life wondering if you can trust me not to drink?"

She reached out to him, her hand scorching him through the thin lawn of his sleeve. "I trust that you will keep your promise to try. I trust in you. That is all I need. If you have a relapse we will face it together."

"I do not think you understand." Every relapse would take a little of her love away from him, until she would finally leave him—in spirit if not in body. "I cannot sentence you to a life like that."

It would certainly give him a reason to try harder, wouldn't it? Her love—to be worthy of such a gift was enough to make any man want to be the best he could be.

Her fingers dug into his forearm. "You cannot sentence me to a life without you, Brahm."

She was too close, her expression too desperate, too dear for him to resist. He caught her by the waist, pulling her closer. He needed to feel her near. "I am afraid, Ellie."

"So am I," she whispered, her gaze wide.

"I could not bear to lose you because I could not control my urges." He meant the urge to drink of course. His urges for her he did not want to control.

She smoothed her palm over his cheek, sliding her hand down to cup his jaw. "I will help you control those urges— and lose control of a few others."

He laughed then, all the fight and stubbornness draining out of him. How well she read him. "It will not be easy," he warned her.

Eleanor smiled. "Nothing worth having ever is. But I am willing to try, Brahm. I will never forgive either of us if we don't at least try. We've both spent so much time thinking of the worst that could happen, but think of the best. Think of all the wonderful things we can share during the rest of our lives. Do you really want to give that up because we're afraid?"

"No. I do not." And he didn't. He would much rather concentrate on all the good things they could share—like a bed.

Her gaze softened, and he knew that she realized she had won. "I love you, Brahm."

Warmth blossomed in his chest as he lowered his head, unable to resist her any longer. "I love you."

Her lips parted eagerly beneath his as he kissed her, welcoming the intrusion of his tongue. He licked the hot, moist hollows of her mouth, tasted the blushed sweetness of her lips. Their tongues twined, their lips moving together in a frantic waltz until he thought his lungs might burst.

He broke the kiss. Gasping for air, Brahm stared down into wide blue eyes dark with desire.

He would give her one last chance to change her mind. A part of him half expected her to do just that. "Are you sure this is what you want?"

She pressed herself against him. Her breasts were heavy against his chest, her hips soft as they cradled his groin. She rubbed her pelvis against his growing erection, the sweet friction bringing a low groan to his lips.

"Yes," she replied. "I want you."

He kissed her, claiming her lips once more before sliding his mouth down her jaw to the delicate length of her throat. His teeth nipped at the fragile skin there, and he swept his tongue along the rapidly beating pulse at the base of her neck, tasting the frantic throbbing of her excitement.

Eleanor's breath caught in her throat as Brahm's hands—his beautiful hands—slid up her ribs to cup her breasts. His thumbs brushed the aching peaks through the satin of her bodice, sending a shiver of delight down her spine. Her nipples tightened, aching for more than just his touch. She wanted his mouth on her flesh, wanted the fierce pressure of his lips and tongue.

She wanted him.

Brahm's hands tightened on her breasts, his fingers squeezing her nipples forcefully, drawing a gasp from her lips. Yes, this was what she wanted, what she craved.

His hands left her, but before she could cry out in protest, his fingers tugged at her neckline and sleeves, lowering both so that her breasts were soon bare, the cool air hardening her nipples even more. Then he lowered his dark head, his silky lips closing around her wanton flesh.

Eleanor shuddered. *"Ohh."* His tongue was rough and velvety as it stroked her. His fingers found the crest of her other breast and pinched it gently, sending a swath of warmth rushing between her legs. Arching her back, she pushed herself against his hand and mouth, watching as his mouth devoured her with such delicious intensity.

His erection pressed hard against the softness between her thighs. She rubbed herself against it, giving herself over to the pleasure that threatened to bruise her tender flesh. Brahm flexed his hips, adding to the sensation. Greedily he sucked at her nipples, his teeth scraping the sensitive flesh. Her fingers clawed at his shoulders through his shirt. She would shred the fabric if she could. Just as she thought she couldn't take any more, he moved to the other breast and repeated the sensuous torture.

Gently he pushed her back, guiding her steps until the backs of her legs met the edge of the bed. His bed. Only then did he raise his head from her chest. His gaze was hot on hers as his hands came around to the back of her gown, deftly opening the buttons there. He peeled the gown down her shoulders, leaving her in nothing but her garters

and stockings. She had dressed with just such an encounter in mind.

No man had ever looked at her as Brahm did. No one
ever made her feel so beautiful and desirable. In his eyes
she saw herself reflected as a goddess, a woman made for
loving.

"You are the most beautiful creature I have ever seen,"
he whispered, brushing the backs of his knuckles along
the curve of her cheek.

She rubbed her face against his hand. "I want you
naked."

He grinned. "As you wish."

Eleanor watched dry mouthed as he grabbed the hem of
his shirt in both hands and pulled it upward over his head.
Her greedy hands claimed him immediately, running over
the springy hair of his chest, reveling in the hard muscle
beneath. He was so warm, so hard, so lovely.

Her hands drifted down, made bold by the knowledge
that he loved her as she loved him. She unfastened the
falls of his trousers, pushing the soft fabric over his hips
and down his thighs. He made short work of them from
there, straightening to stand before her gloriously naked,
while she still wore her earrings, stockings, and shoes.
She kicked the shoes off.

One of his knees came up to settle on the mattress as he
slowly lowered her. The coverlet was soft against her
back, a delicate friction on her skin. Brahm hovered above
her, beautiful and golden in the lamplight. Glancing
down, Eleanor saw the full length of him poised between
her thighs. How could Fanny Carson have neglected the
word "magnificent" when describing Brahm in all his
maleness?

He lowered his head toward her as his palm brushed her

belly, his fingers teasing the curls at the apex of her thighs. Eleanor arched instinctively, sighing in pleasure as his fingers parted the damp flesh aching for his touch. His thumb brushed her most sensitive spot, lifting her hips off the bed as she bit her lip to keep from crying out. She felt so hot, so liquid and ready.

"You like that, don't you?" His breath was hot against her lips as he stroked her with his thumb.

"Yes." Her voice was low and raw to her ears. Her legs spread wider, opening herself up completely for his hand. He slid a finger inside her and her body clutched it, bringing a moan of pleasure to her lips.

His fingers worked her until she was gasping and writhing beneath him. Then he withdrew his hand and replaced it with his satiny erection. The blunt head nudged the opening to her body and she shoved against it, wanting to take it all inside her—needing it inside her.

"You are so wet," he murmured, shoving himself against her heat. "So beautifully tight."

Eleanor raised her legs, bending her knees to take him even deeper as he slid within her. He filled her, completed her. "I cannot believe how good you feel inside me."

Her words, her sincere admission, drew a low growl from him. "I can't believe it either."

She raised her hands to touch him, but he caught them in his own, pinning them above her head as he slowly moved inside her. There was nothing else but the wet heat of their bodies, the pure, sweet friction that drove Eleanor to the brink of madness and brought her back again.

He teased her, easing himself inside her, only to withdraw, her muscles clenching to pull him deeper. Digging her heels into the mattress, Eleanor lifted her hips, taking her weight onto her shoulders as she gasped for more.

He did not deny her. Brahm's back bowed as he shoved deep inside her, burying himself to the hilt. His pelvic bones dug into her thighs as he filled her, thrusting into her as though his life depended on it.

Eleanor raised her knees even farther, spreading them to take him as deep as she could. Brahm released her hands, his fingers seizing her by the waist. Without breaking the rhythm of their bodies, he rolled them over so that he was on his back and she was atop him.

Eleanor sat astride him, his body still buried within hers. She was wondrously stretched, deliciously filled. Not just in body, but in spirit as well. Brahm filled her, seeped into every part of her, heart and soul. They were no longer two separate beings, but the same creature.

She lifted herself up and down on him, her thighs trembling with tension. Sparks of pleasure shot through her as the aching, swollen nub between her legs brushed against him. She wanted to grind herself upon him until the sparks became a complete blaze, but something made her go slow and savor every excruciating thrust.

Brahm stared up at her from beneath heavy lids, his hands cupping the curves of her breasts.

"Bend down," he ordered, his voice low and hoarse.

Trembling, every nerve in her body alive with sensation, Eleanor did as he bid. She leaned forward, lowering herself upon him so that her mound rubbed against his pelvis. The ache intensified. She braced her hands on either side of his head, bringing her torso down so that her breasts were above his face. She knew what he intended and wanted it as much as he did.

Brahm's hands pressed on her back, forcing her the rest of the way down until one nipple brushed the stubble on his chin. She gasped at the abrasion, bucking her hips savagely against his. He opened his mouth, taking the quivering peak into his hot mouth.

Eleanor cried out at the sharp tugging of his lips, the gentle nipping of his teeth. He sucked ruthlessly as she ground her pelvis against his. She rode him with abandon now, unable to maintain control any longer. She spread her thighs as far as she could, taking the length of him as deep as she could, thrusting herself down upon him in her quest for climax.

She moaned as the tension mounted inside her. She wanted the release at the same time she wanted this moment to last forever.

There were so many things she wanted to say. She wanted to tell him how he made her feel, but there were no words to describe it. He was heaven inside her, the world around her. He was everything.

But she said nothing, the gift of speech having been stolen from her by the desire driving her. She shoved, lifted, and churned against him with an intensity that made colors burst behind her eyes. She arched her back, thrusting her breast into his mouth and her hips down on his. She could feel the dampness between them, and it thrilled her. She rode him with abandon, trusting that he would be there when her control snapped, and that he would be there when she regained it once more.

She stiffened when the spasms hit, plunging her shivering, shuddering body mindlessly on his until she felt him buck beneath her. She cried out against his hair, unable to do anything but let pleasure take her where it would. He released her nipple, his own moans of release muffled by her shoulder as he held her tight against him, his body emptying itself in hers until they collapsed in a boneless heap.

How long they stayed like that, she had no idea. It could

have been minutes or hours, she didn't know and she didn't care. She wasn't going anywhere. She had never planned to. Her announcement that she was leaving had been nothing more than a bluff—although she would have had to leave had this not happened. God love Brahm's sisters-in-law for their advice.

"I think you killed me," he murmured later, his voice edged with humor.

It took all of Eleanor's strength to lift her head so she could look at him. She was still half on top of him, and her body refused to move. "You had better not be dead. We cannot do this again if you are dead."

"Again! Good Lord, woman. It will not be happening tonight."

She sagged against him. "Oh, thank God."

They laughed together, a sound that made her heart sing.

Warm fingers traced circles on her back, stroked the curve of her hip. "You were not really going to leave me, were you?"

She yawned. "I did not want to, but I would have, had you forced my hand."

"Whose idea was it, Blythe's or Octavia's?"

"I thought of it on my own," she replied honestly, and not without a little pride. "Although I do believe it was Octavia who pointed me in the right direction."

He chuckled. "I knew it. How North lives with that woman I will never know."

The answer was simple enough, and Brahm knew it as surely as she did, but she said it anyway. "He loves her and she loves him."

The fingers clasped around her hip squeezed gently.

"You never answered my question," she reminded him.

"Yes," he murmured, tightening his arms around her.

His words caused her heart to leap with joy. "Yes, my love. I will marry you."

Happily ever after

He was drunk.

Not on alcohol, but on happiness—if such a thing were possible. The sun was shining, the birds were singing, and all was good and right with the world.

It was the perfect day for a wedding.

Creed House was already bustling with activity when Brahm's family arrived that morning. He was sitting at the table, sipping a cup of coffee and enjoying a large breakfast.

"How can you eat?" Wynthrope demanded, gesturing at the heaping plate. "You are getting married in a few hours!"

Moira smiled at her husband. Her face was blessed with that radiance that only woman in the first flush of pregnancy seemed to possess. "Just because you could not eat anything the morning we were married does not mean all men are like that."

"I can always eat," Devlin remarked, offering Aidan to Brahm so he could pick off his brother's plate. "Bacon, Moira?"

"Oh yes!" Moira had an appetite that could rival even Devlin's at the best of times. She was even more ravenous pregnant. Many women lost their appetite in the first few months, but not Moira. Secretly Brahm though Wynthrope liked watching his wife grow fat with child. He watched her eat with a smile that only a man who appreciated soft women could achieve.

"Save some for me," Octavia chimed in, easing herself

into a chair at the table. She was very pregnant now—so pregnant that Brahm had his doubts as to whether his new niece or nephew would wait until after the ceremony to arrive. There would be hell to pay if the child arrived before Eleanor said, "I do." They had waited so long and gone through so much to get to this day, nothing was going to prevent it from happening.

Brahm pushed his plate toward his sister-in-law with the arm that didn't have a baby in it. "Help yourself."

North, who was standing back from the scene, merely grinned at his wife's gluttony. It must be a family trait to like women with ferocious appetites. Lord knew he did.

"Here," Brahm said to him, offering him Aidan. "You need more practice at this than I do." He didn't add that he hated seeing North standing back as though he wasn't part of the family. He was as much a Ryland as Brahm was, and North was as dear to him as either Devlin or Wynthrope—perhaps even more than Wynthrope.

North took the infant without fuss. "I give you four months tops, and then you will be on your way to joining the rest of us in fatherhood."

Brahm only smiled. Now was not the time to tell them that it would be less than four months. Eleanor's monthlies had not arrived when they should have. She said it was just because of the excitement of the wedding, but in his gut, Brahm knew the truth. She was already carrying his child—who would be publicly declared premature when he—or she—arrived.

He was going to be a father. Eleanor would be a mother. It seemed they had already raised two families, but caring for their siblings was nothing compared to what lay ahead of them. A child. An heir. A little person that would be half him, half Eleanor. Could there be anything more amazing?

Whoever would have thought that he would actually marry and become a father? Certainly not him. He had gone to Burrough's estate hoping to win Eleanor's forgiveness, not allowing himself to totally hope that he might win her heart. If only he had been patient with her then instead of running off as he had, things might have turned out so much smoother for the two of them.

But he was done living his life on might-have-beens, should-haves, and could-haves. It was a fresh start for both of them. It would not be easy to change those things within themselves that made him and Eleanor doubtful and fearful, but together they could overcome any obstacle.

"It is time to go," he told them, consulting his watch. Eleanor and her sisters would be at the church by now.

It had been hell allowing her to stay with Arabella the last few days, but they had to salvage what propriety they could. Of course, their engagement negated much of the damage done by her staying with him unchaperoned. There would always be those who whispered about them behind their hands, but as Viscount and Viscountess Creed, they would still find doors open to them, no matter what. Brahm was fortunate in his choice of friends, as was the rest of his family. He and Eleanor would have a social circle if they wished it. And being infamous had the advantage of affording one real friends without the bother of superficial acquaintances.

They took three carriages to the church as Brahm's would be needed afterward for him and Eleanor. Moira took bacon wrapped in a napkin with her for the ride. Wynthrope fed it to her with a grin as Brahm watched, shaking his head with a joy that would not let him rest.

He might not always like or agree with Wynthrope, but there was no denying that his brother was a good husband and would be a good father. In time, Brahm thought, he might even call Wynthrope a good friend.

The church was far from full—only family and close friends had been invited. Rumor had it that there were those who wouldn't have come even if they had been asked. Of course, rumor also had it that there were many among the *ton* who wished they could be present. Some said he was only marrying her because he had ruined her. Others were already counting the days till the first child was born, eager to see if it would be before nine months was up. That would be the next scandal.

But Brahm never had paid much mind to the gossips. Other than his brothers, there was only one person whose opinion mattered that deeply to him, and she was standing beside him, holding his hand and smiling as the vicar droned his way through the ceremony.

She was beautiful—the most beautiful bride ever—in an ivory gown and veil. Her flowers were white and pink roses—her favorites. She stood next to him, her gaze locked to his, her smile rivaling the sun for its brightness.

She had asked her sisters to attend her, and all but Lydia had agreed. In fact, Lydia had refused to come to the wedding at all. Brahm couldn't say she was missed, but he knew Eleanor felt her sister's rejection. Perhaps in time, that too would fade. Perhaps Eleanor and Lydia would be able to be friends again.

The vicar pronounced them husband and wife, and Brahm kissed his bride in front of God and their family and friends. Holding Eleanor tightly by the hand, he led her from the church, through the throng of well-wishers cheering them on.

They climbed into their carriage and waved as they pulled away, toward Creed House where the wedding breakfast would be served—much to Moira and Devlin's pleasure.

Eleanor squeezed his hand. "Happy, Lord Creed?"

He squeezed back. "Very, Lady Creed."

She leaned closer, pressing her lips to his as the open carriage rolled through Mayfair. People passing by no doubt stared at them, but neither Brahm nor Eleanor cared. Pulling her onto his lap, Brahm held his wife tight against him, kissing her for all of London to watch if they so desired.

When he got her home to Creed House, he pulled her into one of the smaller, unused rooms on the first floor. Laughing, she lifted her skirts while he dropped his trousers. They made love against the wall. It was awkward and Brahm's leg made it all the more precarious, and afterward, as they went to join their guests, his limp was even more pronounced, but it was one of the best moments of his life because it was the first time he made love to Eleanor as her husband. He finally had everything he had ever wanted enough to fight for.

It had been a struggle, but he had made certain his brothers were happy. He had made amends to them for mistakes of his past. He had gone after Eleanor and won her heart, fulfilling the dream he had harbored for so very long. He loved her and she loved him, and together they could face anything.

Their courtship might not have been the stuff of fairy tales, but they finally had their happy ending.

Don't miss October's offerings from
Avon Romance. . .

A Matter of Temptation by Lorraine Heath
An Avon Romantic Treasure

Victoria is nervous, yet thrilled, to be plucked from the many debutantes who vied for the hand of Robert, the Duke of Killingsworth. What Victoria doesn't know is that the man who she became engaged to is not the man she has married. But what will happen when she finds out the truth?

Flashback by Cait London
An Avon Contemporany Romance

Haunted by the suicide of her sister, Rachel Everly goes back to the place where everything went wrong, only to find Kyle Scanlon, a man who seems to hold all the answers. But the closer Rachel comes to getting the truth, the closer she draws to the path of a horrifying serial killer.

Scandalous by Jenna Petersen
An Avon Romance

Katherine Fleming is devastated to discover the nobleman she's engaged to has a secret he's kept from her: a wife! Suddenly Katherine is tainted by scandal, and is forced to accept a most unconventional proposal from the notorious seducer Dominic Mallory, her faithless fiance's brother. He is precisely the sort of rake she has always tried to avoid, but can't resist!

Rules of Passion by Sara Bennett
An Avon Romance

Marietta Greentree could care less about society's restrictive rules—not when she can become a courtesan like her mother. But when Marietta sets out on her first task—to seduce the darkly handsome and aloof Max, Lord Roseby, she finds that falling in love can often be an unavoidable consequence of seduction. . .

CEDAR PARK PUBLIC LIBRARY